West River

Books by Bill Bishop

Barton Family Saga Series

TWO HEARTS
The Tale of Cole Younger's Sweetheart

BEYOND THE HORIZON
Riders of the Mauvaises Terres

WEST RIVER
A Story of the Badlands, the Black Hills, and the Last Pioneers

West River

A Story of the Badlands,
the Black Hills, and the Last Pioneers:
A Barton Family Saga

BILL BISHOP

RESOURCE *Publications* · Eugene, Oregon

WEST RIVER

A Story of the Badlands, the Black Hills, and the Last Pioneers: A Barton Family Saga

Resource Publications
An Imprint of Wipf and Stock Publishers
199 W. 8th Ave., Suite 3
Eugene, OR 97401

www.wipfandstock.com

PAPERBACK ISBN: 978-1-6667-1237-7
HARDCOVER ISBN: 978-1-6667-1238-4
EBOOK ISBN: 978-1-6667-1239-1

VERSION NUMBER 02152022

This book is
dedicated to my mother,
Velda Iona Bishop,
one of the last pioneers

Contents

Preface

IN NORTH AMERICA, THE 100th Meridian serves as the dividing line between arid lands to the west and wetter more fertile lands to the east. As it turns out, this natural boundary runs directly down the Missouri River in South Dakota, cleaving the state into two distinctive halves known as East River and West River by the people who live there. This natural line of demarcation not only leaves each half of the state with its own unique climate but has left each half with its own distinct character and history. *West River* is a story that spans the lives of three generations of the Barton family in the western half of South Dakota.

John Barton moved his family from Webster County, Iowa, to homestead some of the first available free land in the western half of South Dakota in the Badlands near Wall in 1907. John's eldest son, Bill, with his wife, Kate, homesteaded the last available free land in western South Dakota on Pilger Mountain in Pleasant Valley in Custer County in the Black Hills near the town of Dewey from 1929. Bill and Kate had three children—two sons and one daughter. That daughter is my mother, Velda Iona Barton, who was born in Creighton, South Dakota, in 1928.

Bill Barton proved up his Pleasant Valley claim in May of 1934 and worked his land until the end of the year, when he was forced to move his family to Custer in search of work. *West River* is a story of the struggles and twisting fortunes of the Barton family over a thirty-year period starting in 1915 through the Great War, the Spanish Flu pandemic, the Roaring Twenties, the Great Depression, and the Dirty Thirties, all the way to the end of WWII in 1945, and the dawn of a new age for America and for themselves.

The thirty years between 1915 and 1945 in many ways carved out the mold from which our current modern age has been cast. To capture the many pivotal events during this turbulent and critical period in our nation's history, I have spun both fact and fiction into this account of the final days of the Old West. I have drawn on historical facts about western South Dakota, the Barton family, and about the times in which they lived. I found it necessary to weave actual historical events into this fictional narrative, believing we are all products of the times in which we live and from which we have been spawned. The Barton family is no exception.

Though this story is packed with actual historical facts and events, this is a work of fiction, none of the characters or events depicted in this story are intended to represent any true persons either living or deceased or their true actions or intentions. This historical fiction is at best a flight of fancy based on family folklore and historical facts surrounding the Barton family and particularly about Velda Barton's life and times.

The author's intent is to entertain, not to inform readers of the accurate recounting of historical persons, facts, or events. The author reserves the right to leave the writing of history to historians. As to those things that may be plausible within their historical context, the author believes the realm of the possible is limited only by an understanding of the facts and one's own imagination.

BILL BISHOP
Rapid City, South Dakota
August 22, 2021

BOOK ONE

December 2, 1916

Three Tree Creek, Pennington County, South Dakota

Huns at the Gate

AFTER PROVING UP HIS badlands homestead in 1912, John Barton focused his efforts on expanding his cultivated land. Putting over three hundred acres of land under the plow, he had come to understand deep down in the marrow of his bones and in every fiber of muscle stretched taunt across his lanky frame what being a sodbuster really meant. His odds for success had always been slim to none. He had known plenty of men who had given their all and much more, and yet, had failed. Far too many men, unwilling to yield no matter the cost, had lost their lives clinging onto a dream that had long since turned to dust.

John started out as a cowboy and loved cattle and horses and riding the open range. He had never grown accustomed to riding around in automobiles, even though they had become the common means of transportation. He vowed he would continue to ride his horse free and easy as long as he was able to step up into the saddle. Though he owned a truck and a Model T, he more often than not rode his favorite horse, a big black Morgan named Midnight, to and from town, especially when there were no passengers to take or supplies to haul.

Returning from a quick morning ride to Wall, he reined up his horse to look down the gentle slope that led to Barton Lake, the small kidney-shaped pond centered on his land near the home he had built for his growing family. From his perch high on the ridge, he could see his sons, Bill and Alva, working in the south forty to put up hay. Bill was his eldest son and had become the man around the place when John was away. Though there was a healthy rivalry between his two boys, with Alva only a year and a half younger than his older brother, they worked well together and seldom argued, leastwise not about anything either boy took seriously.

John had four daughters, Arvella, who had been the first Barton born on the homestead in 1907, Myrtle Bell born in 1909, Matilda born in 1910, and little Lucille born only the year before. Seeing Arvella, Myrtle, and Matilda playing in the yard near the house brought a smile to John's face. He had high hopes for his daughters. He also had high hopes that the child his wife, Sarah, was now expecting in the spring would be another boy, if for no other reason than having three boys and four girls just seemed like a good balance. With the couple not getting any younger, John had agreed with Sarah that their seventh child would be their last.

He recalled the first time he discovered his hidden valley with its kidney-shaped pond in the winter of 1887 when the land was still part of the Great Sioux Indian Reservation, that had covered the western half of South Dakota, with the exception of a fifty-mile-wide strip of land running down the western edge of the state which included the coveted Black Hills. Thirty years had passed since he first piled up his stone marker on the land, he had hoped to settle one day. Though he had to wait twenty long years before he was able to legally stake his claim in 1907, it felt as though it were only yesterday.

He smiled with satisfaction as he thought back over the past ten years since he officially staked his claim under the Homestead Act, and moved his family out from Webster County, Iowa. It was still hard for him to believe that his boyhood dream of staking a claim in the mysterious Mauvaises Terres, now known as the Dakota Badlands, had become a reality. He had molded his boyhood dream into that reality with his own bare hands by mixing the sweat of his brow with the land's dusty soil. Holding up his hands, he looked at his callused palms and thought of his sons and the growing calls for America to join the war in Europe. Whether his sons would one day be called on to fight unknown enemies on the other side of the world was, John knew, a matter of fate beyond his control.

John had heard a lot about the horrors of war from his father, who had fought in the Civil War. He knew firsthand what killing another man could do to a man's soul from his own experience of having had to kill more than one man during his wilder days in the untamed lands of the West. He prayed his sons would never be forced to take another man's life.

Since the outbreak of war in Europe in 1914, America had stayed clear of getting involved. President Woodrow Wilson had pledged America would remain neutral and away from any foreign entanglements. Even in the face of gruesome atrocities and reports of millions of soldiers and civilians alike being slaughtered, America had remain firmly rooted in its isolationism as the war in Europe dragged on without an end in sight.

John believed America needed to stay clear of getting in the middle of old-world rivalries that had nothing to do with America or its destiny. America, unshackled from old-world grievances, was a country that had been carved out of the wilderness of a new world and populated by people who had left their old-world concerns far behind. For John, America was filled with self-selected pioneers, people who had chosen to leave the old behind and who dreamed of building something new.

John feared however since Wilson's reelection, the president's tone had changed. He also had come to realize that though America may wish to turn its back on the old world, the old world was reaching out to remind the new world that there really is only one world, a world growing smaller by the day from which no country nor man could escape.

The May 1915 sinking of the British ocean liner the *Lusitania* without warning by German U-boats off the coast of Ireland killing nearly two thousand passengers, including over one hundred fifty Americans, had touched off anti-German rhetoric and calls for war. Rumors of America entering the war in Europe gripped the nation.

Newspapers had fanned the flames of anti-German sentiment, which had spread like a wildfire, scorching the landscape across the nation and leaving no city, town, or hamlet, no matter how remote, unscathed. Germany was now the enemy, and all things German suspect and anti-American. The barbaric Huns had to be stopped at all costs.

Nearly all of John's neighbors were recent immigrants of German descent and were, in many ways, the commercial backbone of the local community around Wall. They had become as American as any wave of immigrants before them. Even so, sentiments against Germany and the actions of Kaiser Wilhelm quickly escalated to violent opposition against all things German, no matter where it might be found.

German schools had been forced to close and German-language street signs had been torn down in towns throughout the state of South Dakota and the country. John had grown up hearing German spoken all around him and had come to understand the language fairly well. To him, it was natural for the German- and English-speaking communities to work together, while living apart.

During his visit to Wall, he quickly learned that spoken German was no longer welcome. He had found the town festooned with American flags. Talk opposing "Kaiser Bill" and the need to stop German aggression had filled the air. Despite more than half the population being made up of recent German immigrants, it became clear to John that his German neighbors, in an effort to demonstrate their patriotism and love for America, had become radically anti-Germany overnight. He noted with surprise that those with the strongest German accents were now the loudest in proclaiming their love for America and their loyalty to the American cause.

He had never heard many of these same gentlemen speak English in public. John couldn't help but wonder, upon first hearing these proclamations of allegiance, just what America's cause might be. Supporting your country was one thing; John had always been a patriot to his core. He believed in the destiny of American and in its uniqueness in the world. Blindly following unbridled cries to join a war on the other side of the world, however, was something else entirely.

With these dark and foreboding thoughts swirling around in his head, John rode down the slope to his home. The air was cold with the feel of winter settling in, he and the boys would need to lay in more firewood for the bone-chilling months ahead. On the frontier, John had accepted long ago that the work never ends. Cut off from most of the country for several months a year, while freezing cold winds pushed temperatures below zero and frequent blizzards blanketed the region, the pioneers who settled the Dakota Badlands had learned that survival was never a guarantee.

Bill had spent the day with his brother Alva, working to put up hay for the coming winter. His sisters had kept themselves busy around the house doing chores for their Ma. Being the eldest child and the eldest son, his Pa's expectations weighed heavily on Bill's shoulders. He prayed his Ma, who was expecting a child in the spring, would give his Pa another boy, a son to one day help work the farm. Bill had already made up his mind that Alva would take over managing the farm one day.

Since his childhood days in Iowa, when his imagination ran wild with his Great-Grandpa Pappy's stories of the Black Hills and the Mauvaises

Terres, Bill dreamed of one day staking his own homestead claim to land in the Black Hills. A child of the barren treeless prairie, Bill longed for the distant ponderosa pine forests of the Black Hills, that appeared as a black ribbon laying ruffled along the western horizon from the higher bluffs around Wall.

Even though homesteading in the Black Hills proper hadn't been allowed, beyond those few settlers who had staked claims early in the history of the white man's occupation of the hills, talk of farmland in the southern hills opening up for settlement had been a matter of speculation for many years. Bill often dreamed of the lush meadows of Pleasant Valley and rolling grassland around Pilger Mountain that his father had often said was the kind of land where a man could set down roots. He remembered the day his father had taken him there when he was ten years old. Upon seeing Pleasant Valley with his own eyes for the first time, the beauty of the place had etched itself forever into his mind and into his heart.

Bill was convinced it was just a matter of time until that vacant land would be filled with land-hungry homesteaders. His biggest concern was whether he would be old enough to stake a legal claim when that time came. Under the Homestead Act, claimants needed to be at least twenty-one years old. Bill wouldn't be twenty-one until 1923.

As Alva turned the wagon around to head back to the house, Bill caught sight of the silhouette of a lone rider high on the ridge to the south. He knew the only farmer in the area who still rode a horse was his Pa. Seeing that the horse could be none other than Midnight, his Pa's jet-black Morgan, standing two hands taller than most horses, confirmed the sighting.

"I see Pa headed this way," Bill said, as he hopped up on the seat of the wagon.

"Yeah, that's Pa, forever the cowboy," Alva said with a knowing grin.

Alva knew Bill planned to set out on his own as soon as land opened up in the Black Hills. What Bill always failed to understand was that he too had plans. Alva had no intention of becoming a farmer. He dreamed of the distant shores of distant lands on the other side of the world. He wanted nothing more than to venture beyond the western horizon to follow the sun as his father had done and his father's father before him as far back as anyone in the Barton family could remember. He too hoped that his Ma would bare a third son for their Pa, a son who would take the reins of the family farm one day.

Pulling up the wagon in front of the house, the two boys watched their Pa make his way down the slope toward home. They were eager to learn the latest news from Wall. They had heard the many rumors of America joining the war in Europe. Bill had mixed feeling about American soldiers actually joining the fight in Europe and about whether he would one day be called to serve. Having just turned fourteen, until recently, Bill had thought of nothing other than graduating the eighth grade in the coming spring. He now wondered how his tiny school would cope with all the German kids planning to attend English-speaking public school for the first time after the winter break. With the sudden closure of all German-language schools throughout the region, English-language public schools were faced with an unexpected doubling in attendance when school-aged children returned after the new year holiday.

Bill knew a number of the German boys in the area. Unlike non-German English-speaking children, German children had always attended their own German-language school and had spoken only German when together. The general custom that had evolved over the years was for Germans to stay to themselves most of the time, mixing with English speakers only when they needed to.

For Bill, this was normal, the way things had always been. With all the anti-German news, Bill had started viewing their German neighbors in a new light. He knew they were good people. He had grown up with them and had made friends. And yet, he had begun to wonder why they insisted on always remaining separate. It was as if they wished to only partake in the bounty of America, while remaining German, separate, and apart.

Over the past year, Bill had noticed more and more that their German neighbors no longer spoke German in public, not even to each other. It seemed as though the Germans were now rushing headlong to embrace the English-speaking community around them. For a teenage boy, with a growing interest in the opposite sex, in Bill's way of thinking, the new openness made German girls fair game for non-Germans, for the first time.

Bill had met his Aunt Nena, his Uncle Benny's German wife, who, Uncle Benny never failed to remind everyone, he first met in Philip, South Dakota, in the spring of 1907 when his brother first staked his claim in the badlands. That Uncle Benny's wife was of German descent hadn't really registered until the new openness between the English- and German-speaking communities had unexpectedly piqued Bill's interest in meeting more German girls, who had heretofore been all but *verboten*.

Bill had seen plenty of German girls in Wall during annual local events, he had even met and talked with a few. Fraternizing between the German- and English-speaking youth however had been difficult with nearly everyone staying close to their own kind and speaking only in their own languages, even in public. Since German- and English-speaking children attended separate schools, Bill had never really had a chance to get to know many German kids very well, especially girls near his own age. He had figured he never would. With the sudden openness between communities, Bill's German neighbors in the surrounding area seemed to now go out of their way to introduce their sons and daughters, something that had never happened before.

The unexpected change was as though a crate of forbidden fruit had fallen in Bill's lap with its lid already pried open. Bill couldn't wait to go back to school where he hoped to get to know what wonders that forbidden fruit might hold. He looked forward to getting to know as many *fraulein* beauties as possible and hopefully someone close to his own age.

Alva, for his part, hadn't yet become so excited about the opposite sex. His brother's sudden interest and endless chatter about girls, girls, girls had caused him to think about girls differently, though he wasn't certain why. He too couldn't wait to go back to school, if for no other reason than to figure out why his brother was so damn interested.

Russia was once the promised land for young German farmers who sought a better life. In the early 1800s, with little opportunity to own land in Germany, thousands of young German farmers gladly accepted the Russian czar's offer of free land. Special rights including the promise of religious freedom, protection of cultural identity, and exemption from military service made the Russian czar's offer irresistibly seductive. Unfortunately, as time passed and policies shifted, the Russian government slowly rescinded the special rights they had granted their German immigrants. Conditions soon deteriorated in German communities throughout Russia. Calls for the expulsion of all foreign settlers on Russian soil soon followed.

With his family selling everything and leaving much behind, Detrick Fremder fled the Black Sea region of southern Ukraine with his parents and siblings after conditions had become unbearable. No longer welcome in Russia and with few opportunities in Germany, single and without prospects, Detrick had no choice but to cast his fate to the wind. Joining thousands of other Russian German immigrants, who dreamed of making a new life in the new world, he set his sights on the United States.

Once again, it was the lure of free land that had helped to ignite the stampede. Scraping together enough money to pay for his passage and, God willing, to purchase enough seed and supplies to set up a small farm once he arrived, he boarded a cargo ship filled with Russian German immigrants and set sail for the United States in the winter of 1904.

Staking his hopes on the promises written in a letter from a distant relative who had already made the journey to America three years earlier, he traveled to Manning, Iowa, with high expectations only to find that all the land in the surrounding area had already filled up with an earlier wave of European immigrants, leaving no room for newcomers. Learning that other recent arrivals from Germany had moved further west to establish a new community in Bloomfield, Nebraska, known as Manning's sister town among Russian German immigrants, he once again had high hopes for a fresh start.

In Bloomfield his hopes were dashed when he discovered, like in Manning, available farmland was a scarce commodity. Russian Germans had indeed settled in Bloomfield and were beginning to prosper. The problem was that they had settled in such numbers that they filled up the surrounding countryside, leaving only wastelands with no water and poor soil for new arrivals.

Determined to find a place to set down roots, Detrick decided he would join with others willing to seek a fresh place to settle in the vacant lands of western South Dakota. After seeing how early settlers, following newly established rail lines, had grabbed the best land ahead of later arrivals in both Manning and Bloomfield, Detrick was determined to be among the first settlers in a region where rail lines had yet to be established. He believed western South Dakota, still wild and untamed, presented him with the best opportunity to do just that.

If he could get ahead of the arrival of a rail line into the unsettled region, he was confident he would be able to secure the choicest land, before other settlers arrived. Western South Dakota was one of the last places to be settled in the western United States, and for Detrick, his last chance to stake his claim to virgin farmland ahead of the rush of immigrants who would flood into the region as soon as rail lines were laid.

After spending nearly two years of backbreaking manual labor in Bloomfield to scrap together a larger grubstake, in early 1906, with the coming of the spring thaw, Detrick Fremder with his new wife, Annie Hamann, and four other families, hitched up their newly acquired covered wagons to teams of oxen and headed northwest. Their small wagon train followed Bazile Creek to the western bank of the Missouri River, far away from the settled towns that dotted rail lines running south and west in Nebraska.

Reaching the western bank of the Missouri River across from the town Chamberland, South Dakota, they found the townsfolk abuzz with stories of the Rosebud Land Rush that had attracted over one hundred thousand lottery entries. Detrick was heartbroken to learn that the land lottery had been held just two years earlier. Had he come straight to South Dakota from Germany, he may have had a chance to enter the lottery. Again, he found himself a day late and a dollar short. From what he could learn, a huge track of virgin land had been carved out of the Rosebud Indian Reservation west of the Missouri River and south of the White River and given away through the drawing of lots. As a result, thousands of quarter sections of land, equaling one hundred sixty acres each, had been parceled out to lottery winners.

Desperate to find a way to get ahead of the growing flood of European immigrants seeking free land, he learned that the government had opened up all of the land west of the Missouri River that lay between the Cheyenne Indian Reservation to the north and the Pine Ridge and Rosebud Indian Reservations to the south. Amazingly, this huge block of land between the Missouri River in the east and the Black Hills to the far west had yet to be settled. In order to open up this vast region known as the Dakota Badlands and to link the Black Hills in the far west with the eastern half of the state, two new rail lines had been proposed and had already begun laying track.

The Chicago, Milwaukee, and St. Paul Railroad Company was building a rail line to run from Chamberlain to Rapid City along the White River through the new towns of Kadoka and Interior. Further north the Chicago and North Western Railway Company was building a rail line to run from Pierre, the state capitol, to Rapid City through the newly platted towns of Philip and Wall. Both railroads were in a head-to-head competition to reach Rapid City before the end of 1907. From what Detrick and the other families in his wagon train could find out, the Chicago and North Western Railway Company would be the first to reach Rapid City in the early fall of 1907.

This meant that their little wagon train was a year ahead of the coming land rush into the vast lands covering the central part of western South Dakota. After a quick discussion, it was decided they would drive their wagons all the way to the future location of Wall, the newly platted town nearest the Black Hills. Considering all their options, settling near Wall would give them access to the Black Hills to the west and a rail link to growing markets in the east.

Detrick was confident, if they wasted no time, they would be able to stake their claims to the best land in the Wall area before others reached the distant outpost. Though there would be no time for plowing and planting crops this year, it was agreed the families would work together to plant gardens, hunt for meat, chop firewood, and build shelters in preparation for the coming winter. Having all grown up in the Ukraine, Detrick's little band of Russian Germans were no strangers to harsh winter winds and freezing cold weather. They knew very well what a harsh winter on the open plains held in store for them.

It was in Philip, a newly platted town slated to be on the new rail line, that Detrick learned that government survey teams had completed mapping all the available land in the region. The coordinates of townships had been fixed with individual sections, measuring one square mile, divided into quarter sections, measuring one hundred and sixty acres each. This meant that the land was effectively open for legal homestead claims. There were already a good number of early arrivals staking claims to the best land around Philip; however, the tidal wave of European immigrants had yet to arrive.

Everyone in Detrick's group knew that homesteaders would soon swamp western South Dakota as soon as the first trains started to roll. With the completion of new rail lines still a year off, Detrick, for the first time in his life, felt his luck had finally changed. Wall had become his and his small band of Russian German families' long-wished-for promised land.

Now after ten backbreaking years since staking his claim to some of the best land for miles around, Detrick looked out over the stubble of his harvested fields and instead of feeling a sense of pride and satisfaction in all he had accomplished, he found his mind filled with worry and concern for the future. He had been forced to flee Russia only to find that his German homeland had no room for him and his fellow Russian Germans. And now, his people were once again faced with the same kind of persecution at the hands of Americans that they had suffered at the hands of Russians back in the Ukraine.

Anti-German propaganda had turned him and his fellow German immigrants into public enemy number one almost overnight. If America sent soldiers to fight in the war against Germany, Detrick feared anti-German sentiment would grow worse, much, much worse, in coming years. With four daughters, the oldest, Kathrine, age nine, born the year after they arrived in Wall in 1907, and Lena born in 1910, Frederika born in 1913, and little Anna not yet a year old, he feared for the safety of his family and of his fellow German neighbors. He knew their future, once so promising, was now shrouded in uncertainty and danger.

As a leader and a member of the five founding families, he knew he had a responsibility to the German community in the Wall area and would do whatever he could to protect them during these dangerous times. He feared that the time may come when he would have to take matters into his own hands and to risk everything to protect his family and his people.

December 10, 1917

Wall, Pennington County, South Dakota

Papers Please

EVERYTHING JOHN HAD PRAYED wouldn't happen, had happened. America had joined the war in Europe, sending tens of thousands of young dough-boys into the teeth of the enemy, an enemy which now cast its dark shadow across the land. With daily reports of mounting battlefield casualties, the war reached into the hearts and minds of every American, awakening their deepest fears.

With unseasonably warm temperatures and needing to pick up additional electrical switches for his new Delco Light Plant at the General Store in Wall, John decided to enjoy the mild weather and ride his favorite horse to town. Though he stubbornly continued to ride his horse in favor of driving his automobile whenever possible, he had no difficulty in adopting other modern conveniences as soon as they came out. John had been one of the first farmers in western South Dakota to install electric lighting in both his house and barn. His Delco Light Plant was his pride and joy and the envy of every farmer in the area.

Arriving in Wall, John rode straight down Main Street, careful to avoid the many trucks and automobiles on the streets. As he approached the General Store, he caught sight of someone waving at him out of the corner of his eye.

"John, John Barton! Hold up a minute," a large flabby bald-headed man yelled as he bounded out of the barbershop's front door waving one hand while wiping shaving cream off his half-shaven face with the other.

John reined up his horse and waited for the now panting red-faced man to catch up with him.

"I thought that was you," the man ventured, catching his breath.

"Good to see you, Tom. What's on your mind?" John said, looking down at his unwelcome pursuer.

"Well, you weren't home last time we dropped by, and me and the boys wanted to have a little talk with you," Tom said as he tried to stare up into John's eyes; a task made nearly impossible by the fact John had turned his horse, putting his back to the midday sun.

John knew anyone trying to look up at him would need to deal with the rays of the midday sun streaming directly into his eyes.

"Sorry you came all the way out to my place without seeing me. What'd you need to know?" John said nonchalantly.

John knew damn well what Tom McFarland and his gang of trouble-makers wanted to know. As members of the American Protective League, a newly formed volunteer national network of civilians run by the U.S. Justice Department's Bureau of Investigation, they had only one goal in mind, they wanted dirt on all the German immigrants in the surrounding area. John had tried to steer clear of pushy amateur detectives like Tom McFarland with their shiny new A.P.L. Secret Service badges; however, as time went on, avoiding the nosy devils had become nearly impossible.

Emboldened by their new powers, they increasingly threw their weight around. In doing so, they soon learned how useful fear could be in controlling other people. Wielding this potent weapon, they sought targets for their hate. At first, they focused on keeping tabs on German immigrants and turning them in as suspected spies and saboteurs. As the months passed, they branched out into investigating anyone they suspected as having dissenting views on the war. For them, with the country at war, there was no room for opposing opinions of any kind, especially any opinions that didn't agree with their own narrow view of the world.

John soon understood that this new army of petty tyrants couldn't be trivialized as some right-wing patriotic fringe group full of crackpots and idiots, even if this described well many of its crudest and cruelest members. The League had the power to destroy any man's life if they chose to single him out for not being fully cooperative with the goals of their patriotic cause. To prove it, they had sent more than one German immigrant accused of espionage to the western region's newly established German detention camp at Fort Douglas, Utah.

"John, we'd like to talk with you about your Hun neighbors. Especially the Hamann family," Tom said with a sneer on his face and a bite in his voice.

"Oh, sure, sure. Happy to oblige," John replied as he stepped down from his horse.

John had hoped he would be able to ride in and out of Wall without confronting any League members. Tom's sudden and unexpected appearance had spoiled that plan. John knew he would now have to deal with the pushy bastard.

After President Wilson's inauguration, things had suddenly changed for the worse in America. Reelected in large part because he had kept America out of the war in Europe, the shocking revelations in the Zimmerman Telegram splashed across newspaper headlines from coast to coast on March 1, 1917, had acted as a wake-up call to the nation. The war was no longer something on the other side of the Atlantic, it had come to America's own doorstep. The telegram sent from German foreign minister Arthur Zimmermann to Heinrich von Eckhardt, Germany's ambassador in Mexico, had been intercepted and deciphered by British Intelligence in February 1917 and revealed Germany's secret plot to forge an alliance with Mexico against the United States.

With newspapers fanning the flames, outraged Americans quickly grew in number nationwide. Calls for war soon rang out from every quarter. By April, just two months after the telegram's shocking revelations had come light, President Wilson, swept up by a rising tide of public sentiment, declared war on Germany. In order to quickly fill the ranks of the military, the Selective Service Law was enacted in May. Almost overnight, the thought of sending boys to join the bloodshed in Europe had turned from being some distant possibility into a reality. By June, the first doughboys had been shipped out to Europe. By October, they had been thrown headlong into the fight.

At forty-nine, John had no concerns for himself or for his two young sons, who were just fourteen and fifteen. The new Selective Service Law targeted the conscription into military service of able-bodied men between the ages of twenty-one and thirty-five.

What worried John more than possible military service for his sons, should the war drag on for years to come, was the new Espionage Act that had been passed in June that provided the American Protective League with real legitimacy and gave their activities real teeth; teeth powerful enough to crush and chew up anyone, German and non-German alike.

John had tried to protect his German neighbors from the most abusive League members since they became active in the community. Helping his neighbors counter false accusations lodged against them by League members however had not made John very popular with the League. With increasingly repressive League actions targeting anyone and everyone they deemed dangerous, he now feared for his own family's safety. The last thing he needed was to be labeled as a person of interest by the local chapter of the American Protective League.

Tom followed John to the porch in front of the General Store, one of the few places downtown where a horse could still be tied up. Trucks and automobiles filled the streets, leaving little room for the bygone days of the horse and buggy.

"Let's have a seat, my friend," John said in a kindly voice, gesturing at the bench in front of the store.

"After you," Tom said with a kindly smile, mirroring John's gesture.

"How can I help," John said as he sat down, immediately regretting having done so.

It was clear Tom intended to stay standing, so he could tower over John while they had their friendly little chat. John could see that Tom loved to play the role of the bully and relished making other men squirm.

"Well, let me get right to the point. It seems the Hamann family has been working for good ol' Kaiser Bill and his barbarian band of bloodthirsty Huns. We suspect old man Hamann has been secretly sending money to support Germany," Tom said as he glared down at John with his eyebrows arched; his breath filling the air with the putrid reek of rotting teeth.

"How's he been doing that?" John said not sure where things might be headed and wanting to avoid letting his guard down.

"He's been sending money to an account at the National Bank in Chamberland that has been forwarding these funds to a German immigrant by the name of Felix Koch in Bloomfield, Nebraska. From there, well, who knows. We suspect the money is being bundled and sent on by Mr. Koch to undercover German agents hiding right here in America to conduct espionage for the German war effort," Tom declared confidently, having connected all the dots he felt necessary to prove his case.

"Didn't old man Hamann and his son recently buy war bonds," John said, knowing the Hamann family, like nearly every other German immigrant family in the area, had been coerced by the League into buying war bonds as a show of their patriotism; a show that had included the requirement that all German males swear a loyalty oath to the United States of America while kneeling and touching an American flag.

"Yes, yes, Hamann bought a handful of war bonds, but you know that doesn't mean a damn thing. These German bastards only support their own kind. They're not like us John. The Hun bastards stick together. Hell, it was only last year they were still sending their kids to their own schools, speaking their own foul language, following their own queer customs, and attending their own churches. They've pushed their Germans-only crap on us for years, and we've had to eat it. No more, my friend, no more. They can't be trusted, John. A Hun is a goddamn Hun. It's time you understood that fact," Tom said, summing up his opinion of all Germans, an opinion shared by League members and increasingly by a growing number of non-Germans in the general public.

"If they want to be Americans and want to live in America, they'll have to become a hell of a lot more American. Can't be German-American. There ain't no room for hyphens in America. They can't have it both ways. They're going to have to choose," Tom growled as he repeated his favorite little speech, his voice rising on every word.

"I couldn't agree more. America's an idea, one we all share. Everyone who lives in or comes to America must embrace that idea. The idea of liberty, freedom, and equal justice for all," John said, wanting to remind Tom that all immigrants who come to America started out as something else, and yet share in the desire to pursue common ideals and values.

For John, the fact immigrants left their homelands and came to America of their own free will demonstrated, for the vast majority, their willingness to embrace the idea of America. Even the slaves, once freed, though they had not come to America on their own volition, now shared in that promise. Indeed, it was the promise of what America stood for, that brought immigrants to its shores to begin with. German immigrants were no different in their desire to embrace that promise.

"Didn't a lot of our Russian German neighbors come up from Bloomfield, Nebraska?" John quickly added, his poker face, a mask of stone, showing no emotional commitment to his statements, one way or the other.

"Yeah, yeah, so they did. So, what? That doesn't mean the money being sent to Koch by old man Hamann ain't for the support of his stinkin' fatherland," Tom retorted and then quickly added, "Many of 'em have the best farmland around here. That's something else we need to look into. How is it that these German bastards have the best of everything, while us red-blooded Americans have been left to make do with the scrapes?"

"Those with the best land got here ahead of the train; it's that way up and down the rail line. As they say, the early bird catches the worm. As for the money, I have no idea where it might be headed. Be good to check out whether old man Hamann was repaying a debt to Mr. Koch. A lot of folks borrowed money from relatives and others so they could make the trip out here," John suggested, holding the expression on his face as neutral as possible.

"Yeah, we'll do that. By the way, you buy any of those war bonds?" Tom said, using the tone of his voice to drive his not-so-subtle point home.

He wanted to be sure John understood the League wasn't only interested in Germans.

"You bet. I think everyone around here is trying to pitch in to support the war effort however they can. Our boys are already fighting over there, we have to support 'em. We have to win this thing and bring our boys home," John said with conviction.

"Damn right. Let's talk again John, and soon. We'd like to keep tabs on the Hamann bunch. Need to watch all their comings and goings," Tom said as he turned to walk back to the barbershop, and then stopped, and looking back at John, added, "Oh, and let me know right away, if you learn anything. Can I count on you, John?"

"Yes, of course. I'll keep an ear to the ground and an eye out for anything suspicious," John said, while trying his damnedest not to let his anger ooze into the tone of his voice.

"You do that, John. You do that. See you soon," Tom said, his voice trailing off as he headed back to the barbershop.

John watched the overweight ape sauntered back to the barbershop with his smug inflated self-importance on display for all to see. Tom McFarland, with his shiny tin American Protective League badge proudly pinned high up on his chest, had trouble written all over him. John knew it would be tough for anyone caught up in his sights to escape the man's need to be right about everything. The problem with Tom McFarland was that if he thought something was true, he knew it must be so, facts be damned. Once he made up his mind, there was no convincing him otherwise.

Settled back into the barber's chair, Tom McFarland relaxed, letting the barber finish shaving the whiskers off the left side of his face.

"Barton claimed he didn't know whether old man Hamann might be a German spy," Tom reported to the other League members who had gathered at the barbershop for their weekly meeting.

"We'll get to the bottom of it soon enough," Ned Cramer said as he peered out the front window of the shop and watched Barton enter the General Store.

Ned liked to keep an eye on the comings and goings on Main Street and was a near permanent fixture at the barbershop, much to the irritation of the barber, Mickey Newman.

"Yeah, and Barton just might know more than he lets on," Bobby Jenkins said, always eager to stir the pot.

It had been due to little Bobby's urging that the local League had accused Christian Shultz and his family of espionage. Though the Shultz family had been a well-to-do and well-establish German family who had played a central role in the building of Wall, the League's flimsy charges of espionage had been enough to have them shipped off to Utah for detention and further interrogation. Watching the whole Shultz family, husband, wife, and three children, rounded up like common criminals and hauled away by U.S. Marshals had been the thrill of Bobby Jenkins' life. Like an addict in need of another fix, Bobby couldn't wait for the adrenaline rush that bagging of another den of Hun scum would give him.

"I told Barton we'd be coming out his way. What I didn't tell him is that we've been keeping an eye on his eldest boy, Billy," Tom said, as he slapped aftershave on his round, puddy, liver-spotted face.

"You mean on the boy's German friends, don't you," Clay Thompson said, wanting to let everyone know, he knew everything Tom knew.

"That's right, Clay. The boy seems to favor hanging out with Germans these days. Seems to have a hankerin' for their fairer sex," Tom grunted, raising his eyebrows.

"I see where you're going with this, Tom. There's no doubt, those filthy Huns are using their women to snare young, impressionable red-blooded American boys to gain favors," Clay said, nodding his head in agreement.

"What's our next move?" Ned said, itching for some action.

"First thing, we'll go out to old man Hamann's place to put the squeeze on the old bastard. He'll slip up sooner or later. Then, we'll swing by the Barton place to see if we can question John and Billy. Never know what we might churn up," Tom said with a knowing grin.

"Yeah, it's always worthwhile to beat the bushes. You never know what you might scare up," Bobby said, his eyes wide with anticipation.

Bobby Jenkins wished for nothing else then for the League to net another poor bastard and soon. He couldn't wait to see their next victim cower in their gasp, like some cornered defenseless animal. It mattered little to him whether their next victim was guilty or innocent; it was all the same to him. He believed the League held the power to decide what was good for the country. He never gave their actions any further thought. That he relished seeing others suffer, well, he figured that was between him and his maker, and as far as he could tell, his maker had no objections so long as those who suffered were German scum or those who supported them.

"Who's next up in the chair?" Mickey said, as he surveyed the assembled League members expectantly.

"Damn it, Mickey, you always seem to be more interested in cuttin' and shavin' and makin' money then in trackin' down Huns," Ned said, not liking the fact that League meetings at the barbershop always seemed to cost him money.

"A man has to eat, Ned. And from the looks of things, you could use a shave," Mickey retorted, seemingly unfazed by Ned's grumblings, which had hit a little too close to the mark.

Fact was, Mickey looked forward to the profits he garnered by holding League meetings at his shop. Though he cared little for the views of the League, Mickey felt he had little choice in the matter. As the country had grown anti-German, he felt he had to go along to get along.

"I think its Clay's turn. I'll keep an eye on the street," Ned mumbled, as he struggled to hold his temper.

"Right you are, Ned, right you are. I'm up," Clay said, quickly getting to his feet, sensing Ned needed a little time to cool off.

"When do you want to pay old man Hamann a visit?" Clay said, looking at Tom as he settled into the barber chair.

"Tomorrow, first thing in the morning. We'll take my car. Meet me here in front of the barbershop at six o'clock tomorrow morning," Tom said flatly, having only made up his mind at that very moment.

"That's kinda sudden notice. I'll have to take a day off," Bobby moaned, worried his boss at the granary might not be so understanding about Bobby taking time off on short notice.

"You're a goddamn League member, Bobby, never forget it. Anyone gives you grief, we have ways to deal with 'em," Tom snapped.

Tom couldn't believe anyone would dare to challenge the League or its activities or any of its members.

"Damn right. No one screws with the League. We have a job to do. Anyone trying to stop us puts himself at the risk of committing sedition. Not a good thing in times like these," Clay reminded everyone.

"Tomorrow morning at six o'clock, gentlemen. Any other concerns?" Tom said, as he surveyed the room slowly.

As the men took in Tom's pinched-brow, beady-eyes, and tight lips, daring any one of them to speak up, to a man, they chose to remain silent. After pointing his fat protruding chin at each of them and receiving no replies, Tom headed for the front door.

Just as he stepped outside, he paused, turned back, and said, "See you all tomorrow morning. Be here, bright and chipper."

With that, he marched off, a big man on a self-appointed mission.

Bill's eighth grade graduation in the spring had been overshadowed by President Wilson's national call to arms. With America's declaration of war on Germany, life for everyone had changed. The anti-German fervor, that had slowly grown in recent years, had gone into overdrive. Hatred for anything German came all to easily for far too many average Americans. Germans had become Huns and all Huns were America's enemy. Bill's desire to get to know his German neighbors better was no longer simply frowned on by the non-German community, it was now viewed as suspicious behavior by members of the American Protective League, whose powers seemed to grow by the day. With no end to the war in sight, Bill worried what the League might have in store for him and his German friends and where it might all lead.

The winter had been harsh in the northern plains. With spring coming late, farmers worried what the year 1918 might bring. Though everyone had hunkered down to survive through the long cold winter, their fear of the League had never been far from their minds. The German community knew that with the coming spring, League activities would once again go into full swing.

Just after nightfall, with the smell of freshly plowed fields in the air, one by one, men dressed in dark clothing slipped though the half-open side door of Detrick Fremder's barn. The barn's interior was pitch black with only a hint of light streaming from under the edge of a closed door near the back of the barn.

Upon entering the barn, each man had stood for a moment to let his eyes adjust to the dark before proceeding toward the dim sliver of light. Taking their seats in silence around a small wooden table, they waited patiently for Detrick to speak as the flickering light from a lone candle in the center of the table danced on their ruddy faces. Detrick had called the meeting and it was only right that he be the one to explain why they had all been urgently asked to attend the secret meeting in the middle of the night, considering the incredible risk they were all taking.

"We were the first Russian German farm families in the area. I don't need to remind you that the Fremders, Meyers, Hamanns, Baumanns, and Zieglers have come to be known as the five founding families in the German community," Detrick began, knowing full well the risk they were all taking.

If the League ever got wind of their secret meeting, they all stood to lose everything they had worked for, and more than likely, their freedom as well. The prospect of being shipped off to Utah or having something worse happen was no longer some uncertain possibility. If it could happen to the Schultz family, with all their connections and considerable political clout, they knew as common German immigrants, they wouldn't stand a chance should the League descend on their secret meeting. Of this, there was no doubt in anyone's mind.

"I know full well, as do you, what the League would do to us, if they found out about this meeting," he went on, looking at each of the assembled faces around the table one by one.

Upon meeting Detrick's piercing glare, eye to eye, each man nodded his understanding. None spoke.

"To survive, we need to find a way to demonstrate our patriotism to the community, while casting doubt on the legitimacy of our League overlords. Keep in mind, Germans are no longer the only ones who fear the League," Detrick said, and then paused to let his words sink in.

"They target anyone and everyone who challenges them. No one is safe. The whole community is living in fear of these self-appointed tyrants. There are many non-Germans in the community who would like to see them discredited and their powers ended," he concluded.

"What can we do?" Hans Meyer said, breaking his silence, and in doing so, cracking the seal on the voices of the other men.

"We know the League has grown increasing dangerous, but how can we do anything about it? Many in the community have turned on us Germans and anything associated with Germans. They might fear the League, but far too many of them also hate Huns," Herman Ziegler said, his voice shaking with every word.

Herman was heartbroken when one by one has neighbors had turned their backs on him and his family. To his horror, people he had once believed to be his friends had turned on him as though he were a stranger.

"Detrick, you know the League is after my father. He sent money to pay off his debit to Felix Koch down in Bloomfield and now they are accusing him of supporting the German war effort. It's crazy talk, but they continue to hound him day and night," Fredrick Hamann said, reminding everyone his father may soon be arrested.

Fredrick and his father had each claimed one hundred sixty acres when they first arrived in the newly platted town of Wall in 1906. Their homesteads, situated just north of Wall, sat side by side. They had each purchased an additional one hundred sixty acres of land, making their combined loadings six hundred forty acres, a full section of land, one square mile. They had good water and soil, and their land was some of the most productive farmland in the region. The League, largely made up of bitter men who had not done well with their own homesteads, had made it a point of targeting German immigrants who had succeeded. The Hamann family with its choice land holdings had become one of their primary targets.

"Yes, yes, I know Fredrick, something must be done, and soon. This is why I've called you all here tonight. I have a plan. And, I think it just might work," Detrick said, his eyes shining in the flickering candlelight.

Detrick Fremder and Fredrick Hamann had grown close since Fredrick's sister, Annie, married Detrick just prior to their departure from Bloomfield for western South Dakota. Detrick knew it was critical that he take action before the League went too far with his father-in-law. The horrible lesson of the Schulz family being hauled off to Utah in the middle of the night to an unknown future had struck fear into the heart of every German immigrant. Considering how easy it had been for the League to dispatch the rich and influential Schultz family, they all realized just how vulnerable they really were.

"So, what is this magical plan?" Hans said, skeptical anything could really be done.

The League had the support of far too many in the community. The Germans were easy targets, and ready scapegoats for any non-Germans that may fall under the scrutiny of the League. All a non-German needed to do was to point his finger at a German to deflect the League's unwanted attentions. The League would gladly do the rest.

"It's not all that magical, but I'm certain it will work like magic just the same," Detrick quipped. "It might take a little time and effort to set up and even more luck to pull off, but if it works, it may end the League's reign of terror once and for all. Or at the very least, loosen the League's strangle hold on this community."

With these words the tiny room erupted with the sound of five men all talking at once, each with plenty on his mind and plenty to say. The men continued to talk through the night and into the wee hours of the morning, turning over every option, mulling over every possible outcome. Two hours before sunrise, the men slipped out of the barn, one by one, into a moonless night. As the men journeyed home, they found themselves more and more convinced that Detrick's plan just might work. Fact was, they had few other options.

Each man had cast his lot with the others. There were times in life when a man had to risk everything, they each had accepted that the League had left them with no choice. If charges were brought against the Hamann family, they were all convinced charges against the other founding families would soon follow. There was no turning back.

With a mother of German descent, J. Edgar Hoover didn't much like all the anti-German sentiment stirred up by the war. In 1917, at the tender age of twenty-two and fresh out of law school, J. Edgar was eager to make a name for himself at the U.S. Department of Justice. He had only recently moved to Washington D.C. and was excited to get started. Tracking down radicals and spies had long piqued his interest and, he believed, it was a surefire way for a newcomer at the Bureau of Investigation to quickly rise through the ranks.

Considering all the time and energy that had been wasted in chasing after poor German immigrants in rural backwaters over the past several years, the Bureau of Investigation, with its legion of American Protective League members, had netted far too many catch and release suckers and far too few trophy catches worth mounting. J. Edger was convinced the Bureau needed to shift its focus to more fruitful targets. He had followed the news of the fall of the Russian czar and the rise of a radical Bolshevik government in Russia with keen interest. J. Edger believed it was this kind of catalyst coming from abroad that may prompt the Bureau to shift its focus, considering the potential threat these kinds of foreign radical elements may pose to the established order in America.

The Zimmerman Telegram had taught Americans they could no longer ignore the world beyond the borders of the United States. All too often, events that happened in distant lands overseas had come calling at America's front door. J. Edgar smiled to himself as he pondered these trends and the likely direction of future developments. He had a hankering to harpoon whales, even trophy catches were not big enough for a man the likes of J. Edgar Hoover. As for the minnows, he had long since decided, he would leave them to others.

July 4, 1918

Wall, Pennington County, South Dakota

Sprichst du Deutsch

PETER BAUMANN, WHOSE HOMESTEAD was located the furthest from Wall in an isolated valley along the Cheyenne River to the west, had learned the art of brewing beer from his grandfather back in Germany. Peter had become the main supplier of beer for the German community in and around Wall. Though many of the men in Wall, German and non-German alike, enjoyed a cold beer, the Temperance Society had been effective in driving the evil brew out of all the diners and boarding houses in the state of South Dakota, including those in Wall. With no saloon in town, the market for beer was effectively limited to private gatherings. The custom of drinking beer after Sunday services among German men in the community had kept Peter busy until the advent of the American Protective League, which soon locked arms with the Temperance Society to increase community-wide pressure on the unwelcome Huns in their midst.

Peter had worked in secret to fulfill his part of Detrick's plan by distilling several gallons of nearly pure ethyl alcohol. Careful to avoid discovery, he had delivered two large jugs of alcohol to Fredrick Hamann's farm the week before the Fourth of July. The plan was for Hans Meyer to pick up the jugs and transfer them to a small storage shed owned by Herman Ziegler located in the alley not far from the rear of the General Store in Wall. Hans had been chosen to transfer the alcohol into Wall, since he ran a delivery business and frequently hauled loads of supplies to and from Ziegler's storage shed. If he transferred the alcohol several days before the Fourth of July, there was little concern that the delivery might draw any undue attention from prying eyes.

They all knew that the League always set up their headquarters tent across the alley directly behind the General Store during events held downtown. Ziegler's shed was well situated for what they had in mind. As was customary, they had learned that Tom McFarland planned to treat his little band of merry henchmen to cold beer, secretly brought in on the train from Pierre, and to ice-cold watermelon as part of their Fourth of July festivities. Detrick's plan was simple, they would spike both the beer and the watermelon with almost tasteless one-hundred-ninety-proof pure ethyl alcohol. Counting on the insatiable appetites of big Tom McFarland and his bully boys for cold beer and iced-down watermelon on a hot summer day, Detrick figured it wouldn't take long before the whole rotten bunch became slobbering drunks.

Detrick and Fredrick had drawn straws to decide who would go into the tent to spike the beer and watermelon and who would act as lookout. Fredrick had seen to it he would be the one to go into the League's tent; it was his father who had recently been officially charged with having used the German language over the telephone. If the League wasn't discredited soon, he feared his father would be arrested and imprisoned before the end of July and that he would be next, along with his whole family. Once the Hamann family was rounded up, the League would waste no time rounding up the rest of the five founding families. Detrick had agreed to act as lookout knowing how Fredrick felt and knowing there would be no way to talk him out of it. He also agreed that the five founding families were like a row of dominos. If the League succeeded in toppling the Hamann family, the other four families would soon fall, one after the next.

On July 3, the two men met at Ziegler's shed and silently watched from a distance as the League's tent was set up and stocked for the coming Fourth of July festivities. Unable to come out of the shed during the daylight for fear of discovery, the two men stayed out of sight and spent a miserable day catnapping in the stale air and sweltering heat of the windowless shed.

At midnight, with their shirts drenched in sweat, they stepped out of their hideout into a cool breeze filled with a chorus of katydids and chirping crickets. Dressed in black and moving on cat's feet the two men made their way to the back of the League's tent where Fredrick quickly slipped under its canvas edge. Detrick, carrying the two jugs of alcohol and an empty wooden bucket, carefully placed each item one at a time into Fredrick's hands every time they were extended from under the tent's back edge. Detrick held up the edge of the tent and waited patiently as each item slowly disappeared under the lip of the canvas.

Detrick laid on his belly at the back of the tent and slithered from one side to the other to keep an eye on the narrow alley between the front of the tent and the back of the General Store. For what seemed like hours, Detrick maintained his vigil while Fredrick worked slowly and methodically to drain a bucket of beer from the large keg of beer set up in the tent and to slowly pour an equal amount of ethyl alcohol back into the keg.

For the watermelon, Fredrick had brought a knife with a long sharp narrow blade to cut a beveled plug out of the huge melon. Pulling out the plug, he then tipped the second jug of ethyl alcohol up so its contents could slowly drain into the meat of the watermelon. When the jug was finally empty, he carefully replaced the plug, like a cork in a bottle. He was confident the plug's cut was clean and fit perfectly. The chance of anyone noticing a plug had been cut into the melon was highly unlikely, especially considering the men who would be slicing up the melon would never suspect anyone would be crazy enough to mess with League property.

When Fredrick finally slipped back out from under the tent's edge, Detrick had never felt more relieved. His relief quickly evaporated when he discovered the bucket now full of beer was still inside the tent. Fredrick realizing his mistake, once again slipped under the edge of the tent to retrieve the bucket. Pushing the nearly full bucket of beer out from under the back edge of the tent without spilling any had taken less than a minute; even so, during this lost minute, the daring duo's luck ran out.

Just as they were ready to move back to Ziegler's shed, an old Model T came puttering up the alley, its headlights ablaze, lighting up the alley on both sides. Detrick and Fredrick froze, not knowing what might happen next. Just when they thought they might be in the clear, the Model T made a sharp turn and pulled up in front of the tent. Lying flat on the ground in the shadows at the rear of the tent, they weren't sure what they would do if someone decided to walk around to the back of the tent.

When the engine finally stopped and the headlight went dark, nothing happened, as silence reigned, causing the two men's hearts to race with anticipation. After several minutes, they heard a man laugh and then the giggle of a young woman as they got out of the car.

"Oh, come on honey, you know I have to be home soon," the woman said, giggling.

"Let's have a little drink and then I'll take you straight home," the man said.

Hearing their voices clearly, Detrick had no doubt that the man was Clay Thomson, the League's number two, and the young woman was Wilma Philips, the feed store owner's eldest daughter, who he knew couldn't be more than fifteen years old.

Listening as the couple ducked into the tent through the front flap, Detrick motioned to Fredrick that they would need to hold tight. Detrick figured they would be able to slip away quietly once the party in the tent got underway. For now, about all they could do is wait.

After a lamp was lit, the sound of mugs being filled from the large keg of beer was followed by a series of creaking squeaks. Fredrick gestured to Detrick that there was a cot set up inside the tent. Both men nodded at one another with knowing looks that more than likely Casanova Clay had maneuvered his young prey onto the cot.

"Toast!" they both said in unison to the clink of beer mugs coming together.

"Oh, I never drank beer before," Wilma said smacking her lips. "It's so strong!"

"Yeah, this stuff does have a little kick to it," Clay said, having never tasted a beer that had such a wallop.

Taking another gulp, he had to admit the brew was stout. He hoped it would have just the kind of kick that might kick-start some real fun. Coaxing his young beauty to drink up, and liking the direction things were going, Clay couldn't help it when a Cheshire cat grin took possession of his face, pulling up the corners of his thin lips.

Outside the tent, Detrick was well aware of the direction things were headed. A young woman, still a naïve child in many ways, was about to be taken advantage of by a man twice her age and who cared nothing for her. He knew Wilma had a reputation of being a loose woman around town but didn't like it one damn bit how Clay was taking advantage of her. Detrick, with five young daughters of his own, faced the horrible dilemma of either standing by and letting it happen or stopping it before it went too far. If he intervened, he risked his own freedom and that of his family's and possibly that of many others. Listening to Clay slyly prod Wilma to have one more swallow of beer after another, Detrick found himself unable to do anything but clinch his teeth in anger.

Frozen to inaction by the terrible cost of intervention, Detrick Fremder was reminded of the lesson many men have learned: a man's morals seldom win out over a man's need to protect his family. War had taught that lesson to legions of men over and over again down through the ages. Detrick was waging war against the injustice of the League; he was in a battle for the survival of his family and his fellow German immigrants. Reluctantly, he accepted that Wilma, innocent or not, would soon become collateral damage in that war. The fact he knew she had a reputation of being less than chaste proved to be a poor balm for his guilty conscience.

With Wilma giggling like a schoolgirl as the liquor worked its magic, Clay whispered, "Give your daddy another one of those sweet, sweet kisses."

"Oh Clay," Wilma purred.

After a long silence punctuated with heavy breathing, Detrick and Fredrick had little trouble imagining what might be happening inside the tent.

Coming up for air, Wilma groaned in earnest, "You love me, don't you Clay?"

The question hung for a long moment until Clay breathing heavily said, "Yes, sweetheart, I said I did, didn't I?"

Following this brief exchange, Detrick and Fredrick heard only heavy breathing for what seemed like several minutes, until Clay said, "Here, let me help you with that."

Hearing the rustling of clothing, Detrick and Fredrick knew things inside the tent were about to heat up considerably. Figuring the two lovers, lost in the moment, could care less about anything beyond the walls of the tent, Fredrick motioned to Detrick that it was time for them to be on their way. Detrick grudgingly nodded, wanting nothing more than to somehow stop what he knew was happening inside tent, yet knowing he had no real options.

Once again moving on cat's feet, they made their way back to Ziegler's shed, careful not to spill the bucket of beer. Pouring the beer into the outhouse hole behind the shed, they quickly rinsed out the bucket and the two large jugs. They then filled the bucket with oats and the jugs with kerosene. They were confident they had covered their tracks. Though these steps seemed extreme and unnecessary, everyone had agreed they couldn't afford to leave any clues behind that could ever connect them to coming events.

As Detrick made his way home, he was confident his plan would work. Clay had tasted the spiked beer and had figured it was just a strong brew.

He hadn't questioned why it was so strong. It was good to know the spiking of the beer wouldn't give things away. He had less concern over the spiking of the watermelon, which was unlikely to be detected by men already tipsy. And as luck would have it, he now had an ace in the hole, one he intended on playing when the time was right.

Clay Thomas was nearly forty years old, old enough to be Wilma's father. More importantly, Casanova Clay was a married man with three kids of his own. Detrick knew this little tidbit was priceless and fit in perfectly with their plan to bring down the League. If Wilma could be convinced that she needed to protect her reputation by claiming Clay had forced himself on her, her public accusation may deliver the devastating blow to the League they were hoping for. For this to happen, Detrick would need to find a way to let Ed Philips know what his daughter has been up to.

Detrick decided he would get to town early in hopes of finding someone in the non-German community he could trust. Ed Philips needed to be informed before the Fourth of July parade, where Detrick figured the League would try to start trouble. His hope was that League members would be drunk by then and probably more than a little belligerent. With the alcohol giving them a sense of invincibility, it would be inevitable that fistfights would break out as League members shoved German immigrants around. He was sure the League had already arranged for Sheriff Johnson and his deputies to close in and arrest as many disorderly Germans as possible. The sheriff had proven long ago he was more than willing to turn a blind eye to League abuses.

Detrick's original plan had been to turn the tables on the League by getting them so drunk that when things exploded into violence, it would be clear to the good people of Wall that it was drunken League members that instigated the trouble. He also hoped that their public intoxication would put their alliance with the local Temperance Society in jeopardy. The plan had always been a little thin, since it relied on Sheriff Johnson doing his duty. If the sheriff chose to ignore the League's drunkenness and quickly whisked both League members and any Germans they rounded up off the streets, Detrick's plan would fail.

If Wilma Philips could be convinced to demand Clay Thomas be arrested for assault when the drunken melee was still in full swing, the seriousness of her charges made in public for all to hear might just be the final straw to break the stranglehold the American Protective League had on the citizens of Wall. With visions of Tom McFarland, Clay Thomas, and the rest of the League's henchmen arrested by a reluctant yet cornered Sheriff Johnson and his deputies dancing in his head, Detrick, exhausted and unwilling to wipe a hopeful grin off his face, fell into a deep, dreamless sleep.

The morning dew burnt off early, as the temperature soared. For weeks there had been nothing but cloudless skies, bone dry winds, and scorching heat. Though farmers had grown disparate as their crops shriveled in their fields, they knew there was little they could do beyond praying for rain and cooler weather.

The war had dragged on for four grizzly years, with American doughboys fighting at the front lines for the past year and half. Nearly everyone knew someone, or knew someone who had someone, fighting in the trenches. As causalities grew into the tens of thousands, the war's soulless tentacles gripped the nation. With the country at war, no one wanted to miss Wall's annual Fourth of July festivities.

Everyone knew that as long as the League prowled the streets, it didn't pay for anyone to be seen as anything less than patriotic. The number of people who had suffered under the thumb of the League had grown steadily. Though Germans were the League's primary target, an increasing number of non-Germans had been brought low. Unsure who to trust, everyone learned to keep their guard up.

"Come on, everybody, let's get on the move," John hollered, wanting to avoid pushing his old Model T too hard down the rutty Market Road to town during the middle of the day, when the temperature was forecast to hit a hundred degrees before noon for the tenth day in a row.

With John behind the wheel, Sarah riding shotgun with little baby Francis, just a year old, on her lap, the four girls piled in the back seat on top of a large picnic basket and assorted blankets, and Bill and Alva riding in the narrow rumble seat, the old Tin Lizzy groaned as it pulled out of the driveway. Reaching Wall by quarter past ten in the morning, John staked out a shady spot in the public park where the family could eat an early lunch before lining Main Street to watch the big parade.

As Sarah spread out two blankets on the grass in the shade of the large cottonwood tree, Annie Fremder, Detrick's wife, happened by. Sarah and Annie had gotten to know one another since their children started attending school together. Having girls of about the same ages, the two women had been friendly until the League had made it plain that non-Germans would do well to steer clear of their German neighbors.

"Looks like you found a nice shady spot," Annie said, admiring the fine picnic lunch Sarah had started to lay out on blankets.

"Yes, we were lucky to grab it," Sarah said, unsure how to proceed with their conversation.

The tension between Germans and non-Germans had grown steadily as the two camps attempted to stayed at arm's length from one another.

"Yes, you were. We brought a tarp, we pitched it, right over there," she said, pointing at the white canvas awning on the other end of the park. "Please ask John to drop by. My husband, Detrick, would like to talk with him," she added before turning to walk away.

"Yes, I'll do that. See you at the parade," Sarah said, wondering what Detrick Fremder could possible want to talk with John about, considering, as far as she knew, the two men barely knew one another.

She suddenly remembered that Annie was Fredrick Hamann's sister. She felt a chill run down her spine when she realized that it was Fredrick's father, Ludwig Hamann, who had been relentlessly hounded by the League for months. That Ludwig Hamann was Annie's father was something Sarah had never really thought about. She now worried whether John, who had always supported and gotten along with their German neighbors, including the Hamanns, was somehow involved.

The League had waited for the Fourth of July with relish. It was the big day on which they had planned to net a whole nest of German subversives. They had slowly tightened their noose around the five founding families, whose prime land holdings had made them a natural target for the bigotry that drove many of the actions of the League and its members. Only one thing could account for an immigrant doing better than a hardworking red-blooded American: they had somehow cheated, plain and simple. To a man, every League member believed it was the League's duty to put uppity foreigners in their place. Targeting the five founding families fit the bill perfectly.

Using the barbershop as their customary rendezvous, League members drifted in one by one. While waiting for Tom and Clay to arrive, Bobby

Jenkins couldn't help recounting recent events with Ned and Mickey, who had arrived early.

"The look on poor old Ludwig's face was priceless," Bobby said with a hardy laugh.

"Yes, old man Hamann couldn't understand what we were talking about. The old fool just kept stuttering in his broken English. It was beautiful, just beautiful," Ned agreed, nodding his head.

"Nailing him for speaking German over the telephone finally did the trick. I knew we'd get the sonofabitch and his Hun coconspirators down in Bloomfield," Mickey said with the broad smile carved into his pasty face.

As the war dragged on, anti-German hostility had grown in South Dakota by the day, which reinforced the League's legitimacy in the minds of a growing number of non-German citizens. The state of South Dakota's prohibition against the use of the German language over the telephone had become the League's newest weapon to ferret out spies and saboteurs. Further strengthening the League's hand was a new state law against public assemblies of three or more persons which had recently been passed. The League couldn't wait to employ this new weapon, the first chance they got.

Tom McFarland figured the Fourth of July celebrations in Wall provided the League the perfect opportunity to catch Huns breaking the new law by the score. Should any Huns gather among themselves in small groups of three or more at the edges of the festivities as the Germans usually did, Tom figured the League would be well within the powers of the new law to pull the slimy Huns in for questioning. If things went as planned, many of the Hun bastards would resist arrest, and Tom had pledged he would make damn sure they did, which would allow the League to use whatever force necessary. Tom couldn't wait to bust a few ugly Hun heads.

Tom had never accepted that any German immigrant could ever really be trusted. Born a Hun, die a Hun, he liked to say. He believed every German thought of themselves that way and that Germans could never become good red-blooded Americans.

Tom and Clay arrived together sporting broad smiles having shared a joke just before stepping through the barbershop door.

"Well, you look like a happy bunch," Clay said, still smiling from his earlier exchange with Tom.

"We were just talking about the look on old man Hamann's face when we cornered the sonofabitch," Bobby said with a chuckle.

"Funny you should be talking about old Ludwig Hamann, Tom and I were just talking about the same thing. It was hilarious seeing the old fool babble like some frightened schoolboy, when he tried to explain why he'd been speaking in German over the phone to his Hun buddies down in Bloomfield," Clay said, shaking his head.

"Well, it's not a done deal yet. We need to round up more of his coconspirators today," Tom said, reminding everyone they had work to do.

"That's right, we need to turn in several of the bastards to make the charges stick. We have to show the U.S. Marshals we have a whole sleeper cell living amongst us here in Wall," Clay added.

"Come on boys, let's have a cold beer and some of that iced-down watermelon. Puttin' the screws to our Hun neighbors this afternoon is gonna be thirsty work," Tom said with a chuckle, motioning for everyone to follow him over to the small tent behind the General Store that would serve as the League's temporary headquarters during the festivities.

The town of Wall was festooned with American flags and red, white, and blue bunting had been draped from every windowsill and banister. Streamers waved in the breeze from every streetlight pole with colorful banners suspended over the parade route down Main Street. Tents with their side panels rolled up had been pitched in the city park to serve refreshments and to protect visitors and townsfolk from a relentless sun that beat down mercilessly on anyone caught out in the open. Fourth of July celebrations had always been a highlight in the life of the Wall community, and everyone looked forward to a fun-filled and relaxing day.

Several marching bands, award winners of the recent rodeo and stock show, and an array of decorated floats had been assembled and would be paraded down Main Street starting at half past noon. Several speeches had been scheduled and a fireworks display planned for early evening.

Tom and his band of merry minions were in high spirits as they guzzled cold beer, carefully staying out of sight of the local Temperance Society. South Dakota had come into the union as a dry state in 1889, and though it hadn't lasted, it was headed back in that direction again, as the probation movement gained momentum statewide following the national trend. Drinking alcohol was frowned on by the local citizenry, especially during family gatherings where young children and wives were in attendance.

Tom knew they needed to tread lightly around the Temperance Society, but felt he needn't be too concerned since, in his swelled-up self-importance, the League had become untouchable. He figured he would let his boys enjoy a few beers and then have everyone stick to nonalcoholic beverages and the huge watermelon he had packed in ice for the rest of the day. There was nothing more delicious and satisfying than a big slice of ice-cold watermelon on a hot summer day.

Little did he suspect that on this fateful day, things wouldn't turn out quite the way he planned. Big Tom McFarland was about the learn one of life's most important lessons, a lesson he would soon learn the hard way: no one is untouchable.

After talking with Detrick Fremder, a man he had never really known, John had agreed to have a talk with Ed Philips. He was sure Ed wouldn't be at all happy about how Clay Thompson had been taking advantage of his eldest daughter, Wilma. He wasn't sure however how Ed might react to the news. He worried that things could go very badly. The last thing John wanted was to get into a fistfight with Ed Philips, a man who hefted hundred-pound feed sacks all day and stood six-five and weighted a good solid three hundred pounds.

"Ed, Ed Philips! Good to see you here," John said, wearing a broad, friendly smile on his face.

Seeing the size of Ed Philips up close, John, a man confident he had the sand to stand up to any man, felt a twinge of doubt about what he was about to do. Ed's reaction was a gamble, a gamble John had agreed to take, he reluctantly reminded himself.

"Yes, it looks like the whole county's turned out," Ed said, burying John's right hand in his own meaty mitt as the two men shared a hearty handshake.

"Ed, I have a private matter I need to talk with you about. Do you have a minute?" John said, deciding there was no reason to beat around the bush.

"Private matter? Why yes, of course. Let's talk over at my store," Ed said, seeing John didn't want to draw undue attention and didn't want anyone else to hear what he had to say.

Ed's mind raced as he tried to figure out what John Barton, of all people, might want to talk privately with him about. Ed led the way as the two men quickly walked over to the Philips' Feed Store just off Main Street. With most of the businesses in town closed and everyone gathering along Main Street for the parade, the side streets were quiet and empty.

"What's this all about John?" Ed said, turning to meet John face to face.

"Let's just get out off the street and I'll let you know," John said, wanting to avoid drawing any undue attention, especially from any League members.

Arriving at Ed's store, Ed quickly unlocked and opened the front door. "After you," Ed said, as he quickly ushered John inside.

Once the two men were off the street and out of sight, John wasted no time getting down to business. He had four young daughters of his own and fumed at the thought of some lowdown Casanova abusing any one of them. John shared Detrick's story, careful not to mention Detrick or how widely the information might be known around town. Ed had stood with his arms folded tightly across his board chest, nodding his head sightly up and down as John recounted what he knew. When he finished, John couldn't help but notice Ed's physical reaction to the unwelcome news. Ed nearly doubled over like a man punched in the guts as a grimmest of pain twisted across his face.

Shaking his head from side to side, his eyes moist and red, Ed spoke slowly with a quiver in his voice, "I feared my little Wilma was under some evil bastard's spell."

Gathering himself, he continued, "She's been sneaking out for weeks. I should've stopped her. That bastard Clay Thompson's been hanging around the store. I saw him eyeing Wilma, but that bastard glares at all the gals, so like a fool, I let it pass. He's League, I didn't want to invite trouble. I'd hoped he'd move on and leave my little girl alone."

"We've all been under the thumb of the League, Ed. We've all been living in fear," John said, wondering if this could bring an end to it.

Ed stood stock still for a long minute until he said with conviction, "Yes, the whole damn town's been living in fear, far too long, but no more. That bastard abused my little girl and he's gonna pay for what he did, League or no goddamn League. One way or another, he'll pay, even if I have to kill the sonofabitch myself."

As mad as the man was, John worried that there was no telling how things might turn out. Ed, a Goliath of a man, could easily rip Casanova Clay into little pieces with his two bare hands.

"There is a way to nail the sonofabitch and to let justice be served. And God willing, to save your daughter's reputation. Ed, if you can get Wilma to cooperate, we can make this happen today," John offered, hoping Ed would be willing to go along with the plan Detrick hoped would rid the town of the League.

After describing what the League and the sheriff's office had planned for the German community during the parade, John outlined the critical role Wilma could play in nailing Casanova Clay, saving her own reputation, and ending the tyrannical reign of the League once and for all.

"You can count on Wilma being there and playing her part. She'll finger that bastard. I'll see to it," Ed said, the tone of his voice leaving no doubt.

"Ed, I'm sorry . . . but . . . I knew I had to . . .," John said, truly sorry he had to be the barer of bad news.

"I know it was tough for you to let me know. I thank you for speaking up and for giving me a way to save my little Wilma. I'll take it from here. Now, let's get back, before the parade gets underway," Ed said, a man eager to get his ducks in a row and hopefully to get his bare hands around Clay Thomas's scrawny pencil neck.

Ed knew he had to save Wilma's reputation. She was young and naïve. In a small town like Wall, a loose woman would be forever marked. If Wilma became the harlot of Wall, the Philips family name would be ruined. The impact on his wife would be devastating. He had to try to save Wilma from herself, even if she was already lost. Leaving his store, Ed was a man on a mission to find his daughter and to set the record straight. With the parade scheduled to begin in less than half an hour, he had no time to lose.

"Give me another big slice of that juicy watermelon," Tom slobbered between chops on the watermelon slice he was already working on.

He had downed two beers and after emptying his bladder behind the tent had polished off several slices of watermelon.

A growing pile of watermelon rinds in the far corner of the tent stood in testament to the relaxing morning spent by League members. Their cheeks flush, their speech slurred, and their voices growing louder by the minute, to a man, they all felt like they had the world by the tail.

"It's ten past noon, Tom. Let's mosey over to the park and get ready to have a little fun," Clay said, feeling a little tipsy, but not giving it a second thought.

"No need to worry, Clay, them Hun bastards aren't going anywhere," Ned said, as he bit into another slice of watermelon.

"Yeah, we cun eat barb-que after round up," Bobby chimed in, his face beet red, his speech slurred.

"You alright, Bobby? I warned you the beer had a kick," Clay said, worried Bobby might not be able to hold his liquor.

Having everyone drink beer on an empty stomach on a hot summer day might not have been one of Big Tom's best ideas, Clay thought; but then, he knew when it was best to keep his mouth shut and such thoughts to himself.

"I'll be fine, just mind your own damn Ps and Qs, Clay," Bobby snapped, his temper flaring as the one-hundred-ninety-proof alcohol coursed through his veins, dissolving his inhibitions.

"Let's just get in place before the parade starts," Clay snapped, shrugging off Bobby's belligerence and trying to take charge, as the alcohol boosted his overinflated confidence. "We'll make our move along the street in front of the City Park, where Sheriff Johnson said there'd be plenty of room to round up as many Hun bastards as we want."

"Slow down, Clay, you're not in charge here. We go when I say we go," Tom barked, reminding Clay and everyone else in ear shot who was in charge. "I'd like to finish this here slice of watermelon 'fore we go," he added, leading back in his chair with a half-eaten slice of watermelon in his hand and juice running down his fat double chin.

Mickey, a small man who had been raised by a mother active in the Temperance Movement, was a teetotaler and had passed on drinking any beer. Strangely, he had noticed he was feeling a little light-headed. He'd never been drunk in his life and so had no idea what it felt like to be drunk. He wasn't sure what was happening to him. He thought it might just be his nervous anticipation of the coming excitement. Though he had noticed the watermelon had a stout taste, he hadn't mentioned it to the others, considering everyone else was enjoying the watermelon and had no complaints. Indeed, everyone seemed to be in good mood. Mickey noted however that as the morning passed, the group had become increasingly loud and rowdy. Nothing alarming, yet Mickey began to wonder if something might be wrong. He knew better than to speak up and contented himself with keeping out a wary eye and keeping his mouth zipped shut.

After finishing off his fourth slice of watermelon, Tom joined the row of men at the back of the tent to relieve himself one last time before ambling over to the park. With Tom taking the led, the motley troop of visibly inebriated hooligans marched directly to the City Park. Pushing their way through the crowd of people lining the street to see the parade, the League made its presence known to everyone.

"Stand back, everyone, we're here on League business," Tom announced, his chest bowed out, his tin badge polished shiny bright earlier that morning, resting high above his right shirt pocket.

"Yeah, get the hell out of the way, we're here to enforce the law," Bobby said, as he sucker-punched Fredrick Hamann square in the mouth.

Fredrick, not completely surprised by the move, came up swinging like a wild man. His first punch cracking Bobby Jenkins's jaw and his second and third blackening both of his eyes. With the first punches thrown and answered, as if on cue, the mayor standing on the courthouse steps announced through a large blowhorn that the Fourth of July parade would soon begin its march down Main Street.

Just as the first drumbeats of marching bands filled the air, all hell broke loose. An all-out brawl between League members and whoever got in their way, Germans and non-Germans alike, surged around the sheriff and his deputies as they struggled to figure out who they needed to arrest.

With punches being thrown in every direction, Ned attempted to get in a few sucker punches of his own. Just as he wound up to swing, his face was met with a balled-up fist that flattened his nose, sending blood flying out in every direction. Bent over with both hands grasping his broken nose, the last thing Ned remembered was a muddy black boot coming up and catching him square in the mouth. Knocked out cold, Ned lay flat on his back with a broken nose and bloody hole for a mouth.

Mickey, seeing things had gotten out of control, decided to tuck tail and run. He liked to think of himself as a businessman and had never fully believed in the League or its hatred of Germans, seeing how Germans had been some of his best customers before the war. With punches flying in every direction, Mickey attempted to slip away before the brawl caught up with him. Stumbling, unable to walk straight as his alcohol-soaked brain caused the world to spin out of control, he soon ran straight into the arms of several brawny Germans who took turns using his limp spongy body as a punching bag. Pummeled senseless, Mickey finally collapsed, curling himself into a fetal position on the ground as he nursed a badly lacerated face and several busted ribs.

Tom McFarland, his face beet red and unsteady on his feet, attempted to hold his ground. Standing in the middle of the melee, a good head taller than most of the other men, Tom swung at everything and connected with nothing. It wasn't long until he came face to face with Detrick Fremder, who was in no mood to take any guff from a drunken German-hating fat man wearing a shiny tin badge.

Tom, feeling invincible, charged forward to battle with Detrick, with alcohol dimming his common sense. Stumbling headlong into a stiff right hand, followed by a perfectly delivered left uppercut that lifted his rotund body clean off the ground, Tom was sent sailing several feet, landing hard on his back right on top of little Bobby Jenkins, who still laid sprawled out on the ground since his earlier encounter with Fredrick Hamann. Pinned under a mountain of blubber, Bobby's talkative nature lubricated by watermelon juice and fueled by nearly pure ethynyl alcohol suddenly went into overdrive as he started jabbering and laughing like a crazed monkey about all the dirty tricks the League had pulled off over the past couple of years. The crowd of townsfolk that had gathered round the brawl were appalled by the outlandish behavior of drunken League members and shocked by Bobby Jenkins's many revelations of horrible deeds.

Having had enough and seeing that the League's members were all down and out, Ed Philips hollered at the top of his lungs, "Everyone! Stop, stop what you're doing right now!"

The power in his voice sent a shock wave up and down Main Street, bringing the parade to a halt and the rowdy crowd to a standstill. Even the sheriff and his deputies stood frozen, unsure what to do next.

Ed then motioned for Wilma to step forward. Wilma, her shoulders shaking, with tears streaming down her elfin face, slowly made her way to her father, who now stood at the center of the assembled crowd.

"Tell 'em, Wilma. Tell 'em. Don't be afraid. Tell 'em what you told me," Ed said, his voice gentle, causing everyone to lean in to hear what Wilma had to say.

"Clay, Clay Thomas, that man laying over there," Wilma cried out, her voice a quivering shriek, as she pointed an accusing finger straight at Casanova Clay, who lay sprawled out on the ground with a number of egg-sized knots on his head, a broken nose, and a rib cage that had been caved in on both sides.

"He tried to hurt me . . . to force me to . . . he's a monster . . . and should be arrested," she continued, her voice trailing off into tears.

Ed, having decided not to strangle the man outright once he had him in his grasp, had beaten Casanova Clay to within an inch of his life. Clay lay wide-eyed and stunned by Wilma's public accusation. He had never figured that Wilma, of all people, a man-crazy girl who had more lovers than she could count, would ever start pointing fingers. Now that she had, he knew his life had taken a very unwelcome detour.

With a growing chorus of voices ringing out in the crowd calling for justice, Ed once again commanded the attention of the everyone present.

"Sheriff, I demand that you arrest Clay Thomas for assault and the rest of these drunken slobs for public intoxication and inciting a riot," Ed said, satisfied the majority of onlookers agreed with him, and hopeful they would look favorably on his little Wilma.

Soon the cacophony of voices grew louder as the majority of the community called for the arrest of Clay Thomas and the rest of the League members. Mrs. Mary Gifford, head of the local Temperance Society, witnessing the change in the community's mood toward the League, was quick to make public that she and her fellow sisters could never condone the League's horrible behavior or their public intoxication and would no longer support their efforts.

Sheriff Andrew Johnson stood stunned as he witnessed the unexpected and sudden turn of events. He knew then and there he wouldn't be able to save the League. They had gone too far and now would have to pay for it. His bigger concern was whether he would be able to save himself. The next sheriff's election was only three months off.

As if a malevolent cloud had been lifted, Germans and non-Germans began freely talking to one another without fear for the first time in far too long. Men shook hands and women embraced; the town had begun its process of healing. With everyone in high spirits, the marching bands with pounding drums and blaring trumpets suddenly came back to life, signaling that the parade, like their life as a community together, was once again back on track and in full swing.

November 28, 1918

Three Tree Creek, Pennington County, South Dakota

Hablas Español

ON NOVEMBER 11, 1918, a little more than two weeks before Thanksgiving, the welcome news came, the war was finally over. The Allied victory brought a pride-filled bounce to the nation's step, as the future looked bright for America and its newfound place among the major powers of the world. There was indeed plenty to be thankful for with everyone looking forward to a special Thanksgiving holiday. Despite the cheerful mood, newspaper headlines across the country warned of a new invisible threat that now stalked the nation and the world like the Grim Reaper himself. This new killer had been dubbed the Spanish Flu.

Reported to be spreading in large cities in America and in several countries around the world, there was a real fear that this new killer could soon spread inland following major transportation routes. For many in South Dakota, the rumor that there had been a flu outbreak in Fort Riley, Kansas, earlier in the year confirmed that the flu pandemic had already reached the Great Plains. Emergency ordinances were soon passed requiring the wearing of masks and prohibiting public spitting.

Though mask wearing had been reluctantly accepted by a war-weary population, fear of surging death totals from urban centers around the country convinced nearly everyone the pandemic was real and spreading rapidly. Numb after having lived in a state of near perpetual fear for the past several years and now thankful the war was finally over, flu or no flu, the nation couldn't wait to celebrate the Thanksgiving holiday with gusto.

The town of Wall was still talking about the Fourth of July brawl and the many revelations that had come to light about League abuses over the past couple of years. Since the incident, German and non-German citizens had all tried to put the war years behind them. The armistice that brought an end to the war had helped to close the rift between Germans and non-Germans across the nation.

Detrick appreciated the role John Barton had played and the personal risk he had taken in ending the abusive reign of the League in Wall. Though the war ended just five months after the Fourth of July brawl, Detrick was convinced that had they not acted when they did, the five founding families may have lost everything.

Over the following months, Detrick and John had met on several occasions, and the two men had grown to like and respect one another. John, the older of the two men, always had plenty of stories to tell about rogues, renegade Indians, desperadoes, and the Old West before the coming of the trains and the fencing of the open plains. Detrick found John's tales of the Old West both entertaining and fascinating. He also soon discovered that John was just as fascinated in his stories about Gypsies, Cossacks, and Tartars around the Black Sea and about his childhood days on his father's homestead in the Ukraine near the Crimea.

In compliance with the new rules to control the pandemic, nearly everyone wore masks to school and when in public as a matter of course. The Barton family, like other farm families, stayed clear of Wall and large gatherings as much as possible. Living at the edge of civilization had its advantages during a pandemic. The chance of meeting strangers from outside the area was slim to none. Steering clear of town added to the quarantine-like existence many homesteaders lived.

With their children attending school together and no reported outbreaks of the flu among farmers in the area, John and Sarah decided to accept the invitation from Detrick and Annie Fremder to share Thanksgiving dinner. With everyone complaining about having to squeeze into the old Model T, John had to admit his little family had grown considerably in recent years both in number and in size, with his children no longer able to fit into their assigned seats without considerable discomfort.

After a bumpy, miserable ride, a disheveled, ill-tempered Barton family was met with an unexpected surprise upon their arrival at the Fremder home. Standing in a row on the front porch decked out in identical blue-and-white three-piece German Dirndl dresses stood the five daughters of

Detrick and Annie Fremder. The sight of the five girls, who so strikingly resembling one another, each standing exactly a head taller than the one next in line, all wearing identical dresses, was so surreal John couldn't help muttering under his breath how much they looked like an unnested set of matching matryoshka dolls. Sarah, overhearing his remark, lightly touched the back of his hand and gave him one of her hold-your-tongue looks, just as the car pull up and stopped in front of the house.

After everyone untangled themselves and piled out of the car, Kathrine, who had just turned twelve, greeted the Barton family and introduced herself and her sisters: Lena age nine, Frederika age six, Anna age three, and little Matilda just a year old, who, Kathrine informed the Barton family, they all called Tillie. After Kathrine completed her introductions, Detrick and Annie stepped out of the house and introduced themselves.

Wanting to follow suit, John motioned to Bill, his eldest son. Bill quickly understood and stepped forward to introduce the Barton children in the order of their ages just as Kathrine had done. He let everyone know he was the oldest at sixteen, Alva was fifteen, Arvella was twelve, the same age as Kathrine, Myrtle was nine, the same age as Lena, and Matilda was eight, who, Bart informed the Fremder family, they all called Matilda, as she was named after her grandma Matilda in Chadron, Nebraska. He then rounded out his introductions by sharing that Lucille was four, and little Francis was two.

Once Bill had introduced the children, John and Sarah stepped forward and introduced themselves. John couldn't help but notice that unlike the near identical appearance of Detrick and Annie Fremder's children, his and Sarah's children had a variety of hair and eye colors and complexion shades. Bill took after John with his dark hair, dark almost tan complexion, and light hazel-blue eyes. Alva took after his mother with a fair complexion, blondish light brown hair, and green eyes. The girls and Francis either favored Bill or Sarah in varying degrees with a mix of hair and eye colors. He realized that when the Germans, who had married only within their own kind, started marrying into the local community, they too would begin to resemble their mix-breed neighbors.

With all the introductions complete, Detrick and Annie welcomed everyone and then opened the front door of the house and, standing on both sides, ushered everyone indoors. The first thing that struck Bill as he entered the Fremder home was the delicious aromas of fresh baked bread, roasted turkey and ham, and the distinctive scents of cinnamon and nutmeg wafting off two large pumpkin pies cooling on the windowsill near the dining table. It wasn't long before everyone settled in, and the children got busy getting to know one another.

Bill and Alva being teenage boys weren't exactly comfortable with a house full of adolescent girls all talking and giggling at once. Both boys couldn't help but notice just how cute Kathrine and her sisters were. Their fair nearly blemish-free complexions, strikingly feline features, strawberry blond hair, and deep blue eyes were hard to miss. The boys also noticed that it wouldn't be very long before Kathrine, already filling out and as big and tall as her mother, would be a full-grown woman. Bill, taken by her beauty at first sight, was determined to get to know Kathrine Cristina Fremder better in coming years.

Both boys had come to realize early on that they were four to five years older than most of the other children in the area, having been born back in Iowa several years before their father settled in the badlands. The majority of the children on farms around Wall were born after the first wave of immigrants arrived in 1907. This difference in age had provided them with many advantages.

Finding work, for one, was always easy, since extra workhands were hard to come by, with most of the children in the area being too young for heavy chores and most sodbusters unable to take on extra work away from their own homesteads. Other opportunities were also aplenty. Bill's plan to start a small general store in Creighton, a newly platted town on the Market Road between the Barton farm and Wall, had met with no real competition. John thought Bill's idea was a good one and a good investment. Bill planned to set up his new venture in the spring of the coming year.

Alva had promised to help out with getting Bill's new venture up and running, but had made it clear to everyone, including his father, that his dream was to travel west and to explore distant lands. He planned to join the Navy as soon as he turned eighteen. Though John had hoped he would stay on to take over the farm, he had blessed Alva's decision, knowing that he himself had left home at the age of sixteen and firmly believed that every man had the right to set his own course in life. As strong as John's convictions were about each man setting his own course, he had to admit, the end of the war had made his decision to let Alva join the Navy a damn sight easier than it might have been.

On the way home, everyone was in high spirits and talked about all the fun they had had at the Fremder place. Even Bill and Alva had found the day enjoyable. Alva couldn't stop talking about how he had won the horseshoe tournament, having defeated Detrick by tossing three solid ringers in a row on his final three pitches of the final round. In coming weeks and months, the Barton and Fremder families grew even closer. Detrick Fremder, not having sons of his own, liked having Bill and Alva visit. He also hoped one or both might take an interest in one of his older daughters. Other farm families also grew close, as the pandemic closed down the country.

By Christmas Eve, newspapers were reporting that nearly a half a million Americans had died of the Spanish flu, making America's appalling losses of over one hundred sixteen thousand men in the Great War seem somehow trivial by comparison. From February through March 1919 a second wave of the flu swept through America, bringing the total American death toll from the Spanish flu to a whopping six hundred seventy-five thousand souls.

Considering the staggering death toll in the country, South Dakota's low population density had helped to limit the flu's spread and saved the state from the worst of the pandemic. When the final figures were tabulated, statewide per capita deaths from Spanish flu were only half the national average, totaling under two thousand, with only sixty deaths in Pennington County, most of which were in or around Rapid City, the largest town in the western half of the state.

Almost unnoticed by a nation in shock, the American Protective League was officially closed down by the attorney general of the U.S. Justice Department on February 1, 1919, with all records transferred to the Bureau of Investigation and straight into the hands of an ambitious J. Edgar Hoover, who had since December 1917 managed the Enemy Alien Registration Section of the Department of Justice. For J. Edgar, becoming the keeper of secrets was a dream come true. With German immigrants no longer the focus, and the fear of Bolsheviks and the ugly head of communism on the rise, J. Edgar knew it was just a matter of time before the Bureau would need to shift its focus to more fruitful targets at home and abroad.

He could almost feel the sea breeze rush across his face as he imagined his coxswain yell, "There she blows!" Aye, he thought, finally a catch worthy of pursuit, as he dreamed of readying his harpoons. There would soon be whales aplenty. He couldn't believe his good fortune.

August 30, 1919

Radical Division, Bureau of Investigation, Washington, D.C.

A 'Ty Goodish' Po Russki

As the nation attempted to rally back as the pandemic receded, Americans learned that events overseas once again were threatening their peace. Bolsheviks soon replaced Germans as public enemy number one as the hunt for communists swept the nation, driven by a growing fear of a new Soviet regime that had risen from the ashes of the Russian Revolution in November 1917.

To address the new threat, the 1917 Espionage Act used to monitor German immigrants during the war was soon expanded with the enactment of the Sedition Act in 1918. Though the Germans were no longer the target, communist and those who criticized the government were now monitored as radical elements with labor union leaders targeted as potential enemies of the state.

Following a series of bombings targeting government and law enforcement officials in the spring of 1919, newly appointed attorney general A. Mitchell Palmer, hoping to leverage his high-profile position in the U.S. Justice Department as a stepping-stone for his own presidential ambitions, conducted a series of well-publicized raids directed at leftist radicals and anarchists. As a result, fear once again gripped the nation, touching off America's first Red Scare.

To oversee efforts to counter the threat of communism, Attorney General Palmer established the Radical Division of the Bureau of Investigation on August 1, 1919. At the ripe old age of twenty-four, J. Edgar Hoover was selected to head up the new division. The Bureau's shift in focus to more subversive radical foreign elements was exactly as J. Edgar had predicted. With whales aplenty and the hunting good, his new role would eventually lead to his appointment as the head of the Bureau of Investigation and his ultimate prize, the keeper of all secrets.

At the age of seventeen, Bill, with the help of his brother Alva, had worked all spring and summer to get his small general store up and running. Investing all of his hard-earned savings and borrowing money from his father, he was determined to make the store a success. Alva, a reluctant partner, had also invested in the store though never failed to remind his brother that he would be wanting his money back with interest in a couple of years.

Both boys were handy with a hammer and with the help of their father had built a sturdy little building that they divided into three sections of equal size. The front third of the building was built to function as the store, with a counter in the back, shelves along the walls, and two long tables running down the center of the room for the display of dry goods and supplies. In the middle third, a storeroom was set up with a door and loading dock attached to south side of the building. The back third of the building had its own rear entry and was divided down its center to create two rooms of equal size connected by an interior door. One room was set up to serve as a bedroom with ample closet and storage space and the other room was set up as a living, kitchen, dining area with a large cast iron cookstove, a cupboard and shelves, and a table and chairs. Bill figured he could always add on to the building if he needed to expand either the store, the storeroom, or his living quarters in the future.

After nailing up the store's freshly painted sign, Bill and Alva stood back to admire their handiwork.

"Barton General Store. I'll be damned iffen it doesn't sound good," Alva said as he looked up stretching out both arms and cupping his hands as though he were holding the new sign between his palms.

Turning to Bill with a big grin on his face, he added, "It was a damn good idea, Billy. I know you'll make it a success."

"There's still a lot to do. I've been trying to convince the Post Office in Wall to let us handle the local mail," Bill said, knowing this was the first time he had shared his well-kept secret with Alva or anyone else.

"Well, I'll be damned. I have to admit, you, my brother, are a hell of lot smarter than you look. You're sayin' your store might become the Creighton Post Office? That's a damn good idea," Alva said, always impressed how his brother seemed to keep one step ahead of the competition.

"Didn't Pa always tell ya, looks can be deceivin'," Bill said, with an impish grin.

"They sure as hell can in your case anyway," Alva retorted with a twisted smirk of his own.

After the boys shared a good belly laugh, Alva added, "So, you might become one of the youngest postmasters in the country. Will I have to doff my hat and bow every time we meet?"

"One step at a time, Alvie. One step at a time. The first step is to become an authorized mail drop. Once I have that, I should be able to work on having my store designated as the Creighton Post Office. Then little brother, you can doff your hat and start calling me, Postmaster William Reuben Barton, thank you ever much," Bill said, as he shoved his nose high in the air, mimicking those high and mighty folks who thought they were better than mere lowly riffraff.

"By God you do have a plan. First a store and then a post office, what next?" Alva said, truly happy for his big brother and believing whatever his brother did would succeed.

"Well, it'll be some time, but I have my eye set on Kathrine Cristina Fremder. She's as pretty as a button. She's only thirteen, but she's already a woman. In three years, she'll be ready to marry. I plan on being the first suitor in line," Bill said, feeling he had everything well in hand.

"I thought you fancied her. She sure as hell can't take her eyes off of you. Every time she's around, her eyes follow you like the eyes of a hungry lioness tracking a lame gazelle," Alva chided his brother.

He had noticed since the first time they met at the Fremder place for Thanksgiving dinner that the two would-be lovebirds had eyes for one another. Since their first meeting they always seemed to find ways to be around one another, whether it was at church or in town or at other social events. It soon became clear to everyone the couple naturally gravitated toward being together.

"I got the impression little Lena's eyes have been trackin' you, little Alvie," Bill teased.

"No, those Fremder girls are damn cute that's for sure, but I have my mind made up. I have a hankerin' to see the world. I'm not lookin' to get hitched," Alva said flatly.

"So, you're still set on joining the Navy?" Bill said.

"I just turned sixteen and plan to join on my eighteenth birthday. That's just two years off. I can't wait to travel to distant lands and to see firsthand what's out there. I guess I'm like Pa, and our Grandpa Bill and our Great-Grandpa Pappy back in Iowa, I have to see what lies beyond the distant horizon with my own two eyes. I can't just read about it," Alva said with the look of a man eager to begin.

"In many ways, I envy you. I often dream of what lies out there in the world; however, in recent years, it seems only chaos and death has come knocking on our door from those distant shores. I wonder where it's all headed," Bill said, his feelings mixed and uncertain.

"America's place in the world has changed, like it or not. Our dough-boys fought and won a war that had gone on far too long. Our military has proven it's second to none. Our navy will soon rule the waves. Our growing territories won in the Spanish American War just twenty years ago include Cuba and Puerto Rico and in the far east, Guam and the Philippines. America has already seized Panama and Hawaii to secure our command of the seas. In recent years, we have taken over the whole island of Hispaniola, both Haiti and the Dominican Republic are now under our control. America is staking claims and marking its boundaries. I want to help push those boundaries as far as possible," Alva said, convinced America would one day rule the world.

"Here in the badlands, it's easy to feel like the world is somehow far, far away. We all know it's not. It touches our lives every day. The Great War and the Spanish flu pandemic reminded us of that fact. We're all in the same boat that's for sure. Unfortunately, we're not all rowing in the same direction," Bill said, thinking about his brother's view of America's rising star in the world and wondering what it would cost Americans in blood and treasure in coming years.

"Getting everyone to row together and in the same direction is America's unique place in the world. Being a nation of pioneers, we must lead those who have been unwilling or unable to break themselves free of their past. Their old ways of thinking and doing must be brought to an end," Alva said, a true believer in America as the shinning city on the hill, the nation with a manifest destiny to bestride the world and hold up its lantern of progress to show the righteous way to the peoples of the world.

Bill knew there would be no way to change Alva's mind. He was far from being alone in his beliefs. America had become a world power; the days of quiet parochial life were over.

In reality, America had always been involved in the world, from its founding down through the decades. With a continent to conquer, it had chosen to ignore the world beyond its ever-expanding domestic borders. Now with a continent in its grasp and a growing number of far-flung territories scattered across the world, America had outgrown its isolationism.

Bill's biggest concern was that America's desire for empire may soon suffer from the same fate suffered by old-world empires time and time again down through the ages. Americans would never again find peace, if the nation remained determined to build and hold onto an empire that stretched across the far corners of the world. He wished Alva well but feared the many wars and years of unrest that would surely follow, if America remained determined to one day rule the world.

Bill wasn't the only young person who thought the grass looked greener on the other side of the fence. Since German children started going to school with the children of the English-speaking community, curiosity in the other, between Germans and non-Germans, had increased by the day. Kate and the older German girls her age found the boys from the English-speaking community oddly attractive. The older German boys, quickly surveying the fresh crop of non-German females, made it clear they thought the same way. After a life of Germans only, German children, suddenly compelled to associate with non-German children every day, felt as though they were visitors in a foreign land. If difference is indeed the spice of life, going to English-speaking public school for German children was like being thrown into a bowl full of spices; for them, it seemed as if their hermetically sealed and self-contained world, that had once been so well-defined and predictable, had suddenly been swept away, and an alien world full of variety and unpredictability had taken its place.

Kate loved going to school with non-German children and having the freedom to make friends outside of the German community. At first, the mannerisms of the non-German children were strange and different. Just the way they moved when they walked and talked fascinated her. She realized just how isolated her people had been from the larger community, and even from what it was like to be an American. She was proud to be German, but she soon understood that she had yet to become an American, or even understand what that meant, something she wanted more than anything.

Kate had noticed that Bill and Alva Barton were older than most of the other children. Bill's high cheekbones, dark hair and complexion, and hazel eyes were somehow familiar and yet exotic in many ways. She had been delighted when the Barton family had been invited for Thanksgiving dinner. She had been even more delighted when she caught Bill staring at her out of the corner of her eye several times that day. It seemed he always found a way to be seated near her. During the school year, she had gotten to know Bill better and had often talked with him at school and at community events. She wished for nothing more than to be his girl.

She knew she had plenty of competition. Bill Barton was one of the most eligible young men in the community. Now that he had started his own general store in Creighton, every family with a teenaged daughter looked for ways to snag the up-and-coming Billy Barton. If Kate had anything to say about it, her shining Prince William would be hers the moment she turned sweet sixteen, a little more than three years off. She had made up her mind that she would do whatever she could to keep Billy Barton looking her way.

Sarah had been walking on air all morning. Her weightlessness had been brought on by the news that on August 26, with the adoption of the 19th Amendment to the U.S. Constitution, women had finally been granted the right to vote.

"Well, John Barton, what'd I tell you back in '84, when we first met. I told you women would be the equals to men someday," Sarah said, proud that women's voices would finally not only be heard, but would be counted. With the vote, women would have the political clout to finally be listened to.

"Must've been because of the bad influence of them troublemakers over in Wyoming," John said with an impish grin. "Them female critters over there have been voting since 1869. Seems they couldn't keep it to themselves."

John liked teasing Sarah about women getting the vote, just to rile her up. With four daughters and three sons, he wanted nothing more than to have all his children to be treated equally and get the same breaks in life. He had agreed with Sarah long before they were married, that women were the equals of men. He was pleased that women had finally gotten the vote.

"Troublemakers? Wyoming critters? Is that what you think of those fine upstanding ladies? Yes, they've had the vote over in Wyoming for the past fifty-years," Sarah said, her voice growing in volume with every word. "And now, finally, the rest of us have it."

"You know I'm just trying to rile you up," John said, his grin still in place. "You're cute when you get worked up over somethin'."

"I know you like a book, John Barton, and I can read you like one too," Sarah said, her arms akimbo, looking down at him with a funny grin on her face as he sat in his favorite chair.

She knew he was kidding, and she loved him for it. He had always supported her and the girls. Frontier life tended to force couples to take on traditional roles. And yet, as true partners, she was happy John saw the work they did as equal and necessary for the good of the family. John had always encouraged his daughters to reach for the stars, even if those stars where to be found beyond the horizons of the badlands.

"Well, let's have a toast to celebrate. We'll have to do it quick, since Congress also passed the 18th Amendment earlier this year and starting next year alcohol will be illegal. I have no problem with women voting. It's about time. Prohibition however is a crazy idea," John said, meaning every word.

"Well, we have a half a bottle of rye whiskey in the cupboard. Better drink it up before we get arrested," Sarah said with a wink in a deadpan voice.

"Why, Sarah Barton, you are a naughty little girl," John said, getting up and heading to the cupboard.

"Ever since you dragged me into that stinky horse stall in Chadron, Nebraska, I've never been the same."

"I dragged you? Wasn't it you who grabbed my arm and sashayed me down main street straight to that lonely horse stall on the edge of town?"

"You really do have a twisted memory of things, Johnny boy. You couldn't take your eyes off me from the first time we met."

"Now, that's a fact, I won't deny. But then, it was you who corralled me in that horse stall. Let's be honest."

"Well, I couldn't help myself, you bein' so damned handsome at the time and all."

"At the time? What're you tryin' to say?"

"Let's be honest, Johnny boy, the years haven't been exactly kind to you. But, all things considered, you still cut a fine figure of a man."

"You're too kind by half, my dear. You're a real charmer, when you wanna be. I guess, it's why I couldn't help falling in love with you at first sight."

"So, now that you've sweet-talked me, Johnny boy. How about that drink?"

Pouring two fingers of whiskey into each of a pair of water glasses and topping it off with a dash of well water, John liked the direction things were headed. With little Francis and Lucille taking a nap and the older girls helping out Bill and Alva at the Barton General Store in Creighton, he figured Sarah just might be in the mood for a little midafternoon frolic.

Handing Sarah her glass, Bill sat down next to her on the couch. Clicking their glasses together, they both took a long slip of the stout brew. Bill savored the whiskey's smooth spicy oaken flavor as it slid down his throat, warming his innards on contact and raising his hopes as to which way Sarah might decide to cast her vote.

January 3, 1920

Creighton, Pennington County, South Dakota

Farewell Toast

THE MORNING WAS CRISP and clear, the temperature just above freezing, only a gentle zephyr moved through the air under the flawless blue bowl of the sky that stretched overhead fastened securely to a cloudless horizon in every direction. The near treeless rolling plain of the badlands was as near to God as a man could get, John thought. But then, he thought with a grin, wherever a man might find himself on such a fine morning, the same could be said.

Bill and Alva had gotten the Barton General Store up and running, which was already doing a brisk business, especially with the change of seasons. Farmers appreciated having a store closer to their farms, saving them the need to run all the way to Wall for everything little thing. What excited everyone even more than having a general store nearby was that Creighton now had its own post office with a public pay telephone.

Bill had worked hard to gather support for his idea of establishing a post office in Creighton. To everyone's surprise, the U.S. Postal Service granted Bill's request and designated the Barton General Store as the location of the Creighton Post Office starting January 1, 1920. The Creighton Post Office was in fact one of several new satellite postal locations now tied to the Wall Post Office, which had been designated as the regional postal hub. Not yet eighteen, Bill had been named the Creighton Post Office's first postmaster.

To celebrate, John, Alva, and Bill had invited every farmer in the surrounding area to gather at the Barton General Store to mark the occasion. Bill and Alva had already put up the Creighton Post Office sign and had covered it with a large tarp that could be pulled off with a rope at the unveiling. Numbered post office boxes had been installed behind the counter in the back of the store and Bill had received training in Wall on how to operate his postal branch. He would receive additional training after the year-end holiday.

Peter Baumann, the head of one of the five founding families, had been the brewmaster for the German community since the founding of Wall. Peter was known far and wide as the beer supplier of the annual German Oktoberfest and for gatherings of German men after Sunday church services as was the German custom until the League, backed by the local Temperance Society, stepped in to forbid such gatherings in 1917. During the reign of the American Protective League, the Temperance Society had been able to end the heathen practice of drinking on Sunday. For them, the drinking of alcohol was evil and had to be stamped out whenever and wherever possible. They believed the drinking of alcohol on Sunday was the worst of all sins, a belief that had helped fuel anti-German sentiment during the war years.

Fueled by anti-German fervor and a desire to restore the American work ethic, the Temperance Movement had gained steam during the war and pandemic years, resulting in the passing of the 18th Amendment to the Constitution on January 16, 1919, imposing the prohibition of alcohol in the United States of America. Congress granted a grace period of one year for the new law to be implemented nationwide on January 17, 1920.

Figuring this may be his last chance to have a drink south of the 49th parallel and because he had always loved the taste of a good beer, John decided to order several kegs of beer for the celebration. Peter had gladly agreed to supply the beer, grudgingly accepting that these would be the last kegs he would ever brew before he had to destroy his brewing equipment to comply with the new law.

Though he lived close to Wall and used the Wall Post Office, Peter wanted to join the celebration in Creighton, if for no other reason than to enjoy one last beer with friends. He spread the word among the German community and hoped besides himself, the other representatives of the five founding families, Detrick Fremder, Fredrick Hamann, Hans Meyer, and Herman Ziegler, would also attend, and that more than a few others in the

German community would join the festivities. He even agreed to supply the beer and to deliver it on site at no charge. Upon learning what Peter had in mind, John couldn't have been happier. He knew Bill and Alva would be more than a little surprised by the size of the likely turnout.

The wet and mild weather over the past several years had allowed farmers to greatly expand their cultivated lands, bringing in bumper harvest several years in a row. Though the war and pandemic had negatively impacted everyone, the market for agricultural produce had grown, year on year. America's booming national economy had helped to boost rural economies to new heights across the nation. A rapidly growing population, due to a soaring birth rate in the region, had brought a newfound confidence. Everyone was convinced that with grit and hard work anything was possible. With high hopes for an endless string of good years ahead, the whole countryside around Wall and Creighton seemed to be eager and bursting at the seams to welcome a new year and a new decade.

With the weather mild and the sky clear, John couldn't resist riding over to Creighton for the afternoon festivities. Riding Midnight, his favorite jet-black Morgan, he was pleased to see automobiles coming and going on the narrow Market Road. Creighton was located about five miles south of his farm and twenty miles north of Wall. Coming over the last rise before Creighton on the rolling country road, John reined up and found himself dumbstruck by the huge number of vehicles parked along the road on both sides and around the Barton General Store.

He knew serving beer would draw a crowd, especially Germans, he had no idea the crowd would be so big. The majority of those gathered in front of the store were men; however, John did take note that there were a few women sprinkled in the crowd. Considering Germans made up more than half the crowd, it was clear that Peter had been more than successful in spreading the word far and wide that there would be beer served at the celebration.

As John rode closer, he could see his son Bill, dressed in his Sunday best, and postmaster Jim Hobbs from the Wall Post Office, also dressed in formal attire, standing on the porch of the Barton General Store in front of the assembled crowd. Alva was standing to one side holding a rope attached to a large tarp draped over the edge of the roof along the front of the building. John had arrived just in time for the unveiling. Reining up in the alley next to the store, he quickly dismounted and tied up his horse. Rounding the building, Bill heard a brass band begin to play the national anthem.

Taking off his hat and standing at attention with his right hand over his heart, John watched with pride as Old Glory slowly rose up the newly installed flagpole in front of the store. With the stars and stripes flapping in the breeze, wearing a broad toothy smile on his round ruddy face, Postmaster Hobbs stepped forward to address the crowd.

"Ladies and gentlemen, I am Regional Postmaster James A. M. Hobbs. I want to thank all of you for attending the grand opening of the Creighton Post Office on this auspicious day," Hobbs said, his baritone voice booming out over the crowd.

"I don't mind telling you I had no idea we would have this kind of turnout today. It seems clear the Creighton Post Office has been long awaited. I am confident we made the right decision to locate this branch of the Wall Regional Post Office in Creighton," he continued.

After thirty long minutes of recounting the history of the U.S. Postal Service since its creation in 1775 by Benjamin Franklin, including highlights of Postmaster Hobbs's own illustrious career, regional postmaster James Alexander Methanal Hobbs finally got around to introducing Bill.

"Without further to do, I would like to introduce your new postmaster William Reuben Barton," Hobbs boomed once again, flashing his now familiar broad toothy grin.

Bill, overwhelmed with the large turnout and with no experience in public speaking, had nervously stood stock-still fidgeting with his shirt collar and the buttons on his suit coat as sweat ran down the center of his back while Hobbs' speech droned on and on seemingly without end. His sudden introduction caught Bill completely off guard, causing his blood pressure to soar, reddening his cheeks. His racing heart, now in overdrive, dried out his mouth and tightened the growing knot in his stomach. If it hadn't been for the uncanny timing and enduring levity of his ever-mischievous little brother, mockingly doffing his hat, bowing, and giving out a shout in a comical Irish brogue, "Postmaster William Rueben Barton, if you please," Bill might have remained frozen indefinitely, a prisoner of his runaway stage fright.

"Thank you all for coming today to mark the opening of the Creighton Post Office," Bill heard himself say.

He wasn't sure how he did it, but by uttering those first few words, he suddenly felt at ease and knew whether a man found himself in front of one person or a thousand, he should never fear speaking out, especially if he has something to say. And speak he did. Bill spoke of his dreams for Creighton and for the region and about the services the new post office would provide. He spoke for more than twenty minutes to a supportive audience that hung on his every word.

Wrapping up, he turned, and gestured toward Alva, who stood next to the porch, and said, "Alva, the honors are yours, if you please."

On cue, Alva pulled on the rope attached to the tarp that covered the Creighton Post Office sign. When the tarp failed to slide off the sign, Alva gave another strong tug to the rope that once again was met with firm resistance. The tarp draped over the edge of the front of the building had gotten hung up on the head of a stubborn nail that held the tarp fast to the edge of the roof.

Unexpectedly, a lanky young man sprang from the crowd and shimmied up one of the supporting columns of the porch, effortlessly swinging up on its roof, and without missing a beat, quickly unhooking the tarp from the offending nail. He then signaled Alva to give the rope another tug. Taken by complete surprise, everyone was stunned by the young man's astonishing series of fluid motions that seemed nothing other than miraculous by all who witnessed them. Tugging the rope, the tarp slid off the new Creighton Post Office sign without a snag to the uproarious applause of the over four hundred people in attendance. In awe of the nimble stranger, the crowd continue to cheer when the young man, still standing next to the new sign on the porch roof, extended his arm to the crowd and with a flourish took a deep bow.

Wilma had watched her husband in disbelief, and now wondered more than ever, who he really was. He had come to town only a month after the Fourth of July brawl. Wilma, having discovered she was with child had been desperate to find a man. Jeffery Engel's unexpected appearance had been the answer to her prayers. Being a stranger to the Wall area, he knew nothing of her past and seemed eager to settle down and start a family. Her dramatic public incrimination of Clay Thompson had saved her reputation and driven Clay and his family completely out of the state; it had also scared off her many lovers and, she soon discovered, any potential local suitors.

Wilma, determined to bury her checkered past, set her sights on the unsuspecting Jeffery Engel. Turning on all of her substantial seductive charms, she soon had her hooks dug deep into Jeffery's hide. After a whirlwind romance followed by a short three-week engagement, Jeffery and Wilma were married, with little Jeffery Junior arriving just seven months later.

Jeffery had staked his homestead claim right in the middle of the badlands just south of Wall. No one could figure out what the man was thinking considering the land in that region was made up of a series of eroded bluffs that were barren, dry, and lifeless. Amazingly, everyone soon learned that Jeffery wasn't all that crazy when they discovered he had devised a way to harvest hay from the flat tabletop plateaus that rose up like an archipelago of lush green islands in the midst of the otherwise eroded and lifeless landscape.

When many of those who applauded her husband's quick actions to save the day had turned toward her to doff their hats and nod politely, Wilma's emotions swelled in her breast, bringing tears to her eyes. As her tears worked their way down her cheeks, she felt her life had finally changed. It had been a long time since anyone had paid her any respect. She hoped with all her heart that her past was behind her; where she prayed, it would stay forever.

Feeling the new life that moved inside her, she felt pride for first time that her and Jeffery's second child would be born in the spring. She prayed Clay Thompson would never return to Wall to remind everyone who Jeffery Junior's father really was. She had decided long ago that she would take that secret to the grave.

Jeffery looked down from the porch roof and soaked in the adulation of the crowd. He missed the days when he was Robert the Great performing on the high wire to adoring fans. Those days had abruptly ended when he had been conscripted into the British Army against his will. After being knocked unconscious by his sergeant major while trying to desert, he had been left behind in the bottom of a muddy trench during an intense battle in which his platoon was completely wiped out. When he awoke, he had found himself in a German field hospital. He had no idea what had happened or whether his attempted desertion had ever been reported up the chain of command. He only knew he was one of a handful of his regiment's survivors.

Frantic to escape, he noted how closely he resembled a badly injured German civilian next to him. When the man died of his injuries in the middle of the night, Robert switched beds with the dead man. Able to speak passable German, he remained in the hospital for several weeks. With so many war dead and the enormous number of deaths from Spanish flu confounding official records, he was able to assume the dead man's identity without raising a single eyebrow.

As Jeffery Engel reborn, he soon made his way to the United States to get as far away from his past as possible. Though he knew Wilma hadn't been honest with him about her past or about who Jeffery Junior's father really was, he figured the two of them deserved one another. He hoped they would both be able to put their pasts behind them. Seeing her standing in the middle of the crowd, her cheeks wet with tears and her belly swollen with their second child, he was confident they would.

Staying out of view of the crowd gathered at the front of the building, Peter Baumann with Detrick and Fredrick had set up and tapped six large kegs of beer behind the store during the lengthy speeches. With the completion of opening ceremonies, the brass band struck up the nation's latest hit song, Paul Whitman's "Wang Wang Blues," as the crowd moved to the back of the building, where volunteers had set up a wide array of refreshments on makeshift tables.

The men, upon seeing the six large kegs of beer set up on the edge of the back porch, soon formed lines as Alva passed out paper cups, an item that had come into common use since the Spanish flu pandemic. Fearing the infection risk of using unsanitary tin cups, the nation had embraced disposable paper cups, creating a boom for makers like Dixie Cup. Quick to capitalize, Bill had ordered a large supply of the disposable cups for his general store, which he could see, thanks to Alva's generosity, would soon be used up before he had the chance to sell a single paper cup.

Once all the men who wanted a beer had one in hand, Peter call for everyone's attention.

"Prohibition will begin in two weeks. It's for this reason we decided to serve everyone one final beer at the ceremonies today," Peter said, his German accent still strong. "And so, I'd like to ask John Barton to propose a toast," he continued, as he held up his paper cup filled with beer and gestured toward John.

At first John was caught flatfooted, but quickly recovered, holding up his paper cup with a smile as he gave Peter a kindly nod.

"Thank you, Peter. Today is a great day for Creighton and a great day for my son, Postmaster William Reuben Barton, if you please," he said as he jokingly doffed his hat and bowed in his son's direction, setting off uproarious laughter and putting everyone in a good mood.

"I can't tell you how proud I am of both my sons, Bill and Alva. Now, before this fine brew goes stale, please lift your cups," he continued, and then lifting his own cup high, he added, "May the nineteen twenties be a decade to remember. Cheers!"

With that, John downed his cup of beer in three big gulps. The beer went down smooth and easy, its slightly bitter yet tangy taste was as good as John ever remembered. John knew, right then and there, he would miss having an occasional beer and wondered how long the country could do without it. The crowd of men followed suit. After quickly downing their first cup of beer, they soon lined up for seconds.

Regional Postmaster Hobbs, hesitant to imbibe in public for fear it would get back to the Temperance Society, contented himself with a cup of fruit punch. Alva, taking Hobbs by his arm, led him inside the store on the pretense of inspecting the postal facilities. Bill had made his way indoors with a tray of beers and was waiting at the counter in the back of the store when Alva and Jim Hobbs came in. Standing around the counter at the back of the store, Bill, Jim, and Alva shared their own private toast.

"I'm going to miss this," Jim said after polishing off his second cup of beer.

"Well, to tell you the truth Postmaster Hobbs, I'd never drank beer until today, but I can truly say, I too will miss it," Bill said matter-of-factly.

"Me too," Alva said with raised eyebrows and a grin on his wily face, causing the three men to share a good belly laugh.

"Well, I have to be on my way," Jim said, and then quickly added, "See you in Wall on Wednesday, Postmaster William Reuben Barton. You still need to complete your training, so I can pin your official U.S. Post Office badge on your chest."

With a big toothy smile once again taking in the bottom half of his face, Jim Hobbs touched the brim of his hat and headed for the front door.

After he left, Alva turned to Bill and said, "You did it, my brother. Not sure how you pulled it off, but you damn well did it."

"We did it, Alvie. I couldn't have done it with you," Bill said, meaning every word.

The two embraced as brothers do; after patting each other on the back, they headed for the door. Without saying another word, they both made a beeline for the beer kegs at the back of the store for one last toast with their Pa, who they knew they would find nearby.

"Well, boys, did you give Postmaster Hobbs a good send-off before he headed back to Wall?" John said as he turned away from a conversation he was having with Detrick and several other German farmers from the area.

"Yes, he seemed genuinely pleased with how things turned out," Bill said.

"Detrick here has been telling me about the young man who saved the day," John said, motioning for Detrick to join them.

"He did that for sure. If it wasn't for his quick actions, we would've been in a real pickle. Who is he? I've never seen him before," Alva said, looking at Detrick.

"His name is Jeffery Engel. He's new to the Wall area, but a damn clever guy when it comes to ropes and pulleys. His skill in that area has helped him farm the grassy plateaus in the badlands, if you can believe it. I've been helping Jeff and Wilma get settled in. Me and a few others in the area bought Jeff's first hay crop this year to get him up on his feet," Detrick said, a little embarrassed to be talking about the young couple.

Detrick had never forgiven himself for not intervening when Casanova Clay had preyed on a not-so-naïve Wilma Philips. Though Wilma had been wild and had more than a few lovers, he could have stopped Clay, and he didn't. He swore to himself, he would try to make it up to her, if he could.

"You can thank Detrick for Jeff being here today. Jeff and Wilma rode out with him from Wall. Detrick told me, Jeff had never been to Creighton and wanted to see the little town everyone in Wall was talking about," John said.

"Is Jeff around here?" Bill said. "I'd like to share a beer with him before you all go back to Wall."

Bill had no more than got the words out of his mouth when Jeffery Engel joined the circle of men and introduced himself.

Jeff's English was formal with a slight British accent, but with so many immigrants in the area Bill paid little attention to foreign accents. Jeff's clear concise speech wasn't the only thing that made him stand out however, his whole manner and smooth movements where those of a performer or professional athlete. Bill was left with the impression there was a lot more to Jeffery Engel than what met the eye. His decisive actions to unhook the tarp, his acrobatic skills, and his carefree manner in front of a large crowd hinted at a hidden side to the mysterious Jeffery Engel.

What also struck Bill as curious was the care Detrick Fremder showed to Jeffery and Wilma, seemingly going out of his way to ensure the couple's success. That they were not related and that there was no other connection between them that Bill knew of, made Detrick's actions seem odd, considering all the Germans Bill had ever known tended to stay out of other people's affairs, especially the affairs of non-Germans. Then again, he figured, the Germans in recent years had been trying to reach out to the non-German community. By helping Jeff and Wilma, Bill figured, Detrick was probably trying to do just that.

Seeing this as an opportunity, Bill decided that now was as good a time as any to see how receptive Detrick might be to having a non-German court his daughter. With his mind on how he might turn the conversation, he heard Detrick going on and on about how he had a house full of girls and how he was growing fat trying to keep up with all the baked goods they made. Seeing this as his opening, Bill decided to drive in headfirst.

"Baked goods? What, like cakes and cookies and pies and such?" Bill said, hoping he sounded nonchalant.

"Yes, yes, cookies, cakes, pies, sweet breads, too much for one man to eat," Detrick said with a chuckle, hoping there were young men listening and hoping his words would fall on fertile ground.

With five daughters to marry off in coming years, he was desperate to rope and corral as many eligible suitors as possible, before other families in the area had a chance to put their brand on them. Though there had been a baby boom in the badlands since 1907, girls outnumbered boys nearly two to one. Eligible bachelors were a scarce breed and would continue to be so for some time to come.

"I wonder if I might drop by sometime to see what Kathrine's been whipping up," Bill said, hoping he hadn't reached too far by naming the target of his desires.

"Yes, yes, I'm sure she'd be happy to see you again. Having the post-master of the Creighton Post Office pay a visit would be our honor," Detrick said, a little too enthusiastically. "When can you drop by?" he added, wishing when he said it he had bitten his tongue before being so forward.

"Would this coming Wednesday afternoon be agreeable?" Bill said without thinking, figuring he would be in Wall to finish his training that day anyway and could easily swing by the Fremder place after his business was concluded.

"Yes, yes, Wednesday should be fine. We'll look forward to your visit," Detrick said, astonished that he may have, without any effort at all, landed one of the most eligible bachelors in the area.

Bill couldn't believe his luck. He had racked his brain for months on how he might find a way to start his courtship of the beautiful Kathrine

Fremder, only to have her father offer her to him on a silver platter, sweet breads and all.

With the beer kegs empty and the refreshments gone, the cars and trucks along Market Road thinned out and before long were soon all gone. After their Pa rode out to return home, Bill and Alva sat down on the back porch to relax a bit before calling it a day.

As the sun reddened the western skyline, Bill shared his plan to visit Kathrine on the coming Wednesday. He also shared why he believed that Detrick Fremder had, in his own way, blessed the courtship of his eldest daughter. Bill went on and on about the many unexpected events that had shaped the day. Listening to Bill, Alva sat quietly nodding his head, deep in thought. After Bill stopped talking, a long silence descended on the two men as the sun slowly melted into the distant horizon.

They watch the once deep-blue sky light up ablaze in shades of orange and red before slowly fading to gray and then black as stars emerged one by one, shimmering high above them, and yet somehow seemingly within their reach. Ever in awe of the raw beauty of nature, Alva turned to Bill and said once again, "You did it my brother. Not sure how you pulled it off, but you damn well did it."

Their laughter echoed off the prairie for miles as the two brothers found it impossible to stop laughing, since every time they stopped to catch their breaths, they would look at each other and started laughing all over again. They both knew the nineteen twenties, with the war and pandemic behind them, were already shaping up to be a decade for the ages. For the two of them, with nothing holding them down and no one holding them back, they knew the sky was the limit and that the stars were indeed within their reach.

BOOK TWO

June 15, 1923

Custer, Custer County, South Dakota

Shangri-La

AFTER HIS FIRST VISIT to the Fremder place, Bill returned on a regular basis, putting on more than a few pounds in the process. Kathrine, who he soon called Kate, had captured his heart. In private, Detrick often reminded all his girls, "The quickest way to a man's heart is through his stomach." Kate's cooking may well have helped seal the deal, however as far as Bill was concerned, he was head over heels in love with Kate for reasons other than her fresh baked cookies, though he had to admit, they were a delicious bonus.

Bill, at the age of twenty-one, and Kate, at the ripe old age of sixteen, walked down the aisle of the Lutheran church in Wall without a single empty seat to be found. The husbands and wives of all five founding families and many other German friends from the surrounding area attended the wedding, filling the bride's side of the church. Filling the pews on the groom's side of the church were the leading non-German families from the surrounding area.

The marriage of Bill and Kate signaled to everyone the coming of future unions between what heretofore had been two separate worlds. Bill and Kate were the first couple of mixed culture and heritage to be married in Wall since its founding.

Kate was among the oldest German children born in the Wall area. The crop of young adults turning sixteen in 1923, though relatively small, was followed closely on its heels by a huge bumper crop of children already in their teens. Kate's four sisters and many other German children would be coming of age in the next few years. With the German and non-German communities growing closer together, year by year, there wasn't a mother or father on either side of the aisle that wasn't thinking about who might become the future spouses of their children.

Having broken new ground, the marriage of Bill and Kate would be closely monitored and scrutinized. It was no secret that in sewing circles in both camps, there was real concern that such a marriage would work out. More than a few held the opinion that the unnatural union could never be successful.

After exchanging vows and attending the largest wedding reception ever held in Wall, Bill and Kate, oblivious to the symbolism attached to their marriage or to the many concerns surrounding its success, boarded the mid-afternoon train for their honeymoon in the Black Hills.

Bill had reserved the bridal suit at the new State Game Lodge in Custer State Park. Built in 1920, the rustic native stone and wood lodge was known for its excellent service and as being one of the most well-appointed and finest hotels in the region. The lodge was nestled in a forest of deep dark-green ponderosa pines. Sprinkled within this dark forest was a complex web of bright freshly leafed-out branches of oak, birch, and aspen, which appeared to float on every shifting breeze. Bill was confident that Kate, a child of the treeless prairie, would fall in love with the rugged granite out-croppings, whispering pine-covered peaks, gurgling natural springs, and rich lush meadows that made up the mystical beauty of the Black Hills. Bill had chosen Custer State Park as the location of their honeymoon hideout because of its relatively close proximity to Pleasant Valley and Pilger Moun-tain, which lay only a day's ride southwest of the nearby town of Custer.

With thoughts of his new wife, and God willing, of their future chil-dren in mind, Bill wanted to show Kate where he dreamed of homestead-ing in the Black Hills, should that opportunity ever arise. Bill had followed closely the calls to open up the remaining public lands in the Black Hills suitable for homesteading. Even if this failed to happen right away, he wanted to ensure Kate would agree and be ready to move quickly when and if the time ever came, a time Bill felt deep down in his bones would come sooner than most people thought.

As the population continued to swell on the prairie to the east, more and more young couples would look to the west for fresh land to settle. The pressure to open up the last arable lands in the Black Hills proper would eventually force the government to offer suitable federal lands for home-steads. Like his father, Bill was certain that the land around Pleasant Valley and Pilger Mountain would be included in those lands.

Bill hoped he might be able to inspect the area around Pilger Moun-tain more closely and, if possible, put up a marker on the land he might one day be able to claim as his own. He remembered the day his father showed him the stone marker next to Barton Lake for the first time. His father had discovered their sheltered prairie valley with its kidney-shaped pond during the winter of 1887 when the land was still part of the Great Sioux Indian Reservation, which had covered all of western South Dakota, excluding the Black Hills. It wasn't until 1907, twenty years later, that his father had been able to return to the land he had marked to finally officially claim it as his own.

His father's original marker still stood next to Barton Lake, as a re-minder that a man should never give up on his dreams. Bill wanted to fol-low in his father's footsteps. His plan was simple, he would find the exact location of his future homestead and place his own stone marker on that spot, so when the land finally opened up for homesteading, he would know exactly where to head.

Waking up late, Bill wasn't sure where he was at first. Feeling a soft warm arm laying across his chest, he turned to find Kate cuddled up next to him. Her blond hair tussled across her pillow framed her elfin face as she slept quietly. He still couldn't believe he was married to the woman of his dreams. Their first night together had been awkward at times, but it hadn't taken them long to discover the secrets of each other's young bodies as only lovers can.

"You awake?" Kate said, her eyes still closed.

"Yes, how are you feeling this morning, Mrs. Barton?" Bill said, know-ing their lovemaking had been the first time for Kate.

"How are you feeling, Mr. Barton?" she said, her eyes now open with raised eyebrows and a funny little smirk on her lips.

Bill turned and held her tight, pressing his naked body against hers as they lay looking into each other's eyes. It didn't take long for Kate to know his answer. When Kate pressed back, Bill had his. After another round of passionate lovemaking, the couple, having skipped breakfast, decided to go down to the main dining room for an early lunch. Looking out across the meadow at the rolling forest that surrounded the lodge, the thick trees seemed to go on and on forever. Bill breathed in the rich pine-scented air.

He couldn't wait to escape the dusty prairie and to build his and Kate's future in the green oasis of the Black Hills.

Exploring the wildlife loop that wove its way through open grasslands and pine-studded rolling hills, Bill and Kate were amazed by the number of bison, pronghorn, whitetail, elk, and mule deer that had taken up residence in the wildlife preserve. Prairie dog towns covering large tracks of land were dotted with tiny sentinels standing on their hind legs perched on the edges of their dirt mounts ever ready to signal to their fellow colony members of any impending danger. Their unique yelping and barking filled the air every time a hawk or an eagle flew too close for comfort.

Among the many other animals in the park were the begging burros. Kate fell in love with the motley gang of begging burros that had taken up residence in the park. The burros were donkeys that had escaped from gold miners who had flooded into the Black Hills during the gold rush in the 1870s. Surviving in the wild, the burros soon found a good living begging for food from the many visitors to the park. The teeming wildlife in the park stood in stark contrast to the relative scarcity of wildlife on the open prairie.

On the third day of their nuptial bliss, Bill and Kate rolled out of bed early and drove to Fourmile Corner, located west of the town of Custer, where Bill had hired saddle horses with bedrolls and provisions for their ride to Pilger Mountain. The trail running southwest from Fourmile Corner through Pleasant Valley had once been part of the Cheyenne Deadwood Stage Route which Bill's father had traveled many times when he rode shotgun on the Monitor Gold Wagon back in the late 1880s. Bill remembered the many stories his Pa told him about Pleasant Valley and Pilger Mountain. He would never forget the day when his Pa had taken him on horseback to Pilger Mountain when he was ten years old. Bill had pledged to himself on that day that he would one day stake his claim to land in that hidden paradise.

Though the road near Custer had been recently graveled, there was no telling how far south the gravel went. With Pilger Mountain roughly twenty-five miles southwest of Fourmile Corner, Bill worried that rain would make the trail impassable by automobile. The rugged trail also made a breakdown a real possibility. That very few people lived deep in the southern hills added to Bill's concern should anything mechanical go wrong. Either way, he figured they would need horses to explore the area around Pilger Mountain once they arrived, which made his decision to ride in on horseback an easy one. Kate had agreed to go in on horseback and seemed eager to explore the hills.

What soon became clear was that Kate hadn't ridden many horses. Bill feared she might be thrown off her mount, as her horse, sensing hesitancy in its rider, began acting up by prancing back and forth, throwing its head around, and fighting its bit. Bill's concerns were soon put to rest when Kate reined up on her big strawberry roan and refused to give him his head no matter how hard he bucked and fought. It wasn't long until her horse, named Jake, settled down.

Kate, taking control, spurred Jake and pointed him due south. At that moment, Bill realized he needn't worry about his new bride. She was no shrinking violet. She was a frontier woman, born of frontier stock, who had lived the same hash life he had. He was damn proud to see that she had as much sand in her as any man, and probably a hell of a lot more than most.

Bill planned for the couple to set up camp on Pilger Mountain, since their ride there and back ride would be a good fifty-mile round trip. Wanting to explore the area around the mountain, he figured they would need to stay on the mountain for two nights. Riding at a good pace straight down the old Pleasant Valley trail, Bill noticed how the soils of the surrounding landscape turned darker and darker red the further south they rode. By midday the narrow trail with lush green meadows on both sides opened up into a wide flat valley rimmed with gently sloping hills covered in ponderosa pine. To their right, Bill and Kate were greeted by Pilger Mountain that rose up as if welcoming the couple home.

High overhead a lone eagle hovered on the warm air turbulence rising up from the valley floor. Bill could feel the breeze that rushed over the tops of the tall grasses making them ripple and flow like waves on an ocean. Floating on every rippling wave, wildflowers danced and bobbed, filling the scene with a mix of dazzling colors. Purple and yellow coneflowers, scarlet gaura, deep violet thistle, pink and light purple woolly verbena, white and purple aster, yellow black-eyed Susan and sunflowers, and many more carpeted the valley floor with their delicate splendor.

"Oh my, this place is so beautiful," Kate gushed, a child of the badlands, she had never seen such a rich, lush, colorful scene.

"I knew you would love this place. And look, an eagle to welcome us to our future home," Bill said, pointing to the sky where the lone eagle hovered high above.

As they watched him hover, almost on cue, he seemed to dip a wing in their direction in silent tribute.

Finding a place just inside the tree line along a gentle slope overlooking the majestic valley that stretched out to the southeast, Bill and Kate wasted no time in setting up their base camp. Using pine poles Bill hewed from a grove of jack pines growing nearby, they put up a tarp to protect them from any possible rain showers. While Bill was building a stash for their food and supplies in the branches of a large Ash tree not far from their camp site, Kate started a campfire, and it wasn't long before they were enjoying a hot cup of coffee and the picnic lunch Kate had packed for their expedition.

"This is quite a treat, Kate," Bill said with a smile.

"Well, thank you, Mr. Barton. We always aim to please," Kate said with a wink.

Bill couldn't help reaching over and pulling her into this lap, where he kissed her deeply.

"You haven't finished your lunch, sir, and dessert won't be served until after dinner this evening," Kate giggled.

"Just wanted to have a sample taste of that sweet dessert," Bill said, as he licked his lips.

The couple shared a good laugh and turned to look out over the idyllic scene, both knowing they had found their Shangri-La. Alone, wrapped in a cocoon of natural beauty, they felt as though they were the only people on earth and that no harm could ever reach them. Pilger Mountain was a treasure, their treasure, one they both now hoped to possess one day.

Rather than ride into the forested hills in the late afternoon, Bill decided to explore the open valley floor. Riding several miles south, Bill and Kate found more of the same, the valley offered a flat level table of land with rich dark black soil, ready for the plow. Several springs bubbled up out of the ground creating small marshy pools of fresh clear water. Bill found it strange that this part of the hills had never been settled, considering the main stage line had once run up through Pleasant Valley to Custer and then on to Hill City and Deadwood in the northern hills. Nearly every gold miner and settler that ever invaded the Black Hills in those early years would have traveled through the wonderland of Pleasant Valley.

What added to the mystery was that on the northern end of the valley flowed French Creek where gold was first discovered in the Black Hills during the Custer Expedition in the summer of 1874. Bill had noticed several mining digs on their way to Pilger Mountain, but none of the operations seemed to be active. Bill figured that after finding little or no gold in the area, the early fortune hunters had quickly moved on into the northern hills where big gold strikes created the legendary wild west towns of Lead and Deadwood. Whatever the reasons, Bill knew that land with soil as rich as Pleasant Valley would not stay fallow and unsettled forever.

Kate hadn't told Bill about her father's hope of one day settling in the Black Hills and his keen interest in learning more about Pilger Mountain. He had asked her to share what she found out about the hidden valley. She wondered how Bill might feel about it. Detrick, with the birth of his first son, Herman, in 1921 and his sixth daughter, Gladys, just two months before Bill and Kate's marriage, was eager to find a second homestead he could develop for his ever-growing family. With all the good land around Wall already taken, he hoped Pilger Mountain would be the answer to his prayers.

On their way back to base camp, Bill spotted a huge mule deer buck with his antlers in velvet herding his harem of six does into the edge of the woods. Just as the largest of the does nearly reached the tree line, the crack of a rifle shot rang out across the valley as the big doe dropped in its tracks, sending the rest of the deer leaping into the trees. Bill's horse, startled by the unexpected sharp retort of a rifle, reared up, forcing Bill to hold on tight as he struggled to bring the skittish animal under control. Surprisingly, Jake held his ground without so much as a flinch as Kate reflexively pulled up on the reins, her heart racing in her chest. It was clear they were not alone in their isolated Shangri-La.

Emerging from a pine-studded knoll to the north, two riders worked their horses down its steep slope, one of them holding a rifle in one hand. Bill wasn't sure what to think, having believed there was no one else in the area. Seeing that the man without the rifle was waving in their direction, he knew they had been spotted and that he now would have to acknowledge the gesture and meet the unwelcome intruders face to face. Looking over at Kate, he saw concern etched in her features.

"Who are they?" Kate said, her voice worried.

"Hard to tell. They might just be out on a hunt," Bill said, trying to sound unconcerned, while his mind raced, assessing all the possible scenarios this chance encounter might yield.

Riding over to where the big doe went down, Bill and Kate stayed in their saddles while the two hunters dismounted to look over their kill.

"She's a big one alright," the short one said, still holding his rifle.

"That she is, Luke," the taller of the two said, and then added as he looked up at Bill, "You folks want a good hunk of venison for your supper tonight?"

"That's a kind offer, my friend," Bill said with a smile on his face. "You folks from around here?"

"I was about to ask you the same thing," Luke said, still gripping his rifle, his knuckles white as he squeezed it tight.

"We're tourist out for a ride. Just passing through," Bill replied, trying to appear as calm as possible.

"We have a dig up yonder about five miles. Been trackin' these muleys. We're surprised to see anybody up here," the tall one said, eyeing Kate in a way that made it plain he had noticed she was a woman.

"I'll bet. Probably not many folks come out this far from town," Bill offered.

"Yeah, especially tourist, that's for sure," Luke said, and then added, "Who's the little lady?"

"My wife, Kate," Bill said, his voice tense.

"Don't mean no offence, just asked to be friendly," Luke said, laying down his rifle.

"That's right, we're just out for a hunt. He's Luke, and I'm his older brother, Jesse," the taller man said. "I didn't catch your name."

"I'm Bill," Bill said, still on edge, not knowing which direction things might break.

"Well, now, let's get to butchering this here doe. I'll slice you off a good chunk of hindquarter for your supper tonight," Jesse said as he pulled a long sharp knife from his boot.

Working with Luke, the two men soon gutted and bled the doe and trussed up its legs for transport. Rather than skin the animal on the spot, they simply carved off a large piece of meat from one of its hindquarters, leaving the hide in place. Wrapping the chunk of meat in an old bandana Luke pulled from his saddle bag, he walked over and handed the bloody bundle up to Kate.

"There you go, ma'am. You put that on a spit over an open fire, and you'll have yourself some of the best eatin' in the Black Hills," Luke said with a gap-toothed grin.

"Why thank you, Luke. I'm sure my husband and I'll enjoy it very much," Kate said, trying to act thankful and as nonchalant as her husband.

Kate was all too aware that if the two gentlemen chose to be less than gentlemanly, Bill would have a tough time holding them off.

"Never you mind, ma'am, we don't see many folks out this way, especially pretty young women, like you," Jesse said with an awkward wink that cause both of his eyes to pinch closed.

"We don't mind sharin'. We know you'd do the same," Jesse added, still gawking at Kate with one eye, while his cocked eye looked off in Bill's direction.

Bill wasn't quite sure who the man was looking at for certain, but figured he had Kate on his mind.

"Well, gentlemen, we should be on our way. Once again, thank you for the meat," Bill said, wanting to get as far away from the two as quickly possible, but deciding it would be better to hold off until the two men rode out so he could see which way they headed.

"Don't mention it. We need to get goin' as well. It'll be dark soon," Jesse said, as he motioned to Luke to grab his end of the doe's carcass, so the two men could hoist it over the back of Luke's saddle.

With the doe secure and the two men back in their saddles, they bid their final farewells and rode due north without looking back. Bill and Kate watch them go until they disappeared, both wondering if that was the last they would see of the two men, and both praying that it would be. Hefting the large chunk of meat up like a trophy, Kate looked over at Bill with a grin.

"Well, it looks like we eat like royalty tonight," Kate said with a glint in her eye.

"Yes, I'm especially looking forward to several helpings of the queen's dessert," Bill said with a knowing glint of his own.

"Seems your appetite for dessert is bottomless," she teased.

"When you're on the menu, it always will be," he quipped.

"Oh, Mr. Barton, do tell, do tell," she said.

"No, no, I'll never tell," he said, triggering the two of them to share a good laugh.

The tension of the chance meeting with the unexpected strangers and the potential threat they could have posed seemed to melt away once they put some distance between themselves and the two men. The men had ridden due north and if they spoke the truth, their dig was nowhere near Bill and Kate's base camp.

Having placed the base camp just inside the tree line, Bill figured the trees would help to hide their location. Bill knew their campfire would look like a beacon from a distance as it shined out into the dark uninhabited valley. To cut down on light spilling out into the valley and to make their campfire more difficult to spot, Bill situated the tarp so that it hung between the campfire and the open valley, blocking any light from escaping. Up close, their campfire would still be able to be spotted. As viewed from a distance, the tarp would help to keep their location hidden. Just in case, Bill decided to sleep with his loaded pistol close at hand.

After enjoying juicy slices of roast venison and a variety of fixings Kate brought out from town, the two snuggled into their soft bedroll where Bill enjoyed several helpings of the queen's dessert. Laying on their backs looking up at the star-filled night sky through the pine boughs, they both dreamed of their future life together. Kate felt that she couldn't be happier than she was at that moment.

She had loved Bill from the first time they met on Thanksgiving Day four long years earlier. That Bill had become a postmaster and had his own general store and now had plans to homestead in the most beautiful place on earth, she felt as though she had hit the jackpot. In many ways, she was a simple farm girl, an immigrant's daughter, but in Bill's arms she never felt more confident that her people were now part of America. She wanted her children to make their mark in this new land called America and to help build its future.

Without checking the surrounding area before turning in for the night, and with his belly full, Bill fell into a deep, deep sleep, after enjoying one last helping of dessert. Just before dawn, he was awakened by a rustling sound not far from where the couple lay. The sound came closer as the hair on the back of his neck stood on end. Slowly he reached under the saddle he was using as his pillow and slid out his loaded pistol. Afraid to make any quick moves, he slowly moved his hand over Kate's mouth and then squeezed her arm. Suddenly awaken, she remained silent as she eased her head sideways to look in Bill's direction, her eyes as big around as cup saucers.

Just as Bill rolled over to see what was sneaking up on them, a full-grown cougar gave out a deep-throated growl and bared its fangs. Without further warning, the big cat sprang forward with its front legs spread wide and its razor-sharp claws unsheathed. In a blur of action, Bill twisted his pistol around and holding it with both hands fired three shots point blank into the crest of the beast as it flew through the air, landing on top of him in a dead heap. Rolling the cougar's limp body off him, Bill scrambled to his feet, with his heart pounding in his chest nearly out of control. Just as the cougar pounced, Kate had let out a primal scream that echoed across the empty valley, bringing the nocturnal sounds of the forest to a deafening silence.

"Oh, Bill! Are you alright?" Kate cried out.

Frightened by the sudden and unexpected violence, uncontrollable tears ran down her cheeks, draining the tension from her body.

"Yes, I'm fine. It was close, damn close, too damn close," Bill said, checking his naked body for cuts and scrapes and happy to discover that the blood running down his chest was cougar blood and not his own.

"He must have smelt the mule deer's blood. I should have buried that piece of bloody hide. I knew better," Bill said, admitting he had made a near fatal mistake.

Raw meat was never anything a person wanted to have laying around a campsite. Fresh blood was the one thing that could be smelt for miles around. If there'd been a kill, predators and scavengers were sure to come calling. Looking down at the dead cougar in the dim light of the dawn, a chill ran down Bill's spine, the animal was full grown and easily weighed two hundred pounds. Had the cougar reached him still alive, the beast would have ripped him to shreds.

Bill held very few superstitions, but he did believe in the power of totems. He had been told his grandmother, Lucy Breeden, had been part Otoe Indian and a member of the Eagle Clan. He had been pleased when a lone eagle had welcomed them to Pilger Mountain and had taken the sign as a good omen. He recalled his father pointing out the eagle feather he had wedged under the base of his stone marker next to Barton Lake to protect his claim until he could return and make the land his own. Bill had brought with him an eagle feather his father had given him for the same purpose. He believed in the power of these things and how they belonged to the deeper mysteries of the universe, mysteries beyond simple human understanding.

Bill felt his confrontation with the cougar, the spirit of the mountain, was no accident and that it held deep meaning. The cougar totem was one of strength and power. The deer peacefully gathers its life from the forest, the cougar preys on the deer, locking the two animal spirits forever in an eternal duality: the deer, gentle and peaceful, the cougar, powerful and fierce, both equal halves of an endless cycle of renewal. He and Kate had been christened by the blood of both.

Looking out over the valley as the golden orb of the sun slowly rose in the east, Bill stood deep in thought as the sun's rays warmed his naked body. When Kate joined him, she slipped her arm around his waist. Without thinking, he slipped his arm around her waist and reflexively pulled her naked body tight against his own. For a long time, without moving or speaking, the couple stood naked, unashamed and unafraid, knowing they now belonged to this place and that they would one day share their lives here, together.

After pulling the cougar's fangs as totems, Bill buried the cougar together with the piece of mule deer hide next to a pair of old, twisted pine trees to serve as a natural marker of their resting place, knowing somehow he would return to the spot someday, and wondering what that day might mean for his family.

Bill and Kate wasted no time in riding up Pilger Mountain to explore what might lie beyond the first tree-lined ridge. Beyond the forested ridge, they discovered several wide, level meadows much like the valley below. Finding these rich, open grasslands confirmed for Bill that these lands would be opened for settlement someday. There would be little need to clear land for farming where so much of the land was already treeless meadows and grassland.

At noon, Bill and Kate reined up at the summit of the mountain to enjoy the view of a broad vista to the north and west. Looking across the rolling hills below, the dark green pines and deep red soil of the southern hills capped with outcroppings of snow-white gypsum created a unique rugged beauty like none other in the world.

"This is an unbelievable view. You'd never believe that a near lifeless, treeless wasteland lays only a few miles to the east," Kate said in awe of the beauty that had been hidden just beyond her reach all her life.

"Yes, it's another world," Bill said, more convinced than ever that Pilger Mountain was their Shangri-La.

"Have you made up your mind," Kate said.

"I think that place with the small spring where we could build our home on the ridge in the trees facing southeast with our farmland on the level grassland below is the best location we've found," Bill said, having thought about all the locations they had scouted and having weighed all the pros and cons of each.

"The one with the small grove of poplar trees to the west?"

"Yes, that's the one."

"It's a beautiful spot. It also has a huge pine tree with a strong lower branch where we could hang a swing."

"You're always thinking of our future kids."

"Aren't you?"

"Yes, every time I look at you, I see them in your eyes."

"You are quite the charmer, Billy Barton," she quipped with a cute come-hither look on her face.

"You're worth all my charms, even my lucky rabbit's foot," he said with a mischievous smirk.

"Ha, ha, you made a funny," she teased.

"I'll make a lot more than a funny, if you step down off Jake," he said, eyebrows raised.

"Right here in front of God and our future children?"

"Where else?"

Their lovemaking was passionate and no longer awkward as they now could sense each other's desires and fulfill them. Exhausted, they lay in the tall grass watching the thunderheads build in the west.

"Looks like rain," Bill said. "We better get on the move. I'd like to mark our claim and get our camp set up for the coming storm."

"Well, Billy Barton, if you could've just held off on your dessert until after dinner like a good boy, we wouldn't be behind schedule."

"Dessert? I thought that was an appetizer. We'll enjoy dessert tonight," Bill said with a chuckle.

"You always have quick little answer," Kate said, enjoying their playful banter and most of all the inexhaustible passion her husband had for her.

After returning to the valley, it didn't take long for them to find the location of their future homestead. Wasting no time, Bill quickly piled up a stone marker next to the large pine tree where Kate hoped they would hang a swing one day. Satisfied his stone marker looked like the one his father had piled up on his homestead next to Barton Lake on Three Tree Creek, he removed the eagle feather he had kept under the inner brim of his cowboy hat and wedged it under the edge of the marker's largest base stone.

Ensuring his stone marker faced due east, he then placed four colored stones at the base of the stone marker that he had brought with him, one at each of the four cardinal points. He knew that for the Lakota the yellow stone represented the east for enlightenment; the black, the west for insight; the white, the north for wisdom; and the red, the south for innocence. For his father, they had also come to symbolically represent the races of the people who now made up America and who would together carry the nation forward.

To complete his marker, he placed small pebbles one by one in a square around the whole arrangement to represent the earth. He then placed pebbles so they emanated out from each corner of the square to represent the four winds. When he finished, he stood back and studied his handiwork. He was satisfied with its *uname* design, one of the Lakota's holiest symbols, in which he had enshrined his stone marker. With his eagle feather as its anchor he was confident the totems were strong. After kneeling to say a silent prayer, he reached into his pants pocket and pulled out a delicate jade double happiness pendent carved long ago in distant China and placed it on the yellow stone, facing east toward the rising sun. His father had found the pendent placed on the yellow stone of his own stone marker and had looked up the meeting of its Chinese characters, which meant double happiness. His father had given the pendent to Bill to place on the yellow stone of his own marker on Pilger Mountain in hopes that the charm would help bring Bill and Kate the same good luck and happiness he and Sarah had enjoyed on Three Tree Creek.

Calling to Kate to join him, they prayed together with all their hearts that they would return and that they would both grow old together on Pilger Mountain in the years to come. They both touched the jade pendent for luck before standing. To ensure all the spirits of the forest had been enlisted to protect his claim, Bill placed the cougar's fangs on top of the capstone, and promised himself, he would retrieve the fangs on the day he returned to officially claim his land.

After enjoying several extra helpings of dessert and spending an otherwise uneventful night, they slept soundly other than being awakened briefly by the rumble of thunder and bright flashes of lightening ahead of gentle rain showers that passed through just before dawn. When they awoke, the air was fresh with the rich smell of ponderosa pine, Bill couldn't get over how different life was in the heart of a pine forest compared to the stark treeless prairie of his boyhood. He could see that Kate too was loath to saddle up and head back to Custer.

As they made their way back north, Bill looked back across the valley and could just make out the tall pine tree that marked the location of his stone marker. He prayed he had secured the location with the same strong totems that had protected his father's land for twenty years before he could stake an official claim. Bill had no idea how long he might have to wait before he and Kate would be able to stake a legal claim to their land, if ever. Deep down, he was convinced that day would come.

As they rode in silence, he looked over at Kate to find she was looking at him. They smiled at one another and then both looked back to catch a final glimpse of their Shangri-La, their hidden valley at the base of Pilger Mountain. Turning once again to face one another, an unspoken truth passed between them. They had become as one, husband and wife, on Pilger Mountain. Regardless of what the future may bring, that truth could never be changed.

November 28, 1928

Creighton, Pennington County, South Dakota

She Came Special Delivery

THE NORTH WIND CUT through his coat when he popped up out of the root cellar with a gunnysack full of string beans, potatoes, and a large pumpkin. It had been freezing cold since the end of October without a break. Settlers of the badlands had grown accustomed to extreme temperature swings, from arctic cold winds one day to balmy summer breezes the next. Unlike previous years, the arctic cold had settled in early and held on tight without any hint of letting go any time soon. Bill quickly made his way back to the house, surveying the many cords of wood stacked up under his makeshift pole barn on the way. If the biting cold continued, he would need to chop a hell of a lot more wood for kindling before winter came to an end, a long four months off.

Just as Bill and Alva had predicted, when the Creighton Post Office first opened, the 1920s had been a decade for the ages. Business had been good with bountiful harvests lining farmers' pockets with plenty of cash to spend year after year. The postal contract had as predicted also been a boon to business for the Barton General Store. Farmers and their families coming to pick up or drop off mail often ended up purchasing additional supplies. With every ring of the cash register, Bill couldn't help but smile at his good fortune.

Bill and Kate had settled into married life with the birth of their first child, Harold Daren Barton, born on March 15, 1924, exactly nine months after Bill and Kate returned to Creighton from their Pilger Mountain adventure.

John Barton, upon seeing his grandson for the first time, christened the boy Bart, rather than calling him Harry or Hal, typical nicknames for a boy named Harold. John told everyone Bart sounded more like the name of a badland's buckaroo destined to be a future tycoon. Bill liked the sound of the nickname and took to calling the boy Bart, as did everyone else. Even little Harold seemed to prefer Bart to any other nickname.

It wasn't long before Bart became the center of Bill and Kate's universe, the axis upon which all else rotated. There were fourteen children between Bart's grandparents at the time of his birth, giving him nine aunts and four uncles, some like little Gladys born a year earlier were close to his own age. In 1926, Detrick and Annie gave him a baby aunt named Dorthey, and on November 11, 1928, just two weeks before Thanksgiving, they give him a baby uncle named Lavern, to round out the count.

Less than two weeks later, on November 28, 1928, a windy, bitter-cold day, little Bart, now four years old, watched his father pace back and forth in their narrow kitchen wringing his hands every time he heard a groan or moan coming from the bedroom on the other side of the wall. Bill had fetched his mother, Sarah, at the break of dawn to act as midwife for the birth of their second child, the same role she had played during the birth of little Bart. Without a clinic within twenty-five miles or a real hospital within seventy-five miles, no one had given it a second thought that the new baby would be born, like little Bart, in the back of the Creighton Post Office, the home of the growing Barton family.

"Push, push! Now breathe, breathe!" Sarah urged, her booming voice carrying through the doorway that connected the kitchen and bedroom in the tight living quarters.

"Please, no more, no more. Just let me rest," Kate complained.

As the next contraction hit Kate hard, Sarah once again barked, "Now push! I see the head! Keep pushing, its coming, its coming, almost there. Push!"

"Ahhh!" Kate yelled in pain and relief, and then fell limp, her second child had entered the world.

Exhausted, the sound of her baby crying brought tears of joy to her eyes.

"It's a girl!" Sarah cried. "But she's come early. She's so tiny. Hurry, we need to keep her warm."

"Bill, quick, bring a bread pan and a clean towel," Kate hollered, with urgency in her voice.

Confused, Bill dug out a bread pan from the cupboard and grabbed a clean kitchen towel from the linen cabinet, quickly taking them into the bedroom. As soon as he entered, he saw a tiny orange bundle in Kate's arms. When he heard it cry, he was shocked that a human baby could be so small.

"We need to keep this baby warm. She came too early. She's very, very small. My Mama had small babies and after losing her first one, she learned what to do," Kate said, holding the baby against her beast.

"We need to keep her warm all the time. The best way is to keep her in the oven's bread warmer when we're not holding her."

"It's a girl? That's wonderful," Bill said, his eyes fixed on the little orange bundle. "Yes, yes, we need to keep her warm. We should put her in the oven right away."

"No, silly, the bread warmer. All warm and dark, it'll be like she's still in her Mama's belly to her," Kate said, trying to reassure her husband and knowing their baby may not survive.

Turning to Sarah, Bill said, "Is she alright?"

Considering the baby was too early and too small, he worried she may have other problems.

"Yes, she got all ten fingers and all ten toes and a pair of lungs better than most," Sarah said with a chuckle and a smile. "If you keep her warm and well fed, she'll do just fine."

Though the little girl was jaundiced, her skin as yellowish orange as an October gourd, Sarah had assured the young couple that this was a common condition for babies born before thirty-eight weeks of gestation. What no one knew at the time was that the little one was also lactose intolerant and wouldn't be able to keep down her mother's beast milk. Fortunately, the baby took to feedings of warm sugar water every few hours, which kept the couple up nearly twenty-four hours a day. Knowing this couldn't continue indefinitely, they started trying other possible formulas.

With Bill owning a general store, they had plenty of supplies on hand to keep trying, one thing after another. It wasn't long before they hit upon Eagle Brand canned soymilk, which the baby took to like a fish to water. Confident their baby would now survive, Kate chose the ancient Teutonic name of Velda because of the baby's inner strength and fighting spirit. For her middle name, Bill chose Iona, which he hoped would balance Velda's fighting spirit with a deep inner peacefulness. Weighing only three and a half pounds at birth, Velda Iona Barton was the smallest live birth recorded in South Dakota at the time.

In the coming months, Velda grew rapidly. Bart, calling his little sister "his baby," had become a common fixture at her side. When John Barton saw his granddaughter for the first time, he froze in disbelief as memories of his mother flooded his mind. He could see that Velda was destined to be the spitting image of her Great-Grandmother Lucy Breeden in nearly very feature. Though Velda's mother was German with blue eyes and light strawberry blond hair, Velda had a darker complexion with brown eyes and light brown hair. Her high cheek bones signaled her more complex heritage. John knew in an instant Velda's Otoe heritage, buried deep though it might be, had found expression, and he hoped, it would again and again, down through the generations.

Bill had watched as the country's commodity and stock markets skyrocketed higher and higher every year. It seemed, if a man was willing to take a chance and make a bet, anything was a good risk. Many had borrowed money to make short-term investments on livestock and land that had paid off handsomely. The rural population had grown, and with it, the pressure for more agricultural land. The children of the prairie were now having children of their own and were eager to make their own way in the world.

Soon after returning from Pilger Mountain, Kate told Bill of her father's interest in finding good farmland in the Black Hills to homestead and his hope that the Fremder family might be able to join Bill and Kate when they struck their claim to land on Pilger Mountain. Though Kate had been worried about how Bill might take the news, she was relieved when he expressed his delight that Kate's patents wanted to settle near them and hoped other homesteaders from the badlands would follow. His only concern was that he and Kate needed to be among the first to a stake claim in the region. Having already scouted out and marked his claim, Bill was confident he would be able to beat the rush of land-hungry settlers, if and when that time ever came.

Quite unexpectedly, the word that land near Dewey, in the southern Black Hills, would be opened up for homesteading came by way of Kate's father, who had learned the news from Jeff Engel of all people. According to Kate, when Jeff first shared what he had learned about land opening up near Pilger Mountain, he had asked Detrick what he thought about homesteading in the Black Hills. Detrick had told him that he was also interested in staking a claim to a homestead on Pilger Mountain and that Bill Barton had already scouted out the best land in the area.

How Jeff had come by the news of land opening up for homesteading in the southern Black Hills was a mystery to everyone, since nothing had been officially announced and no one thought Jeff Engel knew anything about the area. According to Detrick, Jeff had told him that the land around Pilger Mountain had been surveyed and the Custer County Courthouse would handle the homestead filings. If the information Jeff had was true, Bill realized that his dream may have finally come to pass.

To get a better understanding of what Jeff knew, Bill asked Detrick to set up a meeting between the three men. Though it had taken two weeks to find a time when all three men could get together, the information Jeff shared was well worth the wait. According to Jeff, he had learned about the upcoming land announcement from a surveyor who had taken a personal interest in how Jeff had devised a method for farming the tops of plateaus in one of the most rugged and desolate regions of the badlands. Unable to believe what he had heard from others; the surveyor had decided to swing by Jeff's homestead to see his operation firsthand. Fascinated by the techniques Jeff had developed to conquer the unforgiving land, the man had stayed over for several days. During their many conversations, the surveyor told Jeff all about his work, and in doing so, had unwittingly divulged the planned public announcement for homesteading on Pilger Mountain near Dewey on May 1, 1929; a sensitive bit of information that had yet to become public.

After their meeting, the three men returned to their homes knowing they needed to get their affairs in order and to gather the necessary supplies for a speedy move into the southern Black Hills. They knew that once word got out, and they had no idea when that might happen, there would be a rush to file claims. Having inside information on the timing of the announcement was an advantage they didn't want to lose. Bill's knowledge of the area was also an advantage, which would help them to select the best homesteads in advance, keeping them one step ahead of the competition. To ensure they cashed in on their advantages, they agreed they would need to be at the Custer County Courthouse before the opening of business on May 1, 1929, so they could be first in line to file their claims.

Jeff had struggled to make a living in the badlands and had for many years wanted a real farm on level ground. Receiving inside information on the Dewey opportunity had been like receiving manna from heaven.

Why this opportunity had come to him out of the blue, he had no idea. He had learned long ago not to ask such foolish questions. When opportunities come, a man just needed to reach out and take hold. Jeff believed that no truer words were ever spoken than "He who hesitates is lost." If he hadn't taken Jeffery Engel's identity when the opportunity presented itself, he would have lost everything long ago. Now, he had the chance to build something new once again. All he had to do is reach out and grab it.

Detrick was as excited as he had been back in 1906, when he first learned that he would be able to beat the land rush to Wall. A lot had happened over the last twenty-three years, and not all of it good. He held onto bitter memories of how Germans had been treated during the war years. For many years, he had longed for a fresh start. Homesteading on Pilger Mountain near his son-in-law and his eldest daughter and his first grandchildren was more than any man could wish for. He and his fellow Russian German immigrants had arrived in America as strangers in a new land. They had become Americans. Pilger Mountain would be the Fremder family's new beginning.

Standing on his back porch deep in thought, Bill looked to the west and heard his boyhood dream calling to him through the darkness. The air on the moonless night was cold, crisp, and clear. Bill could almost feel the earth spinning around the sun as it rode on the outer edge of a pinwheel of stars that turned on the axis of the galaxy. Stepping back inside, he turned to take one last look up at the countless stars of the Milky Way that flowed like a mighty river of sparkling diamonds down the center of a pitch-black sky. Reaching up, he could almost feel the stars gliding across the palm of his open hand.

Hearing little Velda cry, he was reminded how small and frail she was and how precious. Giving up his secure post office income and all he and Kate had built together in Creighton to suddenly run off to chase a boyhood dream had thrust upon him the toughest decision he had ever had to make in his life. The lesson his father had taught him long ago was that a man seldom has the luxury of choosing when things happen. In many ways, the opening up of land around Pilger Mountain couldn't have come at a worse time. But then, the more he thought about it, there never would be a good time to uproot his family to move to a homestead in the middle of the wildness.

The more he thought about it, he knew his focus had never been on the uprooting of his old life, it had been on the establishing of new roots, in a new place, and the challenge of building a new life there. He had been powerless to choose the timing of the move; however, he was confident he had the power to choose how things turned out. He and Kate had made up their minds long ago, when they held each other tight on Pilger Mountain, that whenever the time came to move, they would meet the challenge head on. "Yes," he said to himself, he would answer the call of his boyhood dream. And come what may, he would succeed in building a new life for himself and his family on Pilger Mountain.

January 15, 1929

Wall, Pennington County, South Dakota

The Lucky Seven

JOHN BARTON WAS AS excited about Pilger Mountain opening up for home-steading as Bill was himself. John couldn't help recounting his long twenty-year wait for the badlands to finally open up for homesteading and the mad dash from Iowa he and his brother, Benjamin, had made back in 1907. Bill had heard the story so many times over the years, he could retell it himself nearly word for word. He finally understood how his father felt, having had to wait for six long years for Pilger Mountain to finally open up for settle-ment. And now that it had, he would be able to pursue his boyhood dream.

Sarah offered to take care of Velda for their first year on the homestead to give the tiny infant more time to grow stronger before being moved to the harsher realities of frontier life. Kate had assured her mother-in-law that with her mother and six sisters living nearby, little Velda would be more than well taken care of on the homestead; in fact, she would be smothered in tender loving care.

Since he would need to leave his farm in someone's hands while he resettled his family on Pilger Mountain, Detrick brought his brother-in-law Fredrick Hamann in on his plans. Fredrick was surprised by Detrick's sudden decision; until he recalled Detrick's insistence on settling as near to the Black Hills as possible when the five founding families first came into western South Dakota. Detrick had spoken of one day settling in the Black Hills proper, often saying that the rocky forest-covered hills reminded him of the landscape around his boyhood home near the Crimea. Fredrick had never really taken him seriously, believing his talk of settling in the Black Hills was nothing more than his way of pining about the loss of his family's farm in Russia, the same way so many other Russian German immigrants often did.

That his son-in-law, Bill Barton, turned out to have the same dream, and that Jeff Engel had been the man who came up with inside information about the possibility of new homesteads in the southern Black Hills was nothing less than one of the queerest twists of fate anyone could imagine. Indeed, it was so unbelievable no one could have predicted it.

Now that the opportunity had come, Fredrick was eager to help his brother-in-law however possible. If all went well on Pilger Mountain, Detrick planned to either sell his badlands farm to one of his daughters' husbands or to one of Fredrick's sons. In the meantime, Fredrick agreed to manage Detrick's farm during the coming year and for as long as necessary. He also proposed having more homesteaders join the wagon train they were planning to put together for the move into the wilderness region around Pilger Mountain. Fredrick believed that settling in the isolated region would be safer in numbers. Mutual support had been critical to the success of the five founding families when they first arrived in the badlands. The same would be true for those who settled around Pilger Mountain.

Fredrick's recommendation was to invite Albert Meyer, the youngest son of the Karl Meyer, brother of Hans Meyer, the man Detrick had worked for back in Bloomfield, Nebraska, before he married Fredrick's sister and set out for western South Dakota. Fredrick's main reason for suggesting Albert wasn't so that Detrick might return a favor to Albert's father, though it might be taken that way by some; it was because Albert's young wife, Emma, was a schoolteacher. With no schools anywhere close to the Pleasant Valley area, Emma would be a godsend to the settlers, who all had or would soon have large and growing broods of children. After discussing the matter with Bill and Jeff, it took no time for the three men to agree on inviting Albert and his wife, Emma, to join their merry band.

With the addition of the Meyers, the subject of adding more homesteaders became an open discussion. Bill suggested inviting Roy Kelly to join their wagon train. Buck Kelly, Roy's father, had arrived in Wall just after the 1907 land rush. Unable to find any good farmland left to homestead, he decided to look for good rangeland. Though he had been a farmer, he set about to build a cattle ranch instead. Settling on a rugged stretch of land with good graze along the Cheyenne River north of Peter Baumann's place,

Buck Kelly, through pure grit and dauntless determination, had been able to build a sizable cattle operation over the past twenty-years.

Buck's eldest son, Roy, wanted to establish a second Kelly Ranch in the southern Black Hills to run sheep. Roy believed sheep would do well in the scrub brush and rocky foothills in that region and had been actively looking for opportunities to buy land. It took the men no time to agree to invite Roy Kelly.

"Well, that makes five. Maybe we should shoot for an even lucky seven," Jeff suggested, looking around the table with a grin.

Jeff had always been a superstitious man and by his nature sought ways to align with the unseen forces that governed the universe, at least as he understood them. It had been his fear in seeing a black raven land on the edge of the trench just as his platoon's sergeant major blew his whistle to charge the enemy that had prompted him to attempted to run in the opposite direction. Considering everyone in his platoon had been killed in that fateful charge, he believed the raven had been a harbinger of death sent from the beyond. He had no idea how or why, but he was convinced it was so.

Seven was a lucky number, of that he had no doubt. He felt good about the direction his life was taking and how well things were going and wanted to conjure up all the luck he could. He knew they would need much more than luck to carve a new home out of the wilderness of the southern Black Hills. He was convinced, however, that without luck they would be destined to fail.

Though the men had initially met at Detrick's place to discuss whether to add Albert Meyer and his schoolmarm wife to the wagon train, now that they had agreed to add Roy Kelly and his sheep operation, Jeff's idea of adding more members was readily accepted.

"Our wagon train from Bloomfield in 1906 had five families. We came to be known as the Founding Five. Maybe this time we can become known as the Lucky Seven," Detrick said with a smile, liking the idea of having more settlers in their group.

He also like the sound of the Lucky Seven, and even more, what the name might portend. Detrick believed a man could never have too much luck.

"Alright, seven it is," Bill said, nodding his agreement.

He too figured they would be needing all the luck they could conjure up.

They all knew, more than luck, having a strong group ready to support one another would better ensure everyone's success. With two slots to fill, the three men mauled over one name after another until Detrick hit on the name Jakob Shultz. Jakob was the eldest son of Christian Shultz, who had been shipped off with his whole family to Utah on trumped-up espionage charges during the war. The once highly respected and prominent Schultz family had returned to Wall in 1920 only to discover the impossibility of rebuilding their once thriving businesses after so many years.

Detrick felt giving Jacob and his wife and three young children a chance to build a new life on Pilger Mountain would serve to help right at least in part the terrible injustice the Shultz family had suffered during the war. Detrick was confident Jakob would jump at the chance to join their group, considering he had been trying to buy a badlands homestead for several years without any luck. Bill and Jeff were in total agreement.

The last slot was the toughest to fill. There were several possibilities; however, none of them seemed to stand out from the others until Jeff suggested they would need a good mechanic being so far from town. The first name that popped into all their minds was Mike Robinson, who had served on the front lines during the war and had eventually drifted west after he was discharged from active duty. In recent years, he had set up a garage in Wall and had established a good business. Jeff, however, thought Mike would be open to the idea of homesteading in the Black Hills.

Jeff had gotten to know Mike soon after he arrived in town. Like so many others, Mike had been fascinated by the ingenious pulley systems Jeff had built to harvest hay from the flat plateaus in the rugged wastelands of the badlands. Jeff and Mike's friendship had grown when Mike started showing up at the Philips's home for dinner every Sunday. It wasn't long until Mike and Bethany, Wilma's youngest sister, announced their engagement.

The reason Jeff thought Mike would accept an invitation was that Mike had told him he had returned to Iowa after the war only to discover his family had died in the Spanish flu pandemic. With the family's farm in the hands of the bank, he took a job at an auto repair shop in Des Moines, Iowa. His dream was to one day return to farming and have a place of his own. Since Mike and Bethany would be married in June, Jeff was convinced Mike would welcome the chance to stake a claim on Pilger Mountain. Jeff figured, Mike would not only be able to build the farm of his dreams, but also have the benefit of a sister-in-law living nearby to help with his children when they came along. All things considered, Mike would have no good reasons not to join the wagon train. Bill and Detrick nodded their agreement. Everyone was confident, they had their mechanic.

"Now we're seven strong," Bill proclaimed. "How are we on wagons?"

"Fredrick said Albert Meyer can bring a wagon up from Bloomfield by rail and I'm sure Roy can use his father's old wagon. It's probably still in tiptop shape, if I know Buck Kelly," Detrick said, liking how their plans were coming together.

"Well, that does it, then. Mike and Jakob can buy a couple of the five wagons we already have," Jeff said, confident they had their ducks in a row.

Breaking out a jug of bootlegged corn liquor, Detrick poured everyone a healthy cup. With Bill and Jeffery hoisting up their brimming cups of the forbidden brew, Detrick raised his own and declared, "To the Lucky Seven!"

With that the three men clinked their cups and took a good swig of the near one-hundred-twenty-proof Dakota moonshine.

Coming up for air, Bill gasped as he struggled to speak, "Damn Detrick, that stuff ought to be illegal."

The remark sent the three men into a hardy belly laugh. Looking at each other's smiling faces as they slipped their prohibited brew, they knew they had cast their fortunes together and that their lives would soon be changed forever.

For several months leading up to their meeting, Fredrick Hamann and John Barton had helped the three men round up as many old, covered wagons as they could. Though some of the wagons hadn't been used for many years, they still had parts that were in fair condition. Cannibalizing the serviceable parts from a number of broken-down wagons, they were able to build five sturdy wagons with freshly mended leather harnesses and new canvas covers. One by one, they moved the refurbished wagons to Detrick's farm, where they could store them as close as possible to Wall's main train depot. When Detrick's neighbors mentioned that the growing number of covered wagons lined up on his place looked like a real wagon train ready to head west, he would only laugh in reply.

The plan was to take the wagons by rail to Hot Springs on the Chicago North Western rail line and from there on to the Minnekahta Station Terminal, where the Chicago North Western merged with the old Burlington rail spur that ran between Edgemont, located on the edge of the southern hills, to the Deadwood goldfields in the northern hills. By unloading in Minnekahta, they would be able to drive their wagon train northwest straight across Barker Flats to Pilger Mountain and Pleasant Valley.

Their other option had been to unload their wagons in the little town of Dewey, South Dakota, near the Wyoming border, west of Pilger Mountain. As the crow flies, Dewey was closer to Pilger Mountain than Minnekahta, the problem with the shorter route was that Pleasant Valley ran down the east side of Pilger Mountain, making the trip over the top of Pilger Mountain with heavy-laden wagons a far more treacherous journey than traveling straight west on nearly level ground across Barker Flats.

Since Bill had scouted the Pilger Mountain area, he knew where good water and the best land suitable for farming were located. Studying the newly issued section maps for Pilger Mountain and Pleasant Valley, Bill had been able to quickly point out a number of one-hundred-sixty-acre quarter sections that would be the most suitable for settlement. Under the Homestead Act, anyone twenty-one years old or older could claim up to a quarter section of land for homesteading. If a homesteader lived on and worked the land for five years, he could receive a free and clear deed to the land.

Bill selected a nice quarter section close to his own homestead for Detrick. Detrick agree on the location, pleased that Kate and Bill would be settling nearby. Bill pointed out that additional land could be purchased under the Homestead Act for a reduce price if they wanted to expand their operations in the future. Bill had every confidence there would be an opportunity to expand his farm in coming years, once the settlers of Pleasant Valley began to market their bountiful produce into an increasingly booming local and national economy.

Out of a handful of possible options, Jeff selected the one Bill recommended as being equal in quality to Detrick's quarter section. Jeff was delighted with his unexpected turn in fortunes. In recent years, with Jeffery Junior already nine, his daughter, Hana, eight, and with twins on the way, Jeff had come to accept that the coward Robert Grant was indeed dead and buried, and that he was no longer pretending to be the wartime survivor Jeffery Engel, he was and always had been Jeffery Engel. He had come to love Wilma with all his heart. She had told him of her checkered past and had confessed that Jeffery Junior was not his child. Freed by the truth, he had told her of his past and who he really was, a coward and a deserter. They both had agreed to leave their pasts where they belonged, behind them. Jeff and Wilma, with their eyes fixed on the future, truly believed that Pilger Mountain would be their fresh start, a rebirth for both of them.

In the coming weeks, Bill and the others met with Jakob, Roy, and Mike and talked with Albert by telephone. All four men were excited about the opportunity to homestead on Pilger Mountain and agreed to join the wagon train. Bill had identified several good options for homestead sites for each of them. After selecting the choicest land for their homesteads and discussing everything they would need to do in coming months, the Lucky Seven made ready for the big day when homestead claims for land around Pilger Mountain would be officially accepted at the Custer County Courthouse.

The Lucky Seven was a group of committed men that Bill felt was a winning team. They had seven wagons and had gathered and patched up plenty of harnesses and tack. They had even sown new canvas covers for each of the wagons. Even so, Bill still had a major problem on his hands. They lacked the necessary horses they would need to pull the wagons to Pilger Mountain. Scouring the countryside for suitable horse flesh, they had come up short. They only had twelve good horses, enough to put together three wagon teams of four horses each. With seven wagons, they would need at least another sixteen horses, not to mention a few spares just in case.

Bill also knew anyone settling on Pilger Mountain would need a good horse just to get around, at least until serviceable roads could be built in the area. In many ways, homesteading around Pilger Mountain wouldn't be much different than homesteading at the turn of the century, before the telephone, automobile, and electric lights. Having scouted the region first-hand, Bill knew life in the isolated heart of the southern Black Hills, cut off from the comforts of civilization, would be spartan in the best of times for some time to come.

Learning Bill needed good horses to move his wagon train to Pilger Mountain, John offered to introduce his son to Joe Bishop, an old friend of his from his days as a cowpuncher. After making several telephone calls, John learned that Joe Bishop had moved from his ranch along the Cheyenne River north of Edgemont to Hot Springs in recent years to take over running the family's growing business empire after the death of his father, E. J. Bishop.

While tracking down Joe Bishop, John learned that the Bishop family owned numerous properties in Hot Springs and most of the land east of the town on both sides of the Fall River. They also had extensive business interests in a number of going concerns, including part ownership in several hotels and in the region's main rock quarry. When John had asked how to find Joe Bishop in Hot Springs, he was told visitors to Hot Springs couldn't miss the Bishop House, which sat up high on a ridge just off Minnekahta Street overlooking the Fall River, the main train depot, and the famous sandstone buildings that lined Main Street.

E. J. Bishop and his bother Roland had built the Bishop House to look like a palace straight out of a fairy tale. Built in a distinctive French colonial style, the elegant wooden three-story home with soaring sandstone turrets had been painted yellow to make it stand out against the white gypsum-caped vermillion bluffs the provided the house's unique backdrop for anyone looking up from the town below.

Setting up a meeting with Joe Bishop at his home, John and Bill traveled by rail to Hot Springs. John was eager to catch up with Joe Bishop after so many years. Though he would have liked to talk over old times with E.J., a man to whom he owed many favors, John couldn't help but smile when he thought about the wily old shyster, who had run the Standard Gage Saloon in the now forgotten town of Burton from the early days of the Black Hills gold rush. The Standard Gage Saloon had been a notorious hole-in-the-wall, one of the wildest bars and whorehouses to be designated as an official stage stop on the Cheyenne Deadwood Stage Route.

Thinking back, John could still see old E.J. standing behind his bar dressed in a fine silk three-piece suit sipping on his best rye whiskey as he held court over a tangled mob of whores, card sharks, cowpunchers, lowlifes, fortune hunters, rogues, and desperadoes. With the arrival of the Burlington Railroad, the town of Edgemont sprang out of the prairie, where Burton had once stood, the same year South Dakota became a state in 1889.

With prohibition the law of the land in the new state of South Dakota, houses of gambling, alcohol, and ill-repute like the Standard Gage Saloon were soon forced to shutter their batwing doors for good. John recalled how unconcerned E.J. had been about being run out of town on a rail.

Flush with cash from over a decade of bootlegging and unregulated business profits, much of which had been made on the shadier side of the law, E.J. soon laid down sizable bets on properties and businesses in the booming town of Hot Springs. It wasn't long before E.J. had become a very well-known and wealthy man. Sending his brother Roland to New York

City to manage the family's stock portfolio and his youngest son, Clarence, to California to seek land investments, E.J. dreamed of building an empire.

Arriving at the Bishop House, John was pleased to find Joe Bishop decked out in a three-piece suit with gold chain and pocket watch, looking every bit the spitting image of his father, E.J., as he played the part of a gentleman. John had to admit the man was a far cry from the one he remembered. Though he looked the part of a genteel businessman, etched into his weathered face were the well-earned creases from the hardships he had faced in his youth when he fought Indians on the northern plains with the U.S. Cavalry and scouted for the cattle baron Tom Burton on the dusty Chisholm Trail.

Joe Bishop's cattle ranch had suffered considerable financial losses in the aftermath of the Great Blizzard of 1887 that had ended the reign of Great Plains cattle barons like Tom Burton forever. Though the cattle barons may have gone the way of the wind, Joe Bishop had proven he was a survivor. He had slowly but surely rebuilt his herd with hardier stock better able to weather the harsh winters of South Dakota. It had taken years for him to rebuild and even more to turn a profit; however, giving up had never been an option for the likes of Joseph Bishop, the son of E.J. Bishop, who had never yielded to anyone or anything.

When America finally joined the war in Europe, E.J. Bishop soon secured a lucrative government contract for his son to supply meat to the U.S. Army. How E.J. had pulled off the coup, when so many others vied for the contract, he declined to share with his son, taking the secret to his grave. When asked, he would simply say with a crooked smile, some things were better left unsaid. Joe used the sudden cash infusion to rapidly expand cattle operations on the Bishop Ranch. Leveraging his new government connections, Joe secured additional contracts to supply meat to several military forts located in the northern plains and to the Pine Ridge Indian Reservation in western South Dakota. In the decade following the war, it seemed everything the Bishops touched turned to gold, gold that flowed straight into the family's pockets.

Joe informed John and Bill that his eldest son, Ross Bishop, now ran the Bishop Ranch. With over three thousand head of cattle on the hoof, the Bishop Ranch covered over ten sections of land and leased another twenty sections from the government, making it one of the largest cattle operations in the region. Joe was sure Ross would have the horses they needed for a good price. Joe was happy he had the chance to meet Bill, John's eldest son. Receiving an open invitation to stay at the Bishop House whenever the Barton family came to Hot Springs, John and Bill couldn't have been happier with the way things had worked out.

To get down to the Bishop Ranch, they boarded the train from Hot Springs to Edgemont. The train, after cutting through the last row of foothills, made a gradual decent southwest across Minnekahta Flats and down the face of the stone dome on which the Black Hills rested. Along the route, the train passed through Minnekahta Station at the western edge of Minnekahta Flats, where Bill planned to unload their wagon train for the final journey northwest across Barker Flats to Pilger Mountain.

Bill's goal was to arrange to have Ross Bishop deliver the horses they planned to buy to Minnekahta Station. The Bishop Ranch located along the Cheyenne River north of Edgemont made it relatively easy to have the horses brought straight north to Minnekahta Station. Fact was, the Bishop Ranch was situated perfectly for their purposes, a stroke of luck John and Bill took in stride without a thought.

It seemed the stars had aligned, and that the heavens now showered down luck on everything that would make Bill's boyhood dream of homesteading on Pilger Mountain possible. Since unexpectedly receiving inside information on the opening of free land on Pilger Mountain and learning his father-in-law had the same dream as his about homesteading in the Black Hills, Bill had been able to pull a good team of men together who all had unique skills and who were all willing to work with one another. He had even landed a schoolmarm eager to serve the new community. Bill couldn't believe how one thing after another seemed to fall into place with little effort.

That one lucky stroke after another could happen without a hiccup, would have been tough to believe, had he not seen things somehow magically come together one after another with his own two eyes. And now, with his Pa's rekindling of his old friendship with the Bishops, the Lucky Seven had found the horses they so badly needed to make their venture a success. Bill had to admit there had been far too many coincidences to believe these things had all just happened by chance. Bill had become convinced there were only good things ahead. He believed more than ever that his move to Pilger Mountain was his true destiny, a destiny long ago written in the stars.

Arriving at Edgemont, rather than renting an automobile, the two men rented horses for the ride to the Bishop Ranch. Bill had reluctantly followed his Pa's lead, knowing the man's dislike of automobiles and his strong desire to die in the saddle someday. Forever the cowboy, Bill figured his Pa wanted to relive his younger days when he had worked for the cattle baron Tom Burton, who had built the brick house where Ross Bishop now lived. After Tom Burton's sudden death following the Blizzard of 1887, Joe Bishop had taken over what remained of Burton's Lazy Cheyenne Ranch, including his brick house.

As the two men rode north out of Edgemont, Bill understood why they called Edgemont the southern gateway to the Black Hills. In front of them the rolling foothills of the Black Hills seemed to sit one on top of the other as they grew in height on the northern horizon. Carved in the face of the ancient stone bluffs that faced south, canyons seemed to beckon to all who dared to enter. Running along the face of these rugged cliffs, the Cheyenne River wound its way east, its opaque waters running pale white with an orangish tint as they stirred up the chalky sediment common to the alkaline-laden soils that surround the southern Black Hills.

The surreal beauty of the scenery captivated Bill as they rode in silence. Noticing his Pa looking up, Bill looked up and saw what must have caught his Pa's eye, a lone eagle hovering high overhead.

"He is marking our way," John said, pointing at the eagle.

"Always a good omen," Bill said, nodding his understanding.

Bill knew his Pa believed they were members of the Eagle Clan and that the eagle was their special totem. Once again, even the omens seemed to confirm he had made the right choice for his family's future and that life would be good on Pilger Mountain.

Before riding up to the brick house, John held up his hand to signal he wanted to rein up their horses. John saw his son understood that he wanted to look over the place before riding in. It had been over thirty years since he had last seen the place. He had many mixed feelings about having worked on the Lazy Cheyenne Ranch and about the outlaw cattle baron Tom Burton, but after so many years most of his memories were only good ones. He had learned that a man needed to take life as it comes. There really was no other way.

John had lost everything after Tom Burton went bust in 1887, having never received the back pay he was owed, or the sizable grubstake he had earned over nearly two years of backbreaking work that Burton had offered to hold onto for him. Even so, he had found a way to start over, and in time, to even fulfill his boyhood dream. Though he would never wish it, he figured his son may have to learn this same harsh lesson somewhere along his path in life. It was a lesson most men had to learn the hard way sooner or later. Though a man could control many things in his life, and often had the power to make his own choices, there would be times when no matter how hard he tried, things wouldn't work out.

Every man has to take life as it comes; it's what he can make of whatever life throws at him that matters in the end. John was certain his son had the sand to face whatever life had in store for him, and not only survive, but find a way to thrive and make something good out of it. Looking over at his son, who had already accomplished much in life, John couldn't have been prouder that like himself, he had chosen to pursue his boyhood dream, come what may.

Stepping down from his horse, John came face to face with Ross Bishop, who had only been a toddler the last time he had seen him. John couldn't believe how much Ross, with his broad shoulders, piercing hazel-blue eyes, stern jaw, and striking Anglo-Saxon features, resembled his father, Joseph Bishop, right down to his firm but friendly handshake. The striking resemblance brought to John's mind the old farmer's adage, "Plant corn, get corn." John had to admit the expression couldn't be more accurate when it came to describing the Bishop family's menfolk, who all looked, spoke, and acted one hell of a lot alike.

Their business with Ross didn't take long once they settled on a price for the horses they wanted to lease and for those they wanted to buy. Ross agreed to deliver seven saddle horses fully outfitted to the Custer County Courthouse on the morning of May 1 with the understanding that the horses would be ridden to Minnekahta Station and would arrive by midafternoon on May 3. The plan was for the seven men to board the morning train back to Wall on May 4 and for Ross to take the horses back to his ranch. Ross also agreed to deliver twenty good horses suitable for pulling wagons to Minnekahta Station by midafternoon on May 15. These horses Bill intended to buy. Ross asked very few questions about why they needed so many horses, having received word from his father that he should give the Bartons whatever they needed at a fair price.

Before they rode out, John and Bill caught sight of a little boy about five years old rounding the side of the brick house running at a full tilt. John could hear Ross's wife, Theresa, calling out from the kitchen for Billy to come back as the boy scampered to his father's side. Billy was Ross's youngest son and the spitting image of his father. John had to chuckle to himself at how the little towheaded boy squinted his right eye almost shut in the bright sunlight just like his father, Ross, and his Grandfather Joe did, and on further thought, John had to admit, just as his Great-Grandfather E.J. had once done. With a grin on his face, the only thing John could think of as they headed back to Edgemont was how much ears of corn all seemed to look one hell of a lot alike.

"What's the grin all about?" Bill said as the two men rode south toward the Cheyenne River crossing.

"Corn," John said, the grin on his face growing a bit wider.

"Corn? What about it?" Bill said, wondering why on earth his Pa was thinking about corn of all things.

"The ears, they all look alike," John said, his grin now breaking into a smile.

Seeing his son was perplexed, John enjoyed the confused expression on his son face, causing his smile to grow all the more.

"That they do. So, what about it?" Bill said, bewildered.

"Damnedest thing, wouldn't you say?" John said, his smile now commanding the lower half of his face.

"Nature's way, I guess," Bill said, trying hard to figure out what his Pa was getting at.

"Exactly," John said, spurring his horse to take the lead as they crossed the Cheyenne River where the river was shallow and the riverbed firm, making it an ideal crossing point year-round.

Bill followed his Pa as he pondered ears of corn and how they all look alike and then had to laugh out loud when it hit him that his Pa was talking about the Bishops. Bill too had been taken aback when he met Ross Bishop face to face. The man had looked like an exact replica of his father, only a younger version. To top it off, his son Billy had looked as though he had also been cast from the same mold.

Shaking his head back and forth, still chuckling out loud, he rode up beside his Pa once they cleared the crossing and said, "They do all look one hell of a lot alike, and I'd swear to that on a stack of Bibles."

"If you'd ever met E.J., you'd be even more convinced than you are right now," John said, sharing the chuckle with his son.

"As they say, 'Plant corn, get corn,'" John said, winking at his son, a broad grin returning to his face.

"Ah, ears of corn. I see now. No truer words, no truer words. . .," Bill said, causing the two men to once again share a good laugh.

They both enjoyed the ride back to Edgemont, satisfied all the pieces were now in place for the big move to Pilger Mountain. With the sun low in the western sky, the scattered clouds lit up the same shade of vermillion as the rugged stone-capped slopes that marked the southern boundary of the Black Hills. With the world bathed in a crimson glow, the sun sent out narrow beams of golden light that streaked the sky as it melted slowly into the distant horizon. The men rode in silence, deep in thought. Though all the pieces were in place, they both knew there was still much to do.

May 1, 1929

Minnekahta, Fall River County, South Dakota

Westward Ho!

Arriving in Custer the day before the announcement, the Lucky Seven were up the next morning at the crack of dawn. Checking out of the Roadway Inn, they enjoyed a hardy breakfast of bacon and eggs with flapjacks and gravy dished up by the ever-smiling Molly Tillerman, the owner of the establishment, who was always ready with a story about her good-for-nothing husband and the history of the Black Hills. One of the first white women to settle in the Black Hills, she had panned for gold on French Creek with her good-for-nothing husband as far back as the mid-1870s, earning enough to build the Roadway Inn. Now in her late sixties, Molly still moved around the serving tables like a younger woman, her deeply wrinkled and weathered face however told a very different story. It was clear she had lived a hard, harsh frontier life and had given it her all.

She had been suspicious of seven strange men suddenly showing up together but had learned to keep her suspicions to herself a long time ago. As long as they paid their bills, she figured, one way or another, it wouldn't be long until she knew what they were up to. Nothing that happen in and around Custer ever got past the long ears and sharp eagle eyes of Molly Tillerman. She had seen it all over the years and looked forward to solving the mystery of the seven strangers.

Just as they had planned, and much to the surprise and bewilderment of Custer County Courthouse clerks, the seven men were the first in line to file their claims even before the Courthouse doors opened on Wednesday morning May 1. With their legal claims duly filed, the seven men, with Bill leading the way, walked out of the courthouse to find Ross Bishop and one of his ranch hands waiting out front with a string of seven fully outfitted horses. Bill was surprised that Ross himself had made the trip to deliver their horses.

"Just wanted to see what you folks were up to," Ross said, greeting Bill and the other men with a broad smile.

"Just filing claims to land around Pilger Mountain," Bill said, the announcement now public.

"Always liked that part of the hills. Great hunting grounds," Ross said.

"There's game aplenty that's for sure. We hope to bring a little civilization to that part of the hills," Bill said with a grin.

"Well, good luck. I always wondered when that part of the hills would finally be settled. For me, I have all the land and cattle I can manage," Ross said, stepping up on horse.

"You be coming out to Minnekahta Station?" Bill said.

"No, Rusty here will pick up the horses on May 3rd," Ross said, motioning in the direction of his ranch hand.

"Good to meet ya, Rusty. We'll see you in the afternoon, day after tomorrow," Bill said, walking over to shake hands.

"I'll be there," Rusty said, a man of few words.

Bill and the other men watched as Ross and Rusty rode out, headed east toward the Dakota Ridge. After sorting out the horses, the men soon stepped up into their saddles. With Bill taking up the lead, they rode at a fast trot west to Fourmile Corner and then straight south on the old Pleasant Valley stage trail to Pilger Mountain.

Arriving at Pilger Mountain, the men got busy. One by one, they measured out and marked the boundaries of their claims. To a man, they found themselves in awe of the valley's natural beauty and its rich black virgin soil. They were all convinced they were among the luckiest men on earth.

Bill, after showing each man the location of his claim, was finally able to inspect his own. Standing in the shadow of the giant pine tree right where he built it, his stone marker stood like a silent sentinel awaiting the return of its master. It had stood in solitude for over six years, the guardian of his boyhood dream with his eagle feather wedged under its base and two cougar canine fangs resting on its capstone just as Bill had left them.

Seeing his stone maker embedded in the *uname* design just as his father's marker had been brought tears to his eyes. His long wait had ended.

In his pocket he held the receipt for his legal homestead claim. He knew it would take five years to prove up that claim, but he was never more confident about his and Kate's future and that of their children.

With the local economy booming, he would get top dollar for his general store and postal contract. He was giving up a lot, but with cash in hand and a tidy nest egg securely tucked away in the bank, he was never more certain of the decisions he had made. He would make a good life for his family on Pilger Mountain, he could feel it in his bones. Looking out over his land, he couldn't wait to get started.

The two days on Pilger Mountain passed quickly as the men went about scouting the area and making plans for their Pleasant Valley settlement. Getting a chance to ride across Barker Flats to Minnekahta Station allowed everyone a preview of the trail they would be following with their wagon train in less than two weeks.

Time passed faster than any of the men could have imagined. Before they knew it, the day of their big move from Wall to Pilger Mountain had come. With a northern Alberta clipper burying the region under a foot of snow and plunging temperatures to below zero, the men had fought high winds and snow flurries all morning to load their wagons and horses onto railcars for the trip into the southern Black Hills.

Just the day before, everything had looked good with blue skies, calm winds, and cold but mild weather. They had all hoped to get underway before the Arctic storm front forecast to blow in from the northwest swept across the northern plains. Bill and the other men had learned long ago that if hope were as valuable as gold, they would all be millionaires.

They knew, all too well, how fickle the weather could be in the high plains, especially in the spring and fall of the year, when the change in seasons created a volatile mix of hot moist air flowing up from the sultry south and cold dry air flowing down from the frigid north. As these massive weather fronts clashed across the Great Plains, they often brought violent storms with torrential rainfall and tornadoes in the summer and fall, and high winds and blizzards in the winter and spring.

Swings in temperature from freezing polar cold one day to balmy tropical breezes the next were not uncommon. Given it was the middle of May, no one was concerned that the snow now piling up in deep drifts would stay on the ground very long. A Chinook wind could turn things around overnight. Should this happen, the warming temperatures could melt off the snow rapidly, leaving the men wading through knee-deep mud rather than battling hip deep snow. If Bill had his way, he would prefer to drive their heavy-laden wagons over hardened snow-packed ground than over wet, soggy ground where they would risk having their wagon wheels bogged down in the region's notoriously slippery yet sticky gumbo.

After hitching their loaded railcars onto a westbound train, they were able to finally get under way. Trains running west out of Wall had to climb a steep uphill grade to the small town of Wasta, which sat atop the natural mound formation upon which the higher elevations of the Black Hills rested. Once their train topped the mound, it continued to slowly climb higher as they moved west. It wasn't long before the deep dark green ponderosa pine-covered peaks of the Black Hills rose up out of the prairie appearing like mounds of jet-black coal on the western horizon. The name Black Hills came from the Lakota Sioux name, *Paha Sapa*, meaning hills black.

Just east of Rapid City, their train turned south, taking the rail spur along the western edge of the Black Hills. As they traveled south, they crossed one river after another that flowed east out of the Black Hills to join the Cheyenne River, which meandered north along the edge of the mound on which the hills rested until it merged with the Belle Fourche River and turned northeast at a point called Two Rivers not too far north from where John Barton's homestead was located. The Cheyenne River, known to the Lakota as the *Wakpa Waste*, the Good River, then cut a muddy path through the badlands straight east all the way to the Missouri River.

The views of the Black Hills from the train were breathtaking as they chugged their way south between the Dakota Ridge to the east and the Black Hills to the west. This natural valley, between the forested hills to the west and the harsh treeless badlands to the east, had been a boon to cattle ranchers since the first white men settled in the region.

Roy Kelly envied the ranchers in the area for having settled some of the choicest grazing land west of the Missouri. If all went well with his Pilger Mountain sheep ranch, he promised himself he would try to find a way to expand his family's Cheyenne River cattle operations into grazing ranges along the Dakota Ridge. He hoped he would be able to get to know Ross Bishop better in coming years, since the Bishop family had been running cattle in the southern hills since the early 1880s.

Ed Philips, the father-in-law to both Jeff Engel and Mike Robinson, had insisted on joining the wagon train to Pilger Mountain, claiming his wife would never forgive him if he didn't help their little girls get settled into their new lives. Ed had his own homestead near Wall that he hoped to pass on to his only son, Jack, who had also taken up running the Philips family's feed gain business.

Ed couldn't have been more pleased about how things had worked out for Wilma, considering the direction her life had been headed in her wilder days. Jeff had turned out to be a good man, a good provider, and a good father to their children. That Bethany would be living near her sister was a coincidence Ed had silently taken in stride lest he jinx his good fortune. Ed had never been a superstitious man, nor had he ever considered himself lucky. With both of his sons-in-law members of the Lucky Seven, he had started to think he just might be luckier than most.

John Barton, Fredrick Hamann, Christian Shultz, and Buck Kelly had also volunteered to pitched in. John, Christian, and Buck wanted to help their sons get settled in and Fredrick wanted to help his brother-in-law, Detrick, and his sister, Annie, with their eight children get set up as quickly as possible. Everyone in the wagon train was committed to helping Albert and Emma Meyer. They had all pledged to pitch in to build a one-room schoolhouse and to have it outfitted and ready to receive the first crop of Pleasant Valley children by the start of school in the fall.

Their schoolmarm upon learning of their plans couldn't have been more elated. She too looked forward to the adventure of settling in Pleasant Valley, if for no other reason than the valley's name seemed to portend a bright and happy future. She wished for nothing more than to have her own children someday and for them to grow up in such a wondrous place.

Following the Chicago North Western rail spur from Hot Springs, they made their way west to the Minnekahta Station Terminal that sat on the western edge of a wide, flat valley that formed the natural southern gateway into the Black Hills. Bill had been amazed at how their train had been able to plow through the drifting snow all day. Now that they had arrived at the Minnekahta Station Terminal, they had no choice but to face the reality of their situation head on. With gusting winds and snow flurries showing no sign of letting up, they had little choice in the matter. They needed to drive their wagon train into the hills as far as possible before dark. Though there would be no way to make it to Pilger Mountain, Bill felt confident they would be able to get halfway to Barker Flats, where they should be able to find a good place to set up camp for the night in the shelter of the trees.

Bill had been unanimously named wagon master in recognition of his knowledge of the lay of the land and his invaluable assistance in identifying and securing the best tracts of land in Pleasant Valley. To a man, they believed that with the nation's economy booming and markets for livestock, wool, farm produce, and timber soaring to all-time highs, their gamble on the lush virgin lands of Pleasant Valley and Pilger Mountain would pay off in spades in coming years. The future of the country looked bright, and for the Lucky Seven, it looked even brighter.

As their train pulled into Minnekahta Station, Bill hopped off onto the platform to meet Ross Bishop and his ranch hand, Rusty.

"You boys sure chose a doozy of a day to be out for a wagon ride," Ross said with a kindly grin and stern look on his face as the wind nearly blew his hat off.

"Yeah, the weather did turn on us a bit, but that's life in the Banana Belt," Bill quipped, returning a whimsical grin while holding down his own hat.

The Black Hills had jokingly come to be called the Banana Belt because of its unseasonably balmy weather during winter months, when a unique combination of meteorological factors pumped warm dry air up from the southwest into the higher elevations of hills. Temperatures in the Black Hills often soared forty to fifty degrees higher than those of the surrounding prairie lowlands during the dead of winter. Though these temperature spikes were often short lived, they were a unique feature of life in the hills and a welcome relief from the bitter cold.

"Indeed, it is," Ross said with knowing nod, shaking hands with Bill.

"We have a couple of riders holding your remuda of twenty horses just over that ridge out of the wind," Rusty said, pointing to the west, as a strong gust of wind swirled around the men kicking up the powdery snow.

"If you gentlemen could bring the horses over, we'll get busy unloading these wagons and gettin' 'em hitched up," Bill said, wanting to keep things moving.

With snow still coming down, they had no time to waste.

Ross and Rusty stepped up on their horses and rode out to the west and soon came riding back accompanied by two other riders. The four riders kept the twenty horses corralled as they gathered them in front of the train station. Holding the horses in place, the riders quickly dismounted and tied the horses to a row of hitching posts. After a short conversation with Bill and John and quick handshake with the other men, Ross and his three ranch hands soon headed out, their transaction now complete. They too had no time to waste having planned to ride back to the Bishop Ranch that afternoon and knowing with the snow still coming down they wouldn't be getting in out of the cold until after dark.

It was late in the day before the Lucky Seven were able to get their wagons unloaded and teams hooked up and readied for the trail. Though there had been breaks in the bitterly cold wind, the snow flurries had continued. Knowing there was no turning back, the men accepted their miserable lot without complaint and boarded their wagons for the final leg of their journey.

Bill, with John riding beside him, waved his right arm in a broad arch and pointed toward the northwest and called out as loudly as he could, "Wagons Ho!"

As the wagon drivers snapped their reins and whistled and barked out encouragement to their reluctant teams, the wagons slowly creaked forward. The team of horses on the lead wagon driven by Roy Kelly was made up of the largest and strongest horses they had in hopes that they would be able to buck through the snow-swept landscape and create a narrow trough-like trail in the near belly-deep snow for the other wagons to follow. Slowly but surely, with the horses straining in their harnesses, the seven wagons ploughed their way over a series of pine-studded knolls that led toward Barker Flats.

The north wind continued to blow straight into the ice-encrusted faces of the men as they fought to keep their unruly teams of horses pushing headlong into the storm. An hour before sunset, the sky cleared as the winds calmed and snow stopped falling. Bill, taking the change in weather as a favorable omen, called out for the wagons to pull up for the night. It was nearly dark before campfires could be lit. Though it had been an exhausting day, everyone was excited that Barker Flats was in sight and their long-awaited promised land was less than a day away.

Bill figured if they got an early start the next morning, they may be able to make it to Pilger Mountain by evening. The last thing they needed now was a Chinook wind to come up and rapidly turn the frozen ground to a sea of mush. He knew the soil in Barker Flats was mostly made up of soft clay and could pose a real problem if it was too wet. Now that there was over two feet of snow on the ground, his only hope was that temperatures would remain cold and the ground hard until they could cross Barker Flats and reach their final destination.

After a fitful, sleepless night, Bill was up at the crack of dawn the next morning. The air was frigid cold. The scene around him was one out of a children's storybook. Everything was covered in snow and frost as the surrounding forest slowly filled with a cacophony of the sounds of life that grew louder with the coming sun. Bleary eyed he watch the blazing ball of the sun climb over the rim of the earth in the east, chased by two sun dogs in close pursuit. The sun dogs with their rainbow-colored hue stretched out in identical arcs on both sides of the sun, signaling the coming of a sudden change in the weather. Absorbing the meaning of the message being sent by Mother Nature, Bill quickly swung into action.

Hearing pots and pans banging around, John rolled out of his bedroll to see what all the commotion was about.

"It's barely daybreak, what's the rush?" John said as he rounded the wagon, coming face to face with his son.

"Sun dogs. We need to get on the move. We have no time to lose," Bill said, pointing to the sky in the east.

John knew immediately why his son was eager to get on the move. If the snow began to melt too rapidly before they reached Pilger Mountain, things could get a damn sight more difficult than they had been.

"You get the others up, I'll whip us up some breakfast," John said. "We'll need to move out as soon as possible."

Without comment, Bill grabbed a tin pot and a metal ladle, turned on his heel, and quickly went from wagon to wagon, pounding on the pot with the ladle, calling for everyone to get up and roll out. Within minutes everyone was up and scurrying around. The men knew what sun dogs meant in the high plains; they also knew what a sudden change of weather would mean for all of them.

In less than an hour, they were underway. The horses labored as they pulled the heavy-laden wagons, their breathing flowing from their flared nostrils hung in misty puffs, like the exhaust of a steam engine, as they plowed their way across the wide tableland known as Barker Flats. The sun seemed to rocket straight to its zenith, its relentless sun dogs merging into a single halo that encircled the sun directly overhead at high noon. With time slipping away, Bill grew increasingly concerned when out of the southwest a warm breeze with a distinct desert scent suddenly filled the air. Rather than stop for their noon meal, Bill rode down the line of wagons, telling everyone they needed to keep pushing their teams forward until they reached Pleasant Valley.

By midafternoon, the snow on the surrounding trees was gone, disappearing into thin air. Hour by hour, the snow on the ground had shrunk.

What had been two feet of powder that morning was now less than a foot of soft, mushy snow in the heat of the afternoon sun. Driving the teams hard had taken its toll with foamy lather covering the sides of the horses as they strained in their harnesses. Just as they reached the edge of Pleasant Valley, with Pilger Mountain's gentle slopes forming its western boundary, a strong Chinook wind swept in from the southwest, melting the remaining snow off the landscape before their very eyes. Within minutes, streams ran full and the smell of spring filled the air. Like a miracle, winter had turned to spring in what seemed like an instant.

The firmer ground in the valley was a welcome bit of luck as the wagons worked their way into the valley and along Pilger Mountain. One by one, wagons soon peeled off from the others, as each man drove his team to the location of his own claim. By late afternoon, though they were exhausted, every man now believed, more than ever, his luck was strong and his success certain.

In coming days, they got down to the business of felling trees and constructing shelters. They had agreed that in their first year, they would help each other to plant a few acres on each claim, so they could all have a small crop to harvest come fall. Putting in sizable vegetable gardens however was their highest priority. More than ever, they needed to be able to produce their own food and to become as self-sufficient as possible in order to succeed in their isolated valley. With the soil rich and the game aplenty, no one worried that they would lack for food, so long as they were willing to put in the work.

Bill had brought along his Pa's old Delco Light Plant which he hoped to get hooked up as soon as he could. His Pa had bought a new one and Bill figured having electric lighting at least some of the time would make the homestead a bit more civilized. He knew getting fuel to run the generator would be tough in the beginning, but he wanted to make life as comfortable as possible for Kate and the children.

With no phone service, and cut off from the outside world, they would have to make do on their own. Should they need to reach anyone on the outside, the closest town with mail service and a telephone was the little town of Dewey, twelve miles due west on horseback over Pilger Mountain. Custer was a larger town but was located more than twenty-five miles north, more than double the distance. The other towns in the region were even further away. Edgemont to the south and Hot Springs to the east were both roughly forty miles away.

The spring and summer passed quickly. The men kept busy, plowing fields, clearing trees, and building cabins on their own claims. As soon as school got out in the spring, the women and children moved from the bad-lands to join their menfolk on Pilger Mountain. Though everyone had to live in or under their covered wagons until their cabins were built, they all pitched in doing whatever needed to be done.

The womenfolk worked as hard as the menfolk, putting in gardens, building chicken coups and pens for their livestock, setting fence posts and stringing wire, and even helping wrestle logs into place as their cabins took shape. All seven men pitched in to construct a sturdy little one-room schoolhouse that was completed just in time and on schedule for the first ringing of the school's bell on the morning of Monday, September 9, 1929.

As more and more families staked claims in the valley, the Lucky Seven welcomed them with open arms. The general consensus being that the more settlers that filled the valley, the higher the likelihood they would get the new county roads they needed and postal and other services they lacked. With the children in school and their first harvest standing tall in the fields, the settlers around Pilger Mountain were flying high.

Bill had sold his general store and postal contract for a good price, which had allowed him to buy a new Roman Eagle cookstove and sewing machine for Kate and enough supplies for nearly a year. Looking over his new place, Bill was proud of what they had been able to accomplish in a single season. His cabin was well built and had four rooms. He had to smile when he thought how his rustic little cabin in the woods was actually larger than their former living quarters behind his general store in Creighton. He was proud that his cabin was one of the few with electric lights, even though he wasn't able to run them more than an hour or two every night. He had also put up two large pole barns, using one of them to store firewood and hay and the other to shelter his horses.

As October rolled around, everyone stayed busy getting in the harvest and chopping firewood for the long winter ahead. The Barton place was abuzz with activity. Kate had labored for over two weeks canning meat, fruits, and vegetables for the coming winter, while Bill laid in firewood and worked on his Delco Light Plant, which seemed to need constant attention. He had wired the cabin and even run wires to both his pole barns. They had given up a lot to move to Pilger Mountain, but he was determined not to give up every modern convenience.

There were however many modern conveniences enjoyed by nearly every American that were alien to the settlers of the vast vacant frontier lands of the upper Great Plains east of the Rockies and west of the Missouri River. The first commercial radio broadcast in America was in 1920 just after the war. Though commercial radio broadcasts began in eastern South Dakota as early as 1922, there were still no commercial radio broadcasters in western South Dakota at the end of the 1920s. Every time Bill exchanged letters with his brother Alva, he was surprised to learn of all the things happening in the world and all the news and programs his brother listened to on the radio. Amos 'n' Andy may have been all the rage in much of America, but they meant nothing to Bill and his neighbors, who had never heard any of their comedy routines or even listened to a single radio broadcast in their entire lives.

Just before their move to Pilger Mountain, Alva had sent Bill a cat whisker crystal radio with several earphones and a long antenna wire. Upon opening the package and seeing the radio for the first time, Bill had to laugh out loud when he thought about how long his antenna wire would need to be to pick up even a whisper from the outside world. The radio, still packed away in its original carton, reminded Bill just how cut off his life had been from the fast-moving changes driving the nation and the world. The people of western South Dakota in many ways lived in a cocoon, protected from the outside world by their own isolation. This had been true during the Spanish flu pandemic that had stalked the nation but never really impacted the sterile, vacant, windswept wastelands of western South Dakota.

His move to Pilger Mountain had been like turning back the clock more than fifty years to a simpler time prior to the modern age. With no real roads, automobiles, phones, radios, or even postal services, Pleasant Valley was like living in a cocoon within a cocoon, that had been hermetically sealed. Deep down, Bill knew that a man could run, but he couldn't hide. The Great War had found every American, even those living at the edges of the badlands. The long arm of the government had reached into every home, no matter how remote.

He knew there was no hiding from the next crisis that may strike the nation. He also knew from Alva's letters the world had gotten a damn sight more complicated since America had decided to step onto the world stage as a great power. Rather than ponder all the things that might happen, he had come to accept that all a man could really do is get on with his own life and deal with whatever might come his way, however and whenever that day came. Little did Bill Barton know, his day was coming, and that day was a hell of a lot closer than he could have ever imagined.

October 29, 1929

Pleasant Valley, Custer County, South Dakota

Black Tuesday

THE MORNING WAS STILL and chilly, the fall leaves were at the height of their glory as they lit up the dark green pine forest with splashes of bright red, orange, and yellow. The sounds of squirrels, chipmunks, and birds, busy making a living, added to the illusion that all was well in the world. The air was fresh and crisp. Bill inhaled the rich pine-scented air deep into his lungs as he stood on his front porch. Life was good in Pleasant Valley. It had truly become the Shangri-La he and Kate had believed it would be.

Looking out over his harvested fields, Bill dreamed of the many bumper crops his fertile land would yield in coming years. His boyhood dream had come true, and he looked forward to building a future for his family in Pleasant Valley. The large pine tree next to the cabin now sported a rope swing at Kate's insistence, which Bart had claimed as his own.

Already five years old, Bart was among the first crop of children to attend their new Pleasant Valley School. Little Velda, soon to be one, was now walking on her own. She had shot up like a weed since her premature birth and was now as tall and as strong as her Uncle Lavern, who had been born to Detrick and Annie just two weeks before Velda's birth. Surrounded by her many aunts and uncles, Velda had thrived. She was no child of the prairie, she was a child of the forest, and Pleasant Valley was her home.

Detrick had built his cabin into the side of a low-lying ridge that faced south. Next to his cabin, he had built a long house where his children and the occasional guest and farmhand bunked. Detrick had also purchased additional land and had decided to hang on to his original badlands homestead, leasing it to his brother-in-law, Fredrick Hamann. Having never owned land, Detrick found it difficult to sell what he owned, especially to a stranger. Land meant more to him than money, much more. His feelings about his land mirrored those of other homesteaders, who had carved their farms out of an unforgiving prairie. Their land was all they had to show for their life of labors. Owning land and building a working farm was what defined a man. Land was something a man could feel between his fingers, something in which he could set down his roots.

Investments in stocks and bonds belonged to the world of bankers and rich men. It was a world the people of the prairie knew little about and cared for even less. Some had bought government bonds to support the war, and some had even purchased shares of stock in local ventures. Most however had never owned a stock or a bond, nor had they ever had the money to do so.

Whether the people of the frontier took part or not, the stock market had grown steadily during the 1920s, reaching its zenith in August 1929. For nearly a decade, speculation had driven the market higher, making more than a few wily investors wealthy beyond their wildest dreams. The first crack in the money machine showed up when banks strapped for cash were unable to liquidate large loans on their books, leaving them with an ever-swelling portfolio of nonperforming debt. A second crack showed up when the agricultural sector, once a safe harbor, had also begun to struggle as commodity prices steadily declined due to overproduction. The third crack was caused by chronically low wages that had, year on year, increasingly acted as a drag on the economy, drying up consumer demand.

The first sign that these cracks may spell real trouble came in September, when stocks prices began a steady decline. As the decline continued into early October, traders became alarmed. By mid-October, the relentless decline in stock prices had driven the market into a panic. With no one wanting to get caught holding the bag, the wholesale dumping of shares began in earnest. On October 24, a day that would come to be known as Black Thursday, a record number of shares were traded as share prices dove to new lows. Banks and investment houses stepped in to purchase huge blocks of stock in an attempt to stabilize the market, which created a brief rally on Friday, October 25. Though these emergency actions seemed to have been effective in halting the decline, the damage to investor confidence had already been done.

On Monday, October 28, the market opened to a barrage of sell orders, sending it into a tailspin. Once again, banks and investment houses attempted to step into the fray, only to discover the market resisted all their efforts to slow down its unrelenting decline. By the end of the day, Monday had turned into Black Monday, a bloodbath that many hoped they would be able to put behind them at the opening of the market the next day. Their wishful thinking unfortunately was met with Black Tuesday, October 29, the day stock prices completely collapsed, wiping out the fortunes of thousands of investors in a single trading session. When the last ticker tape was tallied, billions of dollars in equity had vanished in the blink of an eye. In a nation hooked on easy credit for over a decade, cash suddenly became king overnight.

Banks caught flatfooted and without adequate capital reserves soon found their lack of cash flow their Achilles' heel. Strapped for cash, banks rushed to liquidate their capital investments. Runs on banks soon followed as depositors sought to pull out their savings in fear of looming bank failures. The rush to withdrawal cash caused the very thing depositors had feared the most, the collapse of the banking sector. One bank failure after another rippled across the country like the toppling of a string of dominos. As banks shuttered their doors, the life savings of many hardworking Americans were wiped out. Without government-backed depositor insurance, depositors were left without any real legal recourse to ever recover their lost savings.

As early as 1858, transatlantic cables had carried communications between America and Britain. By the turn of the twentieth century, cables linking Britain, France, Germany, and America had formed a complex web of telegraphic communication, allowing the news of the downturn in commodity markets and the collapse of the American stock market to be sent around the world at the speed of light, instantly triggering panic in every corner of the globe. As if suspended in another age, the news that had shaken the foundations of the global economy had arrived in Pleasant Valley nearly a week late and on the back of a galloping horse.

Roy Kelly had ridden to Dewey early on the morning of November 3 to pick up his weekly mail when he learned all about Black Tuesday. He also heard rumors of the growing number of bank failures sweeping the nation, since the stock market collapse. According to the newspapers, hard times were coming. Though Roy may not have had all the facts exactly right, what he had shared had been more than enough to put a sizable knot in the pit of

Bill's stomach. If the First National Bank in Wall ever failed, his life savings, his family's nest egg, money that had taken him a decade to earn, would be lost, leaving him flat broke.

As he watched Roy ride out toward Detrick's place to spread the news, Bill knew he had to learn more about what was happening beyond the serene bubble of Pleasant Valley. He also knew he had no time to waste. From the sound of things, the outside world had found a way to reach into their peaceful life in Pleasant Valley and tip it upside down. Bill made up his mind right then and there, he would ride out for Wall first thing in the morning. His hope was that he would be able to withdraw his life savings before it was too late. Considering the market had collapsed the week before, he knew his chances of reaching Wall in time were slim. Fact was, he knew it was probably too late already.

Roland Bishop sat in his mahogany-paneled Manhattan office tabulating his stock trades over and over again and coming up with the same sorry answer. After covering all the margin calls, he had racked up over the past week, the family's substantial holdings had all but evaporated. He had bought stock for pennies on the dollar all day Thursday, as the market fell, and again on Friday picking up one bargain after another, as the market rallied back. By the end of the day, he had calculated he would be able to nearly double the family's fortune come Monday morning with a few quick trades. When the market declined from its opening on Monday morning, Roland decided to once again borrow money to buy into the falling market, picking up huge blocks of stock for next to nothing. He was convinced the market would charge back in coming days, as it had always done in the past.

By Tuesday afternoon, with the market in free fall, his attempt to undo what he had done became impossible. The market was full of sellers dumping shares for whatever price they could get with buyers as scarce as hen's teeth. When the dust settled, the tale of the ticker tape was undeniable, the Bishops were busted.

When he called his nephew, Joe Bishop, in Hot Springs to inform him the family's fortune was gone, rather than being met with a string of cuss words, he was met with silence on the other end of the line. When Joe finally spoke, he told Roland that he had already been informed of their stock market losses and had also been notified that the banks in Hot Springs and

Rapid City had gone bust. The sizable cash deposits the Bishop family had in both institutions had been wiped out, down to the last penny.

Joe warned Roland creditors would be on his heels and that he should pull up stakes in Manhattan and head for California as quickly as possible. Joe's youngest son, Clarence, had been sent to California to invest in land, a move Joe had always figured was the family's ace in the hole. Joe assured Roland they would be able to rebuild if they cut their losses and got out now. Joe would join Roland and Clarence as soon as he could unload the Bishop House and get whatever he could for its furniture and artwork.

Without the need to discuss the matter, they both knew Ross would be hit especially hard by the bank failures, but they figured he would still have the ranch and could sell his cattle for cash. Their other land and business holdings in Hot Springs had been leveraged long ago to invest in the booming stock market. Rather than get entangled in all the legal challenges that were bound to come, now that they were busted, Joe decided the family would walk away from the properties and leave them for the taxman and a long line of creditors to sort out.

While the Bishop family, like so many others, frantically went about performing financial triage by liquidating what they could and dumping the rest, the nation began its slide into a major economic downturn. With bank failures soaring, the sudden lack of both cash and credit forced one business after another to close its doors. The road to the great depression had, like so many other roads leading to damnation, been paved in good intentions, at least that's what those who had been blinded by their own greed told themselves when the dust finally settled, leaving them to sift through the rubble left behind in the wake of the market collapse.

News of the stock market collapse had caught John Barton as flatfooted as it had everyone else. At the age of sixty-one, John was no longer a young man. He had lived a hard frontier life. As hard as his life had been, it had been the life he had chosen. Fact was, he wouldn't have lived it any other way. He had been dealt a lot of tough hands to play over the years and had nearly always found a way to make his cards into a winning hand. The hand life had dealt him this time around was one he wasn't so sure he could turn into a winner no matter how hard he tried.

Beyond his worries about falling commodity prices and the real possibility that his life savings may have already been lost, John's immediate concern was for his wife, Sarah, who had grown increasingly frail in recent weeks. The doctor had informed them just two months before that Sarah had an advanced form of cancer and had less than a year to live. Growing paler and weaker by the day, John feared they may lose her before Christmas.

Focusing his children's attentions on their mother's failing heath, John had kept the condition of his own health to himself. His biggest worry was his worsening eyesight. The one thing John feared more than anything else was ending up a blind man. He had seen other men who had gone blind on the frontier. He never wanted to end up a burden on his family, the way those men had. His youngest daughter, Lucille, was turning fifteen and already had a serious suitor. He knew Lucille, like her older sisters, would be getting married and leaving home before her seventeenth birthday.

With Francis, his youngest son, not yet thirteen, John had no one who could take over the farm should anything happen to him. He had wanted to sell his farm when the prices for farmland were high but decided to wait until Francis was out of school. Now with the economy in a nosedive and commodity prices low and headed further south, he wondered what a place like his, sitting in the middle of the badlands, might be worth, if anything.

Fearing he may have lost his life savings, John decided he would ride into Wall first thing in the morning. With no way to reach Bill in Pleasant Valley, John wondered if his eldest son, who had sizable savings in the bank after selling his general store and postal contract, had heard the news and whether he too was on his way to Wall. John could only hope they both made it to the bank in time.

Ross Bishop, upon hearing the news from his father that he would have to go it alone from now on, wasn't sure how he felt about having the whole family run off to California, leaving him to sort out what was left of the Bishop family fortune in the Black Hills. The Bishops had been among the first white men to settle in the Black Hills in the late 1870s, not long after gold was first discovered. It was difficult to accept that after becoming one of the most prominent families in the region, the Bishops were now penniless paupers.

Ross knew he still had cattle and though he had lost most of his government contacts in recent years, he still had a chance to sell beef to cover the cost of operations, at least for a while. With beef prices hitting new lows, it would be a tough slog, but he felt he had plenty of cattle and good range land and that he was up to the challenge.

He didn't much like being left behind but understood why his father was grabbing whatever scraps of the Bishop fortune he could before hightailing it out of the state. Without a doubt, he figured his father already had a passel of hungry creditors hot on his heels. Come what may, Ross was determined to rebuild the Bishop fortune in South Dakota. He figured, like his Grandpa E.J., all he needed was a little luck, with a dash of larceny.

August 15, 1932

Three Tree Creek, Pennington County, South Dakota

Bone Dry

RAIN WAS THE ONE thing men had never figured out how to conjure up. Since the beginning of the drought, plenty of men had sent up prayers and some had chanted and danced in circles, and yet, nary a drop of rain had fallen from the void of a cloudless clear blue sky that day after day greeted a vast prairie wasteland. The weather had been bone dry all summer. For the third year in a row, each year having offered less rain than the last, John would be left to harvest the stubble of yet another sorry looking corn crop. With his oats looking just as pitiful, he decided to hay his whole crop, oats and corn alike.

Like too many of his neighbors, John had ploughed up and planted nearly every square inch of the land he owned in an effort to cover the downturn in commodity prices and a long string of losses. He wondered how long he would be able to continue working land that never yielded a crop and running a farm that never turned a profit.

He had been able to make it to the bank in Wall in the nick time to withdraw his life savings after the stock market collapse on October 29, 1929, only to watch those precious dollars slowly dwindle away as he struggled to make a living, year after year. After Sarah's death and Lucille's marriage, John and his youngest son, Francis, had continued to work the farm. Despite their best efforts, there was just no way to make crops grow under a blistering sun and rainless skies in a land starved for water.

The Great Plains had turned into a dust bowl. The overcultivation of the semiarid region could not have come at a worse possible time. Future historians would report that the period from 1930 to 1936 was the driest on record in the Great Plains in over a thousand years. With the jet steam frozen in place too far south, the weather anomaly it created pumped dry air into the region while holding at bay the wet moist air that had, in past years, flowed up from the Gulf of Mexico, providing the seasonal rains that fed the water-starved vegetation of the Great Plains from Texas to North Dakota. With the disruption of the region's natural cycle of life-giving moisture, the semiarid grasslands of the Great Plains soon became a barren desert.

John's eyesight had rapidly grown worse. No longer able to see things at a distance, he feared he would slowly go blind. Though Francis, at age fifteen, was as big as a grown man and could do a man's work, there would be no way for him to continue working a farm that no longer yielded a crop, while looking after a blind man. Francis wanted to stay on and save the farm, come what may. He had begged his father not to give up on the only place he had ever known. John knew, no matter how hard his son toiled day and night, the soil without water would never provide him a living.

It had been twenty-five years since John staked his claim in the badlands, fulfilling his boyhood dream. He had to admit, it had been a good run. He and Sarah had carved a good life out of the forbidding prairie, and though the land never provided them with bumper crops, it had provided them with a bountiful harvest of strong, healthy children, each one prefect in his or her own way. John still felt a deep spiritual connection to the badlands and knew he always would. At his core, he was however a realist and knew the time had come for him to move on.

Finding his old stone marker next to Barton Lake, John knelt in front of the marker's mysterious reliquary of religious symbols and prayed for one last time. Drifting dirt had nearly covered the marker, causing John to wonder whether it might become like the Great Sphinx of Egypt, an unsolvable mystery, to be accidentally stumbled upon by explorers thousands of years in the future. Having such a fanciful thought brought a light-hearted grin his face, something his face had not worn in far too long.

He had always marveled at the many totems and amulets that adorned his marker, left by travelers from many religious backgrounds who had somehow discovered his stone marker on their way through this distant corner of the badlands. He was pleased his eldest son had made a replica of his stone maker and had embedded it, like his own, in a Lakota *uname* design.

The thought that his marker would survive long after his death gave him comfort, knowing most men pass through this world without leaving a trace. Reaching down, he picked up the delicately carved turtle amulet that rested on the maker's capstone and pocketed the Lakota good-luck talisman. For John, markers and talismans would forever link the Barton family to these mysterious lands.

On his way back to the house, a strong gust of wind came up, carrying a wall of dust in its wake. Hurrying the last fifty yards, he wondered how many of his neighbors had already given up fighting what had long ago become a lost cause. The region's meager topsoil had always required considerable good luck and a lot of coaxing to yield any kind of crop. Its rock-hard surface broken open by the plough had loosened the soil, freeing it to take flight on the relentless winds. Stripped off furrows turned over by the plough, topsoil filled the air, drifting in mounds like sand dunes piled up on a waterless desert. Fence posts, sheds, barns, houses, abandoned automobiles, and farm implements were soon buried with only the tops of the tallest of things able to poke out from under the shifting soil.

Finally getting word to Bill and Kate in Pleasant Valley after nearly a week of trying, John informed them that he and Francis were giving up on the farm and would be heading their way. Back in 1926, John had reluctantly traded in his old 1914 ventage Model T Ford for a used 1924 Chrysler Model B-70, the Chrysler company's first mass production vehicle. As it turned out, Sarah fell in love with the shiny new automobile the instant she saw it. She couldn't get over its roominess, its deep diamond blue color, and its fold-down convertible top. She had always enjoyed driving every chance she got, though she never liked the old Model T, which she had to hand crank more than a few times to get started. The Chrysler with its electric starter was like owning one of the seven wonders of the world to Sarah.

Shuttling her daughters around for one reason or another and often for no reason at all, Sarah behind the wheel of her diamond blue Chrysler became a common sight, roaring up and down Market Road. In jest, the diamond blue Chrysler was christened the Blue Demon by Sarah to spite John, who had complained that she drove like a demon possessed. The Blue Demon soon gained a reputation on the Market Road. Whenever the weather was warm enough, regardless the time of year, Sarah, with the convertible top down and her daughters, Arvella, Myrtle, Matilda, and little

Lucille, holding on to their colorful bonnets with ribbons streaming, could be heard laughing out loud by neighbors along the road as Sarah sped by pushing her Chrysler's team of seventy horses into a full gallop.

A wide grin returned to John's face when he thought about Sarah's Blue Demon roaring down the Market Road to Wall one last time with all seventy horses galloping full bore. John stood looking out over the vacant land nodding to himself as he thought of all the good times he and Sarah and their children had shared together in their prairie paradise. Though times had taken a bad turn, the good times they had shared would forever survive in their hearts and minds. Yes, he thought, on that last trip down Market Road, he and Francis would put down the top and laugh at the wind all the way to Wall. From Wall, John had decided, they would make their way following the shortest course possible to Pleasant Valley. The Barton family's time in the badlands had come to a close.

The drought hadn't just wiped out farmers, it had decimated ranchers as well. Faced with a wasteland stripped of graze and pocked with bone-dry mud-cracked watering holes, ranchers had been forced to sell as many animals as possible at whatever price they could get. Ross Bishop had seen some tough times in his life but had never experienced anything that could have prepared him to survive year after year in a land without graze or water. With no way to feed and water his starving cattle, he had been forced to sell into a market already glutted with beef. In desperation, ranchers throughout the Great Plains had rushed to sell whole herds of cattle in an effort to cut their mounting losses. Prices for beef plummeted, leaving many ranchers without cattle and with little cash to show for it.

As Ross looked out over the dry riverbed where the Cheyenne River had once meandered along the southern boundary of this ranch, his mind wandered back to memories of his younger days. He remembered how proud he was to join his father on the last cattle drive up the western Chisholm Trail in 1900. Not long after that final drive, the stringing of barbed wire soon crisscrossed and chopped up the land from Texas to the Dakotas, barring any future attempts to drive cattle on the open plains. He had been sixteen years old and full of vim and vigor. Now at forty-eight, he wondered how he would be able to start over again with a house full of children still too young, and a wife at her wits' end and on the brink of filing for divorce.

To compound his troubles, he didn't have near enough cash to hold on to what few assets he still had. Though he had always been an optimistic man, Ross saw only dim prospects in the days ahead.

Pleasant Valley, nestled in the heart of the southern hills, surrounded by a thirsty forest of ponderosa pine, hadn't escaped the drought that gripped the prairie lands that encircled it. The higher elevations of the Black Hills, surrounded by flat prairie lands that stretched in hundreds of miles in all directions, had in previous years created its own weather patterns with higher annual precipitation forming a natural oasis. With only dry air pumping into the region, the once lush Black Hills became a tinderbox. The biggest concern of the settlers around Pilger Mountain soon became the ever-looming threat of forest fires.

Protected from the worst of the relentless winds that pounded their prairie counterparts, farmers in Pleasant Valley hadn't lost all of their topsoil. Even so, like their prairie counterparts, they too had been unable to grow a marketable crop for three years in a row. What had started out so promising for the Lucky Seven, and all the families who had rushed to homestead around Pilger Mountain, had turned to dust before their very eyes, leaving them to fight a grueling daily battle for survival.

The only member of the Lucky Seven who seemed to prosper while others scraped to make a living was Roy Kelly with his herd of sheep that were able to make a living grazing on the rugged hillsides, whether it rained or not. With the larger game in the area growing increasingly scarce, as families took to hunting to make ends meet, graze suitable for goats and sheep became increasingly abundant.

Bill hadn't been able to reach Wall before its bank had failed. Though he had lost all of his sizable savings, he had been allowed to access his safety deposit box where he had fortunately stashed roughly one hundred dollars in coins for a rainy day. Heartbroken, he had returned to Pleasant Valley desperately hoping that he would be able to recoup his losses by cashing in on bountiful harvests in coming years.

With one bad year following the next since the market collapse, Bill wondered whether he would even be able to stay on his land long enough to prove it up. When they entered Pleasant Valley in 1929, five years seemed like a short amount of time to work the land to make it his own. Now just three years later, each year drier than the last, working his claim for five years seemed like a near impossibility.

Seeing how well Roy's sheep where doing, Bill and Detrick scraped together enough money to purchase a small herd of goats, which required little tending, as the unruly critters took to eating nearly anything and everything that came in their path. Another advantage for raising the stinky beasts was that, unlike thirsty cattle that never seemed to get enough to drink, goats and sheep could go without water for long periods, a big advantage in a world without rain.

Though Velda was only four years old, whenever she was allowed, she took to following her nine-year-old brother, Bart, and their black and white collie, named Sandy, to tend the Barton family's little herd of goats along the ridges of Pilger Mountain. Like all children everywhere, Velda's world was the one that surrounded her every day. The tough, unforgiving frontier life she had been forced to live was nothing out of the ordinary for Velda, she had never known anything else. Making do, doing with little, or simply doing without, was just the way things were and had always been. In later years, Velda would come to understand, being a pioneer was not something you learned, it was something you lived, something that became part of the very fiber of your being.

BOOK THREE

August 30, 1933

Pleasant Valley, Custer County, South Dakota

Child of the Frontier

AFTER NEARLY AN HOUR of nonstop nagging, Velda finally got her way, she would be able to tend the family's goat herd all day with her brother on the steep slopes of Pilger Mountain southwest of the Barton homestead. Bill had no problem with Velda joining her big brother. Kate, however, had other plans for Velda's day and was initially against letting her run off and play all day. Secretly, Velda wanted nothing more than to escape the reach of her mother, who always had something that needed to be done.

The weather was clear and mild and so it was finally agreed it would be a good idea for the children to enjoy the day together. Bart went along with the idea, though he would have preferred to not have his little sister tag along. To Bart's way of thinking, babysitting his little sister wasn't his job; it was his mother's.

Hiking along the upper slopes on Pilger Mountain, where they planned to graze the goats, Bart stubbornly refused to slow down to let his little sister catch up. Velda, determined to show her big brother she was up to the job, never complained, often having to run to keep pace. Before long, the goats were left to graze freely while Bart and Velda watched over them from higher up on the slope.

After a lunch of homemade cheese sandwiches, dried venison strips, and crab apple tarts, Bart decided to return to the game traps he had set earlier that morning. He figured even Velda should be able to watch goats graze on her own for a while.

"Velda, watch the goats. I'm gonna catch us a rabbit or two for supper," Bart said, acting like the big man he imagined himself to be, as he handed her his shepherd staff and marched up the sagebrush-covered slope toward the tree line.

They had seen fresh rabbit scat and tracks near an old tree stump on a ridge just beyond the tree line earlier in the day. Bart was convinced the rabbits were still around and decided to set up a couple of homemade traps near the old tree stump. He was sure the traps, made just like his grandpa had shown him, would do their job. He had baited the traps with dried apple slices, something he figured hungry rabbits wouldn't be able to resist.

Velda watched as Bart headed off until he disappeared into the trees. She was used to being left alone and taking care of herself. Growing up in the wilds, children were expected to grow up fast and to pitch in like everybody else. The shepherd staff, long, thick, and heavy in her hand, made her feel important in her role as protector of the flock. In Velda's young mind she was playing the same role Jesus did in the Bible. Of course, Jesus watched over sheep and not goats, but for Velda, that minor detail made little difference.

Soon to be five years old, it had been decided that Velda would start school in September, a year ahead of other children her same age. Her Uncle Lavern, just two weeks older than her, would also be sent to school when Velda started. Like twins, the two of them had grown up together and were nearly inseparable. Everyone had agreed that sending them to school early, so long as they would be together, would be good for both of them. Velda couldn't wait to start school with the other grownup children.

"Come on, Sandy, let's move 'em further down the slope," Velda said in a husky little voice to her big black and white collie while motioning for him to bunch the goats and move them down slope.

With the command understood, Sandy soon ran in a wide arc around the goats, herding them into a tight bunch and then barking and running back and forth at the edge of the bunch as the goats slowly and reluctantly at times moved down the slope. It was then that things quickly took an unexpected and violent turn.

Out of the trees, a full-grown cougar suddenly bounded, running at full speed straight at the goats. Velda knew that Roy Kelly and several other settlers had seen a she-lion roaming in the area in recent weeks. According to Roy, the cat had acquired a taste for mutton. He had lost two sheep and was on the hunt for the hungry cougar, which had cost him real money.

John had warned Bart and Velda that they shouldn't try to stop the cougar if she decided to take down one of the goats. John had reassured Kate and the children that they shouldn't have any trouble with the big cat during the daylight, since cougars usually hunted at dawn or dusk or more commonly during the dead of night.

The charging cougar had taken Velda by complete surprise. Gripping her staff with both hands, she began running and yelling at Sandy to watch out for the cougar. Sandy, alerted by her calls, hunched down as he surveyed the area just as the cougar ran headlong into the herd of goats, scattering animals in every direction. Sandy, enraged by the attack, ran directly at the cougar, barking and baring his fangs. Startled by the charging dog, it was the cat's turn to be surprised.

With a goat firmly in her clutches, the cougar hovered over her prey, torn between finishing her kill or turning to confront the oncoming threat. Velda, running in the direction of the bleating goat, watched in horror as Sandy bowled directly into the cougar's side, knocking her off her prey and sending the she-lion flying twenty feet down the slope.

Flipping back onto her feet in a single fluid motion, the enraged cougar took a fighting posture as she hunched down on her haunches with her front legs spread wide, her claws unsheathed. The cougar, growling from deep in her throat, charged forward, swiping the air with her huge claw-tipped paws, and then quickly retreating to a defensive posture every time Sandy, barking wildly, charged forward baring his fangs. Velda yelled in vain for Sandy to get away from the cougar. Incensed by the cougar's attack, Sandy had whipped himself into a frenzy, his hair stood on end down the middle of his back as he confronted the menacing creature. Sandy could no longer hear his master's commands, his mind focused solely on the unwelcome intruder.

Velda's approach diverted Sandy's attention for only an instant but just long enough for the big cat to sense a possible weakness in its opponent and an opportunity. Without warning, the cougar broke off her standoff with Sandy and pounced directly at Velda with her front legs spread wide and her claws fully extended. Velda, holding her staff like a baseball bat, caught the cougar's motion out of the corner of her eye and without thinking, reflexively swung her staff around with all her might in a wide arc, meeting the big cat in midair square on her jaw. The crack of the oaken staff meeting the cougar's lower jaw echoed out over the valley below.

Velda had swung the heavy staff around so hard that when it struck the cougar's lower jaw, the force knocked the cat flat on its back and threw Velda backward onto her rump. Momentarily knocked unconscious, the big cat painfully rolled back up on wobbly legs as she shook her head, stunned by the blow. Sandy, still enraged, charged the wounded cougar, sending the frightened animal dashing off up the slope, with her lower jaw dripping blood and swinging loosely back and forth with each bounding stride. Reaching the tree line, the slack-jawed she-lion looked back and then stumbled sideways before disappearing into the shadow of the trees.

Velda, not sure exactly what had happened, found herself sitting in the tall grass still holding onto the heavy staff with both hands in a death grip as she tried to catch her breath. Sandy soon joined her, licking her face as she hugged him tightly around his neck.

"Sandy, you crazy ol' dog! That ol' she-lion coulda killed ya," Velda cried, hugging the big collie hard as tears streamed down her face.

At the time, Velda didn't think much about all that had happened. She was just glad the cougar was gone, and Sandy was alright.

The little goat had been injured, but not too badly. After Sandy licked the little goat's wounds, Velda sent him running back to the herd. The little goat had no more than returned to the herd when Bart emerged from the tree line with his chest pushed out carrying a tree branch over his right shoulder with two large rabbits dangling on its end. The broad grin that creased his narrow face from ear to ear signaled to Velda her big brother was pretty proud of himself; the familiar smug look on his face was one she had seen all too often in her short little life.

"So how was your afternoon? Been keepin' busy?" Bart said with a dismissive smirk on his face.

Bart believed his sister was more a hinderance than any real help when it came to tending the goats. He felt being four years older than his sister left the two of them with little in common.

"Well, that she-lion came around," Velda said flatly, knowing the news would send her brother into a tizzy.

She knew very well how her brother felt about having his little sister tag along when he tended the goats. He never stopped complaining about it to their Ma and Pa.

"What?! Don't lie about things like that. Ain't no cougar gonna come around during the daylight. Do you remember what happened to the little boy who cried wolf too many times?" Bart scolded.

He knew Velda liked to make up stories, many of them coming straight out of the tall tales told to her by their Grandpa John, who had come from the badlands with Uncle Francis to live with the family. Bart had soon discovered that his Grandpa John had a tall tale for everything and that Velda seemed to remember them all, word for word.

"I'm not makin' up stories. She attacked one of the goats. Sandy chased her off," Velda said, putting her hands on her hips, like her Ma often did, and fixing a stern look on her elfin face, in an attempt to wear one of her Pa's serious expressions.

"No way. Just drop it, Velda. There wasn't any cougar. And if there was, Sandy here wouldn't be able to run it off," Bart said, frustrated that his sister never seemed to give up when she insisted on sticking to telling one of her whoppers.

"What do you think of my fat rabbits?" Bart said, wanting to change the topic and wanting his sister to acknowledge her big brother's marvelous achievement.

"They look like fat ones. We'll eat good tonight," she said and then added, "Let me show you the little goat the cougar laid into. Sandy licked his wounds, so he should be alright in a few days."

With that, Velda turned on her heel with staff in hand and walked toward the herd grazing nearby. Bart, without saying anything further, laid down his rabbits and reluctantly tagged along.

"Here he is," Velda called out.

Upon seeing the little goat with bloody claw marks running down both sides, Bart found himself speechless. There was no doubt that a big cat had attacked in broad daylight when his little sister had been left alone to tend the goats. If anything had gone wrong, if the cougar had turned on Velda, he wouldn't have been there to save his little sister. Sandy had saved not only a little goat; he had saved his sister's life.

Reaching up to touch the cougar fang given to him by his Pa that hung on a leather strap around his neck, his belief in its power would never be stronger than at that moment. He knew his sister wore an identical totem around her neck. He was convinced that it was her cougar totem that had protected her. He had been told the story of how his Pa had been baptized in the blood of a cougar right here on Pilger Mountain and that their totems had been made from the fangs of that same cougar. Bart's belief in the power of their cougar totems was unshakable and, at that moment, no one could have convinced him otherwise.

Taking the staff back from his sister he noticed blood smeared on its hooked end. Looking more closely, his mind raced as it struggled to sort out what he was looking at. In the center of a broad blood splatter that covered the end of the staff were what looked like three broken teeth lodged into the wood with their bloody jagged stubs poking out in a row. Touching the stubs, he discovered that the teeth had been driven so deep into wood he was unable to budge them, even when he applied all the pressure he could muster, with his two thumbs.

With his mind reeling, Bart looked at his little sister in a new light. There was only one way those cougar teeth could have gotten lodged into the end of his staff, and it wasn't Sandy who put them there.

"Velda, tell me about the cougar attack," Bart said, wanting to understand what really took place, and marveling at what must have happened.

"So, you believe me now," Velda said, cocking her head sideways and looking up at her brother

"Yeah, I believe you, little sissy. Did you know there're three of that ol' she-lion's broken teeth lodged in the end of this here staff?" Bart said, turning the hook end toward Velda so she could see.

"I hit her with it. Pretty hard, I guess," Velda said flatly.

"You sure as hell must've. Tell me what happened," Bart said, truly wanting to know how his little sister, weighing no more than forty pounds, had fought with a full-grown cougar and come out victorious.

His little sister had always just been there under foot, always in the way, always a nuisance. Realizing what must have occurred, he found himself seeing his sister as a person who could stand on her own, a person able to earn his respect, a real person for the first time in his life.

The story of Velda's battle with the cougar became part of Barton family lore, with the story being told and retold year after year, each time becoming a little more sensational with the telling. To her parents, her battle with the cougar was the day Velda lived up to her name, and the day she took her place as a full-fledged member of the Barton family.

Velda enjoyed the attention and praise she received for battling the cougar, even though her encounter was no more than a blurry swirl in her mind. Fact was, she really couldn't recall exactly how she had fought and won; she only knew she had. More than the attention she received for her victory was the boost in confidence the experience had given her. Though she had always had a great deal of self-confidence, she now had a confidence that stood ready to take on any challenge head on, a confidence that would be one of her hallmarks for the rest of her life.

November 30, 1933

Pleasant Valley, Custer County, South Dakota

Stinkin' Bear

THE SITUATION FOR FARMERS and ranchers had become increasingly desperate since the collapse of the stock market and subsequent wave of bank failures that had dried up credit and wiped out savings across rural America. Most farmers, having never invested in the stock market, were caught by surprise by a market failure caused by speculators in New York City. Many wondered how their lives could be so negatively impacted by problems caused by folks back east. To compound the mounting troubles that surrounded rural America on all sides, right on the heels of the unexpected man-made economic disaster, a natural disaster of growing magnitude took hold of the land. For four long years, severe drought had battered farmers and ranchers, turning the Great Plains into a dust bowl.

A year had passed since John and Francis made their way from Three Tree Creek, John Barton's original homestead in the badlands, to Bill Barton's homestead on Pilger Mountain in Pleasant Valley. The journey from Fourmile Corner just west of the town of Custer to Bill and Kate's homestead down a rutty, heavily potholed, rock-strewn dirt trail had been a bumpy bone-jarring ride. The Chrysler high centering more than once along the way sustained considerable damage to its undercarriage as it made its way down the old Pleasant Valley stage trail.

Leaking motor oil from a banged-up oil pan ripped full of holes and hobbling on a broken left front strut, the old Chrysler, with steam pouring out from under its hood, rolled up to the big pine tree next to Bill and Kate's cabin, where it sputtered one last gasp before it unceremoniously died. Without enough money to make necessary repairs or to even buy enough gasoline to turn over the engine, the Blue Demon was left to sit jacked up on blocks on the very spot where it had died. Becoming a permanent yard ornament, the abandoned automobile soon became a playhouse for the children.

President Franklin Delano Roosevelt, elected in 1932, took office in March 1933 and quickly got down to business in his first one hundred days by launching the New Deal, an aggressive series of programs and projects with the aim of restoring American prosperity. With more than fifteen million workers unemployed and over nine thousand failed banks since the collapse of the stock market in 1929, Roosevelt moved to stabilize the economy and restore confidence. To kick-start the rural economy, the Civilian Conservation Corps was created with the goal of employing up to five hundred thousand young men. By July 1933, little more than a month after the new program had been signed into law, two hundred fifty thousand young men between the ages of eighteen and twenty-five had been enrolled in the CCC, making the effort the largest peacetime mobilization of men in American history.

Because the program targeted young men, Bill Barton at thirty-one was too old to enroll. Francis at sixteen was too young even though he had tried to volunteer, so he could earn the thirty-dollar monthly CCC salary, money the family badly needed. Most of Bill's neighbors in Pleasant Valley found themselves in the same boat with their menfolk either too old or too young to enroll in the CCC.

The other New Deal programs, including the Federal Deposit Insurance Corporation (FDIC) that aimed to protect bank depositors, meant little to Bill and his neighbors who had already lost everything and had neither the money nor means to deposit anything in any bank.

For four long years, the Barton family had struggled to hang on to their homestead on Pilger Mountain with each year growing more desperate than the last. The arrival of John and Francis had initially put a strain on the family's meager resources. Francis soon made himself useful, as he could do the work of a full-grown man and was eager to pitch in. John, whose eyesight had rapidly declined since their arrival, was the family's biggest concern.

Not wanting to become a burden on the family, John looked for ways to continue to pitch in and pull his own weight. His most ingenious innovation was a network of rope lines that ran from the cabin to the chicken coop, livestock pens, pole barns, and garden. Unable to see where the ropes led, John had tied a different number of knots into the end of each rope, which allowed him to know which rope went where and what he would find at its other end.

Limited to chores that could be done on his own near the cabin, John took on the responsibly of feeding the chickens and livestock and tending the vegetable garden. He also looked after the children as best he could, when they weren't looking after him. Velda enjoyed spending time with her Grandpa John. The times she enjoyed the most were those when her grandpa crawled in behind the steering wheel of his Blue Demon and took his passengers on wondrous make-believe adventures. Velda never tired of hearing his wild stories and about the many places he had traveled and things he had seen and done. Those times were John's favorite times as well. In retelling his stories, he found that he could see again as he relived his adventures in his mind's eye. Pretending to steer his Blue Demon down a distant highway in a far-off land, he could reel off one story after another for hours on end. Often interrupted mid-sentence, he never tired of answering Velda's many and endless questions. In so doing, he taught Velda patience, an ability that, when paired with her tenacious nature, would make her a formidable opponent in coming years.

Her grandpa's stories took root in Velda's young mind as she began to understand how large the world was beyond the narrow confines of Pleasant Valley. She yearned for the day when she would see that bigger world with her own eyes. Having started school in September, her exposure to so many older children forced her to grow up even faster. Having competed, tooth and nail, with her older brother since her birth, she now found herself surround by stiff competition on all sides. If there was anything that prodded Velda to do her best, it was when she felt she was in competition with others bent on beating her.

With Velda's fifth birthday and Thanksgiving only a couple days apart, it was decided the family would celebrate both occasions together, as they had done every year since Velda's birth. They would have their Thanksgiving meal and birthday cake too. Though her parents felt this had always been a good way to combine the festivities, Velda didn't liked the idea of having her day celebrated on Thanksgiving Day every year. She wanted to have her birthday celebrated, like her brother's, on the day of her birth.

What Velda didn't know was that this birthday would be a special one. Having started school in September, Velda had needed a way to travel back and forth to the schoolhouse located over three miles north of the Barton place. The obvious solution to her parents' way of thinking was to have Velda ride double on her brother's horse. The idea may have seemed simple enough to Bill and Kate; for Bart, it had been tough to accept. Grumbling all the way, Bart had made it clear to everyone for the past two months, he wasn't a willing partner in his parents' master plan.

With the economic downturn, the promised roads in the region never materialized, leaving settlers on Pilger Mountain to rely on horses to get around. Without graveled roads and with money being scarce, an automobile was the last thing settlers in Pleasant Valley needed or could even afford. A farmer could always find enough graze or feed to take care of a horse or two, gasoline however cost money and the nearest gas station was a good day's ride.

With the Barton family gathered around the dining table, everyone sat patiently waiting for Grandpa John to say grace. Velda couldn't wait to have a piece of her birthday cake and to open her birthday presents. She wondered why her parents were acting so strangely and why they kept peeking out the front window of the cabin. With grace complete, everyone soon swung into action with platters and bowls flying around the table as everyone loaded up their plates and put on their feedbags.

"This turkey turned out pretty juicy for an old stringy tom," Bill said, digging into a plate piled high with roast wild turkey, sweet potatoes, canned peas, mashed potatoes and gravy, and Kate's famous sugared gooseberries.

"Yeah, he's not bad for a gobbler. Tried to get a big fat hen, but folks around here have completely cleaned out the game on Pilger Mountain," Francis said, having hunted for several days before finally bagging the lone gobbler.

Wild game, once thick around Pilger Mountain, had become increasingly scarce by the year. With everyone struggling to hold on, the families of Pleasant Valley had come to rely almost entirely on wild meat as their main staple.

"Did Detrick send over his newspaper?" Bill said, wanting to read the new president's Thanksgiving Proclamation.

Detrick bought a copy of the *Rapid City Journal* every Friday and shared it with Bill, who in turn shared it with Roy Kelly, who had become a close friend. Roy in turn shared it on down the line with other settlers in the valley. Eventually, the well-worn newspapers found their way to the schoolhouse, where they were kept as part of the settlement's small library.

Over the years, it had become a custom for presidents to issue a Thanksgiving Proclamation. Now that the nation had a new president and a New Deal focused on getting the nation's economy back on track, everyone was interested in what Roosevelt had to say on nearly every topic. His first Thanksgiving Proclamation was of special interest as it would signal the direction of the new administration's policies in the coming months and years ahead.

"Yes, Pa, I rode over this morning to pick it up," Bart said, acting the part of a grown-up.

At eight going on nine years old, Bart was growing taller and broader by the year. It was clear to everyone that it wouldn't be long before he was bigger than his Pa.

"Well, let's hear what the man has to say," John said, knowing he would need to have someone read the newspaper to him at some point and figuring now was as good a time as any with everyone interested in the new president's Thanksgiving Proclamation.

"Well, let's take a look," Bill said, taking the newspaper from Bart and opening it up to the president's proclamation.

Clearing his throat, Bill read out loud like he was the president himself giving a speech. By pretending to be so formal, everyone quieted down to listen to the president's words. Even Velda settled down to listen, though she wasn't sure who this Roosevelt fella was or why everyone seemed to want to know what he wrote in the newspaper.

I, Franklin D. Roosevelt, President of the United States of America, do set aside and appoint Thursday, the thirtieth day of November 1933, to be a Day of Thanksgiving for all our people.

May we on that day in our churches and in our homes give humble thanks for the blessings bestowed upon us during the year past by Almighty God.

May we recall the courage of those who settled a wilderness, the vision of those who founded the Nation, the steadfastness of those who in every succeeding generation have fought to keep pure the ideal of equality of opportunity and hold clear the goal of mutual help in time of prosperity as in time of adversity.

May we be grateful for the passing of dark days; for the new spirit of dependence one on another; for the closer unity of all parts of our wide land; for the greater friendship between employers and those who toil; for a clearer knowledge by all nations that we seek no conquests and ask only honorable engagements by all people to respect the lands and rights of their neighbors; for the brighter day to which we can win through by seeking the help of God in a more unselfish striving for the common bettering of mankind.

"I like the part where he recognizes the courage of those who settled the wilderness. The thing is, people out here in West River are still doing just that. The work of taming the wilderness is far from over," John said, knowing deep down in his bones that there was nothing tame about the wilds of western South Dakota.

"He speaks a lot about the passing of dark days and a new spirit of dependence one on another and for closer unity and yet we've received damn little aid out here in western South Dakota," Bill said, frustrated by all the fancy language and the lack of real action.

Though the banner on the front page of the newspaper proclaimed in bold letters the payment of the first government checks to CCC enrollees, having been unable to enroll in the CCC, the Barton family wouldn't be receiving a check and had seen no real benefits flowing from the new government in Washington D.C. Indeed, the same could be said by too many families in Pleasant Valley.

John understood his son's frustration, the Barton family had always settled where others had yet to settle. They had always carved their lives out of virgin lands. One generation after the next, they had lived at the edge of what others called civilization, a civilization that owed its very existence to those pioneers who had, through self-reliance and perseverance, honed it out of the wilderness. He knew his son was nearing a breaking point with no real prospects for things getting better. If relief didn't come soon, he wasn't sure how the family could continue to survive in Pleasant Valley. Beyond the valley, with the country in a deep depression, John feared the future for the family was as dim as his eyesight.

Their feast complete, Kate brought Velda's birthday cake in from the kitchen with five lit candles blazing on top. After a hardy rendition of the birthday song, Velda made a wish and blew out the candles.

"What did you wish for?" Bill said with his eyebrows raised high and a funny grin on his face.

"Oh, nothing much. Just wished I had a horse of my own," Velda said in a forlorn little voice, and then quickly brightened up and added, "I know I will someday, so it's alright. I can wait."

Velda knew her Pa didn't have the money to buy another horse and like it or not she would be riding with her brother to and from school. What helped to cheer her up was the thought that her Uncle Lavern might get a horse and she might be able to ride him someday soon.

Just as they were finishing up their cake, Bill handed Velda a big colorfully wrapped box with a big red ribbon tied around it. Velda was surprised and thrilled by the size of her birthday present.

"What is it?" she cried. "It's so big."

"Open it up," Kate said with a big smile on her face.

Velda took the present and slowly unwrapped the colorful paper, fold by fold, careful not to rip it. The paper had been used for her brother's birthday present and would be used again come Christmas. Finally opening the box, she found a shiny new horse bridle and a handmade riding cape inside. Seeing her presents, Velda wasn't quite sure what to make of them. She could sure use the riding cape now that the weather had turned colder, and she liked its patchwork colors. She knew her Ma had made it special for her. The bridle, without a horse, seemed like a strange gift.

"Oh, thank you, Pa. Thank you, Ma," she said, giving each a big hug.

"Here's my present, little sissy," Bart said, shoving a brown paper bag into her hands with a mischievous twinkle in his eye and a crooked grin on his face.

Opening the bag, Velda found it full of carrots.

"What's this, you goof? I'm no rabbit," Velda said, as she turned to stare at her big brother with a sour look on her face.

Figuring her big brother was pulling another one of his pranks on her, she nearly threw the bag of carrots back at him, until she noticed big smiles on everyone's faces. Unable to keep straight faces any longer, everyone broke out in laughter. The whole family had been in on a secret, a secret Velda was soon to learn. Confused, Velda wasn't sure what to think as she looked from face to face. A rap on the front door brought the room to silence, while Bill went to answer it.

"Who could that be?" John said in Velda's direction. "It just might be Santa Claus."

Hearing her grandpa's strange remark, Velda had to look over at him and wonder if her grandpa was alright. Velda worried the old man might not know Christmas was still a month off.

Looking back at her grandpa, when her eyes met his, he winked and smiled and said, "I think your special birthday gift has arrived."

His remark confused Velda even more. She wasn't sure what was going on or what her grandpa meant. When she looked around, standing just inside the front door was Ross Bishop, who had ridden up from his ranch north of Edgemont to share Thanksgiving dinner at Roy Kelly's place.

"Is there a Velda Iona Barton in the house?" Ross said, and then pretended to look around the room in search of the missing girl.

"I'm over here. That's me, mister," Velda said in a stout little voice.

"Well, I'm pleased to meet ya, ma'am. I'm Ross Bishop from down yonder a piece and I think I found something that belongs to you," he said, pretending to be as confused as she clearly was.

Though Ross Bishop didn't look much like Santa Claus, Velda suddenly realized that her wish just might have come true. Springing into action, Velda grabbed her new riding cape, and like a whirling dervish slipped it on. Scooping up the sack full of carrots, she headed for the front door at full tilt, practically bowled over Ross, who quickly stood aside and held the door as she ran outside. She had no more than stepped off the porch when she came face to face with an old saddle pony that had been used as a packhorse on the Bishop Ranch in recent years. Though he was nearing twenty years old, the old paint, looking a bit on the mangy side, was still in good health. It was his gentle temperament that had convinced Ross that the old Indian pony would be the perfect gift for a young child.

Ross had made a deal with John Barton for the horse, knowing, like everyone else in the valley, the Barton family was light on cash. The bargain they struck was for Francis to help Ross clean out his brick house. In exchange, Ross agreed to give them the old pinto and that he would bring the horse to their place on Thanksgiving Day.

"What's his name?" Velda said, nearly jumping up and down with excitement.

"Well, we always called him Stinkin' Bear," Ross said, pushing back his cowboy hat and scratching his balding head.

Until that moment he hadn't really considered the horse's name nor what a terrible name Stinkin' Bear was for a little girl's first horse.

"Stinkin' Bear! Stinkin' Bear . . . Stinkin' Bear," Velda repeated several times, as if willing herself to come to terms with the less-than-flattering handle. "Does he like carrots?"

"Loves 'em," Ross said with a wide grin, regretting that it was too late to change the horse's name.

Taking a carrot out of the paper bag, she offered it to Stinkin' Bear, careful to avoid having her fingers bitten by accident. The old horse using his lips sucked the carrot up out of the palm of her hand and was soon contentedly munching away. Velda was thrilled. Patting the horse on his jowl, the horse bent down his head. When he did, Velda gave him a big hug. At that moment Stinkin' Bear and Velda had bonded for life. For Velda, there would never be another horse in the whole wide world as smart and as loyal as Stinkin' Bear.

After Ross left, knowing Velda would never stop asking when she could ride her horse, Bill, Francis, Bart, and Velda saddled up for a short ride up Pilger Mountain before dark. With sunset only an hour away, they rode to the high point on the mountain just west of the Barton place for a clear view of the western horizon. As the sun sank toward the edge of the horizon, the sky caught fire in a dazzling display, its beauty beyond words.

At that moment, Bill, sitting astride his horse, with his children beside him, wanted nothing more than to hug his children and tell them everything would be alright. He knew the family may have to give up their Shangri-La on Pilger Mountain, sooner than he would have ever believed. He would stick it out at least another year, until he proved up his claim, but he knew without a miracle, they may have to sell out and move to town to find work.

Ross rode back to the Kelly place with the wide grin Velda had put on his face. He could still see the joy dancing in Velda's eyes and in her smile. He was especially happy about how well old Stinkin' Bear and Velda had hit it off. Doing something good for someone helped Ross deal with his own grief, of which he had plenty.

Finally running out of options, Ross had turned over the Bishop Ranch to the bank and sold everything in the brick house. To scrape up as much money as possible, Ross had even sold the brick house off, brick by brick, to local merchants in Edgemont for a penny apiece. In less than a week, the once proud home of Tom Burton, the cattle baron who had originally settled the region, ended up as nothing more than an abandoned foundation on a dusty windswept prairie.

Selling off everything would have broken Ross's heart, if his heart hadn't already been broken when his wife ran off with Chuck Bronson, the cattle buyer, who had bought out the last of his starving cattle for a song, leaving him with nothing to show for a lifetime of hard work but empty pockets, a sore back, and two callused hands. Knowing his wife wouldn't be coming back, he now worried about his children. Abandoned by their mother, Ross found he was unable to care for them by himself. In an act of desperation, he had sent them back to Oskaloosa, Iowa, where the Bishop family still had kinfolk. His problem was those distant kinfolk were having tough times of their own and had made it clear they wouldn't be able to care for his children for very long.

Roy Kelly had invited Ross up for Thanksgiving dinner knowing he had nowhere else to go. Ross and Roy had become friends in recent years. Ross had gone out of his way to help Roy find good land in the southern hills where he could expand, once the drought let up. Roy appreciated the help. The plan was for Ross to share Thanksgiving dinner and spend the night at the Kelly place, before returning to Edgemont on December 1. From there no one knew where Ross was headed, not even Ross.

Bill knew all about Ross's troubles and wondered when he rode off after delivering Stinkin' Bear whether he would ever see the man again. He found it hard to believe how far the Bishop family had fallen since the collapse of the stock market. They had lost everything. He had heard about people going from rags to riches, but never believed a family as wealthy as the Bishops could go from riches to rags so quickly.

He appreciated that Ross had gone out of his way for Velda, which brought the memory of Ross's youngest son, Billy, to his mind. The little boy had been full of life on the day Bill first met Ross Bishop at his ranch. Bill couldn't imagine all the problems Ross must have faced to have finally been forced to send his youngest son, Billy, and all of his children away. Bill wasn't sure he would survive if he ever lost his children. He wondered if Ross would be able to.

January 5, 1934

Pleasant Valley, Custer County, South Dakota

All Roads

GROWING SUPPORT FOR THE repeal of the 18th Amendment surged as the Roosevelt Administration took the reins of government. Looking for new sources of revenue to support its ambitious social programs, Prohibition became a target when increased household spending, originally promised by the law's temperance movement advocates, never materialized. Instead of the promised consumer boom, illegal speakeasies had flourished and with them a number of undesirable and unintended consequences. Tainted alcohol had become a growing health crisis that had resulted in countless cases of blindness and over a thousand deaths a year, while crime syndicates fueled by illicit bootlegging profits had increased crime and lawlessness nationwide. With the arguments in support of Prohibition proven faulty, rather than continue to lose billions in potential tax revenue in the middle of a depression, the argument for repeal soon won the day.

In June 1933, Roosevelt ordered the reorganization of the U.S. Justice Department Division of Investigation to include the Bureau of Prohibition, with J. Edgar Hoover to remain its director. As the year 1933 came to a close, on December 5, the 21st Amendment was ratified, bringing Prohibition to an end. Thirteen years, ten months, and nineteen days after the 18th Amendment had prohibited the production, distribution, and sale of alcohol in the United States of America, President Franklin Delano Roosevelt is reported to have proclaimed, "What America needs now is a drink."

Though J. Edgar Hoover had thrived during Prohibition, he saw fresh opportunities to greatly expand his powers under the Roosevelt Administration. With Roosevelt wanting to end Prohibition and to mold the Bureau of Investigation into a federal agency with the power to reach across state lines, J. Edgar worked to highlight America's soaring crime rate that had been aggravated by the double punch of Prohibition's unintended consequences and the deepening depression.

Hunting down crime bosses had provided J. Edgar with a steady crop of whales to harpoon during the 1920s. With the Roosevelt Administration's desire to further expand of the Bureau of Investigation's federal powers, hunting grounds were bound to expand, making hunting all the easier, and God willing, the whales all the larger. J. Edgar could only dream of how these changes would bring him even more notoriety as his domestic powers continued to grow.

Looking out his office window to the east, he pondered developments beyond America's shores. With Hitler's proclamation of a Third Reich in Bavaria, it was only a matter time before Hitler's radical National Socialist Party seized control of the country and once again plunged Germany into war. The thought brought a smile J. Edgar's otherwise serious face as he pondered the prospects for further expanding his Bureau's international powers in coming years.

News of the repeal of Prohibition came to Pleasant Valley on the back of a galloping horse, in much the same way news of the collapse of the stock market had come four years earlier. The curious twist came in the form of the messenger. Like the other families that lived around Pilger Mountain, the Meyers used horses to get around. The trail to Dewey over Pilger Mountain had become a well-worn path as riders made their way back and forth. On December 6 it was Emma Meyer, the local schoolmarm, who brought back the news from Dewey that alcohol was legal once again. Upon hearing the news, it didn't take long before a throng of thirsty riders headed for Dewey at a fast trot.

With over half of the state of South Dakota's CCC camps located in the Black Hills, the region suddenly found its coffers overflowing with government cash. Though the thousands of CCC enrollees received only a dollar a day, with most of the money being sent back home, they spent whatever was left in their pockets in the local communities throughout the hills. The sudden infusion of cash brought with it an economic boom, creating new businesses to meet the new demand for services. Many old businesses long since left for dead found new life.

Counties soon faced stiff competition as they vied for their share of the increased commerce and government project moneys. With most of the CCC program budget earmarked for shovel-ready projects like roads, bridges, stock dams, landscaping, timber clearing, and the like, the settlers on Pilger Mountain saw an opportunity to finally have the roads built in the region, that had been long promised.

An unexpected boost to the chances for their Pleasant Valley Road petition came when the drilling of test holes for possible oil deposits was announced for Barker Flats. According to local news reports, there was a high likelihood that the Barker Dome formation contained a sizable oil deposit. Test hole drilling was scheduled to start during the coming summer. With the need for heavy equipment to be moved into the area to conduct drilling operations, the Pleasant Valley Road project had become a priority CCC project.

Everyone looked forward to having crews of young men with cash in their pockets set up their CCC camps in the area. The young teenage girls in the valley, who outnumbered teenaged boys nearly two to one, were particularly interested, though they tried to hide their excitement. For those who had been unable to find work, the opportunity to earn cash money either working on the road or working in the oil fields was high on their minds.

Bill, Detrick, Jacob Shultz, and Albert Meyer had all found themselves without work, since Roosevelt's announcement of his New Deal. They were all too old to enroll in the CCC, leaving them in search of odd jobs wherever they could find them. Their problem was the work often paid very little and almost never in cash.

Jeff Engel and Mike Robinson had, on the other hand, done well in recent years. Jeff with his knowledge of winches, pulleys, and ropes and Mike with his mechanical skills had been hired on by Gutzon Borglum, a sculptor who had landed a contract to carve the faces of four U.S. presidents into a solid granite mountain by the name of Mount Rushmore. The mountain was located high up in the Black Hills, where huge naked granite domes of stone soared up out of the surrounding forest. Many of the granite spiers reached up out of the forest toward the sky like the fingers of a drowning man. These unique formations came to be known as the needles and soon became a favorite sightseeing destination for visitors to the Black Hills.

Borglum had selected Mount Rushmore for his sculpture because of the quality of the formation's solid granite stone and its nearly flawless flat vertical surface that faced southeast in perfect alignment to catch the morning sun. This feature had not been missed by the Lakota people, who had called the mountain *Tunkasila Skpe Paha,* meaning Six Grandfathers Mountain, long before Charles E. Rushmore, an early tin mine operator, had named the mountain after himself. According to the Lakota people's origin story, the mountain had been named for the six Lakota warriors who had been led to the surface of the world from the depths of Wind Cave by the first Lakota man, Tokahe, who himself had been tricked to come to the surface by the shape-shifting spider, Inktomi. The seven men became the founders of the people of the Seven Council Fires, known as the *Oceti Sakowin,* the tribes of the Great Sioux Nation.

To the Lakota people, the mountain was sacred and key to the origin story of their nation. In coming years, whether just or unjust and for better or worse, to the peoples of the United States of America, the mountain would become a sacred shrine of democracy and key to the origin story of a new nation.

After calling a meeting of the Lucky Seven to discuss the community's Pleasant Valley Road petition, Bill and Detrick had ridden over to Dewey to bring back a small keg of beer. They figured that after nearly four long years of nothing but struggle and drought on Pilger Mountain, the Lucky Seven would agree unanimously with President Roosevelt's reported sentiment concerning the other dry spell that had lasted far too long.

The men filed into Detrick's longhouse and took their seats at a large table that had been positioned in the middle of the main room. As Bill surveyed the faces of the men gathered around the table, he took inventory of the toll the last four years had taken on each of them. The drought had not only sucked the moisture out of the land, it had sucked the cocksureness of youth out of the men. Despite their best efforts to put on a show of jovial solidarity, a pall hung over the men, each wondering how long he would be able to continue to pursue a dream that had already turned into a nightmare. Knowing everyone else around the table faced the same bleak reality, it was obvious to anyone willing to admit it, the Lucky Seven weren't feeling so damn lucky anymore.

Unsure whether anything could turn around their string of misfortunes, they had laid their hopes on the completion of the Pleasant Valley Road. With a good road into the valley, they would be able to travel to and from Custer, the county seat and the largest town in the area. Having a vital link to civilization held the promise of bringing many benefits, most of all, badly needed jobs that paid cash money.

"Gentlemen, good to have everyone attend," Bill said, opening the meeting. "We have a lot of ground to cover."

"First things first," Detrick said, pretending to interrupt. "You men look thirsty."

"I could drink a glass water, I guess, if you have any handy," Roy said.

"Water all around," Detrick said, as he hustled off into the next room. "Bill, could you help me?"

"Sure, sure," Bill said, as he rose from the table to join Detrick in the next room, playing along with the ruse.

Before long, the two men return with two large trays of glasses filled to the brim with amber-colored liquid topped by white foamy heads spilling down their sides. The men around the table stood and cheered as Bill and Detrick ceremoniously distributed the glasses of foam-topped beer around the table. Once everyone had a glass in hand, Bill raised his glass and nodded to the others. With their glasses raised, the men echoed in unison, "Cheers!"

They then all took long pulls of the cold, bitter brew, enjoying the unexpected surprise as it slid down their suddenly parched and eager throats. Almost on cue, to a man, they wiped the thick foam off their upper lips with the back of their hands. The mood in the room shifting to one considerably more light-hearted than it had been. With that, Prohibition ended in Pleasant Valley, never to return.

The main reason for holding the meeting had been to find out how many of the other settlers in the valley were planning to pull out and how many would be staying on for the coming season. With the completion of Pleasant Valley Road and the possibly of having working oil wells on Barker Flats, combined with the prospects for employment opportunities in Custer that would pay cash money, the chances of things getting better had improved. It was agreed that the members of the Lucky Seven would hold on for at least another season. After suffering such a long string of bad luck, the men were convinced they were due for a break, even a little luck would be better than none at all.

The beer had been a hit and it was agreed that they would take turns providing the brew at future meetings. Though no one said so, the men were relieved when Mike volunteered to bring beer for the next meeting. Mike and Jeff were the only two of the seven men that had steady cash incomes. Beer might be inexpensive, but it did cost money, something most of the men had seen very little of in the past four years. Like Bill, they had all lost their savings when the Wall bank failed.

Many had wondered how Bill and Detrick could have scraped up enough money to buy beer for the meeting. What Bill and Detrick had decided to keep to themselves was that they had paid for the beer with goat meat. Fact was, it had been some time since either man had two cents to rub together.

Detrick however believed he had come up with a way to earn money and saw the new road as a real opportunity to reach lucrative markets beyond the valley. He had studied the art of taxidermy for several years and felt confident that his creations would sell well. His challenge had been to find a way to get his creations in front of potential buyers. If he could find a way to market them to the growing number of tourists visiting the Black Hills, he was confident he could start earning real money again.

Unable to find work to earn badly need money, Bill felt his youth and his dreams slipping away. He had owned and run his own general store and at the age of eighteen had been appointed the youngest postmaster in the state. His future had looked bright, and he had believed there was nothing he couldn't succeed at.

He was twenty-seven when they arrived in Pleasant Valley, a young man ready to fulfill his boyhood dream. At the time, he had been certain he had the world by the tail. He had money in the bank, a young wife and children, and one of the finest pieces of land in the southern Black Hills. In the beginning, Pleasant Valley had been everything he and Kate could have wished for. It had been their Shangri-La.

All of that had ended when economic forces beyond his control and the fickle whims of Mother Nature had conspired against him at every turn. Now, at age thirty-one, he found himself flat broke and with few prospects. He had to shake his head at how silly life could be at times. Though he had worked from dawn to dusk for four long years, he had come out worse off than when he started. Like it or not, his last chance to hold onto his boyhood dream had come down to having a good road to Custer.

Bill had talked with Mike about how much it would cost to repair his Pa's old Chrysler. Once the road was built, having an automobile would once again become a necessity, especially if he wanted to find steady work outside of the valley. Custer being over twenty-five miles from Pilger Mountain had made it impossible to run back and forth on a regular basis on horseback. With an automobile and a good road, he would be able to drive to Custer and return the same day. Considering all the times he had gotten his hopes up only to have them dashed, he had to admit, with the completion of a good road to town, his prospects were definitely looking up for a change. He refused however to let his hopes get too high, having learned, far too many times in recent years, nothing is a given.

August 31, 1934

Pleasant Valley, Custer County, South Dakota

Last Bite

AN EARLY SPRING HAD allowed the CCC crews the opportunity to get the Pleasant Valley Road project underway a month ahead of schedule. From early April to mid-July the valley from Custer to Pilger Mountain had been plunged into a constant flurry of activity as the road slowly took shape. Bill had been able to hire on as a surveyor's assistant, a job for which he soon discover he had a knack. While working on the project, he learned that there were a number of highway projects in the Black Hills. One project that interested him more than the others was the Iron Mountain Road project that had recently got underway not far from Custer. The builders had the ambitious goal of cutting a scenic path between Custer State Park and Keystone, the small mining town near the base of Mount Rushmore.

The plan for the new highway was to incorporate a number of pigtail bridges to traverse the tight valleys along the way and to cut several tunnels through solid stone in such a way as to align their openings with the presidents' faces carved on Mount Rushmore. Promoters were confident the new road would become a major attraction for the growing number of visitors touring the Black Hills. Tourism was quickly becoming a thriving industry for the region. With Mount Rushmore taking shape, local residents became excited about the future for the first time in a long time.

Frequent spring rains in the hills had also boosted everyone's hopes. By mid-summer, the fields in Pleasant Valley had never looked so good. To top it off, word had spread like wildfire that oil had been discovered in

Barker Flats. With all the good news, Bill started to feel that things where indeed back on track.

Velda loved all the activity in her valley. Every chance she got she rode Stinkin' Bear over to Barker Flats to watch drilling operations. The huge machinery and men running everywhere reminded her of an anthill with each ant working independently and yet working together all at the same time. Bart often rode over with her. At the age of ten, he couldn't wait to leave Pleasant Valley to join the ranks of men like those he watched working on the oil rigs. To the youth of Pilger Mountain, the Pleasant Valley Road was like the snake that slithered into the biblical Garden of Eden. It didn't take long before the young feasted on this new Tree of Knowledge. Cocooned in their isolated Eden, they had been content with their lot in life, not knowing any better. Seeing the many wonders brought in from an unknown world beyond the valley, they soon longed to have more than the valley would ever provide them.

As quickly as they had come, they were gone. Oil had been discovered in Barker Flats, but the well-heads had been sealed and the drilling rigs pulled out without explanation. Some claimed the deposit was too small, others speculated the government capped the wells as part of a national strategic reserve. Rumor had it that there were many such capped wells on federal lands in southwestern South Dakota. The fact that oil had been discovered was easy to prove considering the number of working oil derricks on private lands that dotted the prairie north and south of the Black Hills.

By the end of summer, the crops in Pleasant Valley began to suffer from drought conditions, but because of above average rains in early summer, settlers looked forward to their first good harvest. Bill had finally been able to tap into Roosevelt's New Deal by qualifying for a Farm Service Agency loan to buy seed, a couple of milk cows, several dozen chickens, and ten more goats. With the income he expected to haul in after he harvested his over a hundred forty acres of corn, Bill felt confident he would be able to repay his FSA loan and give his family a very merry Christmas. The thought of Christmas stockings filled with goodies for his children brought a smile to his face. With a third child on the way, he had high hopes for a new beginning. The Barton family was once again on the rise.

The morning sky had been clear, the weather hot and dry. Looking to the southeast Velda noticed a strange shimmering cloud near the horizon that seemed to be growing, though the sky was clear in every other direction. The strange-looking cloud was like nothing she had ever seen before.

"Ma, come look," Velda said with some urgency in her voice.

Busy canning beans from the garden all morning, Kate was in no mood to chase after her children. The first month of her pregnancy had been difficult, with bouts of morning sickness coming several times a day. Stepping out on the porch, she looked to the horizon where Velda was pointing. Bill came around from the back of the cabin where he had been chopping wood to join them on the porch. All three watched as the shimmering white cloud quickly filled over a third of the southern sky.

"What do you think it is?" Kate said, turning to Bill and fearing his answer.

She had seen plenty of grasshopper swarms in the badlands, but nothing on the massive scale of what they were witnessing.

"Not sure, but it's definitely getting bigger," Bill said, not yet alarmed but increasingly fearful of what it might be.

He too had seen clouds of grasshoppers before and knew the havoc they could wreak. He had never seen a swarm of grasshoppers big enough to blot out the sun, however. Ballooning larger by the minute, the strange cloud soon looked more and more like the kind of mega-swarm that could do just that. With the shimmering cloud coming from the southeast, the natural gateway into the hills, it became clear the swarm was headed straight in their direction.

Mesmerized by the pulsating shimmer of the swarm, Bill's mind was snapped back to reality, when he heard the familiar sound of a horse and its jangling tack coming hard in his direction. Reining up in front of Bill's cabin, Roy Kelly looked like a man who had just seen a ghost.

"Hoppers! Millions, millions of 'em! Got word from a rancher near Edgemont. They're wiping out everything in their path. Quick, we all need to get fires going with plenty of smoke. We need to try to drive 'em off," Roy Kelly yelled, and without so much as a by-your-leave, galloped off up the valley to spread the alarm.

Without exchanging words, Bill and Kate quickly sprang into action. Kate sent Velda to get blankets to cover the garden. Bill recruited Bart to help dig pits and to pile them full of firewood, coal oil, and green pine boughs. His hope was the smoke from smoldering fires, up and down the valley, would create a nasty, foul-smelling cloud that might drive the swarm further north. Bill knew that shielding fields of sun-ripened crops ready for harvest from a swarm of hungry hoppers numbering in the millions was a fool's errand. Even so, he knew he had to do whatever he could to save whatever he could. It was his family's last hope.

Francis, having grown up on the prairie and having seen the damage a grasshopper swarm could do, knew he needed to find shelter for their livestock and fast. Grasshoppers had been known to land in such numbers that they could blind animals caught out in the open or even suffocate them. With the help of Sandy, the family's faithful collie, who took charge of the goats, Francis drove the livestock into a natural box canyon deep in the forest over a mile from the open fields of Pleasant Valley. Leaving Sandy to guard the animals and keep them from straying off, Francis returned to the cabin at a full gallop to help out however he could.

Looming on the horizon, the grasshopper swarm had fanned out and grown larger and darker by the minute. Smoke filled the valley as multiple smoldering fires turned the pristine mountain air into blackened soot. The grasshopper swam, having traveled across the barren prairie in search of vegetation, had gathered along the banks of the Cheyenne River north of Edgemont at the edge of the Black Hills. Following the natural gateway into the hills leading to Minnekahta Flats, the insects fed on the narrow strip of vegetation that led them northwest deeper into the hills flanked by dense pine forest on both sides. Like following a trail of bread crumbs in hopes of finding a house made of gumdrops and candy canes, the hungry insects moved northwest with a vengeance.

Unfortunately for the settlers around Pilger Mountain, this natural causeway led the insects directly to Barker Flat and on into Pleasant Valley, following the same flat treeless path the homesteaders had taken to reach their valley paradise. Descending on Pleasant Valley by the tens of millions, the grasshoppers set about devouring everything in their path. Smoke or no smoke, there was nothing that could have deterred the ravenous creatures from their feast.

Velda huddled with her family in the main room of their cabin, as the insects poured down from the sky, peppering the cabin's tin roof and windows. The roar of their hard exoskeletons striking the tin roof was louder than any hailstorm they had ever experienced. Looking through the mob of grasshopper bodies that clung to the cabin's windows, Bill watched as the blankets that had been spread over the garden disappear along with the garden and any other organic material.

"My God, look! We have to save 'em!" Francis yelled, as he ran to his bedroom and soon came out wearing a pair of roadster goggles. Throwing an old coat over his head and tying its arms under his chin, Francis bolted outside, quickly grabbing one of John's ropes tied to the guidepost just outside the front door.

Everyone watched in horror as Francis, wearing roadster goggles with an old coat tied over his head, ran headlong into the swirling onslaught, his whole body soon completely enveloped by the growing swam. Following the rope line to the chicken coop, he started chasing down and picking up chickens encased in grasshoppers. Knocking off as many of the clinging mass of insects as possible, he lifted opened the heavy wooden door of the root cellar dug in the ground nearby and threw in the chickens, one by one. As the frantic rescue continued, Bill could see that many of the chickens no longer had feathers, their bodies having been completely stripped clean by hungry hoppers. Had Francis not taken action when he did, they would have lost the whole brood.

By the time Francis returned to the cabin, his whole body was caked with grasshoppers as they tore at his clothes. Striping off the coat tied around his head, he rubbed his back on the porch post while grabbing gobs of grasshoppers by the handful off his chest and legs before diving headlong back into the cabin. With the door once again slammed shut, Bart and Velda were soon running in circles as they pounced on the torrent of grasshoppers that bounded off Francis's body. Bill and Kate also took to smashing and gathering the unruly beasts as the critters sought to escape into every corner of the room. For several minutes, mayhem ruled as everyone battled the sudden invasion. John, unable to see well enough to chase after the hoppers, pitched in by dispatching those unruly critters unfortunate enough to randomly land in his lap.

Francis, laying just inside the front door, was a sorry sight. His clothing was riddled with holes, his hair half eaten, and his whole body from head to toe speckled in black hopper spittle. Setting spread legged on the floor with his back up against the front door, the whole family joined in, when Francis, after assessing the damage the legion grasshoppers had done to him, broke out laughing uncontrollably at the incredible absurdity of the situation they had been plunged into and the hilarious sequence of events that led to his sorry state. The good belly laugh shared by all helped to ease the tension in the cabin, allowing everyone a chance to reset their perceptions of the frightening events that had befallen them, and that continued to swirl out of control beyond the safety of the cabin's walls.

The swarm continued to arrive in numbers beyond counting, blackening the valley floor from one end of Pilger Mountain to the other. In little more than four hours, as if on cue, the swam took to the air and was gone as quickly as it had arrived. Emerging from the cabin, the once beautiful pristine valley with crops full and ripe and ready to harvest had been reduced to nothing more than a greasy smear and acres and acres of gnarled stubble as far as the eye could see. The smoke they had hope would save them now hung heavy, fouling the air over an apocalyptic scene of utter destruction.

"My God, what next," Bill said, unable to understand what he could have possibly done in his life to have such vengeance exacted upon him, time and time again.

No matter what he had tried since arriving in Pleasant Valley seemed to have been destined to fail from the beginning. His crop was no more, and with it, his bountiful harvest. He knew he had no way to pay back his FSA loan. It would be just a matter of time until the bank came calling to collect money he would not have. He had seen it happen to others; the bank would take everything. His only consolation was that before this final blow, he had been able to hold his claim five years, giving him full title to his land, the only asset he would have left once he cleared his debts. Fact was, he wasn't sure if he would have anything left, including his land.

The old Chrysler's cloth top was gone, along with its leather seats. The grasshoppers had chewed through anything edible in their path. Freshly cut fence posts had been gnawed down to stumps, leaving the metal barbed wire and nails lying on the ground. Only scattered buttons lying under the clotheslines provided a hint that laundry had been hung out to dry earlier in the day. Even the paint and varnish on buildings and tools had been stripped clean. The chickens once released from the root cellar were a sight to behold, their feathers only stubs shooting out like the needles on a porcupine.

Francis had sent his horse running back into the forest before joining everyone in the cabin. He now went to fetch him and to round up their livestock, which he had thankfully taken deep into the forest. John had been unable to pitch in and had been left to wait in the dark for the inevitable news. He knew what grasshopper swarms could do and had lost more than one crop to the ravenous critters over the years. With the long string of misfortunes that had befallen his son, the news John expected to hear was that his son would now be forced to sell out and move the family to town.

His daughters, Arvella, Myrtle, Matilda, and Lucille, had all offered to share the responsibly for taking care of John several times over the past year. Knowing he now had no other options, John decided he would take them up on their offer, freeing Bill to get his family back on their feet without the need of worry about taking caring of a blind man. He also knew Francis would be turning eighteen in the coming year and had been itching to strike out on his own for some time. The last thing John wanted was to stand in the boy's way. Francis had sacrificed enough for the family. It was high time he made his own way in the world. When John discussed the matter with Bill earlier in the year, they had agreed to let Francis go. Homesteading on Pilger Mountain had been Bill's boyhood dream, he had no right to keep his little brother from pursuing his own.

With his crops ruined and with few options left, Bill looked down at the new Pleasant Valley Road, knowing it led to Custer and an uncharted future. Mike Robinson had assured him that the old Blue Demon had been fixed up enough to hobble down that road. He knew he would now have to steel himself to the plain truth that the Barton family's time on Pilger Mountain may have come to an abrupt and unavoidable end.

November 29, 1934

Pleasant Valley, Custer County, South Dakota

Full Circle

WITH WINTER COMING ON, Bill was relieved the bank had left him alone. If he was going to move the family, he would need folding money and wasn't sure where he could earn some anytime soon. He had his hundred-sixty-acre homestead and had lived on it the required five years to make it his own. On May 1, his fifth anniversary on his claim, he had visited the Custer Country Courthouse with the rest of the Lucky Seven to secure his free and clear deed to his land.

In the wake of the hopper invasion, Bill had called a meeting of the Lucky Seven to discuss everyone's plans for the coming year. Bill learned that the Meyer and Shultz families would be pulling up stakes in Pleasant Valley. The Meyers planned to move to Hot Springs at the end of the school year. Albert had been hired by the railroad and hoped to finally start a family after they settled into their new home. The Shultz family had decided to move out to California, where Jacob's brother had done well growing almonds in Capay Valley northwest of Sacramento. The grasshopper invasion had been the last straw for both families, and now, the Barton family would follow them into an unknown future, turning the Lucky Seven into the Surviving Four. Bill wondered if anyone would ultimately survive and make Pleasant Valley their permanent home.

Detrick seemed confident he could make a go of it. He still had his badlands homestead and hoped to continue to earn leasing fees, when the weather returned. His taxidermy business had started to pay real money and he had hopes of making it a real business. His investment in a small herd of British saddleback pigs had been a good bet as well when the animals turned out to be a hardy breed and good foragers that ate nearly anything and everything and yielded both bacon and ham.

Steady work on Mount Rushmore had provided Jeff Engel and Mike Robinson with reliable incomes. Not having to depend on their homesteads to make a living, they had decided to hold out until wetter weather returned to the region. Roy Kelly's sheep ranch had been a struggle but had started to turn a small profit, due to an increased demand for wool and meat. Roy planned to expand his operations to include cattle along the Cheyenne River in the former location of the old Bishop Ranch, when more reliable water and graze returned.

With settlers planning to continue in Pleasant Valley, Bill hoped his homestead might sell for a tidy sum. With the money from the sale of his homestead, he figured he would have enough to move his family and put down roots in Custer. The fly in the ointment was his need to repay his FSA loan, which he hoped he could put off as long as possible.

Bill worked and reworked the figures and felt he just might be better off than he initially thought. The family still had their livestock and Kate had been able to make some money selling eggs in Custer. With the surrounding economy booming from CCC activity, she had also been able to find full-time work at the Evans Hotel Laundry in Hot Springs during the summer months. Bill worried at the time about her taking the job considering she was only able to come home on the weekends, but the extra money had been hard to turn down. The laundry had expanded services to all the CCC camps in the area and provided living quarters for its laundry workers. The situation hadn't been ideal for anyone. Bill was as happy as Kate when she decided to quit her job at the end of August just before the start of school. With their third child expected in early March, the couple was relieved they would be able to stay on their cozy homestead over the winter.

Once again, with Thanksgiving Day falling on November 29, the holiday and Velda's birthday were celebrated together. Rather than wild turkey, of which there were none to be found on Pilger Mountain, the family feasted on a juicy ham courtesy of Detrick. Bill had been warned by the bank not to slaughter any of his livestock, as everything he owned was now tied up in the bank's lean on his property.

When Velda went to bed that night, she feared the family would be forced to leave their home in Pleasant Valley. Though her Ma and Pa had tried to talk about other things, it was her Grandpa John's comment that he would be moving to live with his daughters that told Velda something was amiss. When Uncle Francis talked about joining the Navy like his older brother Alva, Velda knew for sure things were changing. Velda liked her world and everything and everyone in it. She didn't want things to change. Going to bed that night, she found she couldn't fall asleep right away for the first time in her life. Tossing and turning, worried about an uncertain future, Velda finally fell asleep hugging her Raggedy Ann doll tighter than ever.

Without warning, the family was awakened at the crack of dawn on Friday, November 30, the day after Thanksgiving, by the sound of Sandy barking and trucks pulling up in front of the cabin. Rolling out of bed, Bill was unable to throw on his clothes before someone was pounding at the front door. Quickly pulling on his pants and buttoning his shirt, Bill called out to the unexpected visitors that the dog wouldn't bite and that he would be right out. Bill's mind raced, as he wondered who in the world would be pulling up to his place in the wee hours of the morning. Before he could get to the door, another loud knock echoed across the front room, causing Sandy's barking to go into overdrive.

Opening the front door, Bill was met with the stern faces of three large men, all of whom were strangers. Upset by all the unnecessary pounding on the door, Bill held his temper. After yelling at Sandy to settle down, he greeted the three men with a smile.

"Good morning, gentlemen. What can I do for ya?" Bill said, unsure who they were or what to expect, and not liking the early hour of their arrival nor their uninvited intrusion.

The man standing in the middle held up a raft of papers in his right hand. Seeing the papers, Bill knew in an instant, the bank had decided to take action. The sheriff's badge on the man's chest merely confirmed his worst nightmare.

"Mr. William Rueben Barton, I'm Sheriff Ed Jameson. I'm here to serve you with foreclosure papers. These gentlemen with me will be clearing out your livestock and farm implements. No one wants any trouble. I'm sure you understand," Ed said, his voice firm, his words delivered in an even timbre, the expression on his face difficult to read.

Taking the papers, Bill felt as though his whole world was crumbling under his feet until he heard himself say, "Thank you. I'll have my wife put on some coffee. Let me grab a coat, I'll be right out."

To quiet Sandy down, Bill called for him to come inside and lie down. Coming into the cabin, the dog, still clearly agitated, quickly laid down on his favorite rug next to the front door.

"If it's alright with you, Mr. Barton, I'll just step inside while these gentlemen load their trucks," Ed said, following the dog into the cabin and signaling for the other two men to get busy.

Bill quickly understood that the sheriff was there to keep things peaceful. To do so, he would keep Bill company in the cabin while the bank's hired goons did what they had been hired to do. Bill had heard about farmers becoming violent when the bank came to haul their livelihoods away.

Bill had convinced himself that come spring the family might straighten things out with the bank and pull off a last-minute miracle. Looking at the papers in his hands, he had to accept that he had fought all the battles he could, and, in the end, he had lost his last skirmish. There was no shame in it; he had given it his all. There were just too many things that had conspired against him at every turn. He knew there was nothing more any man could have done.

His problem was simple. Without money, his luck had run out. Even though the bank foreclosure might take everything, he figured he still had his health and a strong loving family. As angry as he felt, he knew now was the time for calm resolve and determination. He had no doubt about his ability to bounce back, despite the fact, at that moment, he wasn't exactly sure how he might do that. He had placed his hope on the bank holding off foreclosure. That hope, like so many others, had evaporated with the morning mist.

"Good morning," Kate said as she came confidently into the front room.

"Good morning, ma'am. I'm Sheriff Ed Jameson," Ed said, uncomfortable that he was about to throw another family out of their home.

The bank had sped up its foreclosures, keeping the sheriff's office busy, and putting him and his men in a tough spot. In his opinion, which he kept to himself, the bank was ripping the livelihoods away from honest hardworking families that were guilty of nothing more than a string of bad luck that no one could have predicted. If it were up to him, he would let the families stay on their places to make a go of it, rather than create so much human misery without gaining anything for anyone, not even the bank.

"Glad to meet you. Please call me Kate. Take a seat. I'll get that coffee started," Kate said, acting as though the sheriff was the local pastor who had dropped by for a friendly social call.

Upset by the unexpected intrusion, Kate had listened from the bedroom and knew the family was about to lose its Shangri-La. She had mixed feeling about leaving Pleasant Valley. Having worked at the laundry in Hot Springs, she had seen how the family might do better, if they could escape from Pleasant Valley and set down their roots in more fertile soil, soil where there were jobs, where they could make a living, where they would once again have the promise of a better future.

Velda and Bart came out of their bedroom to find Sheriff Jameson and their Pa and Ma sitting at the dining table drinking coffee. Confused, they sat quietly in their seats as the adults conducted business, as if they weren't there. The sound of men yelling as they herded animals onto trucks could be heard inside the cabin, which brought Francis and John into the front room with concern etched across their faces.

"What's going on?" John said as Francis led him to his place at the table.

"The bank's foreclosing on us today," Bill said, deciding there was no need to sugarcoat things.

The hammer had already come down and the whole family would all now have to deal with the consequences.

"Foreclosed? I thought they were going to wait to give us a chance to turn things around this spring," John said, confused by the sudden turn of events.

"I guess they have other ideas," Bill said dryly.

"What's the sheriff doing here?" Francis said, eyeing Ed.

"Keeping the peace, son. Just keeping the peace," Ed said flatly, sensing possible trouble brewing. "Do we have a problem?"

"Nope. No problem here. Just wondering why anyone would think there would be any," Francis said, not liking the sheriff calling him "son" one damn bit.

"Well, son, some folks don't take kindly to having the bank foreclose on their farms. Sometimes, things get downright unfriendly," Ed said, looking straight at Francis and then turning to Bill. "I've been asked to remind you to read the papers carefully. Since the bank has a lean on your homestead, they want you to vacate the premises by the end of the year. You have a month to move out."

"What? We can't move in the middle of the winter. Can't we stay on until the place sells or at least until spring," Kate said, surprised the bank could be so heartless.

She couldn't understand what trouble there would be in allowing them to live in their own place until it was sold.

"Sorry ma'am, it's not up to me. The bank spells everything out in the papers there," Ed said, not liking his role as enforcer for the rich and heartless.

He could see that Kate looked like she was expecting. He could also see that the family had two young children, and an elderly grandparent who was obviously blind. Throwing people like these out of their home in the middle of a harsh frigid Dakota winter was beyond heartless, it was downright cruel.

"What do they expect us to do? We have no place to go," Bill said, looking at the order to vacate written on the front page of the documents he held in his trembling hand.

"Again, I'm just the messenger. I have no control over these matters," Ed said without emotion.

A long silence followed with everyone deep in thought. Velda wondered why everyone stopped talking. Though she wasn't quite sure what was going on, she did understand that there were men outside loading livestock onto trucks. The urgency of this thought prompted her to speak up.

"Are they goin' to take Stinkin' Bear?" Velda said, with a quiver in her voice.

The way her little voice sliced through the silence nearly brought a tear to Sheriff Ed Jameson's eye as her question's sad helplessness reverberated deep within his soul. His deep emotional reaction surprised him since he had never really been an overly emotional man. Seeing the concerned look on the little girl's face had ambushed his emotional defenses. He knew he had to do something for this family but wasn't sure what he could lawfully do within his power.

"Yes, honey, they're taking all our livestock, except a dozen chickens and one Jersey cow," Bill said, reading over the papers.

"Sheriff Jameson, would it be alright if Velda here could say goodbye to her horse?" Kate said, knowing the horse meant everything to her daughter.

"I'll have to ask the men if it would be alright, ma'am," Ed said, looking at Kate and then at Velda. Turning to Bill and Francis, Ed added, "I'll have to ask that all of you folks stay seated at the table while I check with the men."

As the sheriff stepped out the front door, Bill's mind raced, realizing he was the only one who knew Stinkin' Bear was not with the other horses. Anne Fremder had come by to borrow the horse the evening before and wasn't expected to bring him back for a couple of days. Since the bank's records couldn't possibly list every animal he owned, he was certain they had no record of Velda's horse, an animal the family had acquired without the aid of any bank loan.

"Velda, honey, Old Red would love to say goodbye to you," Bill said, trying to give his daughter a hint that Stinkin' Bear was not with the other horses and that she should say goodbye to Old Red, one of the workhorses they used for plowing.

"Old Red? My horse is Stinkin' Bear," Velda said, proud of her horse and not understanding why her Pa should want her to say goodbye to Old Red.

"I know you call him that, and Anne likes riding Stinkin' Bear too," Bill said, just as the sheriff stepped back into the cabin.

The sheriff told Velda she would be able to say goodbye to her horse before they left. He also told Bart he would be able to bid his horse farewell, if he wanted. After a few minutes, one of the men came to the door to let the sheriff know the trucks were loaded.

"What's your horse's name again?" Ed said, looking down at Velda as they walk out of the cabin toward the trucks.

"She calls Old Red, her favorite horse, Stinkin' Bear most of the time," Bill said, trying to head off an answer from Velda and hoping she could understand what he was trying to do.

Velda wasn't sure why her Pa kept insisting that Old Red was Stinkin' Bear, but she soon caught on quick enough when Stinkin' Bear wasn't to be found on either truck or anywhere else. When she found Old Red loaded on the truck nearest the cabin, she looked at her Pa with an expression on her face full of questions. Bill, needing her to play along with the ruse, gave her an encouraging wink and nod. Unsure what was happening, but understanding she needed to pretend Old Red was Stinkin' Bear, she reached out and patted the old horse's nose.

"Goodbye, Stinkin' Bear. I'll always love you," Velda said with such emotion she even surprised herself when she felt real tears ran down her cheeks.

Seeing Velda's tender farewell to her horse and her crocodile tears streaming down her little cheeks nearly broke Ed's heart. He hated what was happening. He had wracked his brain to find an answer to Bill Barton's desperate cry for a place to take his family. Now more than ever he dug deep to find an answer. Just as the tailgates on both trucks were latched into place, an answer came to him, though he wasn't sure how Bill Barton might react to the only option he had to offer.

After the trucks pulled out, the sheriff turned to Bill and said, "I think I have a place where your family could hole up until you can get back on your feet."

"What're you saying?" Bill said, caught flatfooted by the unexpected offer of assistance.

"There's an abandoned mining shack at the Minnie May Mine up Little Italy Road west of Custer. It ain't much of a building, but it's solid and has a tin roof. You could settle in there until warmer weather," Ed said.

"What about the mine owners?" Bill said, worried the family would only find themselves in more trouble.

"No worries there. The mine's been shut down and the sheriff's office is in charge of overseeing the place," Ed said, confident it was a workable option.

"So, you'll let us squat there for the winter," Bill said, hopeful.

"I can only look the other way until the end of February, beginning of March at the latest. The owners will be back to inspect the property at the end of March," Ed said, knowing it wouldn't take the family through to spring, but might allow them time to get back on their feet.

"You have yourself a deal," Bill said, extending his hand to seal the bargain.

It wasn't the best of options, but it was the only one the family had in hand on short notice.

After the sheriff left, Bill gathered the family to discuss what they were up against and their limited options. They had thirty days to vacate the homestead, and without the money needed to rent a place, they had few options where they could go. With four adults and two children and one on the way, moving in on someone in the dead of winter would be a lot to ask, even of kin. Bill still had an ounce of pride left and wanted to take care of his own family, if he could. The one thing he couldn't abide was to live off someone else's charity. To Bill's way of thinking, a dog might gladly accept table scraps, a man never should.

Staying with Detrick and Annie was the first option that came to everyone's mind. It wasn't the best of options, however. Though Lena and Fredrika had both moved out when they married, the longhouse remained a crowded place with seven of the Fremder brood still living at home, including Anne age eighteen, Tillie age sixteen, Herman age thirteen, Gladys age eleven, Dorthey age nine, Lavern age six, and Arthur age two. Even so, Bill and Kate knew Detrick would welcome them with open arms, if they asked. Everyone agreed, however, if they had any hope of finding work, living in Custer would be their best option.

They had no idea what they would find at the Minnie May Mine, but all prayed the mine just might provide the family with the fresh start they needed—even though the old gold mine itself had went bust when the vein of gold the miners had so greedily chased ended up petering out into nothing more than a false vein of iron pyrite, a common mineral known as fool's gold in the Black Hills that had been the downfall of many a prospector during the gold rush.

Landing at the failed Minnie May Mine at the end of their Pilger Mountain adventure was more than befitting for the Barton clan, Bill thought. Like the miners of the Minnie May, the Barton family had sought to strike their fortune in Pleasant Valley, and though they had given it their all, they had ended up with nothing but a fistful of fool's gold to show for their efforts. After unanimously deciding they would stake their claim on a new future at the Minnie May Mine, they ended their discussion with a renewed hope that by spring, the family would somehow find a way to get back on its feet.

Bill decided to walk over to Detrick's place with Velda, following the meeting. Velda wanted to see Stinkin' Bear and Bill needed to let Detrick know what had happened and what the family planned to do. Arriving at Detrick's place, he asked Velda to have Anne give her a ride back home after she had a chance to spend some time with her horse. He also reminded her that Stinkin' Bear would be staying at the Fremder place from now on. He promised that Velda would be able to visit Stinkin' Bear from time to time, but they could no longer take care of him. Velda was relieved that Stinkin' Bear hadn't been taken by the awful men who had taken away all their livestock. She was also heartbroken that Stinkin' Bear was no longer her horse but would now belong to her Aunt Anne and to the rest of her many aunts and uncles.

Stinkin' Bear had been the only thing that was hers and hers alone in the whole wide world. Now he was gone. Thinking about the pained look she had witnessed on her Pa's face when they hauled his livestock away, she understood how he must have felt to see what used to belong to him suddenly taken away. She promised herself she would never let anyone take her things from her ever again. She could feel the raging heat of her fighting spirit burning within her. Though she couldn't fully appreciate it at the time, there would be many times she would need to call on her fighting spirit in the months and years ahead. As the Barton family looked to Custer and a brighter future, none of them fully realized what a long, hard struggle it would be for the family to finally find its way back on its feet again.

After explaining things to Detrick, Bill borrowed a horse that he could use until the family moved to Custer. Instead of heading straight back home, Bill rode alone has he worked his way along the tree line to the location of the two twisted pine trees where the spirits of the cougar and mule deer forever dwelled in an endless cycle of renewal. Stepping down from his horse, he stood in front of the twisted pines and wept for the first time in many years. Rather than hold back the tears, he gave his pent-up emotions free rein. For five long years, he had bound up his emotions deep inside himself stoically fighting one battle after another and losing them one by one. After a good shoulder-shaking bawl, he found himself on his knees. Taking several deep breaths to steady himself, he wiped the tears from his face. Standing up, he felt renewed and ready to face the world head on, come what may.

Like the spirits of the cougar and the mule deer, he had played the role of both predator and prey in his life. His life had been an endless cycle of ups and downs, one propelling the other ever forward, each cycle giving birth to the next. He knew it was time for him to feed the hunger of his failure that now gnawed in his belly. Shedding the role of the prey, fearful of the wolves ever at the door, he had been reborn, freed of such concerns. He was now a hungry predator on the prowl once again.

Riding back to his homestead and into the arms of his loving family, he knew leaving Pilger Mountain would be bittersweet. He had lived his boyhood dream and had come to terms with all that had happened. His and Kate's Shangri-La would forever be a Pleasant Valley bathed in sunlight on a warm spring day when wildflowers blanketed the ground, and the scent of sweet pine filled the air. Knowing he and Kate and their children would be able to visit Detrick and Annie in coming years somehow softened the blow of his own failure. He accepted that staying in Pleasant Valley was no longer an option. If he was to survive, if he was to provide for his family, he would need to find new hunting grounds and learn new ways to bring down fatter game.

December 14, 1934

Pleasant Valley, Custer County, South Dakota

Paradise Lost

IT HAD NEARLY BROKEN her heart, when Velda learned Stinkin' Bear would no longer be her horse. She didn't understand why they had lost everything nor why they would have to move out of their home. All she knew for sure was she wouldn't be returning to the Pleasant Valley School after the new year and would be moving to Custer, a place she had been before, according to her Ma. Fact was, she had no memory of Custer. Custer to her was a place people only talked about. Like Hot Springs or Edgemont, Custer seemed as distant as New York City or Chicago in her young mind. She only remembered going to Dewey several times and knew nothing of any of these other far-off places. She had grown up on Pilger Mountain, the only place she had ever known.

That night, she had gone to Stinkin' Bear's stall with his shiny bridle in her hands and sat on the mound of hay where he had slept the last night he had spent in his stall. She had been given the bridle as a birthday present just the year before, when Stinkin' Bear had first come into her life. She knew throwing a fit when you didn't get your way never changed anything. She had shed only fake tears for the strangers to see, knowing she wasn't saying goodbye to Stinkin' Bear at the time. Now, in the privacy of his narrow horse stall, her real tears finally found their release. Stinkin' Bear meant everything to her. Once again, she felt the raging heat of her fighting spirit burning within her. Once again, she promised herself she would never accept losing anything ever again.

Detrick had come over to help Bill move his Roman Eagle cookstove and his Delco Light Plant. Bill had bought the stove when he sold his general store and brought the old light plant out from Creighton. He decided to take them with him to the Minnie May Mine, knowing they would need to have a way to cook and a way to heat the old mining office that was little more than a tar paper shack with a single sheet of tin for a roof. He wasn't sure when he would be able to hook up the Delco Light Plant but was determined not to leave anything of value behind. The bank might have the right to take his land and his cabin, there was nothing in the foreclosure papers that indicated they had any legal hold on his furniture and personal effects.

Borrowing a truck from Mike Robinson, Detrick had agreed to haul their cookstove, the Delco Light Plant, and all their furniture to Custer. Stripping the cabin, they soon had all the Barton family's worldly goods loaded on the truck. It was decided that since the old Blue Demon no longer had a roof and only had horse saddles thrown on top of bare springs for seats, Kate, now nearly seven months pregnant, would ride with her Pa in the truck. Though the weather was clear and calm, the air was freezing cold, sure to give anyone riding in the open car a bone-chilling thrill all the way to Custer. Before piling into the vehicles for the journey to Custer, everyone took one last look around the cabin they had called home for the last five and a half years. Detrick and Kate followed in the truck, as the Blue Demon set out toward Custer on the Pleasant Valley Road.

When they drove by the Fremder place, Annie and her whole brood of seven children lined the road waving their farewells. Seeing them standing in a row reminded Bill of the first time he saw the Fremder girls all dressed alike, each a head taller than the next. He also remembered his Pa's remark before he was shushed by his Ma. Even now, the Fremder children all standing in a row really did look like a matching set of matryoshka dolls. Shouts of encouragement and luck, goodbyes and best wishes soon faded as they headed north to Custer and an uncertain future.

Bill sat behind the wheel and John rode shotgun with Sandy at his feet. Francis, Bart, and Velda wrapped up in blankets huddled in the back seat with no place to hide from the relentless wind. With the top gone, chewed off by hungry hoppers, John started laughing out loud at the freezing cold wind swirled around everyone in the car as they rolled down the road. Looking over at his Pa, who had a huge smile on his face as he laughed at the wind, Bill had to admit the old man was as crazy as a pet coon. He also had to admit that was why he loved him so much. Bill reached over to pat the old man on the leg to let him know he understood and started laughing himself. Before long Francis, Bart, and Velda joined in the frivolity.

Without a word between them, they all recalled the stories of Sarah driving her Blue Demon up and down the Market Road to Wall with its top down and her daughters holding onto their bonnets while they all laughed at the wind with gusto. John had shared the story of his and Francis's final trip down that very same Market Road to Wall with the Blue Demon's top down, laughing at the wind all the way to Wall and on to Pleasant Valley. It was only fitting that they traveled the Pleasant Valley Road for the last time with the top down, laughing at the wind. They all agreed that it had now become a Barton family tradition which made them laugh all the harder.

With the wind roaring around them, John yelled out to remind everyone, the past was the past, if they cared to look back, they would see it growing smaller with every mile. The road ahead would lead them into their future, a future they had yet to write. John believed that starting anew was a time when a man was his freest. With the past behind him, his future was a blank canvas awaiting his fancy. Life was what a man made of it; starting anew, without the burdens or obligations of the past, allowed a man to pursue his heart's desire, indeed it allowed him to purse any option he might choose within his reach. He believed this to be true for a woman as well. He made sure Velda understood that she was the author of her own destiny and that she should believe that starting anew in Custer would be the adventure of her life, as it would be for her brother, Bart, and the new baby as well.

John hated the thought that he would soon no longer be able to help raise his oldest grandchildren. He was glad he had had the chance to watch them grow up and to have shared with them the lessons he had learned in life. Having been raised on the frontier, he knew Bart and Velda had the sand to overcome anything. They were children of the frontier, the last of America's pioneers. For that, he was grateful.

Detrick followed the Barton clan and marveled at how they could all laugh in the face of the freezing wind as they made their way up Pleasant Valley Road. He understood how people on the frontier learned to laugh in the face of a hard life that provided little comfort with its endless series of chores and hardships. Frontier people could find humor in misery. The fact that their survival was a daily struggle made the little things in life precious, whether it was the sight of a wildflower, a clear blue sky, thunderstorms on the horizon, bees gathering pollen, fall leaves, sunsets and sunrises, or just the rustling of the wind through the tall grass.

Painful blisters, broken limbs, cuts and scrapes, sore backs, chapped skin could all be seen as funny, as comical misfortunes, as a matter of course, as things a person simply shrugged off. Such misfortune was a part of life. The struggles a person might have were the same struggles everyone shared. It was because of this common bond, this common suffering, that such misfortune could be seen as comical and a topic of jokes and jest. Detrick smiled watching the Barton family shrug off their misery. They had lost everything and yet they forged forward undaunted. They were pioneers. They had lived on the frontier and eked out a living in the harshest of conditions. They were survivors. Looking over at Kate, Detrick had no fear for his daughter's future. He knew her husband's people, like his own German countrymen, were not the kind of people to ever give up. They would find a way and they would grow strong again.

When they arrived at Fourmile Corner, they turned east on Highway 16 until they came to Little Italy Road. Taking a left, they headed north into the forest. The further they went, the rougher and narrower the Forest Service trail became. Bill was thankful the weather was clear, fearing there would be no way to get the fully loaded truck up the narrow dirt road in snowy weather. Over two miles from Highway 16, they finally caught sight of the Minnie May Mine atop a rocky knoll. Surrounding the main mine shaft was a collection of rusted winches, cables, and other mining equipment. Just south of the mine shaft stood a shack that leaned precipitously to the east, a clear indication of the strength of the prevailing westerly winds that flowed around the contours of the rocky knoll to the north.

"Oh my," Kate said upon sizing up the dilapidated shack as she stepped out of the truck.

"She's not pretty, but she's still standin' and in one piece," Bill said, and then quickly added, "Don't fret, Kate, we won't be here long."

Of course, Bill had no idea how long they would be there, other than knowing the sheriff would be forcing them to move on in little more than two months.

"Well, let's get things unloaded and set up," Detrick said, having learned the hard way, the best way to move forward was to take the next step.

They had no time to worry about what they didn't have, they needed to deal with what they had right in front of them and to keep moving forward. He knew Bill was in a tough spot, and he was concerned for his eldest daughter, especially with her expecting in a couple of months. He found some comfort in knowing that Bill had a good head on his shoulders and still had a strong back. Most of all he knew Bill was his father's son. Getting to know John Barton during the war years and the years since, Detrick had come to believe, any son of John Barton couldn't be anything other than as tough as nails. He knew Bill had been taught how to survive whatever life threw at him.

Detrick had agreed with Bill and Kate that it would be better for them to live near town where work was more available. Though Bill's boyhood dream had been to be a farmer on Pilger Mountain, and no one could ever say the man hadn't given it his all, Detrick, having witnesses the last five years, had to admit, Bill was better suited to making a living using his head than running a farm. Bill had been a good businessman running his own general store in Creighton and had been appointed the youngest postmaster in the state. Detrick was confident Bill would soon be back on his feet now that he had put farming behind him.

After unloading the truck and moving the heavy cookstove into the shack, Detrick said his farewells and promised to bring the rest of their things and their Jersey cow and chickens the next day. As Detrick drove off, Bill prayed the weather would hold long enough for them to settle in. He also prayed he would be able to find work as soon as possible. He wasn't sure when he would be able to get around to it but didn't look forward to calling Arvella with the news that he would be no longer be able to take care of their father. He was relieved to know, however, when he did, Arvella would spread the word to her sisters, and they would work out the details for John's care between themselves.

By midafternoon, everything had been set up, with the old wood cookstove's smokestack rammed out through a rough-cut hole in the east wall of the shack. With an elbow joint in the stack, smoke drifted straight up and off to the east carried by a steady westerly breeze. The tiny one-room building was soon warm, though cold air seeped in around every window and door. Considering the large gaps around all the windows and along the roofline, Kate wondered just how warm the place would be on a windy day. She had maintained a positive attitude for the benefit of the children. Deep down she was afraid for their future. If Bill couldn't find work, she wondered what would become of them. Life had been so promising when they started. Pleasant Valley had been a lush paradise, neither of them could have imagined that their Shangri-La would turn into such misery.

After Bart chased all the mice and other varmints out from under the shack, Sandy had been stationed in a makeshift doghouse next to the front door. With sheets tacked up for curtains, beds set up lining the walls, and their dining table and chairs setting in the middle of the room, Velda thought their new cottage in the woods looked quite cozy. Taking her Grandpa John's words to heart, she believed she was on the adventure of a lifetime. She intended to live life as it came. That they had no electricity, running water, and used an outhouse that was a good hike from the shack was nothing new to Velda. She took it all in stride and looked forward to what the next day would bring.

The shack sat next to the mine shaft on five acres of open land that had been cleared for mining operations. Surrounding this clear-cut treeless area was a thick forest of ponderosa pine on all sides. Bill, Francis, and Bart got down to work by first dragging deadwood from the surrounding forest into a heaping pile north of the shack. Once they had plenty of fallen tree trunks and branches to work on, Bill and Francis started sawing and splitting firewood while Bart gathered up the chopped wood and stacked it into cords under a pole barn roof located near the mine shaft that had been used by the miners to store materials out of the rain and weather. With the worst of winter ahead, they would be needing to lay in plenty of firewood.

Bart was ten years old and growing up fast. He had gotten into the habit of hanging around his Uncle Francis whenever he could. With only seven years difference in their ages, Bart looked up to Francis more as a big brother than as his uncle. He knew Francis planned to join the Navy when he turned eighteen. He too wanted nothing more than to find a way to strike out on his own. He never liked homesteading in Pleasant Valley and was happy the family had finally moved to town. He remembered his life in Creighton and Wall before his Pa brought the family to Pilger Mountain. The last five years had been hard on Bart with endless chores to do and little else. The crews of men who worked the oil rigs on Barker Flats had fascinated him. The men's talk of life outside the valley had stirred in him the wanderlust his Grandpa John's stories had planted in his mind. Bart often daydreamed about Mexico, Texas, and the wild west and about his relatives who had traveled further west to settle in California, Oregon, and even Alaska.

Always scraping to get by, never having enough, and worrying about every nickel and dime was not the life Bart dreamed about. He had sworn to himself he wouldn't accept living a life of poverty. He never wanted to go without anything ever again. He would find work. He would earn money. He would follow his uncles into the service. Letters from his Uncle Alva spoke of a world full of wonders. Bart wanted to follow his uncle's example and see that world firsthand.

BOOK FOUR

December 17, 1934

Minnie May Mine, Custer County, South Dakota

Everybody Works

GETTING MOVED INTO THE mining shack was only the first step in getting the family back on its feet. Bill knew they needed money and badly. Detrick had come back the day after the move to deliver their Jersey cow and chickens. Bart set up a chicken coop near the pole barn. With milk and eggs and the canned meat, fruit, and vegetables Kate had put up in the fall, the family would have enough to eat for the winter, if they rationed their supplies. To supplement their diet, Bart and Francis had set up several traplines in the forest around them. With luck, they hoped to snag an occasional rabbit or squirrel. They also planned to do a little trout fishing in French Creek and at the nearby new one-hundred-twenty-acre Stockade Lake that had just been built by the CCC the year before.

Grateful the weather continued to hold, Bill and Francis drove to town the next morning to look for work. The two men made quite a sight driving around Custer all day in their vintage Chrysler convertible with its top down in the dead of winter. Nearly every place they asked about work seemed to be looking for people but wouldn't be hiring until after the first of the year or early spring.

While buying gas at the local filling station with one of the last dollars in his pocket, Bill struck up a conversation with Ben Minke, the station owner. Ben was a big, broad-shouldered, bear-like, bearded man with a bulging beer belly. Just as Bill hoped, the station owner knew just about everybody in town and once he got wound up was more than willing to share everything he knew. Bill soon discovered, however, above all else, Ben Minke loved the sound of his own voice. According to Ben's way of thinking, he knew just about everything about everyone and every topic. There was no doubt that the man was a fountain of information about comings and goings in Custer and developments in the region. Bill soon appreciated what a useful resource Ben might become, if he could muster up enough patience to listen to the man drone on and on before he got around to sharing anything useful.

Desperate to find work, Bill became an attentive listener. Coaxing Ben to continue talking only required never interrupting him. By nodding, smiling, and throwing in an occasional grunt, Bill learned a great deal from Ben, much of which he soon suspected he would need to digest with a large grain of salt. Being new to town, Bill found it difficult to distinguish between what seemed to be Ben's opinion, of which he had many on every subject, and what the actual facts might be on any given matter.

Bending the conversion toward possible opportunities for employment, Ben had several ideas, all of which Bill had already checked on and had come up empty. Having had the chance to talk nearly nonstop for over an hour, Ben was in a good mood when he shared that he was looking to expand his business, something he had kept to himself for fear of competition. With tourism growing, Ben wanted to cash in on the coming boom once Mount Rushmore was completed. He owned the land behind his filling station and was looking to hire a couple of carpenters to work through the winter to build a row of ten motor lodges for the coming tourist season. He planned to add more lodges in coming years, if everything worked out.

Bill, having always been handy with a hammer, convinced Ben that he and his brother were carpenters and could do the work. Though Ben didn't think Francis looked experienced enough, Bill convinced him Francis was a professional and promised it would speed up the work, if they could work as a team, something they always did. Much to their amazement, Bill and Francis drove away with the agreement Ben would supply all the materials and would pay them each a dollar a day until the project was completed. Ben insisted that they start on the project first thing the next morning.

Just a week before Christmas, Bill's goal was to get the motor lodge project underway before the year-end holidays. Ben made it clear, he needed to have the lodges built by the end of May. Bill had assured him they would have them ready by then. In making the agreement, Bill had no idea how long it might take to build ten lodges but figured they would cross that bridge when they came to it. All he knew was that his empty pockets would soon no longer be strangers to money.

Bill couldn't believe their dumb luck. He had literally spent one of his last dollars on gasoline when they landed the job. He knew his Pa had a few dollars tucked away in case of emergency but had wanted to avoid tapping into the family's last and only cash reserve. Landing a job that paid a dollar a day meant he wouldn't have to. Driving back to the Minnie May Mine, Bill felt a hell of a lot better about the family's prospects, than he had earlier that morning.

Feeling the pressure of charting a new course for his family, he could almost hear the ticking of a clock in the back of his mind. He had only two months before the sheriff would come knocking. He needed to find permanent lodging for his family, and pronto. With the baby coming soon, there really was no time to lose. According to Ben, the Forest Service was selling off their old squad tents, having been issued new ones from the CCC. Bill had noticed that young CCC enlistees seemed to be everywhere. Known as the "Tree Army" with their green uniforms and spruce tree shoulder patches, the CCC had set up camps all over the Black Hills to work on a long list of Forest Services projects. Bill figured if CCC enlistees could live in heavy-duty squad tents year-round, so could his family, at least, until they had something better.

As his mind sorted through everything he needed to do, he recalled Ben mentioning that a rancher named Lyn Blay was selling quarter acre housing lots on the south end of his property holdings along Little Italy Road just off Highway 16. Already living at the upper end of Little Italy Road, Bill thought the lower end of the road would put the family less than two miles west of downtown Custer. Bill thought the location would be an ideal place to set down roots. If he could buy one of the lots, he would be able to set up a squad tent and work on something more permanent over the coming year. Feeling the urgency of his situation, he decided to swing by to talk to Lyn Blay the first chance he got.

With these and many other thoughts swirling around in his head, Bill turned onto Little Italy Road. Bill's mind was snapped back to the present, when Francis frantically urged him to pull the car over. Looking where Francis was pointing, Bill couldn't see anything of interest beyond a large pile of rusted junk that had been left stacked up in the bar ditch. Stopping the car, Francis quickly jumped out, saying he thought he could see two old bicycles laying under the pile. Finally spotting the bikes, Bill could see that the tires were flat on both bikes and their metal frames were rusty and in petty rough shape.

With no one around to object, Bill and Francis worked to untangle the bicycles from the rest of the junk. Once they were liberated from under the pile, Bill had to agree with Francis that they weren't in that bad of shape and could be fixed up. Wedging them into the open trunk of the car, Bill tied down the trunk lid to keep things from bouncing around. Doing a quick three-sixty to ensure no one was around, they hopped back in the car and made their way home.

With Custer's Primary School a good four miles from the Minnie May Mine, walking to and from school would be tough on the kids, especially during the winter months. Bill couldn't be happier about his brother's eagle eye. Spotting the old bicycles under the junk pile had been next to impossible even when Bill knew they were there. On the ride back to the mining shack, the brothers agreed that once they patched up the tires, they could work on fixing the seats, and with a little grease and tender loving care, the old bikes just might be good enough to ride again.

Bill figured the kids could use the bikes to get to and from school, at least in good weather. Bart, soon to be eleven, was also old enough to work. Bill hoped that having a way to get around might help Bart find a part-time job. To Bill's way of thinking, the family, strapped for cash and with its back up against the wall, needed everybody able to work to get a job and help pitch in.

Turning onto the narrow trail leading to the mining shack, Bill thought about the bikes and the kids and couldn't help but laugh out loud.

"What's so damn funny," Francis said, looking over at his big brother.

"The kids," Bill said, between chuckles.

"What about 'em?"

"They've never owned a bicycle. I'm pretty sure they don't know how to ride one either."

"Come to think about it, I've never ridden one of the wobbly two wheeled-critters myself," Francis admitted sheepishly.

"Hate to tell ya little brother, neither've I," Bill howled, knowing it was going to be a real hoot getting the kids up and balancing on two wheels, when no one in the Barton family had ever ridden a bicycle before.

Catching their breath as they pulled up to the shack, the men were in high spirits but damn near frozen to death after riding around in the open car with outdoor temperatures ranging well below zero.

"We have to get a roof on this jalopy or we're goin' to catch our death. There's no way we can go through the winter without one," Francis said, his ears stinging from the cold.

"Tomorrow is another day. Maybe ol' Ben has something we can use that won't cost us an arm and a leg," Bill said as he untied the rope holding the trunk lid down.

"What should we do with these," Francis said, as he lifted the bikes out of the trunk.

"Let's tuck 'em out of sight just inside the mine shaft entry. I'm pretty sure the kids won't go pokin' around in there. I'd like to see if we can get 'em fixed up before Christmas," Bill said, knowing without money, Christmas gifts would be scarce this year.

"By God, you'd think we're brothers. I had the very same idea," Francis said with a grin, as the two men each grabbed a bike and hustled it over to the mine shaft.

"I'll take the wheels off tonight and throw 'em in the trunk so we can get 'em fixed at Minke's sometime this week," Francis said, liking the idea that the bikes would be a Christmas surprise for the kids.

Francis was nearly eighteen and looking forward to leaving Custer and the Black Hills far behind him in just six months' time. He knew the years ahead for Bart and Velda would be tough, a damn sight tougher than any he had ever experienced as a kid. The badlands homestead had been a constant struggle, and for a kid growing up not a lot of fun, but he always had a roof over his head and the family had never been completely broke. He knew Bill's kids had an uncertain future ahead of them and they would have to do without for some time to come. He was determined to do what he could for them before he left. He had to admit to himself, however, as far as learning how to ride their bikes, they were on their own.

During the coming week, Bill and Francis were able to make progress on the Minke Motor Lodge. Ben had a rough set of blueprints drawn up which provided the dimensions for the basic lodge structures he had in mind. Though the blueprints left much to be desired, they were good enough to figure out how to tackle the project. Since all the lodges would be identical, Bill decided the work might go easier, if they first built a jig for each of the four walls. By building the walls as modular components, they could do the framing quickly, without the need of building each lodge from the ground up, before starting the next.

As Christmas grew closer, the men took turns fixing up the bicycles a little bit every day. By Christmas Eve, the bikes even had a fresh coat of green paint, which they hoped no one would notice matched exactly the color of the metal trim on Minke's filling station. With tires repaired, chrome polished, and handmade leather seat covers stretched into place, Bill and Francis had to admit the bikes looked almost brand new.

Bill had let John and Kate in on the secret and they decided they would each make their own contribution to the effort. John customized a couple pairs of saddlebags that could be strapped onto each bike's rear rack. The saddlebags would work well as bookbags, just as they had when the kids rode their horses to school in the valley. Kate knitted new mufflers and mittens for the kids from the last balls of yarn she had. The finished products were a mishmash of every color under the sun. Pleased with the result, she wondered how the kids would feel about them.

Following the Barton tradition, the opening of Christmas presents followed dinner on Christmas Day, with Santa having visited the night before. After a Christmas dinner of roasted rabbit and squirrel, presents from under the small Christmas tree they had wedge into one corner of the room were all piled on the dining table. Once presents were handed out, everyone set about unwrapping their goodies. Bart and Velda each got a Christmas stocking filled with mixed shelled nuts, a few peppermint sticks, and an orange. They also each received a colorful set of mittens with matching muffler. Bill, Francis, and John each got a new pair of socks. Kate got a new hairbrush.

"Like your presents?" Francis said, looking at Bart and Velda.

"I always liked oranges. They grow 'em in Florida. I'd like to see that someday," Bart said, trying to put a happy face on a sorry Christmas.

"Yeah, oranges are tasty," Francis said and then added, "How about you, Velda?"

"I like oranges too," she said, knowing their Christmas was very different than in previous years.

She could see in the sad eyes of the adults that the family was in trouble. She wanted to believe every day was an adventure like her Grandpa John said, but feeling cold every day and having no friends had started to take a toll. She looked forward to school, though she worried about meeting all the new kids. She had heard the Custer schools had twelve grades and divided their students between primary school and secondary school, with different teachers, unlike the Pleasant Valley School that had one room and one teacher with everyone studying together, from first to eighth grade.

After a long pause, Velda added, "I also like the mittens and muffler Mama knitted. They're so colorful."

"Well, thank you, honey. I wasn't sure you'd like 'em," Kate said, pleased and relieved.

"I like 'em too, Ma. It'll be a long walk to school, and they should keep us warm," Bart said, not really liking the girly colors but understanding the family was broke.

His Pa had already told him he needed to find a part-time job. His problem was how he would be able to get around Custer on foot. They could ride to town with their Pa in the morning. Walking from Minke's to school would easy enough. The problem was the long hike home in subzero temperatures. Bart knew that though he might not like their rainbow colors, having a warm woolen muffler and mitts in the dead of winter would come in handy. It was already cold, and winter had only just begun. He didn't look forward to the year ahead.

"I thought Santa had a few more things on his sled this year," John said, pretending to look around confused.

"No, grandpa. We got everything," Velda said, worried her grandpa couldn't see well enough to know everyone had their presents.

"No. I'm sure there was something more," John insisted.

"Should I look outside?" Francis said, playing along.

"Yeah, I think we better look around. I thought I heard someone out there," Bill said, adding more confusion to the ruse.

"Should I help?" Bart said, wondering why the adults were all acting so strange.

"No son, you stay here. We'll look around. No tellin' what we might find," Bill said, putting on his coat.

Both Bill and Francis ducked out of the shack and banged around outside making noise and talking loudly. They knew the kids would be wondering what was going on.

"Hey, you! What are you doin' there?" Bill yelled, loud enough to be heard inside the shack.

"Hurry! He's a big fat man and he's gettin' away!" Francis yelled, almost giving the ruse away when he tripped over a stump and fell flat on his face and started laughing.

Holding back his laughter, he rolled back up on his feet and dusted himself off. No worse for wear, he followed Bill over to the mine shaft. Pushing the bikes back to the shack, they knocked on the door and called for the kids to come outside.

"Kids, we saw an old fat man run off, but he left a couple of things behind," Francis yelled.

"Yeah, he said they belonged to Bart and Velda Barton," Bill added, stiffing a laugh.

Bill and Francis were having fun with their little ruse and couldn't wait to see the look on the kids' faces when they discovered what all the commotion had been about.

Kate insisted the kids buddle up before going out in the cold. She helped Velda wrap her new colorful muffler around her neck before letting her loose. As the kids rushed out of the shack, they were dumbstruck at the sight of the two shiny new bicycles. Getting such a wonderful gift was the last thing the children ever expected.

Much to the men's surprise, Velda and Bart hopped on their new bikes and rode around the cleared area in front of the shack without much trouble, other than having to navigate the bumpy, rock-strewn ground. The only thing they needed the men to do was to adjust the height of their seats. Bart's was too low and Velda's too high.

"Where'd you kids learn to ride a bike?" Bill said, amazed at the two of them.

"Mrs. Meyer had a bike and taught all of us kids how to ride," Velda said, as though everyone knew how to ride a bike.

Bill looked over at Francis and shrugged with a grin on his face, he hadn't known Emma Meyers rode a bike or that she had taught all the kids how to ride one. Catching the expression on Bill's face, Francis started to laugh, realizing there was probably a lot of things they didn't know that the kids already knew.

The two-month grace period given to them by Sheriff Jameson passed quickly. Bill, badly in need of money, had to sell their Jersey cow, one of the family's only assets, to get the cash enough to buy a used Forest Service squad tent and make a small down payment on one of Lyn Blay's quarter-acre housing lots on the south end of Little Italy Road. The plan was to set up the tent and get it ready to live in. He had learned from the Forest Service that the thing to do was to pile sawdust and wood chips around the walls of the tent, leaving only the pitched top of the tent uncovered. The tent had a well-insulated hole in one side designed for a stove pipe, so using their wood cookstove inside the tent would be possible.

After first putting down a plank floor, made up of a mosaic of scrap wood borrowed on a permanent basis from the Minke Motor Lodge project, Bill and Francis put up the tent and, following the Forest Service's advice, piled up saw dust and wood chips on all sides. Borrowing a truck from Tim Russel, the owner of the sawmill who Bill had gotten to know, they moved the family and all of its possessions on March 1, much to the relief of Sheriff Ed Jameson.

Their move had been just in the nick of time. After no more than getting settled into their new home, Bill had to rush Kate to the local hospital where she gave birth to a bouncing baby boy, who they name John, after his grandpa. With the family in need of money to pay for the housing lot and to cover the cost of living, Kate took a job at Molly Tillerman's Roadway Inn as a short-order cook. With Bill and Francis working on the Minke Motor Lodge all day and the kids in school, John was assigned chief bottle washer and babysitter for the newborn. Unable to see well, John took to letting his namesake sit on his lap all day. The once good-natured well-behaved baby boy everyone had come to call Sweet Johnny, after being held on his grandpa's lap all day, soon became Rotten Johnny, a monster of a brat who insisting on being held all the time. What made matters worse was that when Rotten Johnny didn't get his way, he cried and raised holy hell until he did.

Though things seemed to be looking up for the Barton family, with everyone working, the family was still barely scraping by. Arvella agreed to take John, but not until the fall. Francis had enlisted in the Navy and would ship out for boot camp near Chicago in June. No longer having Francis's income would put a hole in the family's finances, but Bill supported Francis's decision to join the military, like his older brother, Alva. He figured Francis had done more than enough to help him get back on his feet. What worried Bill most was that with the Minke Motor Lodge project coming to an end, he would once again need to find work, and fast.

Bart had tried several part-time jobs to make money. He had worked at the sawmill building shipping pallets after school, which a lot of the old kids did. The sawmill supplied hammers, nails, and the cut boards and paid workers three cents a pallet. Hammering pallets together, Bart found he could make up to a dollar a week, if he worked two to three hours after school every day. It was backbreaking work outside in the cold, but he hadn't been able to find anything better. His only consolation was that by working after school every day, he had been able to avoid listening to Rotten Johnny, who never seemed to stop crying.

Velda liked their new tent home. It was her duty to feed the chickens and collect eggs every morning. She had set up a small business selling eggs for twenty cents a dozen to their neighbors along Little Italy Road. Though Grandpa John took care of Rotten Johnny during the day, babysitting chores fell to Velda when she was home. Her biggest problem had been keeping Rotten Johnny's hands off the tent's canvas canopy. Every time he touched the underside of the canvas, which he couldn't seem to keep his hands off, it dripped water for hours until the spot froze again. With summer coming, Velda looked forward to exploring the area around Custer. If she was indeed on the adventure of a lifetime, like her Grandpa John said, she was determined to live every moment to its fullest.

June 1, 1936

Little Italy, Custer, Custer County, South Dakota

Hearts of Gold

SHERIFF ED JAMESON HAD to admit the new Minke Motor Lodge looked pretty damn good. The Barton brothers had done a better job than anyone in town thought possible. The rumors that had been spread around town from locals who had watched the two men work through the winter even in the middle of snowstorms were that the Barton brothers had no idea what they were doing and sure as hell weren't carpenters. At times the project had looked more like a complete disaster area than a construction site, with partially built walls and roof trusses piled everywhere and every which way. Bill's idea of building the lodges with prebuilt modules was something no one had ever seen done before. His idea of tying all the units together with connecting carports between every unit had been a unique touch that wasn't fully appreciated until all the lodges where completely built.

Being the first motor lodge of its kind in the region, Ed had heard the Minke Motor Lodge had become a gold mine. Ben always liked to talk a lot and always had a lot of cockamamie ideas but hadn't been the kind of guy to take action on much of anything. Seeing one of Ben's ideas become a reality had changed Ed's opinion of the man. Ed knew that without the Barton brothers, the Minke Motor Lodge would still be another one of Ben Minke's pipe dreams; however, now that it had been built and was a smashing success, the man looked like a genius.

Ed had kept an eye on the Barton family after they made their move to Custer. He had to smile to himself thinking about all the petty crimes they had committed. He knew from eyewitness descriptions of their car that it had been Bill and his brother Francis who had taken the two broken-down bicycles from old man Jack Thornton's scrap metal pile, though he had told old man Thornton he had no idea who could have done such a thing. Ed had also noticed that the forest green color of the Barton kids' bicycles matched the color of the metal trim on Minke's filling station. Ed was also sure that Ben Minke, starry eyed over all the money he would make with his new motor lodge, hadn't noticed nor cared that all of the scrap lumber and materials from his motor lodge project had ended up on a housing lot over in Little Italy where the Barton family was living in a used Forest Service quad tent.

Ed had no problem overlooking a little petty theft considering the tough times folks around Custer had gone through. It had been five years since many of the people living in the area had steady work. The CCC had provided work to many of the younger men in the area since Roosevelt became president. The new government programs had done nothing for older farm laborers like Bill Barton. After completing the motor lodge and working over a year on and off on a string of odd jobs, Ed was pleased to learn that Bill had finally gotten a break and landed a full-time job.

With changes made in the government's jobs program, Bill had been able to sign up for his first six-month tour of duty in the new WPA to work on improvements being made to the newly built Iron Mountain Road, a scenic route for tourists that led from Custer State Park over Iron Mountain to the town of Keystone at the base of Mount Rushmore. The road built by the CCC in 1933 had seen several improvements every year. According to Bill, they would be adding guardrails and other signage to the steep winding road. Bill had been hired as a surveyor's assistant. Ed wasn't sure what a surveyor's assistant did but guessed it might be better than leaning on a shovel.

The Work Progress Administration had initially been set up to employ out-of-work laborers, artists, writers, and musicians, mostly in urban areas. With so many farmers in rural western states suffering through drought conditions, farm workers were finally approved for WPA projects at the end of 1935. In the Black Hills, it was decided that WPA enlistees would work alongside CCC enlistees on CCC projects at the same dollar-a-day wage. WPA jobs were welcomed by older men living in the badlands and hills who couldn't find steady work. Unlike the CCC, where the focus was on organizing younger men to work in teams to engage in pick and shovel labor, a key goal of the WPA was to retrain unemployed older workers to give them new skills for possible future employment opportunities.

Though these government programs were a godsend, they paid only a dollar a day and tended to hold down local wage rates at the same level. Bill had never been unable to find steady work since leaving Pleasant Valley. He would have liked to have found a full-time job in town for more than a dollar a day, but search has he might, there simply were no such jobs to be found. Bill figured the advantage of enlisting in the WPA was that the work was steady, and though the wages were low, the job provided food, lodging, and most importantly for Bill, new work clothes free of charge.

After years of hard labor without the money to buy new clothes, Bill's clothing was covered in a collage of patches and was beyond tattered and worn out. By enlisting for a six-month tour in the WPA, Bill would be issued two full sets of work clothes, a bonus tough to pass up. The disadvantage was that he would need to live away from the family during his six-month tour from the middle of June to the middle of December. Knowing he had little choice but to make the sacrifice, he hoped Christmas would be a happy one and that 1937 would bring fresh opportunities.

Seeing the sheriff's patrol car parked in front of the Minke Motor Lodge, Bill pulled up at a distance on the other side of the road. Curious to find out what was going on, Bill watched Sheriff Ed Jameson nodding his head up and down while scratching his chin as he walked around and looked over the lodge from every angle. Bill had just returned from Hot Springs, where he had met with Albert Meyer, who had sent word to Bill that he had found a wrecked 1925 Chrysler convertible Model-B70. Though the car was a year newer than the Blue Demon, it was essentially the same model right down to the last screw. After suffering through two freezing winters and the embarrassment of riding around in the Blue Demon without a top, Bill had been excited about the chance to finally get his car fixed.

Bill had wasted no time in deciding to drive down to Hot Springs. What Bill hadn't expected was the hefty price tag of fifteen dollars for the convertible top demanded by the owner of the junkyard. The owner, unwilling to haggle, left Bill with little room to negotiate. Reluctant to part with his hard-earned money and yet wanting the convertible top, Bill had struggled to make a decision until he remembered the ten-dollar bill Francis had given him to, in Francis's words, "fix the damn car." Having already received his orders to report to the U.S. Navy Great Lakes Training Command in Chicago, Illinois, in June of the previous year, Francis had insisted that Bill accept his parting gift, reminding Bill with a chuckle that one winter without a top on his car was enough suffering for any human being, even one as ornery as his older brother. Unable to find a replacement top that would fit before the snow flew once again, Bill had suffered through a second winter without a top on his car and was determined not to suffer another one. For Bill, a man who made only thirty dollars a month, fifteen dollars was a fortune. Without further hesitation, Bill slapped down fifteen dollars for the convertible top with a smile, silently thanking Francis for helping to make up his mind.

Bill knew Francis had never liked the sheriff but had begrudgingly admitted the man had done the family a good turn when he let them stay at the Minnie May Mine until they could get on their feet. Bill shook his head in satisfaction knowing the Minke Motor Lodge would serve as a constant reminder to all the doubters in Custer what the Barton brothers could do when they put their minds and their backs to it. Bill was proud of what they had been able to accomplish together.

Even so, at times, Bill found it difficult to believe that they had actually completed the project on schedule. There had been plenty of times he had had his doubts. Looking at the Minke Motor Lodge, Bill had to admit, the place had real curbside appeal. One thing was certain, old Ben never had a problem keeping it fully booked, year around.

Easing the Blue Demon back out onto the road with its new cloth convertible top pulled up and buttoned into place, Bill headed home with a smile on his face and, for the first time in a long time, without the need to battle a relentless wind.

Kate had been working all afternoon on preparing a special dinner to celebrate Bill's new WPA job. The front tent flaps had been tied open to let the heat out and the fresh air in. Life at the Barton place had fallen into a rhythm. Living with none of the modern conveniences enjoyed by Americans from coast to coast, no one complained. Fetching water, using oil lamps, using an outhouse, and heating and cooking on a wood stove was not much different than life had been in Pleasant Valley. The biggest difference was that they hadn't been able to hook up the Delco Light Plant since moving to Custer.

Grandpa John had returned to spend the summer to help out with the children, while Kate worked at the Roadway Inn. With Kate busy working on her special dinner, he had spent the afternoon bouncing Johnny on his knee, while telling stories to Velda and Bart. He told several tales from his days as a cowboy riding the western Chisholm Trail. He had also told them how all the land in the Black Hills and the surrounding region had once been controlled by Lakota Indian tribes and their Cheyenne allies.

"You might say the Gordon Stockade right here in Custer was the white man's original sin," John said, recalling the stories about the Black Hills his Grandpa Pappy had told him as a boy.

Pappy was Joseph Breeden, John's maternal grandfather, who had ridden with Lieutenant Gouverneur Warren during the U.S. Army expedition to survey and make maps of the Missouri River and the land around the Black Hills in 1856 and 1857. Though Lt. Warren had attempted to enter the Black Hills at several points, he had been turned back on every attempt by hostile bands of Lakota warriors. During the long expedition that circled the Black Hills and surveyed the Mauvaises Terres all the way to and from the Missouri River, Pappy fell in love with the lush forest of the Black Hills and the haunting beauty of the Mauvaises Terres, the French name by which the prairie lands east of the Black Hills were known at the time. It was Pappy's many stories of the Mauvaises Terres, later renamed the Dakota Badlands, that had instilled in John's young mind the desired to one day homestead in the region.

It was only after gold was discovered in 1874 during the U.S. Army Black Hills Expedition led by Lieutenant Colonel George Armstrong Custer that white men invaded the region in large numbers. Cheyenne, the capitol of Wyoming Territory and an important rail station on the Union Pacific Transcontinental Railroad, became a natural starting point for the first trail north to Ft. Larime, located on the upper North Platt River. From Ft. Larime, miners traveled northeast through Mule Creek Junction to the town of Burton, later renamed Edgemont, and then straight north across Minnekahta Flats into the southern Black Hills. Early fortune hunters first settled in and around Custer, where gold was first discovered along French Creek. After the discovery of richer gold strikes in the northern hills in 1876, the tidal wave of new miners coming from the east cut a new trail from the town of Bismarck, which straddled the Missouri River, on the Northern Pacific Transcontinental Railroad, to Bear Butte on the eastern edge of the northern Black Hills. To the Lakota, this notorious trail, from the Missouri River to the Black Hills, that carried an endless flood of miners, rogues, and desperadoes into the northern hills came to be known as Thieves Road. John was only eight years old when he first heard these tales and could remember clearly how he couldn't wait to get to the Black Hills himself one day.

John first arrived in the southern Black Hills in the summer of 1884 and had lived in the area until 1890 when he had return to Iowa. In 1907, he returned to western South Dakota to homestead north of Wall. He had seen the Gordon Stockade on French Creek east of Custer many times over the years and had come to view the rough-hewn log fortress as a reminder of the white man's permanent occupation of the Black Hills, a symbol that had stood in silent defiance since its illegal construction in 1874.

John had accepted long ago that there was no turning back history nor undoing the many wrongs that were now part of it. Alongside the Lakota people, people from every background now lived in western South Dakota. He himself had made the Black Hills his home for over fifty years.

Though the land no longer belonged to any one people, John had always felt that its spiritual roots would forever belong to the native peoples who had inhabited the lands long before the first white man happened to pass this way. He had come to understand the significance of this from the multicultural collection of symbols that adorned the mysterious shrine that had been assemble overtime on his own homestead and the replica his son had built on his homestead in Pleasant Valley. Though he might be old and nearly blind, John had no doubt about his ability to see the truth clear enough.

"Like in the Bible, grandpa?" Velda said, bringing John back to the present.

"In a way, only this sin was not about forbidden knowledge, but about gold and greed," John said thoughtfully.

"Gold? Like what Pa told us they were looking for at the Minnie May Mine?" Velda said.

"That's right. It was near here on French Creek that gold was first discovered in the Black Hills during the Custer Expedition in 1874," John said.

"Is that why they named the town of Custer after General Armstrong Custer?" Bart piped in.

"Actually, no. I thought that as well, but the name of the town happened another way," John said.

"Oh, it must've been because Custer was killed at the Little Bighorn," Bart said, sure he had the answer and wanting to show his grandpa he knew a lot about the region's history.

"Well, I once thought that too, but the truth is, according to Molly Tillerman, that is, the town's name came about after the original founders, who were split nearly fifty-fifty between former Union and Confederate soldiers, voted on the names of two Civil War heroes, Custer and Stonewall. The name Custer won by the slimmest of margins. Since this happened in the summer of 1875, it happened a year before Custer's Last Stand at the Little Bighorn in June 1876," John said, recounting what he had learned.

"So, Custer led the expedition into the Black Hills that discovered gold right here in Custer and later died fighting the Indians, but the town of Custer got named for him because he was a Civil War hero?" Bart said, finding the story unbelievable.

"The timing says that's probably how it happened. It was 1875, just ten years after the end of the Civil War. Folks back then were still hurting after the war and had come west to start a new life. What they couldn't run away from was their terrible memory of the over six hundred thousand soldiers who died and so they held up their war heroes in an effort to forget," John said, thinking about the six hundred seventy-five thousand Americans who had died from the Spanish Flu and the over one hundred sixteen thousand doughboys who had died in the Great War during his own lifetime.

"Is there still gold in French Creek?" Velda said, wondering if she might find some.

"The short answer is, probably. The problem is, it's tough to find," John said flatly.

"We were told in school, there was grassroots gold in the hills. Miners came and pulled up the grass and they found gold clinging to the roots," Bart said, excited by the thought.

"That's right. Places like Rockerville swarmed with miners when they first discovered grassroots gold there. It didn't take long for the miners to find out that the gold ran no deeper than the tiny flakes that clung to the roots of the grass and soon petered out. Miners are always chasing rainbows in search of the next pot of gold. When they fail to find it, they soon move on. There's more than one boom-and-bust ghost town in the Black Hills," John said flatly.

"Why isn't Custer a ghost town, if there's no gold here," Bart said.

"Actually, Molly told me that when the news of rich gold strikes in Deadwood Gulch were announced in May 1876, all but a handful of Custer's entire population of over ten thousand rushed to Deadwood. No longer the center of the gold rush, it took many years for Custer's population to come back to little better than half that total in recent years. Without large gold strikes in the area, Custer's boom days were over," John said.

"So, there's no more gold?" Velda said, still wanting a clear answer.

"There's gold alright, you just have to work to find it," John said.

"How do we find it?" Velda said, eager to learn more about where they might find gold.

"Well, the gold they found clinging to the grassroots and in the sand and soil along French Creek is called placer gold. Placer gold is the little flakes or nuggets of gold that shed off rocks through natural erosion from the wind and rain. These tiny grains of gold are often carried by rivers, and because they're heavier than most other minerals, they fall to the bottom and collect with other heavy minerals in pockets of black sand in and along riverbeds. By sifting through the black sand, you can find gold," John said, recounting what he knew.

"Was there a lot of black sand around here?" Velda said, pushing her grandpa to learn more.

"When prospectors first came to the Black Hills, there was a lot of placer gold to find in the undisturbed riverbeds. Once they sifted through all the pockets of black sand they could find, placer gold soon became harder and harder to find."

"Did they find where the placer gold came from?" Bart said.

"Well, yes and no. The miners at the Minnie May Mine were looking for gold still embedded in the rocks, rocks that might have been a possible source of the placer gold in French Creek. Hard rock mining is called lode mining, unlike placer mining that searches for sediments, lode mining searches for veins of ore that run through solid stone like the veins in a leaf or the veins that run through the human body."

"Veins in the rocks?" Velda said, looking at the blue lines running up her underarms and wondering how this could be.

"Different minerals melt at different temperatures. Like when ice melts in a bucket when the sun shines on it, but the bucket doesn't melt. Hot water underground combined with intense pressure can melt gold and force it into the cracks and crevasses of other rocks. Quartz is a mineral that is often carried by hot water under pressure in the same way. Quartz often crystallizes in the cracks of other rocks. That's why gold is often found embedded in veins of quartz. The Black Hills have lots of underground hot water and lots of quartz."

"Do you think there's still placer gold in French Creek?" Bart said.

"Well, they haven't been panning for gold in French Creek for nearly fifty years. There's bound to be some gold that's washed into the river since the last time anyone looked," John said, as he raised his eyebrows.

He figured if there was gold fifty years ago, there was a good chance new deposits had built up over the past fifty years.

"How do we get started?" Bart said, wanting to know more.

"Well, you need to build a sluice box and get a gold pan and such," John said.

"A sluice box?" Velda said, having never heard the word.

"That's right. It's like a washboard with its ribs bent a little in one direction so there's a little crease on one side at the base of each rib. You set it up so your slurry, that's your mixture of river sand and water, can run over the ribs of your sluice box in the same direction of the bend in the ribs. Because gold is heavier than the other rocks, gold flakes fall out of the slurry stream as it passes over the gaps between each rib and settles in the creases," John said, having seen plenty of sluice boxes in his day.

"Can we build one grandpa?" Bart said, excited at the idea they might be able to hunt for real gold.

"By golly, I think we can. We got plenty of wood and such. Let's give it a try," John said, pleased his grandchildren were doers.

Talk was easy, the fun was in the doing, and the Barton family had always been doers. Though he had never built a sluice box nor panned for gold, he figured they could hammer something together. Just as the kids were ready to head outside to gather the boards and tools they would need to build their sluice box, Bill pulled up in the Blue Demon.

"Hey, Pa! Grandpa's goin' to show us how to build a sluice box so we can pan for gold!" Bart said, as he bounded out of the tent excited to get started.

Velda, leading John by the hand, came out of the tent just as Bill stepped out of the car.

"What's this about gold?" Bill said, feeling the children's bubbling excitement.

"I think the kids got the gold fever," John said with a wink and a chuckle.

"We're goin' to build a sluice box," Bart said, as if he knew all about it.

"Before we start building something none of us has ever built, let's go over and talked to Molly Tillerman to see if she might know how best to get started. She was one of the original prospectors to enter the Black Hills and to work French Creek. I'm sure she may have a secret or two to share," Bill said with a wink and a grin.

With everyone excited to get started, they quickly piled into the Blue Demon. With Bill behind the wheel and John riding shotgun, the same seat he had always ridden on the famous Monitor gold wagon back in the 1880s, the Barton clan took off for the Roadway Inn, forgetting to tell Kate what was going on or where they were headed. By the time Kate was able to step out of the tent, all she could see was the back of the Blue Demon headed for the main highway. Not sure what had gotten into everyone or where they might be running off to, all she knew was that they'd better hurry back soon, her special dinner would be ready in an hour.

Molly had plenty to say about there being gold yet to be found in French Creek. She swore she knew for a fact there was gold there. The prospectors had turned away from searching for limited and illusive placer gold deposits in favor of lode mining after the news of huge gold strikes around Lead and Deadwood spread throughout the hills like wildfire. She had been sixteen years old when her good-for-nothing husband, hearing the news, ran off to Deadwood without a word, never to return. With the two bags of gold dust her good-for-nothing husband had absentmindedly left behind, she had been able to start the Roadway Inn, and as she often said, the rest was history.

She had kept an eye on the Barton family after their arrival in Custer just before Christmas two years past. She remembered the first time she met Bill Barton and the group of men he had brought to the Roadway Inn who had all filed homestead claims on land around Pilger Mountain in Pleasant Valley seven years earlier. It was obvious, Bill Barton had gone bust, like so many others she had watched, one by one, make their exodus from the fledgling settlement around Pilger Mountain. She had heard the final blow for the Barton family had been the massive grasshopper swarm that had penetrated deep into the Black Hills, descending on homesteads carved out of the forest for the first time in anyone's memory.

With all the CCC activity in the area, Molly had hired Kate Barton to help out as a short-order cook over the summer months. She had been surprised to learn from Kate that the Barton family was living in a used Forest Service squad tent with two young children and an infant. Everyone in town had seen the Barton brothers driving around in the dead of winter in an old topless Chrysler convertible.

The town had also watched in disbelief as the two men worked every day through the winter, even in the middle of snowstorms, on building the Minke Motor Lodge. That the Barton brothers had finished the motor lodge and that it was one of the finer-looking developments in town had left townsfolk shaking their heads in wonder. Molly too had looked over the construction of the motor lodge and had to admit the Barton brothers were damn good carpenters.

It wasn't generally in her nature to worry too much about strangers, she had always figured things would shake out one way or another without her sticking her hand into the middle of things. Witnessing the plight of the Barton family made her angry. The Barton family like too many others worked hard but never seemed to get ahead. She knew life wasn't fair; she also knew, it didn't have to be cruel.

Seeing how eager the Barton kids were to pan for gold, Molly, feeling generous and wanting to help the Barton family in some way, decided to give them several old gravel screens, a couple of rusty gold pans, and a dilapidated sluice box she had kept behind the Roadway Inn for far too many years. She remembered the many hours she had helped her good-for-nothing husband run rich black slurry down the sluice while standing knee deep in the ice-cold fast-flowing waters of French Creek. Though the sluice box was only a foot wide, it was twelve feet long. She had to smile when the Barton clan had to lower their old Chrysler's newly installed convertible top to balance the unruly contraption on the tops of the car's seats to haul it back home.

She could feel the excitement and energy in the children and remembered how excited she had been the first time she scooped gold dust out of the bottom of her gold pan. Like a whirlwind, the Barton clan had loaded everything up and were ready to go. Along with the mining equipment, Molly shared several hints on where they might have luck in finding gold along Upper French Creek and on Ruby Creek west of town. Standing in front of the Roadway Inn, Molly bid the Barton clan farewell as the Blue Demon headed back west toward Little Italy, where the scarlet light of the western sky seemed to swallow them whole as they drove directly into the orb of the setting sun.

Returning inside, Molly thought back over her earlier years in Custer. One character she would never forget was old Horatio Ross, the man who had first discovered gold on French Creek during General George Armstrong Custer's Black Hills Expedition in 1874. She smiled at the thought of his long bushy beard with upturned combed-out mustache. His tall rail-thin frame covered in tattered work clothes was a common fixture around the Gordon Stockade next to the U.S. Calvary's Permanent Camp, first established during the Custer Expedition.

Though news of his discovery of gold had been the spark that had ignited the Black Hills gold rush, he never struck it rich himself. Holding a number of the first mining claims on the alluvial lands along French Creek, he spent thirty long years digging up sediment and panning for gold on those claims until his death at the age of sixty-six in 1904. In his later years, it was said that he made more money from tourists interested in seeing where he discovered the first gold in the Black Hills than from any flakes of gold he may have found in the bottom of his gold pan.

She had to chuckle at the thought of men like Horatio Ross and her good-for-nothing husband. She had seen the likes of such men too many times over her long life. She knew there would always be those who would forever chase rainbows looking for their long-promised pot of gold, and those who just got down to work and built their fortunes from the ground up.

November 26, 1936

Little Italy, Custer, Custer County, South Dakota

Wake-Up Call

BILL HAD COME HOME for several days to celebrate Thanksgiving with his family. His work with the WPA had kept him away all summer and everyone looked forward to catching up. As had become a Barton family tradition, Thanksgiving and Velda's birthday would be celebrated together. At eight years old, Velda had become resigned to the fact she may never have a day of her own to celebrate her birthday.

As soon as Bill arrived back home, he set to work running an antenna wire up the tallest tree on his place. He had learned that the first commercial radio broadcast from Rapid City would go live on Thanksgiving Day. Under the call sign KOBH, standing for the Kall Of the Black Hills, the broadcast would come from the penthouse on top of the Alex Johnson Hotel, the tallest building in western South Dakota. Bill wasn't sure the old cat whisker crystal radio given to him by Alva would be able to pick up the broadcast but thought he would give it a try. The radio had been stored in its original wooden box which had been banged up considerably after all the family's moves. The radio had several sets of earphones which Bill hoped would allow the whole family to listen at the same time.

With his Delco Power Plant up and running and its batteries fully charged, Bill was confident he had everything set to receive the first radio broadcast from Rapid City. The irony of western South Dakota celebrating the arrival of radio at the same time the rest of the country and world was celebrating the arrival of television's first broadcast at the 1936 Berlin

Olympics was not lost on Bill. Since leaving Pleasant Valley, he had come to realize just how far behind western South Dakota was from the rest of the country.

Busy scraping a living out of his isolated homestead for nearly six years, Bill had come to rely on Alva's letters to keep him up to date on developments in the world. Now that he had been exposed to new things every day for the past couple of years, his interest in world events had grown considerably. Always on the lookout for the latest trends, getting the latest news had become more important to Bill than just about anything else. Having a commercial radio broadcast in the Black Hills was bound to change peoples' lives in ways hard to predict.

The biggest news over the summer had been the four gold medals won at the Berlin Summer Olympics by the American track and field athlete Jesse Owens. Owens, being black, had caused quite a stir in Berlin where Hitler had wanted to demonstrate to the world the superiority of the Arian race. In America feelings were mixed about Jesse Owens being crowned the fastest human on earth, with many people happy an American held the title, but not so pleased about the title being held by a black American.

The thing that bothered Bill most wasn't that the dictator Adolf Hitler had snubbed Owens in Berlin by refusing to shake his hand, it was that President Roosevelt hadn't taken the time to even meet with Jesse Owens when he returned to the United States after the Olympics. Fact was, Roosevelt never congratulated Owens for his unparalleled accomplishments. That an American hero couldn't receive a handshake from his own president because of the color of his skin was unacceptable to Bill. Jesse Owens's support for the Republican candidate, Alf Landan, for president in the 1936 presidential election may have caused Roosevelt a degree of discomfort at the time; however, Bill figured it was Roosevelt's need for support from his white southern state constituents that guided his decision to avoid having any photograph taken of him embracing a black man just before the election.

These kinds of thoughts always brought Bill back to the four colored stones he had placed at the base of his stone marker on his homestead in Pleasant Valley and the meaning his father had given them when he first saw them at the base of his own stone marker by Barton Lake in the badlands so long ago. Though they would forever retain their Lakota meanings, seeing them as representing the four races that made up America had given the four colored stones a deeper significance. Until everyone in America accepted the deeper truth that the four colored stones represented, the nation would forever be chained to a past mired in inequality and unable to form that more perfect union promised in the nation's founding documents.

Until Francis had departed for the Navy the year before, Bill hadn't realized how close he and his younger brother had become. Bill also recalled the day he drove John to Rapid City to live with Arvella, and her husband, Tom Overby, when John had given him a delicately carved turtle amulet that he had taken from the top of his stone maker in the badlands. With all the bad luck Bill had experienced, John hoped the Lakota good luck talisman might help turn things around. Bill felt the amulet in his pocket and trusted in its mystical powers. Bill, like his father, believed, if nothing else, the amulet would forever be a Barton link to the mysterious lands in and around the *Paha Sapa*.

Detrick had become a frequent visitor to Custer as his taxidermy creations found ready buyers among the many tourists who now made summer sojourns across the surrounding wastelands to the Black Hills and its oasis of ponderosa pine. Over the past summer, Detrick, with his eldest son, Herman, now fifteen years old, helped dig a basement near the squad tent on Bill and Kate's quarter-acre lot on Little Italy Road. Bill had gotten the basement started before he left to serve his six-month enlistment in the WPA. Detrick and Herman, with Bart and Velda pitching in, continued the project with pick and shovel until by summer's end they had an eighteen-by-twenty-foot hole carved five feet deep into the rock-hard ground. Bill's idea was to finish the basement, put in a staircase and slap a pitched roof on the whole shebang before winter so that the family could get out of the flimsy squad tent and into the warmth of a basement home before the first winter snow flurry. Bill figured they would be able to quickly build a house on top of the basement during the coming spring by hammering together modular wall components over the winter months, using the same construction methods he and Francis had worked out when they built the Minke Motor Lodge.

After the family had feasted on a meaty corn-fed turkey with all the fixings, everyone was in the mood for a big piece of Velda's birthday cake.

Rotten Johnny, going on a year and half, had become a terror on two wheels. Not having his Grandpa John around to hold him all the time, he had quieted down considerably, especially when he found out there was no one willing to run after him every time he squawked. Blowing out the candles on her cake, everyone wanted to know what Velda wished for.

"I wished for my own bedroom in our new house," she said, having helped out all summer to get the basement of their new house dug.

She couldn't wait to get out of the tent and into a house again, even if it was a basement house. She wondered sometimes on bone-chilling nights in the dead of winter when she burrowed deep under a pile of heavy blankets and homespun quilts whether she would ever be able to feel warm again.

"I promise you'll have one as soon as we can get it built," Bill said, and then added, "First we have to get the basement finished and then the house on top. After that we'll add bedrooms for everyone as soon as we can."

"I'll be happy just to get out of this godforsaken tent," Kate said, her arms akimbo as she stood at the stove where she had been preparing a second slice of cake for everyone.

"I'll second that," Bart said, wanting nothing more than to get out of the tent before it became a further embarrassment for him at school.

Now twelve years old, he had started looking at girls differently. He didn't want everyone to know that his family lived in a tent, like common hobos.

"What's this about you and Velda finding gold?" Bill said, wanting to know what the kids had been up to all summer.

Kate had told Bill the kids wanted to show him their gold. Considering how excited they were about what they had found, Kate herself was more than a little curious to find out.

"We worked that old sluice box, off and on, all summer up on Ruby Creek, right where Molly told us to, and we found gold!" Bart said, his voice raising on every word.

"How much gold?" Bill said, finding it hard to believe.

"Well, sir, this is what we found," Bart said, pulling a sizeable, corked medicine bottle filled with water out of his pocket.

The bottom of the bottle was more than half filled with a mound of tiny gold nuggets with suspended delicate flakes of gold dancing in the water in the upper half of the bottle. The sight of sparkling flakes of gold catching the light as they danced captivated everyone with their nearly weightless movements. When Bart shook the bottle, the gold flakes rose up and slowly spun in space, settling back down like the flakes of artificial snow in a snow globe. Bill understood for the first time in his life why the beauty of native gold swirling weightless, pure and delicate, had driven men mad down through the ages.

"Have you had it weighed?" Bill said, wondering what it might be worth and knowing the government had just raised the price of gold the year before, to a walloping thirty-five dollars an ounce up from the old rate of twenty-one dollars an ounce set back in 1834, a hundred years ago.

"We wanted you to see it first. Isn't it pretty?" Velda said, loving the way the gold flakes flickered when they twisted weightless in the light.

"Do you think there's more gold there?" Bill said.

"Not much in that spot anymore, we worked the black sand until we couldn't find any more, but we have some other places we scouted out," Bart said, a man with a plan and fully in charge.

They had hidden the sluice box under tree branches and hoped to go back to move it to a new spot after the end of school in the spring.

"We'll take the gold over to Hot Springs to have it weighed tomorrow. Wouldn't want folks around here nosing around," Bill said, thinking it might be best not to advertise the kids' gold find in Custer.

"We haven't told anyone," Velda said, understanding the need for secrecy, a point her brother never stopped reminding her about.

"What'd you think, Bill," Kate said, curious what the gold might be worth.

"I'd say they have over an ounce. It's probably worth forty, maybe fifty dollars," Bill said, realizing, when he said it, the shocking fact that fifty dollars was nearly equal to two months of WPA wages.

Kate too was surprised. With gold now worth thirty-five dollars an ounce, nearly double the old rate, it became clear that gold mining in the hills might pick up in the near future.

After catching up on everything that had happened in Custer over the past five months, Bill shared that he had received additional training as a surveyor's assistant, and like when he worked on the Pleasant Valley Road, he had found he had a knack for the job and enjoyed learning the technical aspects of the profession. He had borrowed several textbooks from an Army Corps of Engineers surveyor and planned to study to become a certified surveyor.

With everyone eager to listen to a radio broadcast for the first time, Bill set the radio box in the middle of the table and had everyone put in their earphones while Bill worked the dials on the cat whisker radio. It wasn't long until he hit on the scratchy sounds of an announcer's voice introducing the Strolling Songsters, "The Gold Dust Twins," Harvey Hindermeyer and Earle Tuckerman singing "The Little Old Log Cabin in the Lane."

Bill had heard the song many times before and knew "The Gold Dust Twins" where two white men who painted their faces black and pretended to be black men as part of their performing act. The song they were singing in a southern drawl was about an old black man who had grown old and feeble and no longer able to work. As a broken-down old man, he is left to pass his days in his broken-down log cabin on the lane. It was an old song that had been sung since the days when the slaves where first set free.

Bill wondered if black men would ever be truly free in a country unable to simply see them as men. The song also reminded him how no matter the color of a man's skin, society all too often provided no other opinion for a man but to accept his lot in life. Bill believed a man could remake himself and start anew. He refused to believe that a man should ever simply accept his lot in life as long as he was above ground and still drew breath.

He had learned, while working on the Iron Mountain Road, with its stone tunnels that framed Mount Rushmore, that the sculptor, Gutzon Borglum, had worked on a carving of the heroes of the Confederate States of America in Stone Mountain Georgia. As the story went, Borglum having fallen out with the organizers of the project after beginning work on General Lee's sculpture in 1923 suddenly quit in 1925, destroying all his original models for the curving. Following these events, there were rumors Borglum had been a member of the Ku Klux Klan, and if not, that he was sympathetic to their views of the black man's place in society.

Whatever his beliefs, Bill was glad Borglum had chosen to turn his back on the divisive Stone Mountain curving and to focus on something that helped to unite the country. Bill could see that Mount Rushmore had already started to attract tourist to the Black Hills. From Iron Mountain Road, the colossal faces of George Washington dedicated in 1934 and Thomas Jefferson, which Bill had witnessed being dedicated on the Fourth of July in 1935, were clearly visible as they faced east to meet the rising sun. Still covered in scaffolding, the faces of Abraham Lincoln and Theodore Roosevelt were taking shape and with a crew of over four hundred men chiseling flakes of granite off the mountain every day, they too would be completed in coming years. The scale of the project was enormous and filled Bill with pride. He reminded himself that he needed to catch up with Jeff Engel and Mike Robinson who had been working on the faces since moving from Wall. He was sure they would have plenty of stories to tell.

The following day, Bill and the kids drove down to Hot Springs. Much to everyone's disbelief, the gold was found to be pure and weighed in at one-and-three-quarters ounces. At thirty-five dollars an ounce, their sum-mer prospecting had earned them sixty-one dollars and twenty-five cents. For kids used to working for nickels and dimes, sixty-one dollars and twen-ty-five cents was a fortune. Upon learning how much the gold was worth, Bill was as surprised as the kids, and probably more so. Though he shared in their excitement, he felt an unwelcome knot forming like a hard ball in his guts. His WPA salary was only thirty dollars a month. As the family's breadwinner, he knew he had to do better, much better.

In the following days, Bill worked on preparing the basement, includ-ing installing a sturdy staircase. To cover his construction site from the ele-ments he tied a large tarp to the foundation blocks he had laid around the upper edge of the basement dig. To ensure water wouldn't collect on the flat, out-stretched tarp he stood up a center pole anchored in the basement to give the tarp a steep pitch, which made the whole affair look a lot like a Mongolian yurt. Before he knew it, he had to return to serve out his WPA enlistment. With promises to be home for Christmas, he was gone.

Bart and Velda were over the moon about all the money they had earned panning gold. The spot Molly Tillerman had sworn they would find gold had actually been the only place they found any. Bart suspected the spot was one Molly had worked in the past and knew the black sands still held gold. After finding gold in nearly every shovelful of sand in the first place they worked, they had worked several other places, but had come up nearly empty every time. Bart would give prospecting another try next summer, but knew he still needed to find steady work after school.

Velda hadn't told her brother that she was being teased at school for being an Indian, because she lived in a tent. She wasn't upset about being called an Indian, having always believed she was part Otoe and a member of the Eagle Clan like her great-grandma, Lucy Breeden. Of that, she was proud. What bothered her was that she lived in a tent when the other kids all lived in nice houses. Their teasing made her aware for the first time in her life that her family was poor and that being poor made her less likable in the eyes of the other kids. She had never thought about liking or not lik-ing someone because they had or didn't have something. In thinking about it, she found she didn't like that kind of small-mindedness one little bit.

December 22, 1936

Little Italy, Custer, Custer County, South Dakota

Never Back Down

PETER FISHER WAS A weasel. He had always been one. Since he was a small child, he had been called a weasel because he was always getting into everything, and always finding ways to get his share, whether he deserved it or not. As he grew up, he continued to be a weasel, refining his wily ways all the way through college. Now as a grown man, he even looked like a weasel. He wore his mousy gray hair slicked back from a sloped back brow, which pushed forward his close-set features and his shifty, dark beady eyes, making his weaselly looks all the more pronounced. That Peter had become a banker surprised no one, since his chosen profession fit his looks and character perfectly. His problem was none of these things; his problem was that his bank had made a major error and he had drawn the short straw; he would need to deliver the news and try to make amends with a man and his family, the bank had clearly wronged.

Peter was confident he could weasel the bank out of any real liability. After all, the man had owed them money at the time, and it was the bank's fiduciary responsibility to its investors that the debit be collected in full. That the bank collected more than it was due was an unfortunate error which had since been papered over. Legally, the bank was liable for damages to the aggrieved party. Peter, however, was sure he could smooth out any ruffled feathers. According to bank records, no one had suffered any real harm and the aggrieved party had seemingly bounced back without complaint.

With no forwarding address and no legal address on record, it had taken several weeks for the bank to track down their target. Peter, with spit-polished shoes and dressed in his best three-piece suit, set out from Rapid City in a shiny new Cord 810 Coupe with all the necessary paperwork he would need to have signed tucked neatly in his favorite patent leather brief-case, a graduation present given to him by his father, James Earl Fisher, the president of the bank.

Riding his bicycle past the Custer Country Courthouse on his way home, Bart noticed a group of boys from school looking at a yellow flier posted on the town's bulletin board. Curious to see what was so interesting, Bart decided to take a closer look. Pulling up, he couldn't help but notice the presence of the bully, Buster Geed. Buster was the same age as Bart and had been nothing but trouble since the first time they met. Buster, a head taller than most kids and weighing in at a good two hundred pounds, ruled the roost at Custer's Primary School. No one dared to challenge Buster, and he knew no one would.

"What're you doin' nosing around here, tent boy?" Buster said with a self-serving chuckle.

"Just curious," Bart said, hating everything about the inflated blowhard.

"Well, you know what curiosity did to the cat, don't ya?" Buster said, standing in front of Bart so he couldn't see what was posted on the bulletin board.

The other boys, all classmates, stood back, sensing a showdown. Bart, sick and tired of having Buster push him around all the time, decided then and there that today was the day it would come to an end, one way or another.

"Excuse me," Bart said as he stepped around Buster.

"Oh no you don't. That paperboy job is mine, tent boy. They ain't lookin' for some hobo trash like you," Buster growled, pulling Bart's arm and swing him away from the bulletin board.

Stumbling to keep his feet, Bart's temper almost got the better of him, but he kept his calm, just as his Grandpa John told him he should. When confronting a bully, he could hear his grandpa say, be sure to stay in control. Bullies are cowards deep down; they seek to impose their dominance by intimidation, his grandpa had taught him. They become confused when their prey shows no fear.

Standing his ground, Bart steadied himself, shifting his feet into a boxing stance before taking the full measure of Buster. He now knew why Buster wanted to make an example out of the outsider, he simply wanted to eliminate any potential challengers among the other local boys for the coveted paperboy job.

"What's this? Tent boy lookin' for a whoppin'?" Buster boasted, looking around at the other boys and confident he had everyone's attention.

"Seems we're goin' find out who's goin' be Custer's first paperboy," Bart heard himself say.

He wasn't sure why he said it, but he knew if they fought, the winner would be the only applicant the *Rapid City Journal* would ever see step forward to apply for the Custer paperboy job.

"You sayin' winner takes all, tent boy?" Buster boomed, puffing out his chest and once again making sure every boy there understood the stakes of his showdown with tent boy.

"That's what I'm sayin'," Bart said, more than a little surprised at how things had escalated so quickly.

"Well, alright then," Buster said, acting nonchalant and then quickly taking a swing at Bart's head in an attempt to catch him off guard.

Bart figured Buster would try something dirty, having seen him sucker punch more than one kid in the past. Bart saw Buster's haymaker coming a mile away. Though he had sidestepped the punch, Buster's big brass ring clipped Bart on the cheek, drawing first blood. Feeling the sharp sting of the glancing blow flipped a switch inside Bart, causing him to see red for the first time in his life. Angered by Buster's endless taunting since arriving in Custer, Bart let loose with a flurry of punches, each one filled with a year's worth of pent-up frustration from being relentlessly teased for being an outsider, for being tent boy, for being one of Custer's poor little ragamuffins.

Bart's first combination connected. His right smashed into Buster's jaw and his left smacked into his right eye. Buster, surprised by the punches, staggered back on his heels. Pushing Bart back with both arms, Buster reset his stance and realized for the first time in his life, he had a real fight on his hands. Full of bluster, Buster sprang forward, catching Bart with a combination of his own. Hitting Bart in the stomach, caused him to bend forward, where Buster delivered an uppercut powered by every ounce of strength he could muster. The massive punch lifted Bart completely off his feet and sent him sprawling flat on his back.

Bart, stunned by the mighty blow, nearly blacked out as he struggled to regain consciousness while desperately gasping for breath. Seeing a size-twelve boot bearing down on his head from his left, Bart rolled to his right and sprang back up on wobbly legs. Unsteady on his feet, he took a boxing stance and started circling Buster, who, playing to the other boys, pretended to lunge toward Bart, causing Bart to flinch at ever mock attack. Figuring he could finish off his prey whenever he pleased, Buster unwittingly gave Bart the time he needed to gather his senses, his strength, and his resolve.

Just when Buster seemed to be readying himself for the final kill, Bart bolted forward, running at Buster headfirst. Hitting Buster in the midsection, he pushed the heavyweight bully backward, driving his spine squarely into the sharp brick edging at the foot of the steep stairway leading up to the courthouse that had been a feature of the building's architecture since it's construction in 1881. As his back slammed into the sharp edge of immovable brick and concrete, Bart's head plunged deep into Buster's abdomen smashing his diaphragm and knocking all the air out of his lungs.

While Buster's face slowly turned an ungodly shade of purple, as he grasped for air like a fish out of water, Bart lit into him with a punishing barrage of punches that turned his once pudgy smirking face into a bruised and bloody mess. Bart finished him off with a jackhammer of a punch that connected directly on the end of Buster's nose, smashing it as flat as a pancake against his already bloodied face.

An audible gasp rose from the other boys as they watched in disbelief as Buster, their hero and their nemesis, the bully feared by every kid who ever attended Custer Primary School, hit the ground face first with a thud, knocked out stone cold. Hearing their reaction, Bart realized he had actually won. He then walked over to the bulletin board, reached up and pulled the yellow flier off its thumbtacks and shoved it into his coat pocket.

Buster, shaking his head as blood ran freely from of his broken nose, made his way back onto a pair of wobbly legs of his own. Without uttering a word, he straddled his bicycle and peddled off as Bart and the other boys watched in silence. Hopping on his bicycle, Bart turned to look at the other boys as he casually adjusted his rainbow-colored muffler and mittens that had been a source of unending ridicule over the last couple of years and that now served him as a kind of badge of honor, knowing no other kid would dare to tease him ever again.

"Well boys, I'll see ya in the funny papers," Bart said with a crooked grin.

Without saying more, he rode west, toward Little Italy and home, his head held high. He couldn't believe he had finally had his showdown with Buster Geed. Taking the advice he had learned from Grandpa John, Bart had looked behind his larger opponent for something sharp and solid and for the opportunity to drive him into it. Grandpa had guaranteed that it was generally a sure-fire way to chop a larger man down to size. Bart had to smile and thank his lucky stars that he had been born a Barton and had the sand to take care of himself and to never back down. Bullies be damned.

Egged on by the taunting of Timmy Geed, little brother of the bully Buster Geed, the other boys in Velda's class whooped and hollered like marauding Indians, as they circled her on their bicycles as she tried to ride home. Getting closer to Velda's bicycle with every turn, Timmy finally stopped his bicycle in front of Velda, causing her to stop mid-peddle.

"Get out of the way, Timmy. Go pick on someone else," Velda yelled, showing a stern face but worried what the little tyrant might do next.

"What kind of lunch box is that?" Timmy said, pulling a coffee can out of Velda bicycle basket. "This dirty Indian carries her lunch in a banged-up coffee can."

Velda and Bart both used coffee cans to carry their lunches, the family not having the money to spare to buy the same lunch boxes carried by the other kids. Velda had never thought anything of it until Timmy made fun of her for being so poor. Even living in a tent, which Velda had taken in stride, she had soon learned made her somehow inferior in the eyes of the other kids, who lived in houses and had nicer things than she did.

Reaching in her coat pocket she felt the knotted end of the old sock she had dropped a good-sized dirt clod into at the beginning of the school year. Grandpa John had taught her that sometimes it was alright to even the odds, especially if you're a girl and your opponent is a boy. He had showed her how to make what he called a slapjack out of an old sock. He warned her never to use it unless you had to, but not to hesitate if you did.

"Give me back my lunch box," Velda demanded.

"Lunch box? This thing is nothing more than a rusty old coffee can," Timmy said, tossing the coffee can into the bar ditch, causing the lid to fly off, spilling the utensils tucked inside.

"Damn you, Timmy! Look what you've done," Velda yelled, angry she had to put up with the little bully every day at school since moving to Custer.

Timmy, wanting to follow in his big brother's footsteps, felt he had to audition in front of the other kids to show them he was a tough guy, just like his brother. When his brother moved on to secondary school, Timmy wanted to take his place as king of the schoolyard.

Getting off her bicycle, Velda went over and picked her coffee can lunch box and contents out of the bar ditch and put everything back in her basket. Timmy, wanting to make one last show, got off his bicycle, walked up close to Velda and took the coffee can back out of the basket and threw it back in the bar ditch. Velda reached her hand back in her coat pocket, gripped the end of her homemade slapjack, and readied herself for action.

"I think you better fetch that and put it back in this here basket," Velda said coldly, stiffening her back.

"What? It stays right where it is. It's just a piece of trash, just like you, isn't it?" Timmy taunted, his nose almost touching hers, his breath as bad as he was.

When Timmy reached out to shove her, Velda whipped the slapjack out of her pocket and swung it around into the side of his head so fast Timmy didn't know what hit him. The dirt clod exploding inside the sock, thankfully cushioned a near lethal blow to the boy's temple that might have laid him out for good. Velda was sure the other kids hadn't seen the slapjack, which she quickly tucked back in her pocket when Timmy went down. Knocked onto his behind and nearly senseless, he stared back up at Velda in utter shock and disbelief.

Ashamed and embarrassed, he quickly scrambled back up on wobbly legs, hopped on his bicycle, and peddled away before the other boys could see he was starting to cry. Freddie Ward, a boy who sat behind Velda in school, went over to the bar ditch and came back with the coffee can and its contents. Putting everything back in her basket, he and the other boys got on their bicycles and made ready to leave.

"It wasn't our idea, Velda. We don't really think you're a dirty Indian," Freddie said, believing he was apologizing.

"I am part Indian, Freddie, and proud of it," Velda said, having always been proud of being part Otoe and a member of the Eagle Clan.

Velda never understood the prejudice of the other kids against Indians who had once been the only people who lived in these lands. Velda's retort left Freddie nearly speechless, not knowing what to think or how to respond.

"See you in school?" Freddie finally said sheepishly, ashamed they had ganged up on a girl and hoping she would forgive them.

He especially hoped Velda would forgive him. He had always secretly had a crush on her. And now, though he would never admit it, he was in awe of her. She had been the only person he had ever seen whip Timmy Geed in a fair fight. Like most of the other boys, he couldn't have been happier about it.

"Yeah, see you in school, Freddie," Velda said, pulling on her multicolored mittens and adjusting her matching muffler.

Taking one last survey of the boys' faces, her stare was greeted by only down-turned eyes. Getting back on her bicycle, she peddled toward home, holding her head high. She had never felt prouder of herself.

Reaching up, she touched the cougar fang hanging around her neck and remembered the day on Pilger Mountain when she had fought a cougar and won. She hadn't really known what happened in that confrontation but had been happy to come out the winner. Her fight with Timmy Geed was different. She could remember her every move. She now understood how remembering every detail made all the difference. She pledged never to forget this day and how it feels to win.

After driving up and down Little Italy Road several times, Peter Fisher soon discovered there were only a handful of crudely built shacks along the dirt road, many of which looked more suitable for livestock than anything else. Unsure which hovel might be the residence of the Barton family, he decided to get directions from the only man he saw working outside. Pulling into the driveway, Peter was met by a large black and white collie that barked nonstop at the unwelcome intrusion. Afraid to get out of the car, he rolled down his window and call out to the man hammering together what looked like roof rafters, though he couldn't see any house under construction.

"Hello, I think I'm lost," Peter yelled in the direction of the man who had stopped hammering and was walking over to his car as he wiped sweat off his brow with a red bandana.

"Don't worry about the dog. Sandy's all bark. He won't bite," Bill said as he walked up to the car.

"I was looking for the Barton family home. I understand they live around here," Peter said, hopeful.

"As it so happens you pulled into the right place. I'm Bill Barton. What can I do for you?" Bill said, having never seen the man in his life and wonder why such a fancy dandy would be looking for him.

"My name's Peter Fisher of the First National Bank in Rapid City," Peter said as he stepped out of the car and extended a well-manicured, soft, callous-free hand.

"It's been over a year since we last heard anything from the bank," Bill said, finding it difficult to hold down his anger, considering everything the family had been through over the past couple of years.

"Yes, yes. An oversight we hope to correct," Peter said in an upbeat tone, sensing tension in Bill's voice and wanting to avoid things escalating into a shouting match or worse.

After getting out of his car and exchanging an awkward handshake with Bill, Peter stood next to his car and held his ground with a friendly smile on his face as Sandy poked his nose up between Peter's legs and sniffed his behind. The indignity of having to deal with people like Bill Barton and his mangy hound upset Peter to no end, but he had a job to do, and he needed to get it done in the bank's favor, of course.

"Correct? What do we need to correct? You already took everything I owned," Bill said, trying like the devil not to blow up.

"That's why I'm here. We sold your homestead and the livestock, and your debit has been completely cleared," Peter cooed in reassuring tones.

"And so? What're we correcting?" Bill said, knowing there must be some urgent reason for an officer of the bank, dressed to the nines, to come all the way to Custer to talk to him in person.

"Might I suggest we have a seat, and I can go over the papers I have brought along," Peter said as reassuringly as he could.

"Papers? What papers?"

"Might we have a seat and I'll show you."

Pointing the way, Bill ushered Peter over to the squad tent and held back the flap and invited Peter inside, "After you."

"Yes, of course," Peter managed to say, not knowing what to think and only realizing at that moment that the Barton family was living in an old, tattered squad tent, suitable for no better than common hobos.

That the Barton family was living in such desperate conditions in the middle of the winter in subzero temperatures sent Pete's mind reeling. Peter knew, if the courts ever got wind of this, the bank would be in real trouble.

"Welcome. I'm Kate Barton and the little one over there is Johnny, our youngest," Kate said, surprised to have such a well-dressed stranger step into their humble abode.

After exchanging pleasantries, Peter, Bill, and Kate settled down at the table over a cup of coffee and apple pie.

"This pie is delicious," Peter said, meaning every word. He had never had pie that tasted so good.

"I bake for the Roadway Inn. I make an extra pie from time to time," Kate said, please the stranger liked her pie and wondering what exactly was going on.

"Well, let's get down to business," Peter said, polishing off his pie.

"You mention the need to correct something," Bill said, letting the words hang between them.

"Yes, yes. Well, as I told you, we were able to clear your debt by selling the livestock and one hundred twenty acres of your land," Peter said quickly, hoping to avoid any interruption.

"One hundred twenty acres, you say. What happened to the other forty?" Bill jumped in.

"Yes, yes. Well, I have papers here that grant those acres to you," Peter said, forcing a broad smile, though his eyes betrayed him.

"So, you're saying our eviction was unnecessary," Bill said, wearing his own crooked smile, though his smile held a more sinister meaning, which Peter had no problem reading.

"We agree, your family's eviction was unfortunate; however, you need to understand that at the time, the bank's calculations indicated the need to sell everything. It was our fiduciary responsibility to recoup the bank's money," Peter said, as a bead of sweat slowly worked its way down his forehead.

"I see. What I don't see is why two years ago in the dead of winter your bank needed to throw my family out into the cold, when my wife was expecting our son Johnny over there," Bill said, having difficulty holding his voice in a calm steady tone.

"Well, we . . .," Peter said, his mind racing to find the words to steer the conversation back on track.

"Yes, as you said you had . . . let me see . . . as you put it . . . your fiduciary responsibility and all."

"Yes, we . . ."

"Yes, you . . . now want us to say all is fine and dandy after two years of living in a tent and even worse."

"Why yes, but . . ."

"Yes, but now, we can have our cabin and forty acres of land back. No harm, right?"

"Well, yes, but . . ."

"Yes, but exactly. What about the last two years that my blind father, my pregnant wife, our young children, and now our infant son have all had to live like a pack of homeless bums?"

"Well, I don't . . ."

"You don't? Don't what, Mr. Fisher? Don't understand what it is to have a heart," Bill said, fighting to keep his emotions under control and knowing if he could, he just might win this showdown.

He had spent the last two years scrambling to keep the family afloat. Finding out they had been thrown out of their home unnecessarily in the middle of the winter, because of an error made by some pompous ass like Peter Fisher was almost too much to accept.

"I came here to try to make things right," Peter said, finally finding his voice.

"Tell us how you plan to do that," Bill said, knowing there was no way anyone could erase the last two years.

"Your debt has been completely retired and you get the free and clear deed to your cabin and forty acres of land," Peter said, as if he himself was gifting the land to Bill.

"You told me that earlier. The fact that we can have the deed to land we seem to already own is not much by way of compensation for our wrongful eviction," Bill said, having learned a great deal about eviction laws from other farmers in Pleasant Valley who had also been summarily thrown off their land.

"Compensation? It was our fiduciary responsibility to recoup the value of your loan," Peter said, shaken by any mention of liability or, God forbid, any need of further compensation.

"So, you were only upholding your fiduciary responsibility, right," Bill said.

"Yes, that is so."

"You just wanted to secure the return of the bank's money, right?"

"Yes, that is so."

"Well, it seems you did exactly that. However, you haven't mentioned the rent you owe me for the use of my cabin over the past two years," Bill said, with a grin on his face and his eyebrows raised.

"Rent?"

"Yes, rent. You know, it's when you pay someone for the use of something that's not yours. You must understand it is my fiduciary responsibility to my family to ensure the most profitable and efficient use of our limited assets."

"Rent? I'm afraid . . ."

"Don't be afraid, Mr. Fisher. I am not asking for moving expenses, wrongful eviction compensation, pain and suffering or any of a number of other possible charges. At the very least, we are owed compensation for wrongful eviction, that much I know," Bill said, making it clear to Mr. Fisher he was not dealing with some uninformed country bumpkin.

"Moving expenses? Rent? Wrongful eviction compensation? Mr. Barton, I came here to present you with the deed to forty acres of land and papers showing that your debit to the bank has been retired. You are free and clear with forty acres of land to boot. Is that not good news?" Peter said, proud of himself for driving home his practiced narrative.

"Look around, Mr. Fisher. Take a good long look around at what you so cavalierly call free and clear. My family's living in a tattered squad tent full of holes in the middle of the winter, Mr. Fisher. Your bank put us here, through no fault of our own. As you say, our debit is clear, and our home and forty acres in Pleasant Valley still belongs to us—and it seems it always has. We shouldn't be here, Mr. Fisher. We shouldn't have been thrown out of our home. Your bank needs to consider its fiduciary responsibility should this wrongful eviction of a blind man and a pregnant woman in the dead of winter ever go to court. I think paying rent on the use of my cabin and forty acres of prime farmland for the past two years would be a bargain, all things considered," Bill said, sensing he might be one lucky sucker out of millions who landed himself the Fisher-man for a change.

"Rent, yes, I see your point," Peter said, not liking how he had gotten on the wrong side of things, but reluctantly understanding how things could get far worse.

"I figure thirty dollars a month, a dollar a day. That's what folks get paid around here these days," Bill said matter-of-factly.

"Thirty dollars!" Peter blurted before gathering himself. "Let me recommend ten dollars a month. I believe I can get the bank to accept this amount when I explain the hardship your family has suffered."

"Let's just split the difference. We demand no less than twenty dollars a month. That's four hundred and eighty dollars for two years. If you can draw up the papers and pay in cash, we can call it free and clear between us," Bill said with a look on his face that told Peter Fisher in no uncertain terms that the time for negotiations was over.

"Twenty dollars a month . . . yes, I'll make a call to the bank from the courthouse and be right back. I'm sure the bank will agree to your terms. We can draw up the papers when I return in an hour. Is that agreeable?" Peter said in haste, knowing the bank would be better off putting the Barton family behind them.

Fact was, if the case ever hit a courtroom, the bank may need to pay a damn sight more than four hundred and eighty dollars.

"Yes, Mr. Fisher. That would be agreeable. Oh and, don't forget, we want our payment in cash, no bank drafts," Bill said, making it clear when they finalized their business, it would be final.

Watching Peter head back to Custer in his shiny new Cord, Bill felt full of energy and hope. The unexpected visit had changed his fortunes in an instant. He not only had the return of his cabin and forty acres of farmland in Pleasant Valley, but he would soon have four hundred eighty dollars in cash, almost three times the money he had earned working full-time for the WPA over the past six months. He would be able to buy the lumber for the house and pay off the loan on the lot. With the basement almost ready to move into, Christmas would be a happy one at the Barton home this year.

Just as Bill was pondering how they would spend the bonanza they would soon receive, Bart rolled into the yard and quickly ducked into the tent without saying a word. Wondering what the trouble might be, Bill started back toward the tent when Velda rolled into the yard.

"Hey, Pa. Is the basement ready yet?" Velda said, wanting with all her heart to get out of the tent and into a house, even a basement house, before the start of school in January.

"Just about. Your Grandpa Detrick will come with your Uncle Herman to help put up the rafters and nail on a roof. We can then move everything into the basement," Bill said, brushing aside Bart's odd behavior.

With the money from the bank, he would even be able to put in the windows he hadn't been able to afford. Having the windows would brighten up the basement a great deal. They might say money can't buy happiness, and this indeed may be true; however, it can buy the things that can help you be happy, of this, Bill believed, there was little doubt.

Turning to follow Velda into the tent, Bill almost got hit by a car with an angry looking driver that had slammed up their driveway and skidded to a stop only a few feet short of the front of the tent. Bounding out of the car was a mean looking battle-ax, with her hair in disarray, and her makeup and clothing clearly thrown on in haste.

Giving Bill the evil eye, the wild-looking woman stormed straight into the tent. Slumped over in the back seat of the car was a large boy whose face looked like it had been put through meat grinder. His nose was clearly broken and bleeding and bend to one side. Before Bill could reach the tent flap, the battle-ax came back out of the tent, stumbling backwards as Kate menacingly waved a rolling pin in front of the woman's nose as she lambasted her for charging into her home uninvited.

"Now what's this all about, Mrs. Geed?" Kate shouted, upset that the high and mighty Betty Geed thought she could invade their home without an invitation or a thought.

Kate had suffered enough indignity since coming to Custer and wasn't about to take any more from the likes of Betty Geed or anyone else.

"Your son's a monster! He attacked my little Buster and beat the hell out of him," Betty Geed screeched.

"Your little Buster is the school bully. He's the one who beats up on other kids, isn't he?" Kate said, having heard all she wanted to about the bully Buster Geed, which everyone in town knew was a no-good kid who preyed on weaker kids.

Bart listened from inside the tent. After exchanging a knowing look with Velda, they both nodded. He knew he needed to fess up about his fight with Buster. What he didn't know was that it wouldn't be long before his sister would have to do the same.

"Buster and I had a fair fight," Bart said matter-of-factly as he stepped out of the tent.

"Fair fight? Look at my son's goddamn face! There's nothing fair about that, you little hooligan," Betty yelled, seeing clearly Bart's face had also been bloodied.

"Let's ask Buster what happened," Bill said, sensing there would be no peace until they got to the bottom of things.

"No need to talk to him. Your son's the one who needs to be punished," Betty groaned.

"Buster, what do you say?" Bill said, as he rapped his knuckles on Buster's rolled-up car window.

"We had a fight," Buster mumbled with his head down, unwilling to look up to meet Bill eye to eye.

"Was it a fair fight?" Bill pushed, staring down at Buster with a stern it's-time-to-tell-the-truth look on his face.

"Yeah, yeah, we fought about who would take the new paperboy job. The job was to go to the winner. Bart . . . well . . . he . . . well, he . . . he won," Buster finally said, the words the toughest words to have ever passed through his lips.

In saying them, somehow, he felt free, truly free for the first time in his life. He had always hated living a lie, having to always be the tough guy. His father had insisted he be the toughest kid in school, just like his father had been when he was a kid. Buster never liked having to pretend to be the tough guy all the time.

"Well, Mrs. Geed. I think we know what happened," Bill said flatly, hoping to wrap things up.

"But look at my son. His face, it's . . .," Betty said, almost pleading for someone to save her from what had happened.

Flustered and not knowing how she would be able to tell Buster's father that his son had lost a fair fight, her face quivered at the thought. She knew there would be hell to pay and that she, like always, would be the one making most of the payments.

"Boys'll be boys. He'll heal up and maybe he'll stay clear of fighting in the future. We'll see to Bart, never you mind," Kate said, her arms akimbo with the rolling pin handle still gripped tightly in her right hand.

Just when everyone had settled down and Betty was about to pull out of the driveway, a bicycle came rolling up, its young rider bleeding from the left side of his head. From the look on Betty's face, Bill knew the drama that had just closed was about to have a second act.

"Timmy! Oh, my God! What's happened?" Betty cried as she sprang back out of the car to embrace her young son.

Timmy had seen the family car turn onto Little Italy Road and decided to try to catch up with his mother so he might get a ride home. The side of his head throbbed with pain as tears streaked his cheeks. All he wanted to do is get home without anyone seeing him crying.

"Nothing, Ma. Just fell off my bike," Timmy lied.

"You haven't been fighting, have you?" Betty said, confused.

Betty knew Timmy had been trying to follow in his big brother's footsteps, just as his father insisted. Seeing a huge red welt, the size of a fist, on the left side of Timmy's head, told Betty clear enough that her son had been fighting. From the looks of things, somebody had caught him with a powerful right-handed haymaker that had damn near taken his head off.

Unable to hold back his tears, Timmy started crying when he realized his mother somehow knew he was lying.

"What happened, mister? You better tell me before I have to tear into your hide myself," Betty barked, upset about Buster and now having to deal with Timmy in front of the whole Barton family no less.

"Barton did it," Timmy blubbered.

"Barton? Did that monster beat you up, too?" Betty said, pointing at Bart, her face beet red with anger.

At that moment, if killing had been legal, Bart may not have lived out the day. Just as Betty wound up to let loose with a fresh barrage of swear words, she was stopped dead in her tracks when she heard her young son's reply.

"No. It wasn't . . ." Timmy stammered, embarrassed.

"It wasn't! Who then? Tell me, mister, who did you fight with?" Betty screeched.

Velda, listening from inside the tent, knew it was her turn to step out and fess up, just like her big brother had done.

"Me," Velda said in a stout little voice, as she stepped out of the tent with her backbone ramrod straight, shoulders thrown back, and her chin held high.

It was plain to anyone who cared to look, Velda was proud of her actions and was the kind of person who never backed down no matter the odds. She might be a girl, but she was no wilting violet. Her clinched fists put a clear double exclamation mark on that fact.

"You?" Betty exclaimed, looking down at Velda and then at the huge welt on the side of her bawling son's head.

"Yes, ma'am. He took my lunch box and threw it in the ditch and then called me names and shoved me. I hit him," Velda admitted and then looked from Betty Geed to her parents and awaited the verdict.

"Timmy Geed, you tell me now, is that what happened?" Betty said, her mind spinning, unable to process what seemed unbelievable. "Did you shove and fight with this little girl?"

How much hell would have to be paid when their father came home, she could no longer calculate. Both sons beaten bloody on the same day by the same family, with one of them beaten by a girl no bigger nor taller than a garden gnome.

"Yes, Ma. Me and the other boys were just having fun. I might've accidently bumped into her, before she hit me," Timmy moaned, not really sure what had happened and not sure how Velda could have thrown such a hard punch and not broken her own hand.

Hearing her son's confession, Betty turned and quickly threw Timmy's bicycle into the trunk of the car, not bothering to tie down the lid. She then grabbed her wounded, whimpering son and strong-armed him into the backseat of the car, where he joined his big brother, who sat hunched over still bleeding from a broken nose. Too embarrassed to meet the glaring stares of the Barton family and without saying a word, she slammed her car door, swung the car around, and spun her tires, throwing gravel in every direction all the way to the main road, where she had to swerve to miss a shiny new Cord Coupe that had just turned onto Little Italy Road. Bucking out onto the main highway, she stepped on the gas and sped toward Four-mile Corner with her trunk lid bouncing up and down on Timmy's bicycle all the way until she was out of sight.

Pulling up in front of the tent, Peter Fisher was surprised to be greeted by the whole Barton clan. He was further surprised when he noted Kate was holding a rolling pin in her right hand like a club, her young son's face was bleeding from what looked like a recent fight, and his little daughter was standing ramrod straight with her arms akimbo with such a cross look on her face Peter couldn't imagine what might have put it there.

From the cloud of dust drifting in the air, it was evident that the car that had nearly run him off the road, with a crazed, wild-eyed woman behind the wheel and two battered kids in the backseat, had just sped out of the Barton driveway.

Assessing the mood of the Barton family before he stepped out of his car, Peter decided no one would be talking about what had just happened. From his own experience with Bill Barton, he concluded that it didn't pay to have a run-in with any of the ornery Barton bunch.

The Barton family's business with Peter Fisher didn't take long. The bank had seen the logic in paying rent on the Barton family's land over the past two years and even made it an even five hundred dollars with best wishes for a joyful Christmas. With the deed to their cabin and forty acres of land in Pleasant Valley signed back over to Bill and Kate, the final settlement for all other debits drawn up and authorized, and the agreed cash settlement handed over, Peter was out the front flap of the tent with a cash receipt in hand and gone faster than a jackrabbit being chased by a hungry coyote.

Bill leafed through the documents and smiled seeing everything was in order. He then picked up the envelope stuffed full of fifty ten-dollar bills and started laughing. Kate soon joined in. She too couldn't believe their good fortune, considering everything the family had gone through over the past two years after being driven from their Shangri-La on Pilger Mountain.

At first, Bart and Velda had sheepishly stayed quiet not knowing what their parents might do to them for fighting. With their patents unable to stop laughing, they couldn't help but laugh at their parents, who were acting silly. Soon everyone was laughing, even little Johnny.

"So, you beat up Buster Geed, the school bully," Bill said, looking at Bart and still chuckling.

"Yep. I think I broke his nose. I'll be applying for the *Rapid City Journal* paperboy job tomorrow. I don't think any of the other boys want the job," Bart said proudly, but still worried his parents might punish him for fighting.

"Well, you shouldn't fight. Unless you have to. I think you already know that much," Bill said sternly. "Let's not have any more fights. I think we can leave it at that."

"And you, Velda. Did you beat up poor little Timmy Geed," Bill said, his voice no longer jovial, though the wide grin on his face betrayed his serious tone.

"He took my things, Pa. He called me names and shoved me. I had to fight back," Velda said, trying to act the part of a big girl.

Seeing the grin on her Pa's face, she knew he was pleased she could take care of herself.

"Did you kids use any of your Grandpa John's ol' tricks, to, let's just say, even the odds some?" Bill said, looking from face to face.

"Yeah, grandpa showed me how to make a slapjack," Velda said, and then added, "I put a dirt clod in a sock. Timmy's bigger than I am."

"I used the brick edging at the bottom of the courthouse steps, just like grandpa taught us. It did the trick. Buster didn't know what hit him," Bart said, wondering why his Pa asked.

"Alright then. I guess you know now your Grandpa John knows what he is talking about, leastwise some of the time," Bill said with a chuckle.

"Now, Bill, don't encourage them. People shouldn't fight," Kate said out of a sense of obligation to say the right thing, more than any conviction in the words.

"Your Ma's right. Velda, you should be more careful not to beat up all the boys. If you do, who'll be brave enough to ask you to the school dance?" Bill said with a chuckle and a wink.

Turning to Bart he added, "And you, Bart, stop picking on bullies bigger than you are."

"Bill, you know these kids shouldn't be fighting. We're not animals," Kate said, not liking the fact her kids had to fight, but proud they had the sand to do so and happy they could hold their own.

"You're right, Kate. The kids shouldn't fight. But like Grandpa John, and his daddy, Great-Grandpa Bill back in Iowa, always said: If you do have to fight, give it your best, and of course, it always pays to win, even if you have to even the odds a bit to do so," Bill said, meaning every word.

They had all fought their battles that day and come out on top. It doesn't always work that way in life, and they all knew it, all too well. They had all failed in the past and they had all lived with their past failures; but this time, everything had worked out, and there was no good reason not to enjoy every delicious second of it. Bill knew such feelings were a rare treat and should be savored. Looking at the happy faces around him, he smiled back with a knowing grin.

June 15, 1940

Little Italy, Custer, Custer County, South Dakota

Igloos on the Prairie

WITHOUT ANY OTHER REAL options, Bill had reenlisted in the WPA in January 1937 and continued to reenlist, year after year, serving seven successive six-month tours until the spring of 1940. Learning that the Army had plans to build an Ordnance Depot south of Edgemont, Bill had been encouraged by his foreman to look into signing on as a surveyor, considering the Army would need to survey and lay out the massive twenty-one-thousand-acre site, before they started construction. To look into possible employment opportunities, Bill decided to drive down to Hot Springs, where the U.S. Army had set up their headquarters for the project. Studying nights for over two years, Bill had been able to pass his final exams and become a certified surveyor in the fall of 1939. He hoped his training might be helpful in landing him a full-time job.

Much to his surprise, he was hired as a surveyor on the spot. Desperate to find men with critical skills in the sparsely populated region of southwestern South Dakota, finding someone trained to be a surveyor was a boon to the U.S. Army's project team. Being welcomed with open arms had been exciting for Bill until he realized he had no idea what the job paid. Flipping through the multipage employment contract, he soon understood the dangers of working around explosive ordnance. Even though there would be risks working on an ordnance depot, he didn't figure it would be any more dangerous than many of the other job available in the region.

Mining, logging, sawmills, and even working on carving faces into Mount Rushmore were dangerous jobs that paid very little. The depression still had a grip on the nation and a stranglehold on western South Dakota, where farmers and ranchers continued to struggle to recover from years of drought. All Bill hoped for was a steady job that paid more than a dollar a day, the poverty wage he had earned for the past five years, since leaving Pleasant Valley.

Getting to the final page of the contract, Bill read the clause about the federal minimum wage, which it stated had been set at thirty cents an hour in October 1939. This news came as a hell of a surprise to Bill who had been working for little better than ten cents an hour. He would have done cartwheels in celebration if he had ever made three dollars for a ten-hour day. Feeling his heartbeat race a little faster, he zeroed in on the wage for the position of surveyor, plus the added hazardous duty bonus for workers on ordnance depots. Reading and rereading the total wage, he couldn't believe his eyes when he read the position paid a dollar and twenty-five cents an hour plus a hazardous duty bonus of fifty-cents an hour for a total hourly wage of one-dollar and seventy-five-cents. This worked out to eighty-four dollars for a forty-eight-hour week; more money than Bill Barton had ever made in his life. He couldn't believe he would be pulling down nearly four thousand four hundred dollars a year, a king's ransom for a man who had scraped by making less than four hundred dollars a year.

Signing on as a surveyor at the U.S. Army's Black Hills Ordnance Depot with a shaky hand, he was ordered to report for work in Igloo as soon as possible. All Bill knew about Igloo was that it was a new town somewhere south of Edgemont, smack-dab in the middle of nowhere, that was being laid out to house personnel who would support ordnance depot operations. On his drive back home, he wasn't quite sure how he would break the news to the family that they had finally hit the jackpot. The downside was that they would have to move from their new home in Custer back into a tent on a treeless prairie south of Edgemont. Asking the family to give up everything they had struggled to build over the past five years to make yet another fresh start wouldn't be easy, but he knew there was no other way. The U.S. Army had made him an offer he couldn't refuse.

Bart had landed the paperboy job after his showdown with Buster Geed and had grown his paper route from the original seventeen customers the *Rapid City Journal* had turned over to him to just over a hundred. At a half a cent a paper, he made fifty cents a day for less than two hours of work. Between his paper route and other odd jobs, Bart was making over two hundred dollars a year, a goodly sum considering it was more than half what his father made holding down a full-time job with the WPA.

At sixteen, he dreamed of graduating the twelfth grade and enlisting in the Navy, like his Uncle Alva and Uncle Francis, or in the Army, like his Uncle Herman. Herman was the first of his mother's German immigrant family to serve in the U.S. military. Bart was proud that Barton men down through the generations had served their country from as far back as any-one could remember.

Arrived back home after completing his round of deliveries, Bart set about doing his chores around the house. He knew that Velda and Johnny were tending Lyn Blay's sheep up on Thunderhead Mountain and would be moving the sheep into corrals near the north end of Little Italy Road for their annual shearing. The two planned to be back home by noon.

He hoped his Pa would have good news, when he returned from Hot Springs. He had driven down to Hot Springs to look into possible job op-portunities with the U.S. Army. According to his Pa, they had advertised for skilled laborers for a project somewhere south of Edgemont. Bart knew there was nothing south of Edgemont but vacant prairie in every direction. He couldn't imagine what kind of work the U.S. Army would have in that desolate corner of the world. If it paid better than a dollar a day, he was pretty sure his Pa would take it. Finding work had been difficult since leav-ing Pleasant Valley and now that his Pa was nearly forty years old, starting a new career was becoming more and more unlikely.

The mountain air was cool, crisp, and clean. Velda could see all the way to Wyoming from her perch high up on a rock ridge overlooking a rich green meadow below. She loved working as a shepherd during her summer holi-days. Sandy was getting on in years but could still manage to corral a large herd of sheep without running his legs off. Lyn Blay, who ran a large ranch north of Little Italy Road, liked to graze his sheep on Forest Service land around Thunderhead Mountain north of Custer, where the meadows were lush and the rounded domes of pinkish gray granite that capped every ridge stood in testament of the forces of nature that had molded them over eons of time. Like the bare outcroppings of granite that shot up out of the forest floor around Mount Rushmore and had come to be called the Needles, the rounded granite ridges that surrounded Custer reminded all who beheld them of the incredible age of the Black Hills.

From the dawn of the Precambrian age down through eons of time, the Black Hills had witnessed the evolution of life itself. Around the Black Hills and in nearly every nook and cranny, the fossilized remains of ancient life could be found, from seashells and ammonites that had once thrived in warm Cambrian seas to the remains of Jurassic dinosaurs and more recent creatures like mastodons and saber-toothed tigers.

The Black Hills had once been an island in the middle of a vast ocean before the continent of North America ever rose from the sea. Worn down to its core granite dome, the Black Hills had remained as an island covered in a rich pine forest in the middle of a vast treeless prairie with rippling buffalo grass replacing the rippling ocean waves that once washed up on the beaches that now made up the Dakota Ridge, the ridge of sedimentary soils that ring the ovular-shaped Black Hills formation. It is this ancient mysterious beauty that captivated Pappy Breeden when he first saw the hills in 1857. It is the same beauty that convinced John Barton and his son Bill Barton to homestead in these unique and enchanting lands.

To Velda, the Black Hills was all she had ever known. Unlike her older brother, she had no memory of living on the prairie. Returning to graze sheep on Thunderhead Mountain every year was like returning to Pilger Mountain, the place that held her fondest memories. Since leaving Pilger Mountain, life had been hard. Living in a single-room squad tent with the whole family had been difficult over the years. She looked forward to finally having a bedroom of her own. She would soon be twelve years old and had noticed her body was changing. She was becoming a woman, and as one, she longed for privacy, a place of her own, something she had never had.

Johnny, now five years old, had insisted on coming along, just like she had done in Pleasant Valley when her brother had the chore of tending to the family's goat herd. Johnny was big for his age and had little difficulty keeping up, which allowed her to tend the sheep without having to tend him as well. It was Johnny who had first spotted the cougar. They had watched as the she-lion made her way to a shallow ravine on the south end of Thunderhead Mountain. Working their way down the slope, they approached the ravine from a ledge high above in hopes of finding out where the cougar had gone.

Silently, they crawled to the lip of the ledge to peek over. Though they couldn't see anything moving, they heard a low growl off to their left. Slowly, careful not to make any quick moves, they turned their heads to see where the growl had come from. Their eyes soon locked onto and tracked the cougar as she nimbly worked her way cross a granite outcropping to a small cave just below them.

Amazed, they watched as two cubs emerged from the cave and greeted their mother. Playfully batting the cubs around, the three cougars wrestled below them, completely unaware they were being observed. Careful to stay silent and motionless, Velda and Johnny remained frozen like statues for several minutes as they beheld a moment in time neither would ever forget. When the mother and her cubs disappeared into the cave, Velda and Johnny worked their way back to Sandy and the sheep.

It was on days like this that Velda had fallen in love with Thunderhead Mountain, believing it would never change. Little did she and Johnny know in the summer of 1940 that in just eight short years a Polish American sculptor named Korczak Ziolkowski, who had worked on Mount Rushmore, and a well-known Oglala Lakota chief named Henry Standing Bear would dedicate Thunderhead Mountain as the future home of the Crazy Horse Monument by blasting the first chunks of granite off its rugged face. Henry Standing Bear, who had witnessed the carving of the presidents' faces at Mount Rushmore, believed that Indians also had great leaders in their past. He wanted the carving of Crazy Horse Monument to serve as a way to immortalize in stone one the greatest leaders of the *Oceti Sakowin Oyate*, the People of the Seven Council Fires, known as the Sioux Nation.

After gathering the sheep, Velda and Johnny drove them across Highway 385, the road leading north from Custer to Hill City, into pastures owned by Lyn Blay located just north of Little Italy Road. With the sheep corrals located on the north end of Little Italy Road, it was easy for them to walk home after corralling the last animal. In coming days, the sheep would be sheared and sent back out to pasture. Velda would once again drive them back across Highway 385 to the meadows around Thunderhead Mountain. She had no doubt little Johnny, her ever-present sidekick, would be tagging along.

Kate had been busy all morning. Her father and mother and all her siblings still living at home were coming to Custer for a visit. They wanted to see the Barton house and the new addition. Since moving to Custer, Bill and Kate had found it difficult to find time to visit Pleasant Valley. After regaining the deed to their old cabin and forty acres of farmland at the end of 1936, Bill had allowed the Fremder family to use the cabin and the farmland in exchange for an occasional delivery of farm-fresh pork and salted cheese. For many of the Fremder children, having the chance to see the world outside Pleasant Valley was an adventure. Even with the completion of the Pleasant Valley Road, the Pilger Mountain area had remained nearly as isolated as it had been when homesteads were first established ten years earlier. Electric power had yet to be run up Pleasant Valley Road and very few people ventured into the remote region unless they lived there.

Arriving at his place on Little Italy Road just before noon, Bill sat looking at the little house he had built with his own two hands over the past several years. He had only recently completed the construction of an addition that had extended the wraparound porch and added a sewing room and two bedrooms to the house, bedrooms he had promised the kids when he first dug the basement for their home in 1936. It was hard to believe but the house had been a work in progress for the last four years. Now having just completed the final additions to the house, he would have to uproot and move his family once again. He knew the announcement of another family move wouldn't sit well with anyone, especially Velda, who had only recently moved into her new bedroom. She had even spent her own hard-earned money to put up new drapes in an effort to make the room her own.

As he sat in the car, he caught sight of Bart sweeping the porch. With the Fremder family about to arrive any minute, Bill figured Kate had sent him out to give the porch a good once over. Stepping out of the car, Velda and Johnny called out and waved from up the road, as Sandy came barking and running ahead of them. He knew they had spent the morning tending sheep over on Thunderhead Mountain. He was glad everyone made it back home before the Detrick, Annie, and their brood all arrived.

Walking into the house, he still wasn't sure how to break the news. He wondered what Detrick would think of his new job. Detrick had told Bill straight out that he would never make good a farmer. Bill had to agree. His five years in Pleasant Valley had proven that fact. Though he hadn't worked out all the details, he had done the math and calculated if he could work for the next three to four years at the wage he had been offered, he would have the grubstake he needed to get back into business and with a little luck cash in on the growing tourist trade in the Black Hills. He had watched with envy the Minke Motor Lodge become a booming business. He was confident he too could be successful if he had the capital to invest. He now believed, landing the surveyor's job at the Black Hills Ordnance Depot may well make his new dream come true. Bill had come to understand what his Pa meant when he told him long ago: a man may have to give up on a dream, but he should never stop dreaming.

Before he could reach the door, a car horn sounded from the drive-way. The Fremder family had arrived. Piling out of the car, Detrick and Annie were followed by their four youngest children, including Gladys age seventeen, Dorthey age fifteen, Lavern age twelve, and Arthur age eight.

Six of Detrick and Annie's children had already left home. Besides Kate, their eldest, four of Detrick's daughters, including Lena, who was now thirty, Frederika twenty-eight, Anna twenty-four, and Tillie twenty-two, had all married and had growing families of their own on farms and ranches throughout the Black Hills and the surrounding area. With his daughters now having their own babies, Fremder descendants were multi-plying by the year. Detrick already had fifteen grandchildren and was sure to have many, many more. Detrick's eldest son, Herman, now nineteen, had joined the Army and was serving on the west coast.

It wasn't long before everyone had squeezed into the house and took seats at a long dining table that had been set up in the living room. Bill sat at the head of the table, with Detrick next to him on one side and Bart on the other, Lavern and Arthur faced each other next in line, then Dorthey and Velda sat across from one another, followed by Annie and Gladys. Kate sat at the far end of the table, with Johnny next to her on a booster seat. Once everyone was settled in and had a chance to greet one another and exchange pleasantries, lunch was served.

Much had happened in Pleasant Valley. The few farmers that had toughed it out had planted crops and had high hopes of finally harvesting a profitable crop come fall. News from Herman and Francis was exchanged, both men having join the service at roughly the same time. As it turned out, they were both serving in the Pacific, much to the relief of everyone, considering the news of a new war brewing in Europe. Britain and France had declared war on Germany after its invasion of Poland in September

1939. As the world entered a new decade, Germany had unleashed its war machine by invading France, Belgium, and the Netherlands on May 10, 1940, followed by Italy's declaration of war on France and Britain on June 10.

Much of the latest news had been shared by Bart, who not only delivered the daily newspaper but read it from front to back every day. Detrick was angry that his fellow Germans had once again been led down the path to war. He only hoped America wouldn't once again question the loyalty of its German citizens. He still remembered the fear he and his fellow German immigrants had lived under during the Great War and prayed they would never suffer such a terrible fate ever again.

Bill warned everyone that Alva, now a senior chief petty officer on the aircraft carrier the *USS Wasp*, believed the Japanese were a real threat in the Pacific. Though the *Wasp* patrolled the north Atlantic against intrusions by Nazi submarines around Iceland, the Japanese had steadily expanded their empire into Korea, Manchuria, and northern China and now had designs on seizing the Dutch East Indies to gain access to badly needed oil, rubber, and other natural resources. Alva was convinced that Japan was a more immediate threat to American interest than Germany.

With the U.S. territory of the Philippines standing between Japan and Southeast Asia, Bill worried that the Pacific may not be as safe as everyone thought. After a long discussion about the designs of Hitler, Mussolini, and Hirohito for global domination, the general consensus was that America had enough problems without getting involved in wars in distant lands beyond its borders.

Time was getting late, and Bill still hadn't broken the news. Unable to figure out how best to break the news, he decided he would just come out with it and let the chips fall where they may. Tapping on his coffee cup with his stirring spoon, he asked for everyone's attention so he could share an important announcement. The room instantly fell silent as everyone turned to look at Bill, curious to hear what he had to say. No one, not even Kate, had a clue of what Bill might want to share that was so important that he had saved it until now.

"I've been sitting here trying to figure out a way to make this announcement. I decided the best way was to just to go ahead and do it," Bill said, as he tried to organize his thoughts.

"Well, we're all ears," Kate said with a smile, hoping the news would be that Bill had landed a good job while he was in Hot Springs.

She had prayed Bill would be hired on somewhere that would pay him enough that the family would no longer have to scrap to get by. Now that they had a respectable house, and with things getting better year by year, she looked forward to living a more comfortable life in Custer.

"Alright then, I've been hired as a surveyor and need to get down to a new town they're calling Igloo south of Edgemont to start work as soon as possible," Bill said, taking note that Kate's initial expression of delight soon turned to one of concern.

"South of Edgemont? There's nothing down that way except sagebrush," Kate said, wondering what kind of job would last very long down there.

"You're right about that. There's nothing down there. Thing is, the U.S. Army is planning to build an ordnance depot down there and they aren't sparing any expense. There's a train depot in the small town of Provo, near where they plan to build the new town of Igloo. With the roundhouse in Edgemont for the turning of train engines just ten miles away, what they don't have down there now, the Chicago, Burlington, and Quincy Railroad will have no problem hauling in," Bill said, glad to be talking about what he believed might turn out to be the opportunity of a lifetime.

"Ordnance depot? Isn't that a place where they store bombs?" Bart said.

"That's right. Seems living in the middle of nowhere has turned out to have its advantages" Bill said with a chuckle.

"That sound like a dangerous place to work," Kate said, not liking what she was hearing.

"No more dangerous than any other work around here. Mining and logging are not exactly safe lines of work," Bill said, and then added, "Thing is, the job pays a lot better than any of those jobs."

"The pay better beat a dollar a day or you'd be better off staying with the WPA," Kate said, not liking the sound of things.

"Well, it pays a bit more. Fact is, it pays more than a dollar an hour," Bill said, letting the words hang in the air, while everyone's mind raced to process what he had just said.

A dollar an hour was beyond the imaginations of people who had never been paid more than a dollar a day.

"What?! Are you kidding us? Who pays a dollar an hour other than the mob?" Kate said, not believing her ears.

"The government. It seems there's a minimum federal wage in this country of thirty cents an hour, since last year."

"Thirty cents an hour is what the government calls a minimum wage?" Kate said in disbelief. "No one makes even close to thirty cents an hour around here."

"Hard to believe, I know. The wages for a professional surveyor are a damn sight more than that. They also pay a hazardous duty bonus. It all adds up," Bill said, not revealing that his total hourly wage would actually be more than a dollar and seventy-five cents, not counting any additional bonuses for overtime, which he thought he would keep between Kate and himself.

"I know quite a few men who would be willing to work with a bomb strapped to their backsides for thirty cents an hour," Detrick said, having held his tongue until Bill and Kate had a chance to mull over Bill's surprise announcement.

"That's what I wanted to let you know, Detrick. If there're folks in Pleasant Valley who could use the work, they need to get down to Hot Springs to apply as soon as possible. The U.S. Army needs workers, and the pay will be better than thirty cents an hour, that I can guarantee," Bill said, happy to be the barer of glad tidings after all the miserable news he had been forced to share in recent years.

"By God, that's exciting news. You can be sure, I'll spread the word," Detrick said, knowing he was too old to run down to Igloo and his boys were too young.

Even so, he was happy for Bill and Kate and knew that government money would soon pour into the region. There would be plenty of ways to make money off such a development. For one, they would need farm produce to feed their army of workers. Detrick and others in Pleasant Valley were well situated to supply the new base.

"One more thing, I'd like to sell you my homestead," Bill said, having decide right then and there he no longer needed to hold onto the last piece of his old dream. He had a new dream to pursue. Detrick had a big family and was already using the cabin and the land; it was only fitting to keep everything in the family and that Detrick take ownership.

"You sure? We can continue to hold onto it for you," Detrick said, surprised.

"No, I want you to have it. We'll fill out a Quick Claim Deed with a transfer price of one dollar. You can pay me the rest whenever you can," Bill said, having already decided to give the land to Detrick.

"A dollar? How much would I still owe?" Detrick said, trying to process the sudden offer.

"Whatever you feel's fair. You can pay us whenever you can. In the meantime, the land would already be in your name," Bill said, feeling he could afford to share his good fortune and knowing Detrick and his young sons wouldn't be able to take advantage of the high government wages in Igloo.

In the coming days, Bill raced around to set things in order before departing for Igloo. When he worked for the WPA, he had been able use the CCC's bus service and leave his car at home. Because he would have to take the old Blue Demon down to Igloo, he spent nearly half his savings to buy a used 1933 Dodge pickup for Kate and Bart to use in his absence. Bart had convinced him to buy a pickup and not another car, so he would be able to take on odd jobs that required hauling things. Bill had agreed without protest. He knew a pickup might come in handy when it came time to move the family down to Igloo, a topic he had yet to broach.

Filling up the Blue Demon for the long drive ahead, Bill learned from old man Minke that France had just fallen to the Nazis. Talk of war in Europe and saber-rattling in Asia filled the air. As Bill drove down to Igloo, he looked out across the sagebrush-studded landscape and wondered about the government's timing for building a massive ordnance depot, covering nearly thirty-three square miles on land in the middle of nowhere. With Germany, Italy, and Japan having formed a joint military and economic alliance, their desire for territorial expansion seemed clear enough. The so-called Axis Powers had dreams of global domination. It seemed the American government had other dreams.

Bill had taken to listening to President Roosevelt's fireside chats since radio broadcasting finally came to the Black Hills in 1936. Roosevelt's fireside chat in May 1940 had taken a very different tone. Nearly the entire broadcast had focused on how much money had been spent on rebuilding America's military. Roosevelt had gone into great detail in listing the number of ships and planes that had been built and how more men now served in the ranks of the military than since the Great War. The broadcast's message was simple, America needed to be ready to defend itself and to prepare itself for all enemies, foreign and domestic. Bill feared America may be entering the war sooner than anyone might imagine.

Arriving at the tiny hamlet of Provo, Bill discovered there was no-where to stay. A handful of early arrivals had set up tents and thrown up a few makeshift tar paper shacks. The treeless prairie reminded Bill of his childhood in the badlands. It wasn't long until his car was met by Dick Shum, who offered to sell him a town lot for fifty dollars. Dick explained that platted lots measured fifty by one hundred feet and where big enough to park his car and build a house. None of the lots had water, but Provo controlled the water district and had the best fresh water well in the region. Unwilling to haggle over price, it soon became clear that Dick owned most of the town's available platted lots. He also made it clear that he knew once the ordnance depot had been laid out and workers began to flood into the area, the price of Provo lots would only go up. Without many options, Bill bought a lot on Wallace Street, leaving him with less than a hundred twenty dollars to his name.

Though he now owned a lot in Provo to live on, he had only his car to live in. The first thing he did was to dig a latrine and pile up a ring of stones to make a firepit. With no other choice, he knew he would have to rough it until he could manage to put up a proper shelter. He had brought the old squad tent with him, but quickly realized that living in a tent exposed to the relentless winds on the open prairie wouldn't work as well as it did in the sheltered valleys of hills surrounded by dense forest. The tent might be good enough for the summer, but he knew he would have to come up with something more substantial before the first snow started to fly.

Standing on his lot, he looked to the west, following the dirt road that led from Provo to Igloo with his eyes, and then pivoted to pan the horizon in every direction. The nearly featureless landscape was the closest thing to the end of the world as any man alive might ever lay his eyes on. After ten years of living in the forests of the Black Hills, returning to the open prairie was like returning home. Taking a deep breath, he drank in the emptiness around him and the limitlessness of the blue dome of the sky that hovered above. He had never felt freer. He had to admit, though he loved the rich green oasis of the Black Hills, he had missed the open freedom of a bleak, near featureless landscape that ran to the horizon in every direction.

He had seen the plans for the over eight hundred bunkers they would be building and understood why they called the place Igloo. Each bun-ker would first be built as an iron-framed dome-like structure and then encased in concrete and covered in dirt. The resulting mound looked very much like an igloo, with its domed top and protruding entry. He realized as he thought more about it, the people who would come to live and work in Igloo might come to be called Eskimos. Shaking his head, he chuckled at the thought. It reminded him of how his Pa and his Grandpa Pappy felt about the raw deal the Indians had received since the first white man set foot in the New World. If Igloo's well-paid residents ever come to be known as Eskimos, Igloo might be the first place the government actually gave the "natives" a fair shake.

In 1924, one of the first things J. Edgar Hoover did after becoming director of the Bureau of Investigation was to create the Identification Division to gather fingerprints from police agencies nationwide to demonstrate the value of modernizing law enforcement. Building on this success, the responsibility for collecting national crime statistics was assigned to the Bureau of Investigation in 1930, much to the delight of J. Edgar Hoover. These expansions of powers had transformed the Bureau of Investigation into a professional agency with interstate and national scope.

With the nation in a deepening depression and with unemployment soaring, the repeal of Prohibition in 1933 brought with it a crime spree that spread beyond the confines of urban centers. As bootlegging profits dried up, gangsters, seeing the countryside as easy pickings, soon targeted rural communities across America, especially in the Midwest, creating a crime wave that swept the nation as bank robbery, kidnapping, auto theft, gambling, and drug trafficking became increasingly common crimes. Local law enforcement agencies soon found themselves outsmarted and outgunned.

By declaring interstate criminals like John Dillinger, Homer Van Meter, Harry "Pete" Pierpont, John "Red" Hamilton, "Baby Face" Nelson, and the lovers Clyde Barrow and Bonnie Parker as "public enemies," the Bureau of Investigation, in its role as federal law enforcer, had been allowed to become more proactive across state lines. With enhanced federal powers, the harpooning of whales went into full swing. By the end of 1935, the gangsters had all been hunted down and publicly harpooned, transforming the Bureau of Investigation and its "G-Men" into household names and pop culture icons.

With greatly expanded powers and Congressional support, the Bureau of Investigation had been renamed the Federal Bureau of Investigation in 1935, with J. Edgar Hoover placed at its helm and in single-handed control as captain, coxswain, and harpoon master.

Starting in 1933, Nazi Germany had slowly expanded the territories under its fascist control. J. Edgar had monitored developments in Europe, as one nation after another capitulated under threats of war as Nazi troops marched across their borders and occupied their cities. For Europe, Hitler's invasion of Poland on September 1, 1939, became the straw that broke the camel's back. Their policy of appeasement toward Hitler had failed. The war for Europe had begun.

As it was with the outbreak of the Great War, that had come to be known as "the war to end all wars," America was determined to remain on the sidelines. Mired in its own domestic challenges, American isolationism, rooted in the nation's founding, tended to direct the focus of its citizens inward, in a vain attempt to ignore the coming storm, much like an ostrich, wishing to avoid danger, hides its head in the sand. When American pro-Nazi groups began to proclaim fascism as the answer to American woes, J. Edgar saw the seeds of a new role for the FBI, one that would bridge both domestic and international borders, where J. Edgar was certain only giant whales dwelt.

J. Edgar had thought the shift from monitoring harmless German immigrants to radical leftists and unionists to halt the rise communism in America had been a good move in 1920, one that had yielded good hunting. Unfortunately, the hunting grounds hadn't been as bountiful as expected, whales had been few and far between. Bolsheviks, the Red Scare, and Soviet spies were all good material for propaganda to frighten the masses and had helped to broaden the powers of the FBI; unfortunately they yielded very little whale meat.

There was no real threat that communism would ever take over America. America's deep libertarian roots would never accept water sprinkled on them from the spigot of a purely socialist ideology. Americans thrived on competition and on the opportunity to get rich, or at least on the illusion such things might be possible. The free market was an American battle cry. American individualism and its pioneering spirit resisted talk of a socialist utopia, the pathos of America was firmly rooted in the free spirit of the individual, not the collective.

Fascism however prosed a new kind of threat, one that if grafted onto American exceptionalism and its anti-immigrant, nativist, and white supremacist stripes, might become a potent unifying ideology for a populist leader. In such a world, democracy would die. J. Edgar worried if a fascist government, controlled by powerful corporate interests, ever rose to power in America, he might be the kind of whale it chose to hunt.

President Roosevelt's fireside chats had helped to sooth the nation's fears and to keep policies on track, and just as importantly, they had also served to plant the seeds for future actions. His most recent fireside chat had planted a critical seed, one that would target a specific subgroup whose people posed a potential national threat. With a cold, calculating grin, J. Edgar reread the excerpt of Roosevelt's speech that had laid the groundwork for things to come.

> *The Trojan Horse. The Fifth Column that betrays a nation unprepared for treachery. Spies, saboteurs and traitors are the actors in this new strategy. With all of these we must and will deal vigorously. But there is an added technique for weakening a nation at its very roots, for disrupting the entire pattern of life of a people. It is important that we understand it.*
>
> *The method is simple. It is, first, a dissemination of discord. A group—not too large-a group that may be sectional or racial or political—is encouraged to exploit its prejudices through false slogans and emotional appeals. The aim of those who deliberately egg on these groups is to create confusion of counsel, public indecision, political paralysis and, eventually, a state of panic.*
>
> *Sound national policies come to be viewed with a new and unreasoning skepticism, not through the wholesome political debates of honest and free men, but through the clever schemes of foreign agents.*

Trojan horses were real. The sowing of discord an old, tried and true, enemy tactic. Looking for spies, saboteurs, and traitors under every bush could easily lead to widespread paranoia where any group might be targeted for a preemptive strike should they be singled out as a potential threat, weather they were or not. J. Edgar understood very well the extraordinary powers this line of thinking could give him and his Bureau. He had to shake his head in wonder at how things seemed to be simply falling into his hands. He never felt more powerful. With new powerful harpoons, faster ships, and fresh hunting grounds teeming with gigantic whales, he couldn't wait to start spearing and pulling in their steaming bloody carcasses.

November 21, 1940

Little Italy, Custer County, South Dakota

Winds of Change

THE SUMMER HAD BEEN a busy one. Bart had taken a job with Ben Minke, who needed help running his thriving gas station and motor lodge. With Roosevelt's face, the last of the four, dedicated on Mount Rushmore on July 2, 1939, the 1940 tourist season was the largest the region had ever experienced. The tourist trade was no longer thought of a short-term boom, it was becoming a vital part of the region's economy.

Bart had turned his paper route over to Velda when he took his job with Minke. At first the *Rapid City Journal* had protested the hiring of a girl paperboy until they discovered there were no boys in Custer willing to take the job. Talk of war grew into a fervor after the government inaugurated the Selective Service and Training Act, America's first peacetime military draft, on September 16, 1940. With every male from age eighteen to forty-five required to register, Velda soon found herself signing up over fifty new customers.

With the unexpected bonanza, her paper route had swelled to over a hundred seventy customers, making her daily earnings over eighty cents for a few hours of work every day. As a result, she found herself making daily wages nearly equal to those of a grown man; a fact she never talked about and guarded carefully.

Kate had turned to working from home, baking for the Roadway Inn, the Minke Motor Lodge, and many others. Working from home had allowed her to take care of little Johnny when Velda was busy with her paper route. Velda also helped out with deliveries of her mother's baked goods. One of the benefits of becoming a makeshift bakery was that the little Barton house always smelt of cookies, cakes, and fresh baked bread.

Bill had spent the summer surveying the layout for the future home of the Black Hills Ordnance Depot. During a rare two-day break, he looked up Roy Kelly, who had expanded his southern hills ranching operations from running sheep on Pilger Mountain to include running cattle along the Cheyenne River north of Edgemont on land once owned by the original cattle baron in the region, Tom Burton. Ross Bishop had also run cattle on the same land. Roy hoped he would have better luck than the land's former owners. Cattle ranching in the Black Hills had been his original plan when he moved to Pilger Mountain. Bill had been glad to see that Roy had succeeded, where he and so many others had failed.

Learning about how Bill was living, Roy introduced him to Jim Salkin, who ran a large sheep ranch just south of Edgemont. Roy figured Jim just might have an old sheep wagon Bill might be able to use. He also figured it would be easy to pull a wagon to Provo located only seven miles south of Salkin's place. Bill had taken Roy up on his advice, and as it turned out old man Salkin had an old sheep wagon to lend to Bill for as long as he didn't need it. According to Jim, any friend of Roy Kelly's was a friend of his. The sheep wagon turned out to be a comfortable home compared to the old, tattered squad tent. Being up off the ground in a wagon with solid walls all around was a godsend. That the sheep wagon looked like the home of an old gypsy fortune teller with its bread-loaf shape added just another twist to his prairie odyssey since arriving in Provo with its challenging living conditions, conditions far more spartan than he had expected when he first signed on to work in Igloo.

Bill returned to Custer for Thanksgiving a week earlier than originally planned. President Roosevelt had made an unexpected proclamation that moved Thanksgiving from the fourth Thursday to the third Thursday in November. Everyone was caught off guard. The government's idea seemed to have been to try to boost an economy still mired in depression. The result had been total confusion as everyone's holiday plans had been suddenly thrown into disarray. Franksgiving, as everyone started to call it, had turned out to be a bust as an economic stimulus.

The only person happy about Roosevelt's decision was Velda, who finally had a birthday without turkey. Kate had agreed with Velda that having a birthday more than a week early was just too much. For the first time in

Velda's life, she celebrated her birthday on her birthdate. Turning twelve, she held her first birthday party like other girls, with presents and cake on a day all her own. She even invited some boys to her party. She had been pleased when Freddie Ward accepted. She had always thought Freddie was cute.

After leaving South Dakota, Ross had headed east, gathering his children along the way, at least those he had been able to track down. He then headed to the southern hill country of Missouri, where the Bishop family had a number of shirttail relations. Ross soon found out that those shirttails were a damn sight shorter than he had hoped. Finding little hospitality among distant relatives who treated him and his children no better than strangers, Ross and his children nearly starved to death, while living on squirrel meat and grassroot soup.

With his daughters marrying young and his eldest son, Joseph, joining the Navy, Ross sent Billy, his youngest son, to live with his sister in California, before he made his way back to the southern Black Hills. Upon reaching Edgemont, a broken man living on his own, Ross learned about the massive ordnance depot being built near the tiny hamlet of Provo. At the age of fifty-six and with no prospects, Ross saw the development as the lucky break he had been searching for. After losing his wife and his ranch seven years earlier, and eventually losing all his children, who were now scattered on the wind in every direction, Ross had begun to believe he had not only lost his fortune but had lost his family forever. Alone and growing old, he had feared he would never get back on his feet again.

Arriving in Provo, Ross was surprised to find the town already had several hundred residents, nearly all of whom were young men who worked on the Black Hills Ordnance Depot or on building the town of Igloo. Buying a single lot facing Bennet Street, the main road running through town, Ross quickly cobbled together a tar paper shack with the front half set up as a makeshift store and rear half as sleeping quarters. Spending the last cent of the meager grubstake he had scraped together over the past five years chopping wood in Missouri, he set up a small general store to sell newspapers and magazines, tobacco products, candy and gum, and assorted canned foods. Products all targeting a young single male workforce. Visiting local ranches and farms, Ross soon expanded his offerings with a variety of local fresh and home-canned farm produce on consignment.

Surrounded by an ever-swelling legion of young single men with money in their pockets and no place to spend it, Ross profited by catering to their daily wants and needs. Calling his new business venture the Newsy Nook, the little store soon became a quick stop for daily necessities. Once he was able to install a soda machine, attached to the only electric line in town run directly from Igloo, the Newsy Nook became the town's gossip hub and a favorite place to gather in the evenings.

Ross learned about his father passing away soon after he arrived in California in 1929 from his younger sister, Beula. Ross had stayed in touch with Beula, the only family he felt close to. Having no children of her own, Beula had agreed to take Billy to live with her in San Diego, California. No one in the family had heard from Uncle Roland since his mad dash out of Manhattan with as much cash in his pockets as he could pull together. With creditors on his heels, many coming from the shadier side of town, the family feared Roland may not have been able to slip their clutches. Privately, Ross held out hope that Uncle Roland had made it all the way to Argentina, where it had always been suspected he had stashed a bundle of ol' E. J. Bishop's ill-gotten wealth, just in case.

After learning of his father's death, Ross had received no further word from his younger brother Clarence. He wondered what kind of investments his brother might have made and whether he had prospered over the past ten years. Even Beula, living in California, hadn't heard from him. Ross figured he may never find out, and had accepted he would have to make his living on his own. His family, once so proud and so close, had become only a fading memory. For Ross, his uncle and his younger brother were like his wife and most of his children; they were no more than dust on the wind. He hoped if all went well with his Provo venture, he might be able to have his youngest son, Billy, come back from California to join him. He also prayed his eldest son, Joseph, would return to the Black Hills one day.

December 7, 1941

Custer, Custer County, South Dakota

It's War!

SINCE BILL HAD GONE to work at the Black Hills Ordnance Depot, it seemed the whole country had started churning out what Roosevelt called vital defense materials, including aircraft, tanks, rifles, canons, and bombs and ammunitions. Almost overnight, America had become the world's arsenal of democracy, supplying any country willing to fight the Axis Powers with weapons of war. Though America had not entered the fight, Roosevelt had stressed that the current emergency was as serious as war itself. He urged private-sector factories to make the investments necessary to expand their productive capacities and to increase employment ahead of growing demand.

In Roosevelt's September 11, 1941, fireside chat, he had railed about the lawlessness on the high seas by Nazi submarines and how their actions were no different than the Barbary Pirates Thomas Jefferson had been forced to confront when he was president. Four American flag vessels had been sunk or attacked, two of which were warships of the American Navy, with the most recent being the torpedo attack on the destroyer the *USS Greer* off the coast of Iceland.

Nazi plots to destabilize or overthrow the governments of Uruguay, Argentina, Bolivia, and Colombia had also been uncovered and smashed. During the broadcast, Roosevelt had avoided declaring outright war on Germany. Instead, he had reaffirmed the American policy to protect the freedom of the seas in the Atlantic, the Pacific, and all other oceans of the world. Bill recalled the words of the president's ominous closing statement: "When you see a rattlesnake poised to strike, you do not wait until he has struck before you crush him. The time for active defense is now." Though America had not officially declared war, it had declared the right of pre-emptive war. Bill knew there was little difference.

The workforce on the Black Hills Ordnance Depot had grown from a few hundred in the summer of 1940 to several thousand by the fall of 1941, a population exceeding that of Hot Springs, once the most populous town in the region. Provo had been turned into a boom town. Tents, makeshift sheds, and tar paper shacks fanned out across the prairie on both sides of Bennet Street, the main road that ran through town. Whole buildings from Ardmore, Oelrichs, Rumford, and other small towns in the region had been moved to Provo. The relocated structures, including a movie theater, a makeshift roller-skating rink, and several diners, saloons, and dance halls, now made up the core of Provo's thriving business district.

With labor in short supply, women had been recruited to join the workforce in Igloo at full pay. Kate, on a lark, had applied for a position at the ordnance depot and, much to her and Bill's utter shock and delight, had been hired as a heavy-duty semi-tractor-trailer driver for a dollar an hour. The only problem with the job offer was that she had never driven a semi-tractor-trailer. Figuring there was no time like the present to learn, she accepted the offer, unwilling to even consider turning down a wage beyond anything a woman had ever been paid. Like Bill, she had been instructed to report for duty as soon as possible.

Thanksgiving in 1941 was held on the third Thursday in November, with Velda, once again, one of only a few people in the United States of America pleased with the early date. Despite the early date, however, unlike the previous year, the family had decided to celebrate Velda's birthday on Thanksgiving Day with turkey and cake following their long-held family tradition. Velda had hoped she would be able to celebrate her birthday on her birthdate, having never had a better birthday than the one she had enjoyed the year before. As it was so often, her hopes were in vain. She had accepted long ago however that poor people didn't have the luxury of having their own way or getting everything they wanted. From her Pa's glowing talk about Igloo and her Ma's excitement at having been hired on as a truck driver, there was no doubt her parents were convinced Igloo had become the Barton family's long-awaited El Dorado.

With the hourly salaries in Igloo too good to pass up, even for a day, the morning after the family's Thanksgiving feast, Kate threw her things into a couple of cardboard boxes and hopped into the Blue Demon with Bill behind the wheel and headed for Provo, leaving Bart, Velda, and little Johnny in Custer to finish the school year on their own. Johnny was in the first grade, Velda in the eighth grade, and Bart in the twelfth grade. Since Velda and Bart would be graduating from the eighth grade and the twelfth grade and Johnny would be completing his first year in school, the plan was for the children to join Bill and Kate in Provo in the spring of the coming year.

Velda's days became hectic after the sudden and unexpected departure of her mother. Between school, keeping up with her paper route, and taking care of Johnny, she had been kept busy every hour of the day. Bart had been put in charge of the household by his parents; however, working late hours at Minke's filling station and often eating out, he had little time to look after Velda and Johnny. Bart not being around had left Velda to look after Johnny on her own. Bart planned to join the Navy as soon as he graduated and had wanted to spend more time with the family. With his parents in Igloo, and his long working hours, he wondered if he would be able to spend any time with the family before he shipped out.

Since Velda couldn't leave Johnny home alone when she delivered her newspapers, she had decided to bring him in as her partner and take him with her everywhere she went. With Johnny sitting in a wooden wagon hitched behind her bicycle, she did the peddling while Johnny hopped out of the wagon and ran the papers up to the houses. Velda soon discovered working together they could complete the full circuit of her ten-mile paper route, from Custer all the way to Fourmile Corner and back, in record time. Though they were often exhausted when they got home, they also worked as a team to prepare their evening meals. After two weeks of living on their own, they had fallen into a new daily routine, though they both wondered how they would survive the next five months until school was out, and the family was finally reunited in Provo.

The morning of December 8, 1941, was not unlike other Monday mornings since her parents left. Rolling out of bed, Velda quickly freshened up and threw together a breakfast of bacon and eggs with wheat toast and gooseberry jam. Over the weekend, Bart had been deer hunting in Pleasant Valley and had swung by Grandpa Detrick's farm, bringing back bacon and ham, not to mention a poached deer carcass that he had hung up to cure in the back shed. There was always a risk Sheriff Johnson would catch wind of the illegal carcass, but then poor folk had to do what they had to do to survive. Never having enough money, the Barton family had lived on poached deer meat for years.

Though she had originally thought taking care of Johnny and her paper route would be a burden, Velda was impressed with how quickly Johnny had caught on to the whole newspaper delivery process. With Johnny pitching in, the two of them were able to work in tandem and complete deliveries much faster than Velda had been able to do working on her own. With these thoughts on her mind, she was surprised to see the *Rapid City Journal* delivery truck pulling up the driveway at a high speed. Velda wondered why the truck had come to her house so early on a Monday morning and why all the rush. She hadn't been shorted any copies of the Sunday paper and she had been able to deliver everything on time. Velda took note that the driver looked more than a little agitated when he jumped out of the truck and ran up to the house. Velda headed for the front door, with the driver's knocking becoming more insistent with every step. Opening the door, Velda was just about to ask the driver why all the urgency, when the driver beat her to the punch.

"You have to get down to the Courthouse right away," the driver barked as he turned and headed back to his truck.

"What's going on?" Velda said, following the driver to the truck, surprised by the strange request.

"It's war! Now get in," the driver said, reaching into the cab of the truck and shoving a copy of the *Rapid City Journal's* Special Edition into Velda's hands. The paper's banner said it all: "IT'S WAR! JAPS BOMB HAWAII!"

Without missing at beat, Velda told Sandy to stay and Johnny to jump in the truck. Johnny hopped in without question and soon found himself speeding toward the Custer County Courthouse with Velda at his side, explaining to him that they had a job to do. It took only a couple minutes to cover the short distance. Once they arrived, the driver threw several bundles of Special Edition papers on the Courthouse steps and had Velda sign a receipt. He then, jumped back in his truck and was gone in a flash, spinning rubber as he took off for Hot Springs, his next destination. The directions taped to the top bundle were simple. Copies were to be sold for five cents apiece—with a one-cent commission per copy to the vender. The note read, "Hold up the Special Edition and repeatedly call out, 'Extra, Extra! It's War! Japs Bomb Hawaii!' until the papers sell out."

She had five hundred copies and stood to make five dollars for a couple hours work. Fetching a couple empty coffee cans from the Courthouse breakroom, she cut the straps on all the bundles of papers, and quickly set Johnny up with a couple stacks of papers and a coffee can, to collect the nickels. She then set up her own empty coffee can and stacks of papers, which she positioned next to the curb at the bottom of the Courthouse steps. With everything in order, she tuned up her vocal cords, straightened her blouse, and went to work.

"Extra! Extra! It's War! Japs Bomb Hawaii!" Velda yelled, as she waved a copy of the Special Edition high over her head.

It wasn't long until people from inside the Courthouse, from up and down Main Street, and from cars passing by soon gathering around her to get their own copy of what they all believed would become a piece of history. Though Americans had tried to ignore the coming storm and had prayed it would never arrive, no one was surprised that the war had finally struck American shores.

Making a penny a copy, Velda had been determined not to stop yelling until she ran out of papers to sell. As it turned out, she sold all five hundred copies in less than two hours. Hoarse and bone weary, rather than head for school, she took Johnny by the hand and headed for the Roadway Inn, where she was certain ol' Molly Tillerman would take care of them. With the proceeds from the Special Edition sales, she decided she could afford to buy a couple blue-ribbon lunches, especially one for Johnny, her new partner in crime. As far as Velda was concerned, though the country might be at war, its Army, in which she and Johnny now belonged, didn't run on an empty stomach.

Just as they crossed the street on the way to the Roadway Inn, Bart pulled up in his pickup and offered to give them a ride. Velda was surprised to see her older brother, who hadn't been around much since their parents left for Provo. Though she had been angry with her brother for leaving her and Johnny to fend for themselves, she was happy and relieved to see him.

"Get in," Bart said with a grin, pulling up to the curb.

"We're headed to the Roadway Inn to get some lunch," Velda said as though it was something they did every day.

"Roadway Inn? I thought you might be headed to school," Bart said, surprised.

"Nope. Thought we might eat out," Velda said matter-of-factly.

"Well alright then. I'll buy. It sounds like a great idea," Bart said enthusiastically.

"You're money's no good with us. We're buyin'," Velda said with a grin.

"That's right. We're totin' two coffee cans full of nickels," Johnny said, proudly hefting his can up for Bart to see.

"Even better. Now, get in," Bart said with a broad smile and chuckle.

It was tough for Velda to stay angry with her older brother. She knew why he hadn't been around the house over the past couple of weeks. Everyone had to work, it was just the way things were for folks who had to scramble for every nickel.

With the attack on Hawaii, the war had come to America. She feared for her uncles serving in the Pacific and no longer wanted her brother to join the Navy. Hopping into the pickup, they soon arrived at the Roadway Inn, which sat off the main road along French Creek about halfway between the Custer County Courthouse and Little Italy Road.

Velda always loved the smell of the Roadway Inn. Molly hung lavender bundles in every corner of the dining room and made her own potpourri that she stuffed into small baskets on every table. The mixture of aromas was rich and helped mask the caramelized oily smells of the greasy spoon. Molly Tillerman was pleased to see the Barton kids and how well they were doing. Molly was eighty-one years old and could still glide around the tables without bumping into too many things. Though folks could see she had lost a step or two, no one was willing to say so for fear she may retire and leave them without any place in town that served their favorite breakfast of eggs and sausage over homemade sourdough biscuits and gravy.

"What a pleasant surprise. You kids are growing up so fast I almost didn't recognize you," Molly said as she waved for them to take a seat in the back near the kitchen, the warmest table in the house.

Never having children of her own, she was always willing to give a helping hand to the poorer children in town. She was especially proud of Velda, who she thought of as one of her own. She could see Velda was a real businesswoman, like herself. She was proud that Velda ran the town's only paper route, a job only boys handled in other towns. She could also see that the Barton kids were the last of a dying breed. They had grown up doing without on the frontier, a frontier not unlike the one she had experienced in the 1800s. Molly could see the strength of their pioneer spirit, something town kids in the age of electricity, telephones, and automobiles seemed to lack.

"We were selling papers," Johnny said, putting his heavy coffee can, full of nickels, up on the table before taking a seat.

"Looks like you sold a lot of 'em," Molly said, seeing the mound of nickels in Johnny's can and noticing Velda had a can full of nickels of her own.

"I had Rupert, my short-order cook, run over to buy several copies of your paper myself," Molly added, patting an open copy of the Special Edition laying on the counter while giving little Johnny a big motherly grin.

"I thought America would go to war in Europe to fight the Germans again. Like when we sent our doughboys to France," Bart said, even though he knew his Uncle Alva had predicted the Japanese may be America's bigger problem.

Now that the war had started in the Pacific, Bart wondered if Francis and Herman would be alright. With both men serving in the Pacific, there was a good chance they would soon be seeing the war up close, if they hadn't already. Considering the Japanese had attacked Pearl Harbor, his biggest concern was for Francis, who may have been right in the middle of things.

"We all did. We were all lookin' east, wondering what Hitler would do next, when we should have been lookin' west. That damn Hirohito, no one thought the Japanese would attack us without warning," Molly said. "We'll just have to go out and lick 'em both. We can't hide from the Hirohitos and Hitlers of the world anymore. It's time for America to kick some butt."

"That's for sure," Bart said, realizing that the war would be fought on two fronts and wondering how long it would take before America sent troops into both Europe and Asia.

"Let me get you kids three of our blue-ribbon roast beef specials, with extra special fixin's," Molly said with a wink.

Dashing off back into the kitchen, Molly would have liked to talk more about the coming war and how it will impact Custer and the surrounding region, but she had a business to run and customers to serve.

"Do you think Uncle Francis is alright?" Velda said, knowing Francis was stationed in Hawaii and had gone on and on in his last letter about how great it was living in paradise.

His picture postcard from Honolulu, with its colorful scene of a beautiful white sandy beach, palm trees, and hula girls, had said it all. She also knew her Uncle Herman was stationed on the west coast in San Diego, the last time they heard. Being in the Army, she wondered where he would be sent next.

"I'm sure Francis and Herman are fine. We shouldn't worry about them until we know more," Bart said, not really believing his own words.

For the first time in his life, Bart was truly afraid. For years, he couldn't wait to join the Navy to see the world. Like his uncles, he felt the seas calling him to travel to distant shores. Now, with the outbreak of war, he knew he may have to go into battle on some distant ocean with an enemy intent on killing him. Thinking over recent developments in America, Bart suspected the government had known for a long time that America would be joining the war.

America's rapid military buildup, its expansion in the production of military weapons, the establishment of America's first peacetime draft, and even the urgent, nearly frantic, construction of the ordnance depot in Igloo, had all been done in plain sight. He could see plain enough now what had been there for all to see, and yet no one had wanted to admit it: America had been planning to enter the war for some time. The outbreak of war had merely confirmed he would be joining the military whether he wanted to or not. There was little doubt his draft notice was already on the way.

Much like the crash of the stock market in 1929, Detrick had learned about the Japanese attack on Pearl Harbor from a man on the back of a horse. His son, Lavern, had ridden over to Dewy the morning of December 8 to pick up the mail. News of the war had been Detrick's worst nightmare come true. Ever since Herman had joined the Army, Detrick had worried his eldest son may be caught up in a war. Little did he suspect that war would start in the Pacific, right where his son was now serving. He was thankful his other two sons were too young to serve.

Lavern was just thirteen and Arthur only nine. He knew that Bill had two brothers serving in the Navy, one in the Atlantic and one in the Pacific, and that his eldest son, Bart, would be eighteen when he graduated in the coming spring. He suspected that John, Bill, and Kate and the whole Barton family were in for a very rough time.

The new draft that had been announced just the year before required all men ages eighteen to forty-five to register. He feared his daughters' husbands may eventually be called to serve. He also wondered, now that

America had been dragged into the war, whether the immigrants from Germany, Italy, and Japan would be targeted as possible spies and saboteurs. It had been little more than twenty years ago when he had been forced to act against the injustice of the bully Tom McFarland and his gang of American Protective League thugs.

Thankfully, the American Protective League had been disbanded soon after the Great War. The scars it had left behind weren't so easily erased. Detrick still held hard feelings about how German immigrants had been treated and for the years of fear they had endured. He never wanted to see such a fate befall any immigrant group in America again. Those who chose to come to America had chosen America, they had cast their lot with their fellow Americans. Their loyalty shouldn't be measured by the origin of their birth or by how many generations their ancestors had lived in America. America was founded on an idea not a bloodline. Being an American had never been something based on ethnicity or race. Indeed, it is the very fact that all men are created equal, written in its founding documents, that makes America great.

In the months following the attack on Pearl Harbor, J. Edgar's office had seen a flurry of activity. Japan had made one advance after another in the Pacific, invading the Philippines, Guam, Wake, Hong Kong, Singapore, Burma, the Dutch East Indies, and the Solomon Islands, among others. The Empire of Japan now bestrode East Asia as its new master. By early March 1942, only three months after Pearl Harbor, Japan had reached out to attack facilities in Darwin, Australia, and an oil refinery near Santa Barbara, California. With these bold actions, Japan had demonstrated it could strike anywhere in the Pacific at any time, shaking American confidence to its very core.

The February 23 strike on Santa Barbara had in a queer twist served to justify President Roosevelt's Executive Order 9066, signed just four days earlier on February 19, which commanded the rounding up and relocation of Americans of Japanese ancestry to prevent potential espionage on American shores. Military zones were quickly set up in California, Washington, and Oregon, all west coast states with large Japanese American populations. In a series of preemptive raids on the Japanese community and its religious leaders, just hours after the December 7 bombing of Pearl

Harbor, the FBI had arrested over twelve hundred Japanese Americans without formal charges. Following Executive Order 9066, the FBI, working with local authorities, soon corralled over a hundred twenty thousand people of Japanese ancestry, disregarding the fact that the vast majority were American citizens. With their assets seized and frozen, they had been speedily transferred to makeshift detention facilities in California, Idaho, Utah, Wyoming, Colorado, and Arkansas.

J. Edgar had high hopes of landing whales aplenty when the FBI's raids were launched but had ended up with only a very small bucket of minnows. That American citizens had had their property seized without due process and that tens of thousands were now languishing in detention camps in America's most desolate wastelands seemed less a concern to J. Edger than the desire for finding whales to hunt, whales that hadn't been found and that everyone now knew simply didn't exist.

Gnawing at the back of his mind, J. Edgar feared he had followed the same failed course his predecessors had followed when they chose to hunt German immigrants, the very thing twenty years earlier he had believed to be a misguided policy that bore little fruit. At that time, he had been right to shift the attentions of the Bureau away from German immigrants to other hunting grounds. Now that he had made the same error on a grander scale, he wondered how his actions might be viewed by history, though he had little concern that any serious historical review would happen anytime soon, if ever. Certainly, there would be no serious review as long as he was the head of the FBI and still at its helm as its unchallenged, captain, coxswain, and harpoon master.

Late evening on December 8, Bill had stopped by the Newsy Nook to pick up a few groceries when he caught sight of the banner emblazoned across the top of a Special Edition of the *Rapid City Journal*: "IT'S WAR! JAPS BOMB HAWAII!" Gabbing a copy from the rack, his mind reeled with thoughts about Francis and Kate's brother, Herman. Both men were stationed in the Pacific, with Francis, his youngest brother, stationed in Hawaii.

"That's nearly the last copy. You're lucky to get one. Those damn Japanese. They snuck up and hit us when we weren't lookin," an older baldheaded man in striped coveralls standing behind the counter said.

"It's hard to believe. I have a brother serving in Hawaii," Bill heard himself say, his mind still reeling.

"Sorry to hear that. We're all in it now. A lot of folks'll be going to fight this one," the man said.

"How much for everything?" Bill said, looking at the man behind the counter for the first time.

"That'll be a dollar thirty," the man said, ringing up the cash register.

When the man looked up, he found his customer staring at him with a look of disbelief on his face. At that instant, both men suddenly recognized one another.

"Ross, Ross Bishop, you ol' son-of-a-gun, is that you?" Bill said, shocked at running into Ross Bishop in Provo of all places after more than eight years since the last time they met.

Bill could see the man had aged and had less hair, and that what little he still had was now nearly snow white. Other than that, he still looked as fit as ever, standing more than six feet tall in his bibbed railroad-striped overalls and weighing in at a good solid two hundred fifty pounds.

"Bill Barton. Well, I'll be. Never thought I'd see you in a place like this," Ross said, truly happy to see Bill again.

Seeing Bill again reminded Ross of Bill's daughter, Velda, and the evening she first met Stinkin' Bear. The thought of the little girl hugging the old pinto pony brought a smile to his face, an alien expression that hadn't creased his weathered features in far too many years. He wondered if she would remember him after all these years.

The two men talked at length about the years that had passed and of the many hardships they had faced since they last met. Both men saw Igloo as a wish come true, as an answer to a long and winding trail of broken dreams. Wrapping up their reunion, they shared a hardy laugh about the bumpy paths they had both traveled that had led them to Provo, a shanty town, clinging to the outer edge of the world.

Hearing that Ross had hopes of having his youngest son, Billy, join him in Provo, brought back Bill's memory of seeing little Billy at the Bishop Ranch when the boy was no more than five years old. He also recalled how he and his Pa had laughed all the way back to Edgemont about how Bishop menfolk, like ears of corn, all seemed to look one hell of a lot alike. He knew if he ever saw Billy again, he would recognize him in an instant.

May 23, 1942

Little Italy, Custer, Custer County, South Dakota

Sudden Departure

VELDA WAS WALKING ON air. The old tradition of holding a formal eighth grade graduation ceremony was still popular, even though children now went on to secondary school to complete twelve years of public education. Graduation from the eighth grade was a rite of passage between childhood and adulthood, a tradition people held dear and were reluctant to give up. Velda would be graduating from the eighth grade and Bart from the twelfth grade on Monday, June 1. Velda looked forward to her parents coming up from Provo for her and her brother's graduation ceremonies, both to be held on the same day.

The Barton kids hadn't seen much of their parents over the past six months. Though Bill and Kate had dashed home for three days at Christmas and Kate had come back for two days in mid-March to check on things, the children had been left to live on their own and take care of themselves. Even little Johnny had matured beyond his years and had come to insist on his new independence. Despite being only six years old, there were very few things he couldn't do for himself.

Since the outbreak of war, Bart had changed his mind about joining the Navy right after graduation. He had decided to wait for his draft notice to join the ranks of the U.S. Army so he could fight the enemy face to face. He had seen how battles at sea ended for the men who lost. He didn't want to die in a watery grave. If he was to fight and die, it would be on solid ground. He also figured it would take some time before his draft number was called. The extra time in Custer would give him a chance to live a little and to sew some wild oats before he marched off to face the enemy. He had a house to live in, a pickup to drive, a good job, and money in his pockets. To top it off, he thought, he was handsome, young, and carefree. He looked forward to living the single life of a bachelor. There was one thing he was absolutely certain about; he wouldn't be going to Provo after graduating.

On the afternoon of Saturday, May 23, Bill and Kate rolled up to their house in Little Italy in a shiny new 1942 Ford Deluxe Four Door Sedan. Bart could hardly believe his eyes when he saw his Pa and Ma get out of the shiny new automobile. He knew the car must have cost at least nine hundred dollars, double a man's annual wages. Things were definitely looking up, if his Pa could afford such a car. Stepping out of the house, he greeted his parents with hearty bear hugs.

"Where'd you steal this beauty?" Bart said, walking over to get a closer look at the shiny black automobile.

"Well, the ol' Blue Demon finally gave up the ghost and I figured it was about time I got a new ride. I talked the dealer into givin' me a hundred-dollar trade in for the ol' wreck," Bill said with a chuckle, proud of his horse-trading skills.

"I still think he paid too much. We might be makin' good money, Bill Barton, but there's no good reason to throw it away," Kate said, carrying on a quarrel that had raged since Bill went out and bought the brand-new car without talking to her first.

"I'm sure Bart doesn't need to get in the middle of our differences," Bill said, trying to drop the subject.

"Well, it sure is a beauty. And Ma, you know you needed a new car. They all cost money," Bart said, not wanting to take sides, but knowing the Blue Demon had been on its last legs when they left for Provo last November.

"Well, I wanted a bright-colored car," Kate said, her arms akimbo.

Though she was upset about Bill buying the car without consulting her first, Kate was actually proud they could now afford such luxuries. Secretly, she liked the black color that made her feel like royalty every time she was chauffeured around in the car.

"Good to have you here a week early. It's great that we can spend more time together before graduation," Bart said, having understood that his parents wouldn't arrive until the day before graduation.

Bart looked forward to the family spending time together, knowing he would soon be drafted and might not see his family again for some time.

"We know you kids were lookin' forward to your graduations, but the country's at war. We need to get back to work come Monday morning. Sorry we'll have to miss your graduations but neither of us can take the time off. This weekend is the only chance we had to come move you kids to Provo," Bill said.

"Move to Provo? Velda was . . ." Bart started to say, surprised by the sudden change in plans.

"Eighth grade graduation ain't as important as it used to be, now that kids go to school longer," Bill said, trying to justify skipping his daughter's eighth grade graduation, and avoiding any mention of the fact they would be skipping their eldest son's twelfth grade graduation as well.

"So, what's the plan?" Bart said, dumbfounded.

"I'm a supervisor now and I have to be on site to oversee operations. Your Ma drives the big trucks that haul the bombs. We're already moving bombs into bunkers down there, day and night. You wouldn't believe it but there must be over six thousand people crawling all over Igloo. The place is a madhouse," Bill said, his eyes wild.

Bart noted the excitement in his Pa's voice and gestures. He could see that the money his parents were pulling down in Igloo was like nothing they had ever earned before in their lives. Their new car said it all. They had caught 'Igloo fever', a malady little different than the 'gold fever' that had driven the white man's invasion into the Black Hills, and that had driven more than a few men stark raving mad.

Molly Tillerman had observed that people who suffered such maladies were willing to sacrifice everything to get as much as they could as quickly as they could. She always added, the problem was they never seem to get enough. Her good-for-nothing husband had come down with gold fever and never recovered, having never returned from Deadwood. Bart wasn't entirely surprised his parents had decided graduation ceremonies weren't all that important, without a thought about how their children might feel. They had placed all their hopes on Igloo, on mining its rich vein of gold for all it was worth. They could no longer see how anything else could be more important.

When Velda and Johnny came home after delivering the evening news, they both wondered whose car was parked in front of the house. It wasn't long until they were greeted by their Ma and Pa and had the reunion they had both looked forward to for many months. Learning they would be departing for Provo the next day came as a quite a shock to Velda. She had hoped her Pa and Ma would bring her a new dress to wear for her eighth-grade graduation. She had imagined them smiling and cheering when she received her diploma. Now she was being told she would miss her graduation ceremony and needed to leave Custer for Provo the next day. She would have no time to say farewell to her friends or do anything else before she left Custer for good.

Unable to believe her own ears, she pleaded with her parents to let her graduate with the other kids to no avail. Her parents claimed they had no choice, they had to be back to work on Monday morning. Since Bart made it clear he wouldn't be going down to Provo, and would be keeping the pickup, the only option for Velda and Johnny was to leave for Provo when their parents departed the next day.

Bart would take over the paper route and turn it over to a new paperboy when the time came. He would also take care of the house and live and work in Custer until he received his draft notice. With Bart staying in Custer, Bill asked him to look into possible buyers for the house and gave him the phone number to his operations office in Igloo. Johnny wasn't sure how he felt about the sudden turn of events. He had never had any say about where he lived or who took care of him. He had no idea where Provo was. All he knew was that Bart, his big brother, wouldn't be going along with them when they left.

Bart had spent a lot of time with Johnny over the past five months. The two had grown closer. Bart had tried to pass on to Johnny everything he had learned from Grandpa John. Johnny had been named after his grandpa and had been raised on his knee when he was just a baby. They often laughed about how he earned his nickname, Rotten Johnny. Bart wanted to make sure Johnny lived up to the reputation of his namesake, John Barton, one of the last of the Old West cowboys who had ridden all the way into the modern age. He told him about their Great-Grandma Lucy Breeden, and of their Otoe heritage. Being members of the Eagle Clan, Bart had presented Johnny with an eagle feather as a good luck totem, which Johnny kept under the rim of his cowboy hat, just like everyone in the Barton family did.

After hearing the story Johnny shared about how he and Velda had watched from the cliff above as a mama cougar played with her cubs on Thunderhead Mountain, Bart declared Johnny an honorary member of the Cougar Clan and had presented him with his cougar fang pendent he had worn around his neck since he was a boy. And though he was certain Johnny had heard his father tell the story many times before, Bart retold the story about how their Pa had survived a cougar attack on Pilger Mountain long before the land was open for homesteading. Johnny had never felt more special. He now possessed one of the fangs from the cougar that his Pa had fought and knew its spirit would forever live in the Black Hills. For Johnny, the only Barton to have actually been born in the Lakota's *Paha Sapa*, the cougar fang meant everything. The Lakota name for Mount Rushmore had been *Tunkasila Skpe Paha*, meaning Six Grandfathers Mountain; the Lakota had also called the mountain *Igmu Tanka Paha*, meaning Cougar Mountain.

In coming years, Johnny would often reach up to touch the cougar fang and think about his big brother. For him, the name Cougar Mountain belonged to three mountains in the Black Hills: Pilger Mountain, Thunderhead Mountain, and Rushmore Mountain. Johnny knew that Bart had been born in Creighton in the badlands and hadn't move to Pilger Mountain until he was five, about the same age Johnny was now.

Like his sister, Velda, Johnny was a child of the hills and forest and knew nothing of the prairie that surrounded them. He had often peered across the vast flatlands beyond the Black Hills from the peak of Thunderhead Mountain and wondered what those empty lands held. He wasn't sure he wanted to find out, but knew he had no choice in the matter. He had been taught that everyone lived their own adventure. In his, the cowboy buckaroo Johnny Barton was about to ride into the prairie. From there, he had no idea where his trail may lead or what new trails he may blaze. What he knew for sure was that in the future the trails he rode would be trails of his own making.

When Kate got up the next morning, she found Velda asleep at the dining table surrounded by stacks of handwritten letters. Velda had stayed up late to write farewell letters to all her friends. She had also penned short notes to each of her *Journal* customers. She had built the paper route to nearly two hundred customers and was proud of the service she provided. She knew every customer by name and had gotten to know many of them as friends. She was now being asked to walk away from the people she had served without saying a word.

Kate understood how Velda must feel and knew how unfair it was for her to ask her daughter to leave her life in Custer behind without having given her fair warning. Unfortunately, they had no choice in the matter.

Igloo had become a pressure cooker since the nation declared war. Everyone was being asked to work ten to twelve to fourteen or more hours a day. The Black Hills Ordnance Depot and the town of Igloo had materialized out of the prairie overnight. Trains of over a hundred cars were arriving at the rail station in Provo every hour, with newly laid rail spurs helping to move munitions at a steady pace into the ordnance depot and on into the over eight hundred bunkers that now dotted the landscape.

Kate was confident that once Velda saw what was happening down in Igloo firsthand, she would understand why her parents had been forced to break their promise. She also hoped that seeing the amount of money her parents were pulling down and how quickly the family's fortunes were changing might open Velda's young adolescent eyes to see one of life's simple truths: a person has to make hay while the sun shines. In Igloo, the sun was up and shining in a blaze of glory, the mowed grass laid neck deep in the fields, and folks were baling hay like there was no tomorrow. The Barton family was determined to get their share.

Over breakfast, Velda had asked Bart to deliver her letters to her friends and her notes to all her customers. Bart knew it was the least he could do for his sister. He feared he may never see his family again. The news of the war in Asia and Europe had not been promising. Japan had taken the Philippines and Burma, defeating both the Americans and the British, and was now poised on the doorstep of India. In Europe, the Germans had continued to push forward, rolling over one country after another. In Africa, Germany had backed up Italy and captured Libya and its key oil resources.

On the bright side, the Germans were meeting with stiff resistance from the Allies in Africa, while the Soviets standing strong in Stalingrad had halted the Germans' eastern advance. Bart suspected the real fighting would come in the years ahead, when American soldiers joined the Allies to not only halt German advances but to push the Germans back into the Black Forest nest from which they had been spawned.

Once the car was loaded, Bill took Bart aside and, holding his index finger up to his lips, slipped three hundred dollars into his shirt pocket as a graduation present. Bill wanted Bart to enjoy himself as much as possible before going into the Army and off to war. Giving his son a long hug where neither man wanted to let go, he then stood back and shook his hand with a firm grip, feeling his son's strength. Reaching into his pocket, Bill pulled out a delicately carved turtle amulet and placed it carefully into the palm of Bart's open hand.

"I understand you gave your cougar fang to Johnny. I'm damn happy you did. It means the world to him. I wanted to give you this Lakota good luck talisman that had been left by an unknown traveler on the capstone of your Grandpa John's stone marker in the badlands. The Lakota use turtle amulets much like Saint Christopher medallions. Keep it close and it'll protect you wherever you go. Never forget that this tiny piece of our past represents the Barton link to these mysterious lands and will keep you safe and help you to return to them one day," Bill said, holding the turtle amulet cupped between his and his son's hand.

Releasing his grip, Bill hugged his son once again, both men no longer holding back their tears, knowing it would be many years until they saw each other again. After a full round of tearful farewells, and once the kids' two old bicycles were secured in the half-open trunk, Velda and Johnny hopped into the backseat. With Bill behind the wheel and Kate riding shotgun, they all hollered goodbye and waved their arms out of their windows, and before anyone had any second thoughts, they were off and soon gone. Bart stood for a long time after their car had disappeared up the road. As the dust settled, he sensed a shift in the balance of the universe. He understood from this day forward, he had become a man and would now chart his own course in the world.

Looking down at the turtle amulet, he sighed, wondering about the soul who made it and its deeper meaning to the Lakota people. Pushing it into his pocket, he could feel its power. He knew it was because he wanted it to be so; but then he thought, who really understood the deeper mysteries of this universe. He prayed the Lakota turtle good luck charm would help keep him safe and bring him back home one day.

As the new shiny black automobile sped smoothly southward, Velda and Johnny stared out their windows and watched the passing scenery as the road descended out of the forested hills through the pine-studded meadows of Custer State Park directly into a featureless flatland that seemed to spread out like pancake batter on a hot griddle until it spilled over the edge of the world somewhere beyond the horizon.

Velda could hear her Grandpa John's words echoing in her mind, she was the author of her own destiny, and like Custer, Provo would be the adventure of her life, and, she thought, her little brother Johnny's life as well. Their sudden departure from Custer was like turning the page of an imaginary dairy. She made up her mind to live her life's adventure as it came to her. She had seen how people made plans and had worked hard to make them come true. She had learned that it was important to have a plan and to try to make it happen. She also knew that plan as you might, life had a way of rearranging best laid plans. When things turn out better than you expect, or more often than not, when they don't turn out at all, a person just has to take life as it comes; no matter how it arrives. In the end, life is what you make it, learning to accept this simple truth made all the difference, or at least, it always had for Velda.

She had once thought Pilger Mountain was a paradise that would never end. Custer had been an endless struggle until the family had overcome their utter destitution and slowly and painfully rose above the hard knocks life had dealt them. She had gone from living in a squad tent full of holes to having her own room with her own drapes for the first time in her life. Now she would meet the challenge of Provo head on, and come what may, she would find a way to move forward to a destiny, not given, but made.

BOOK FIVE

June 15, 1942

Provo, Fall River County, South Dakota

Ellen

AFTER THREE WEEKS OF getting up at five in the morning to move from the car to the sheep wagon, Velda and Johnny had had enough. Sleeping in the car was bad enough, having to move at the crack of dawn every day, so their parents could drive to work, was beyond ridiculous. Though their father promised to build a house, they knew there was little likelihood this would happen anytime soon. Their parents worked twelve to fourteen hours a day nearly every day of the week, including weekends. There would be little free time for their father to build a house, considering the last one he built had taken him over four years.

People in Provo spent little time worrying about their living conditions, they slept in their cars, tents, piled-up munition crates, tar paper shacks, lean-tos, and nearly anything with a roof. Bill had set up the old, tattered squad tent, but the relentless wind made it less than ideal. There was no denying, the old tent's canvas had seen its better days. Riddled with holes and covered with patches, the squad tent was little more than a rag pulled over poles.

Velda and Johnny decided to search for a more workable option. It wasn't long before they found one in the form of a wrecked car body that had been left unceremoniously wedged deep in a bar ditch just outside of Provo on the road to Edgemont. Hard to see from the road, they had discovered the car during one of their forays into the sagebrush to hunt jackrabbits.

As it turned out, the ordnance depot had been overrun by jackrabbits and had offered a bounty of twenty-five cents a head. The exploding jackrabbit population was an unintended consequence of ranchers killing off all the coyotes and wolves in the region. Without predators to maintain a balance, jackrabbits had multiplied out of control.

Unable to use firearms anywhere near the ordnance depot, an army of bounty hunters soon fanned out across the prairie with nets and clubs in search of jackrabbits. At twenty-five cents apiece, ever the wily entrepreneurs, Velda and Johnny soon armed themselves with baseball bats and gunnysacks and joined the hunt. At first, using Sandy to gently herd the critters their way, they had been able to bag a dozen jackrabbits a day. Pulling down three dollars a day, they too soon became infected with the same Igloo fever their parents suffered from. They had never made so much money so fast and so easily. They could think of nothing more important than getting their hands on as much of the loose cash as possible.

The brush around the new ordnance depot teamed with jackrabbits, and the pesky critters seemed to sense no danger from humans, often allowing Velda and Johnny to walk right up to them. It didn't take long however for their numbers of decline sharply, with an army of bounty hunters combing the brush looking to earn twenty-five cents a head. It also didn't take long for the jackrabbits to learn to fear humans just as they had their natural nemesis the coyote. As their numbers declined, and their fear of humans increased, bagging jackrabbits became more and more difficult and less and less profitable by the day.

Returning empty handed after a long day in the sun hunting jackrabbits, Velda and Johnny spotted a man nosing around their sheep wagon. Keeping Sandy quiet, fearful the stranger might be up to no good, they circled around behind him to get a closer look.

"What're you kids doing over there?" the man said, catching sight of them as they circled the lot.

"We're wondering what you're doin' pokin' around our wagon," Velda said, keeping her distance.

"I'm Jim Salkin. I owned this here sheep wagon," the man said, pointing at their wagon.

The man had the look of a cowboy with bowed legs, worn cowboy hat, and western snap button shirt. He was thin but looked stout, his face was creased, weathered, and rough, though his eyes and his manner spoke of a gentler man.

"My folks're workin;" Velda said, unsure what the man might want.

"No trouble. I came by to let your Pa know I'll be needin' the wagon late fall when I move my sheep. Your Pa said you kids might be around," Jim said, and then added, "Could you let him know I dropped by?"

"We'll let him know," Velda said, and then added, still suspicious, "So, you and my Pa are friends?"

"Yeah, Bill was introduced to me by a good friend of mine, Roy Kelly," Jim said.

"Roy? He was a good friend to us in Pleasant Valley," Velda said, surprised to hear the familiar name.

"Your Pa told me all about losing his homestead up there. Damn shame. Banks can be rough on a guy," Jim said, shaking his head.

Sensing Jim Salkin was the good-hearted helpful sort, Velda ventured asking him for a favor.

"There's a car wedged in a ditch up the road we'd like to have pulled onto our lot here," Velda said, not sure what kind of response she might get.

"Oh, that old wreck. That was Tim Janson's car. He got drunk and ran off the road one night. I understand he crawled out of the car and walked on into Provo and told anyone who cared to listen that he'd never drive another Hudson," Jim said with a chuckle. "Said he was leaving the car in the ditch as a reminder to folks that Hudson cars were no damn good."

"So, he doesn't want the car?" Velda said, hopeful.

"No, he's done with it," Jim said flatly.

"Would there be any way to pull it out of the ditch? We'd like to have it pulled over here," Velda said, fishing for a yes.

"Your Pa alright with that?" Jim said, surprised and wondering why anyone would want a wrecked 1932 Hudson Terraplane sitting in their yard.

"Yes, he said if no one owned it, we could have it," Velda lied.

"Alright then, I think I can get her back up on the road. Shouldn't be too hard to pull her over here; it's not much more than a mile," Jim said, rubbing his chin. He then nodded his head once to himself and wave his arm and added, "Get in."

Leaving Sandy back at their lot, it wasn't long before they arrived at the car wreck, where Velda and Johnny helped Jim by crawling under the front of the wrecked car to tie a thick chain to the car's frame under the bumper. Once everything was set, Jim gunned his truck's engine and threw the transmission into low gear. Slowly he eased the wreck back up on the road. To everyone's surprise, all four ties were still inflated. The front right tire, however, was bent horizontal to the road, having crumpled under the car when it slammed into the ditch. Jim soon solved the problem by clapping a metal skid under the bent tire. Since it was only a little over a mile to Provo on gravel roads, Jim figured the skid would hold up long enough to get the job done.

Sparks and stones flew as the metal skid raked across the hard-packed gravel surface of the road, carving a friendly grove all the way from the site of the crash to the Barton family lot. Provo was nearly a ghost town during the day, with everyone working on the ordnance depot west of town. Those few who stayed in town were busy either out hunting jackrabbits or inside restocking their businesses for the evening rush. Velda was relieved there was no one in sight when they pulled the wrecked Hudson straight down Bennet Street until they made a right turn onto Front Street that ran parallel to the railroad tracks at the end of town. They then turned north up Wallace Street to the Barton family lot not far from the railroad crossing that led west to Igloo. After jockeying the wrecked car body into place along the back of the lot, Jim unhooked his chain, hopped back in his truck, and bade the kids farewell. As he drove away, he couldn't for the life of him figure out why Bill Barton would want the old wreck pulled into town, but then he never understood a lot of things folks seemed to want that made little sense.

"I don't remember Pa ever saying anything about this wrecked car," Johnny said, turning to his sister.

"Well, he might've, iffen he knew," Velda said, giving Johnny a crooked grin accompanied by a conspiratorial wide-eyed look with her chin tilted down and her eyebrows raised high.

"Right. That's right. I'm sure he would've, iffen he knew," Johnny said, wondering what his father would actually think when he discovered the banged-up car body parked in the yard.

With the Hudson in place, Velda and Johnny spent the day cleaning it out and working out what they needed to finish the job. Their idea was simple, they would convert the interior into their private sleeping quarters, thus saving them the need to get up at the crack of dawn every morning when their parents left for work.

Once they laid the front seat flat to meet up with the edge of the back seat, they found the interior roomy. Though the windshield and rear window where still in place, the car had no windows in any of its four doors. To keep the weather out, they would need to seal up the windows and make them watertight. Johnny came up with a simple and affordable solution for the broken windows.

Johnny remembered they had a similar problem covering holes when they lived in the squad tent that they had solved by using thick cardboard bread boxes that were covered in wax on one side. Johnny thought they could slide sheets of wax-covered cardboard into the window slots on each door and then seal up the edges with tar. Velda had to admit the idea was a good one. Fact was, Velda thought the idea was genius coming from a boy of only seven years old.

With plenty of daylight left, they decided to head to Igloo. With the huge volume of materials and resources pouring into the area for the building of the ordnance depot and all the housing and facilities in the new town of Igloo, the massive project had become a kind of cornucopia. Lumber, building materials, pipes, boilers, water tanks, and nearly every other item under the sun seemed to find its way off the depot and into the surrounding countryside. Ranchers and townsfolk surrounding the depot had come to rely on the newfound bonanza. The government, everyone soon discovered, wasn't a very careful bookkeeper and always seemed to have plenty. With most folks having lived hand to mouth all their lives, seeing the level of waste tolerated by the government was at first hard to stomach. In time, feeding on government waste, became a way of life for more than a few.

Velda and Johnny knew where they could find stacks of wax-coated bread boxes in Igloo. To keep an army of men hard at work, the ordnance depot had built a huge mess hall that served meals around the clock. With so many men to feed, crews ate in rotation twenty-four hours a day. As supplies were consumed, the empty boxes and containers were stacked behind the mess hall to be taken away when fresh supplies were delivered. Velda and Johnny wasted no time in gathering as many empty bread boxes as they needed. Knowing no one would complain or care, they tied their flattened boxes into a bundle with twine and shoved them on edge into the bed of the wagon they had brought with them.

On the way back to Provo, Velda couldn't believe her eyes when she caught sight of a pile of brand-spanking-new mattresses that had been unceremoniously thrown off a loading dock onto the ground. Leaving their wagon parked behind an island of sagebrush, Velda and John walked over to the fence that surrounded the supply depot for a closer look. Sure enough, the mattresses looked unused. From the look of the water stains on some of them, it was clear the mattresses had somehow gotten wet during shipment.

All Velda knew was that she had slept on far worse. The problem was the mattresses hadn't been thrown outside the depot's security fence. Velda knew from what her Pa had told her that much of what the government threw away, they tried to keep out of the reach of the civilian economy, so as to avoid disrupting local commerce.

The thought was that too much government surplus would kill local businesses. In a region where there was no local commerce to speak of, Velda saw no reason to waste anything. The people in the surrounding area agreed wholeheartedly with Velda's way of thinking, which was why they had no reservations about tapping into Igloo's endless stream of valuable goods and materials, which poured out of its gates all free for the taking.

"Johnny, do you think you can shimmy up that post and get over the fence?" Velda said, figuring if Johnny could get over the fence, she would have no problem following him.

Her plan was to drag one of the mattresses to the fence where they might be able to boost it over. Johnny looked at the fence post and the towering height of the fence that stood a good eight feet high. Climbing the fence in broad daylight was a risk, but he figured since it was noon, the men working on the docks were probably having lunch.

"I can get over. How do we get the mattress over?" Johnny said, having doubts and wanting to hear more about the plan.

"If you can get over, I'll be right behind you. We can drag a mattress to the fence and between the two of us try to push up it over the top," Velda said with more confidence than she felt.

Seeing the height of the fence up close, she had serious doubts of her own whether they could simply push a mattress over the top.

"Alright, let's get to it," Johnny said, and without further word, shimmied up the post and down the other side.

Velda followed, soon realizing her brother was a better climber than she would ever be. Struggling to get over the top, she prayed no one was watching. Once they were both on the ground, they made their way over to the pile of mattresses. The docks were empty, but the voices of men joking and laughing could be heard from inside the docking bays. With the smell of cigarette smoke drifting on the air, Velda figured the men were on break. She knew they would have to work fast.

Looking over the mattresses, they picked one out that looked to have only the smallest of stains on one of its corners. Picking it up, reality struck. The mattress was heavy, nearly too heavy for them to even move. Dragging the mattress to the fence, they muscled it up on edge until it stood length-wise up against the fence. Velda could see that the top of the fence was almost two feet higher than the length of the mattress. She had to admit to herself that there was no way the two of them could ever push the heavy mattress over the top of an eight-foot fence.

Just when she was ready to tell Johnny they needed to leave the mattress behind, she noticed that there was a latch on the main gate that worked from the inside. All they would have to do is drag the mattress to the gate and take it straight out on the main road. She also knew, if they didn't want to get caught, they would have to get on the move, and quickly.

Dragging the mattress to the gate took nearly every ounce of strength they had. Unlatching the gate, they quickly dragged the mattress out and re-closed the gate. Sweating profusely, they weren't sure how they were going to get the mattress any further until Johnny discovered the rope handles on each side of the mattress. Grabbing the handles, they were better able to pick the mattress up and wrestle it down the road and over behind the sagebrush island where they had parked their wagon not far from the fence. Exhausted, they laid down on the mattress to take a rest and get out of sight. Stretching out on the new mattress, they looked up into the clear blue sky and felt as though they were floating on a cloud.

"This is a mighty fine mattress," Velda said, enjoying the luxury of something so fine.

"Gettin' this thing home ain't gonna be easy though," Johnny said.

"Nope. But you have to admit, we got ourselves a mattress from heaven," Velda said with a sigh and a chuckle.

"Damned sure iffen we don't" Johnny said with a chuckle of his own, sounding more and more like his Grandpa John every day.

"We'll come back after dark to fetch it. Let's cover it with some sagebrush branches and take our breadboxes back, for now," Velda said.

"Sounds good. We can get the windows fixed, so everything will be ready when we put in the mattress. And sissy, I don't know about you, but I'm mighty hungry," Johnny said, getting back on his feet.

The sun was low in the western sky when Bill and Kate returned from work. At first, Bill wondered whose car was parked at his place. Pulling in, he noted that the car had boarded up windows and one of its front tires folded under the front of car.

"What in the world?" Bill said, looking over at Kate.

Just then, Velda and Johnny ran up to their car to welcome them home.

"Whose old car is that?" Bill said as he got out.

"Ours," Velda and Johnny said in unison.

"Jim Salkin pull it over here for us and we fixed it up," Velda added.

"Jim Salkin?" Bill said, trying to hold his temper.

"What do you kids need with an old wrecked car for?" Kate said, upset and confused.

"It's our sleeping quarters. It's tough getting up every day when you go to work so early in the morning and sleeping on those car seats isn't all that great either," Velda said.

"I've told you kids a dozen times; we're going to build a house soon. You don't need that old thing," Bill said, frustrated they would go out and do something like this without talking to him first and wondering how Jim Salkin figured into it.

"Well, we better get that house soon; Jim said he'd be needing his sheep wagon back this fall," Velda said, remembering why Salkin came by.

"Oh, well, we have a new home comin', there's no need to find an old wreck to live in," Bill said, hoping the Sears Modern Home he had ordered months ago would arrive soon, before the family lost the only shelter they had to live in.

"Come look at our new sleepin' quarters," Johnny said, knowing these kinds of family squabbles tended to go nowhere and take too much time.

Bill and Kate cooled down when they saw how nice the old Hudson was inside and how the kids had fixed it up. Even the use of waxed breadboxes and tar to repair the windows had been a job well done. When they learned the kids had snagged a brand-new discarded mattress, the project seemed even more ingenious. Necessity truly was the mother of invention. People on the frontier had learned to live lives where nothing was simply thrown away, where everything was reproposed, and where waste was a dirty word.

Bill had been acting high and mighty since he started making money hand over fist, he understood however how dear money had been and how carefully they had treated everything that came their way. Waste had always sickened him. With the sudden abundance of things being wasted or thrown away in the mad rush to build the ordnance depot, Bill had forgotten that his children's minds had yet to be poisoned by the reckless wastefulness going on in Igloo. They still lived in a world of scarcity, where there was a use for everything, and nothing went to waste. He was proud of them for their ingenuity. He was glad they had reminded him of what he was made of and where he had come from.

Later that evening after dark, Bill and Kate helped to fetch the wayward mattress, no questions asked. They also helped to wedge it into the Hudson. The fit was nothing less than amazing. Even Bill and Kate had been tempted to try and trade places with the kids before decided the kids had earned their reward.

That night, Velda and Johnny slept snug in their Hudson Terraplane as they floated on a mattress stitched together by the hands of angels; at least, they swore it must have been. They had never slept on anything so comfortable in their lives. Waking up, they noticed how hot it had gotten inside the car. Stepping outside, they realized it was already high noon.

"Looks like we need to get ourselves an alarm clock," Johnny said, rubbing the sleep out of his eyes.

"Well, I'll be damned, if it ain't one thing, it's another with you," Velda said, and started laughing at her little brother, whose hair was sticking up in every direction.

"You ain't so cute yourself," Johnny said, with a hardy chuckle of his own.

Looking in the Hudson's side mirror, Velda could see that her hair was also sticking up in every direction, looking no better than her little brother's, causing her to laugh all the harder. Having slept on straw-filled matts since they were born, all they knew was they had themselves a real honest-to-goodness factory-made mattress and a real bed for the first time in their lives, and they couldn't have been happier about it. That they had overslept, they figured, was just the price they would have to learn to pay for getting a good night's sleep.

Hearing a loud scraping sound coming straight down Bennet Street right past the Newsy Nook, Ross had watched out his front door with curiosity as Tim Janson's 1932 Hudson Terraplane was dragged through town. The car had been lodged in the ditch just north of town since Ross arrived in Provo. Ross learned the story about how the car ended up in the ditch north of Provo straight from the horse's mouth. While shooting the breeze with a local rancher named Tim Janson one day, Tim had shared with Ross the real story of why his Hudson had ended up in the ditch and why he had decided to leave it there.

According to Tim, he been drinking a bit at the Pronghorn Bar in Edgemont when he set out for his ranch south of Provo in a snow flurry. He was confident his 1932 Hudson Terraplane could handle a little snow and decide to push on home. Tim called his car Ellen, after his one and only sweetheart, the woman he had planned to marry, until she up and ran off with a fast-talking Fuller Brush salesman. Broken-hearted, he took to talking to his car the way he used to talk to his sweetheart Ellen, when they were inseparable lovebirds.

Well, it seems Tim often had arguments with his lovebird Ellen when they drove down long lonely country roads. It was right when the snow was picking up, making it difficult to see the road ahead, that Ellen chose to give Tim a piece of her mind. With her insults flying, Tim became distracted, which to hear him tell it, caused him to lose control of Ellen, landing them both in the ditch. Surviving the crash, Tim decided it was his turn to up and leave Ellen, once and for all. Without so much as a fare-thee-well, Tim crawled back up on the road and walked to Provo, where he stayed the night until he could hitch a ride back to Edgemont to buy a new car the next morning. He swore from that day forward, he never wanted to see either Ellen ever again, neither his long-lost lovebird nor the one he left in the ditch.

Ross couldn't figure out why Ellen had been pulled out of her ditch and dragged over to a lot on Wallace Street. He knew sooner or later he would learn the whole story; he always did. There wasn't much that happened in Provo that Ross Bishop didn't eventually know about. Though Provo had a population larger than most towns in West River, it had no elected government and no city council. Still an unorganized township, things got done by those who took charge to get them done.

In many ways, Ross Bishop had become the de facto mayor of Provo, since he was the only person in town who knew where the water pipes had been laid and where the bodies were buried, so to speak. The reason why Ross knew and no one else did was that nearly everyone else worked in Igloo. The only people who actually lived in Provo were a few hobos, business owners, and railroad retirees. To everyone else who called Provo their home, it was just someplace to sleep until housing in Igloo could be built.

The Newsy Nook had done well serving the thousands of workers living in Provo. Billy would be turning eighteen and Ross worried that he might be drafted before Christmas. He wanted to see his youngest son again before that happened. After talking to his sister Beula and Billy by phone, he sent money for his son to travel from San Diego to join him in Provo. Ross couldn't have been happier when Billy said he was eager to come home. The last letter Ross had received from Joseph, his eldest son, had come from Britain. He was relieved that Joe, trained as a medic, hadn't been sent into battle and prayed he never would be. He wanted nothing more than to have his two sons back. Ross was afraid however his daughters may be lost to him forever.

Billy had been eager to join his father in Provo. He had lived in many places over the past nine years. His last move to San Diego had been like moving to paradise after the miserable time the family had endured in the hill country of Missouri. Since the start of the war, finding work hadn't been a problem. Though he had only an eighth-grade education, he had been able to gain skills in a wide variety of professions, from carpentry and heavy equipment operator to welding and mechanical repair. A true jack-of-all-trades, there were very few things Billy couldn't do.

Reading his father's letter, he could see how he might do very well in a place like Igloo, where formal education was not the measure of a man but rather whether he knew how to do things. He also understood the pay was good. Saying farewell to his Aunt Beula, Billy hopped on the train in San Diego with a ticket that would take him all the way to Provo. The last time he had been in South Dakota was on the day he and his sisters were sent on the train from Edgemont to Oskaloosa, Iowa, and into the hands of complete strangers. He had been nine years old, half a lifetime ago, and had thought he would never return to the land of his boyhood. Deep down, he really wasn't sure how he felt about it. All he knew was that Provo might be a new beginning for himself, his father, and the Bishop family.

Sunsets at sea never lost their enchanting allure for Alva. He had grown up on the prairie, where the buffalo grass rippled in the wind like the waves on an ocean. He could often see mirages of those lonely wastelands hovering on the whitecaps of the waves as he stared across the endless choppy waters of the north Atlantic. In April 1942, the aircraft carrier the USS *Wasp* had been assigned to ferry aircraft to Malta in support of RAF British operations in the region. In July, due to heavy losses, the *Wasp* had once again been called on to ferry additional aircraft to the island. In mid-July, having no more than returned to the Atlantic, urgent orders directed the *Wasp* to steam at full speed to the South Pacific to support the American invasion of Guadalcanal in the Solomon Islands. Arriving in early August, the *Wasp* found itself in the middle of a full-scale battle with the invasion of Guadalcanal already underway.

The *Wasp*'s aircraft, including Avengers, Douglas SBDs, and Wildcats, were quickly sent out to strike enemy positions and to down as many enemy aircraft as possible. Scoring a string of successes, the *Wasp* had been on a roll, until on September 15, in support of the landing of the 7th Marine Regiment on Guadalcanal, it was hit by torpedo strikes directly into its magazine, causing huge explosions from ammo and gasoline. Within minutes, the *Wasp* was lost beneath the waves.

Though two hundred men had lost their lives in the attack, Alva had survived the calamity. Plucked out of the water by the aircraft carrier the *USS Hornet* and a number of support ships, Alva and the rest of the surviving crew were eventually transferred to Honolulu. Alva had no more than arrived in Honolulu when he learned the *Hornet* had also been sunk at the Battle of the Santa Cruz Islands on October 27.

Unknown to Alva at the time, the battle for Guadalcanal Island had marked the beginning of the end of World War II in the Pacific. By February 1943, the Japanese would be forced into a slow, yet inevitable, retreat, as their early territorial gains in the Pacific would be trimmed off their expanded empire, one by one.

When Alva joined the Navy twenty years earlier, he had believed that America's greatness came from its growing empire. Now that he had seen firsthand how the same kind of thinking ended for the Japanese, he could see the folly of such an idea. Like Japan's defeat at Guadalcanal in the Pacific, in Europe, the defeat of German troops in Stalingrad in early 1943 marked the beginning of the end of the Third Reich. These events would be known as key turning points in the war. The good news was that these events signaled that the Allies would eventually win. The bad news was that America's resounding victories held the potential of swelling American pride and triggering a fresh round of American empire building.

Alva feared that in such a world, the war machine America had built would never be willing to beat its swollen arsenal of spears back into plowshares. America's new place in the world as the guardian of world peace would turn it into something unrecognizable to most Americans. The massive behemoth America had created to defeat its enemies had been built to feed on the prosecution of war and on the production of weapons of destruction. Alva wondered if it would ever be possible to tame the insatiable appetite of such a beast when so many Americans had come to depend on it for their livelihoods.

What course this leviathan, soon to bestride the world, would chart, was unknown. And yet, the course it chose to steer would impact all the peoples of the world, especially Americans, who had yet to discover they would be responsible for the peace and security of a new world order, soon to be known as Pax Americana.

January 9, 1943

Provo, Fall River County, South Dakota

Boom Town

AT THE BEGINNING OF the school year in September 1942, the original thought had been to send Provo's children to Edgemont schools until the new Provo schools, being built on the Igloo Base, were ready to use. The large and growing number of children in Provo caused the Edgemont school district to have second thoughts about hosting such an unwelcome influx. Eventually, deemed to be too disruptive by Edgemont's leading citizens, the Provo school district relented in their request and made do by holding split day classes in a converted barracks just inside of the gate of the new town of Igloo on the Black Hills Ordnance Depot.

Without fanfare, the government moved Thanksgiving back to the fourth Thursday in November in 1942, making the whole country happy again. Velda had resigned herself to sharing the celebration of her birthday with the trappings of Thanksgiving as long as she lived at home. Rather than fight it, she had enjoyed having turkey with all the fixing followed by a generous piece of birthday cake. At the age of fourteen, she had begun to notice how the boys at school looked at her and her new best friend, Babe Olsen, who never stopped talking about boys. Velda could see in the mirror, she had grown over the summer. She was no longer a little girl. She was becoming a woman.

In spite of Edgemont's lack of hospitality to Provo's children, the town had boomed since the ordnance depot's arrival, as had every other town in and around the southern hills. In Edgemont, new businesses had sprung up along Second Street, the main road that ran through town parallel with the railroad tracks that headed straight south to Provo and Igloo. Though a movie theater, several bars, and dance halls had been moved into Provo from surrounding communities, none of these shabby cobbled together tar paper shacks could compete with Edgemont's thriving business district, with its paved well-lit streets lined with brick-and-mortar buildings.

A huge new civic center, named the Armory, had been built to hold basketball games, concerts, dances, and other community gatherings. Edgemont had become the entertainment center of the southern hills. With their newfound wealth, workers flocked to Edgemont looking for a good time, something many, having suffered through hard times during the long depression, had done without for far too many years.

Edgemont represented civilization to young people living in the makeshift town of Provo. With Provo's wild west atmosphere, its entertainment establishments tended to focus mostly on the wallets of single men, much like gold rush towns during the early settlement of the Black Hills. Edgemont offered a more cultured band of entertainment with something for the whole family. The challenge for young people without any means of transportation was the ten miles that separated Provo and Edgemont. This obstacle was solved when it was discovered that by hitching a ride on a passing freight train in Provo, the distance could be covered in little more than twenty minutes, free of charge.

With trains running both ways on a regular schedule, hitching rides became a popular way to travel between the two towns, for the daredevils brave enough to jump onto moving trains. Since trains always slowed down at railroad crossings, the preferred method for rail riders was to jump on at the Wallace Street crossing in Provo and jump off at the 2nd Street crossing just outside of Edgemont. Riding the rails soon caught on with young people eager to test their wings and prove their independence as a kind of rite of passage in a world run by adults.

Velda and Babe had never ridden the rails but had been told how to do it from frequent rail riders. According to the experts, riders needed to be careful not to be seen by the bulls that patrolled the trains to guard against free riders. The best method was to jump between boxcars and to sit on the narrow ledge of the lead car. To stay put and balanced, riders needed to push their backs against the boxcar and rest their feet on the coupling between the cars. Riding tucked in on the backside of the boxcar, riders could stay out of the wind as the train moved down the track. The only drawback of riding the rails was the weather; should it rain or snow, it was tough to stay dry.

Bill had built a small house in Provo as promised. Delayed more than eight months by the growing scarcity of building materials brought on by the war, the Sears Modern Home finally arrived with precut lumber, roofing shingles, and all the plumbing hardware. With the foundation poured and ready when the kit home arrived, it had taken less than a week to nail it together. The house was small, with only five rooms, a living/dinning combination, a kitchen with panty, a bath and laundry room, and two small bedrooms. Though Velda didn't get a bedroom of her own, she was happy they didn't have to go through winter without heat.

The old Hudson had made a great bedroom in the summer. Without any way to easily heat the interior, it wasn't a suitable shelter for the winter, however. As soon as the house went up, Velda and Johnny wasted no time putting the old Hudson up for sale. With housing at a premium, just having a dry place to sleep was in high demand in Provo. It took less than a day to pocket fifty dollars for the old Hudson. Much to their surprise, the new owner, Mick Monger, was a mechanic and asked them to let him work on the car a few days before he moved it. Before long, Mick, covered, in grease from head to toe, jacked the car up and soon fixed the broken front strut and straightened the front wheels until he got all the tires to point in the same direction. He then took to working on the engine. After a week of daily repairs, with blue smoke belching out from under the hood and out of both exhaust pipes, Ellen, the jilted and discarded lover of Tim Janson, had been miraculously resurrected and now had a new beau to see to her needs. Coming out to see what all the commotion was about, Velda and Johnny stood on the front porch of their new home and stared in disbelief as the old Hudson under its own power made its way out of the yard and up the street to its new home on Dakota Street, east of Bennet Street, where makeshift shanties, tents, and car bodies littered the countryside.

With the ordnance depot closed for the weekend, everyone looked forward to a chance to relax after months of nearly continuous work. On Saturday morning, Bill and Kate were invited over to the Olsen's home for an afternoon of cards. With Velda and Babe inseparable friends and spending nearly all their free time together, the families had naturally gravitated toward one another. Fred and Judy Olsen had moved to Provo from Hill City, a small mining town north of Custer. Fred and Judy both worked on the ordnance depot, giving the couples a lot in common.

With Hollywood churning out one motion picture after another and movie tickets costing only ten cents, going to the movies soon became a favorite pastime for nearly everybody. Velda and Babe had gone to several movies at the movie theater in Provo, which they had enjoyed. *Bambi* had been a wonderful, animated film. Velda was still having nightmares after watching *The Mummy's Tomb*. With nothing to compare it to, the Provo movie theater seemed a wonder to kids living in Provo. Having heard that the Edgemont theater was better than Provo's, Velda wanted to see for herself. She also wanted to see the new Humphrey Bogart and Ingrid Bergman movie *Casablanca* that had just opened in theaters all over the country but wouldn't be coming to Provo anytime soon.

With no other way to get to Edgemont, it didn't take much to convince Babe it was time they joined the ranks of the rail riders. Grabbing their coats and scarves, they told their card-playing parents they would be at a friend's house, before dashing out the door. They headed directly for the Wallace Street railroad crossing, where trains slowed down and where they had been told it was easiest to hop on. Rather than stand out in the open, they decided to stand back from the track behind a small storage shed where they could stay out of the wind and more importantly out of sight. After waiting for nearly twenty minutes the girls realized just how cold it was. It had snowed the night before and the surrounding countryside was a white featureless void where powered snow swirled up in columns like dust devils on a dry summer day.

The clanging of the crossing bells alerted them of the coming train long before it arrived. When it came into view, it seemed to be moving a lot faster than they had been told. As it approached the crossing it sounded its horn and slowed down but not nearly as much as they had expected. Seeing no one watching the crossing from the station depot or surrounding houses, they both bolted at a full run toward the crossing. As they approached, they found they needed to run parallel to train and to try to match its speed. Deciding it was worth a try, Velda grabbed the bar just under the rear of a passing boxcar. Struggling, she used her other hand to grab the upper edge of the boxcar frame, which allowed her to quickly pull herself up onto the narrow ledge behind the car. She then turned to see how Babe was doing.

Surprised they were already over fifty yards from the crossing, Velda sensed the train had started to accelerate. Babe had yet to grab the bar just under the rear of the car and was running as fast as she could with her right arm extend and the fingers of her right hand stretched to their limit. Seeing she wouldn't make it, Velda bent down while holding the edge of the boxcar with one hand and reached out to grab Babe's hand with the other. With the ground along the track getting increasingly rough, Velda knew Babe wouldn't be able to keep up with the train much longer.

"Grab my hand! Hurry!" Velda yelled, with fear and urgency in her voice.

Babe could see it was now or never. With one last burst of speed, Babe literally jumped, leaving her feet to grab Velda's hand. Snagging Velda's hand, their clasped hands came together in a death grip. Holding on with all she had, Velda pulled Babe toward the bar welded along the under edge of the boxcar. Grabbing the bar with her other hand, Babe was able to gain purchase and pull herself up next to Velda on the narrow ledge behind the boxcar. Resting their feet on the bouncing coupling between the cars, the girls hugged each other and began to laugh and cry uncontrollably, both of them knowing just how close they had come to being badly injured or even killed. Shaking from the adrenaline coursing through the bodies, it took several minutes for them to finally clam down.

"That was close," Velda said with a shaky voice, breaking the silence as she looked through tear-filled eyes at her friend, who had never looked more pale and frightened.

"Too damn close," Babe said, shaking her head back and forth. "Next time, I get to hop on first."

The remark landed between them like an armed hand grenade, its detonation causing them to burst out into laughter all over again. This time there were no tears of fright, only tears of joy.

"This thing was moving a hell of a lot faster than we were told," Velda said.

"I knew that damn Davy Felon couldn't be trusted. I don't think he's ever ridden the rails himself," Babe said.

"Yeah. Davy's always been a big talker. Mr. Know-It-All," Velda said, damn happy they somehow survived. "He's probably never done any of the things he claims he's done."

"No doubt about that. By the way, it's damn cold out here. And just so you know, I'm not going to try to hop on another train today. We need to think about how we're getting home," Babe said, making it clear they needed to adjust their plan.

"Folks in Provo go to Edgemont all the time. We'll catch a ride from someone goin' back to Provo. If not, we might have to hop another train,"

Velda said, though she wasn't confident of their success in getting home using either option.

After twenty minutes, the train slowed down right on schedule. Hopping off at the 2nd Street crossing just outside of town, Velda and Babe were happy to be off the train and in one piece. Walking straight down the main road into Edgemont, the girls had never felt more alive. They had tempted fate; they had ridden the rails. They had proven to themselves they had the moxie to do it. At fourteen, they were two young ladies out on the town. Reaching the main business district, the clean orderliness of Edgemont was very different than the dirty unkept hodgepodge of Provo.

Wasting no time, they headed directly for the largest movie theater in town. Buying two matinee tickets for *Casablanca*, they didn't have long to wait before the movie started. Lining up to buy sodas and buttered popcorn, they couldn't believe they had actually ridden the rails to Edgemont on their own. They had never seen anything as beautiful as the interior of the Elks Theater, with its beautiful art deco decor interior of simple, clean geometric shapes and streamlined curves. The plaster castings that adorned the walls depicting bold bare-breasted women in flowing garments were something the girls had never seen displayed in public before. Velda felt the soft velvet cover on her seat and believed they must be in one of the finest places on earth.

The civilized elegance of Edgemont seemed a world away from dingy tar paper shacks of Provo. Whether it was the whole experience of being out on the town on their own or the sterling performances of Bogart and Bergman on the silver screen, neither girl could ever say; all they knew was that *Casablanca* was the best movie they had ever seen in their lives. Neither girl had wanted the movie to end; and both had wanted Rick and Ilsa to fall into each other's arms and to run off together at the end of the movie; the war, the world, and Ilsa's husband, Victor, be damned.

As they walked out of the theater and back onto the street, Velda, acting like Ilsa in the movie's final scene, said, "But what about us?" Pretending to be Rick, she answered Ilsa's question in a deep manly voice, "We'll always have Paris."

Babe laughed and got a serious look on her face, continuing Rick's part by saying, "That's right, Toots, our problems don't amount to a hill of beans in this crazy world." Cupping her hand under Velda's chin, Babe added, "Here's looking at you, kid."

Both girls got a kick out of their role playing and had a hard time not laughing out loud as they made their way down the street. It was getting late in the afternoon, and though the sun was still high in the sky, it was quickly sliding toward the western horizon. The weather had turned colder. Edgemont unlike Provo had trees, though most of these were large, twisted cottonwoods long since denuded of their leaves. With a steady north wind whistling through their branches, the trees provided little protection against the steady blast of freezing arctic air. Looking up at the sky, Velda worried that with the clouds hanging so low, there was a good chance of a snow flurry breaking out at any moment.

Buying a bag of hot roasted nuts and a couple cups of hot chocolate, the girls made their way to the city park, where a large domed gazebo acted like a magnet as it drew people to it. Edgemont had hosted the visits of two former presidents, Teddy Roosevelt in 1903 and William Howard Taft in 1911. Velda and Babe had been taught about the presidential visits at school and wanted to see the famous gazebo up close where both presidents had given speeches.

The lure of Black Hills had attracted several presidents over the years. Calvin Coolidge had made the Custer State Park Game Lodge his summer White House in 1927 and had inaugurated the start of work on Mount Rushmore. Velda even remembered when Franklin Roosevelt visited the Black Hills in the summer 1936. Her Pa had shared the story of how his WPA work team had watched the presidential processions come through Keystone when they stopped at Mount Rushmore. It was that Thanksgiving that the family had its first chance to listen to one of Roosevelt's fireside chats, one of the first commercial radio broadcasts in the Black Hills.

The girls soon discovered that the gazebo was a popular gathering spot for Edgemont's teenagers and young people. At first, they didn't recognize anyone in the milling crowd. With kids in Provo unable to attend Edgemont schools, very few kids from the two towns had ever met. Among the large group of adolescents, they finally recognized a couple of girls from their school in Igloo. Spying the twin sisters, Betty and Debbie McDonald, didn't come as a great surprise, considering the two had come to be known as the biggest rebels and rabble rousers in their school.

"Let's find out how they got here and how they plan to get back," Velda said, worried that if it snowed, the road might become impassable for hours.

Getting the twins' attention, Velda and Babe made their way over to them.

"What're you gals doing here?" Debbie said, truly surprised to see Velda and Babe in Edgemont, having believed the two were not the type to be running around.

"Well, we hopped a train and thought we would take in the sites," Babe said, acting like they did it every day. "How about you two?"

"Hopped a train? I don't think so," Betty said, having her doubts.

She had heard about kids hopping trains but had never known any girls who had ever done it.

"We did it, that's for sure. Not sure we'll ever do it again, however. It was pretty wild and more than a little dangerous," Velda said, not wanting to argue, but proud that they had actually ridden the rails and survived to tell the tale.

"The boys always talk about it. Not sure so many of 'em have actually done it," Betty said.

"You know boys, they're all talk," Babe said with a giggle.

"You can say that again," Debbie said with a knowing giggle of her own.

"You come here a lot?" Velda said, wanting to get to the point.

"We come when we can catch a ride," Betty said, sizing Velda and Babe up and seeing the two girls in a new light.

"How do you get back?" Babe said.

"Easy, there're always folks headed back to Provo," Betty said, acting nonchalant.

"See those two guys over there. The one on the left is George and the other one is Billy. I think he came from California or something. They'll be headed back soon. They said they wanted to beat the weather," Debbie said.

"You ridin' with them?" Velda said, hopeful.

"Yep. You gals lookin' for a ride?" Debbie said.

"Do you think we could squeeze in with you?" Velda said.

"Sure. If the guys don't mind, neither do we," Betty said. "What happened? You two decide not to hop another train?"

"Yeah, well, hoppin' a train might be possible but we're thinkin' once was enough," Velda said matter-of-factly.

"More than enough, my friend. I'm the one who damn near got killed," Babe whined with a twisted face, causing a laugh to ripple through the foursome.

George and Billy had no objections to having the four young ladies squeeze into George's 1938 Ford Two Door Sedan. The back seat being narrow could only fit three. Babe got in first, followed by Velda and Betty, with Velda in the middle. Since George had been drinking, Billy got in behind the wheel with Debbie crawling into the front seat between Billy and George, who rode shotgun. With everyone settled into their seats, Billy set out for the ten-mile drive to Provo. Just as everyone had feared, they had driven no more than a mile outside of Edgemont when the wind picked up and snow started to fly.

The road between the two towns was narrow with very little shoulder on either side before dropping off into steep bar ditches, leaving little margin for error. Billy drove at a good clip but paid careful attention to staying centered in his own lane. With a car coming at high speed up from behind, Billy frequently checked and rechecked his rearview and side mirrors. Just as the car zoomed past, Billy and Velda's eyes locked in the rearview mirror for what seemed like an uncomfortable length of time. Though the glance had only been for a second, they both felt a blush of embarrassment, but said nothing.

Debbie enjoyed being squeezed between the two grown men. She flirted by pushed herself up against George, who had swung his left arm over the back of the front seat behind Debbie to make more room. Betty, watching the attention her sister was getting, did her best not to be outdone. To get her share of attention, she became a chatter box and talked all the way to Provo in an attempt to flirt with Billy, who seemed not to notice.

"Of all the gin joints, in all the towns, in all the world, she walks into mine . . .," George said out of the blue, as he squeezed Debbie's shoulder, pulling her closer to him.

George was a long way from being drunk but was feeling good and liked how things had turned out. Debbie giggled and snuggled closer to George. When Billy glanced into the rearview mirror, he once again caught Velda's eye. When he did, he ever so slightly shook his head from side to side with pursed lips, indicating he didn't think much of the McDonald twins. Without thinking, Velda narrowed her eyes ever so slightly in reply. Velda didn't know what to think about her silent communication with Billy, but she knew it made her feel different somehow. She had thought about boys but had never really been around boys in her new role as a woman.

When they arrived in Provo, the snow was coming down hard. Dropping off the girls by the water pump on Bennet Street, near the center of town, Billy and George poked their heads out their car windows and bade the four young ladies farewell, before speeding off.

Turning to George, Billy said, "George, do you recall what Rick said to Louis at the end of *Casablanca*?"

"I think this is the beginning of a beautiful friendship," George said with raised eyebrows.

"Yes, just who'll befriend whom, my friend," Billy said with a chuckle.

"Indeed," George quipped, though he already had his sights set on Babe, she was the prettiest girl he had ever seen, and he wouldn't stop until she was his girl.

Like Billy, he had no interest in either of the pushy McDonald twins. They were cute, of that there was no doubt. Their problem was, their reputations proceeded them. They were nothing but trouble. Velda had struck a chord in Billy, though he wished he would have had more time to talk with her to get to know her better. He figured, it would be just a matter of time before he would catch sight of her again. If nothing else, he was sure she would drop by the Newsy Nook; sooner or later, everybody in Provo did.

Velda and Babe came bounding into the Olsen house, just as their parents had put away the cards and decided to share dinner together. Telling their parents that they had been hanging out with their friends seemed to raise no suspicions. The only thing on their parents' minds was how the snowstorm might impact work on the ordnance depot. The last thing anyone wanted was to miss a single day of work. No one believed that the Igloo cash gusher would continue forever. All they knew was as long as it kept throwing out cash, they needed to grab as much of it as they could.

Velda and Babe both wondered who George and Billy were and whether they would ever see the two young men again. Men their age were few and far between, with most of the young men between the ages of eighteen and twenty-five off fighting the war. They agreed to watch out for George's car in hopes of getting to know the boys better. They also agreed life had got a lot more interesting since they decided to hop on that train to Edgemont. The ride had changed everything. It had taken their lives in a new direction. They both knew there was no going back. With their eyes now opened to the ways of the world, they were uncertain about what the future may hold for them. The one thing they knew for sure was that they had left the innocence of their childhoods behind forever.

July 15, 1943

Igloo, Fall River County, South Dakota

Prairie Paradise

NEVER BEFORE IN AMERICAN history had men and women worked shoulder to shoulder as equals the way they did at Igloo and other military bases and arms factories throughout the country. Rosie the Riveter was more than a slogan, she was a reality. With America's men at war, women had been asked to step up and fill the roles of men, and many of them had without missing a beat. On the Black Hills Ordnance Depot, Women Ordnance Workers, known as WOWs, made up over 40 percent of the workforce. Kate, like Rosie, wore a red and white polka-dot bandana as part of her uniform. The difference for women ordnance works was that their white polka dots weren't just round polka dots, they were white silhouettes of bombs with lit fuses.

Kate loved her WOW uniform with its blue coveralls and red bandana and all that it meant. She had become a skilled semi-tractor-trailer wrangler, able to back her big rig into the tightest loading docks without a nick or a scrape. Even her male counterparts had to admit she was one of the best drivers at Igloo. Kate also loved the freedom her job gave her. Her income was equal to that of a man's. Most of all, she loved that her money was hers to manage for the first time in her life. With such independence came a level of self-confidence she had never known.

To fill the labor shortage, the government had actively recruited potential workers from the nearby Pine Ridge Indian Reservation. The Lakota experience of working for white men had not always been good. All too often, the wages paid for Indian labor were far less than those paid for white labor. Since their defeat, the Lakota had also experience decades of discrimination outside the boundaries of their reservation lands.

With few opportunities for work on the reservation, eventually over a hundred fifty Lakota accepted the government's offer of employment and joined the ranks of workers at Igloo. Much to their surprise, the government went out of its way to welcome them to Igloo by providing an area for teepees and Lakota traditional activities. Those few educated Lakota wanting to live like the white man were allowed to live in the same housing units as whites. It was the first time in history the Lakota had been treated as anything close to equals.

Despite the entrenched discrimination that remained alive and well beyond the gate of the Igloo Base, for workers at Igloo, the same wages were paid to all workers whether they were men or women or white, Indian, Hispanic, or black. One of the first things Bill noticed about working at Igloo was that when people are employed and making good money, no one seemed to care who they worked with or who they lived beside. Igloo was like returning to the Garden, where the sins of men had yet to be committed and yet to be etched into their hearts. The guiding principles of humankind, too often blindly followed, of prejudice, bigotry, misogyny, and racism, all simmered just below the surface, ready to sprout and branch and grow with the slightest encouragement. What amazed Bill was how these all-too-common demons could be caged by simply treating everyone equally and with respect, and by giving them a chance to work at a fair wage.

The first housing units completed in Igloo were the huge barracks buildings for singles and young married couples without children. As the barracks went up, teams poured the foundations for fourplex and sixplex housing units to be built for married couples with children. All plumbing, electrical, and gas hookups were included in the foundations, so when the modular units arrived, they would be able to be bolted directly onto the foundations, providing move-in-ready housing almost immediately, much like the Sears Modern Home only on a grander scale. Unfortunately, like the Sears Modern Home, the modular units had been delayed due to material shortages brought on by the war, causing the Barton family and many others to wait over the summer for their new home in Igloo to arrive.

Along with new housing units, a whole new town with all the amenities had seemingly sprouted out of the prairie fully formed, including a well-stocked post exchange and commissary, an Olympic-sized swimming pool, a bowling alley, a roller-skating rink, and a gymnasium that could seat over two thousand people. To round things off, Igloo also had primary and secondary schools, an office complex, a fire station, a hospital with doctors' offices, and a whole variety of small shops. Though the community, as a military installation, was closed to outsiders, it had everything, and everything it had was brand spanking new.

When the citizens of Igloo moved into their new housing, everything was clean, shiny, and modern. The houses were equipped with indoor plumbing, hot and cold running water, flush toilets, central heating, ice-boxes, and even washers and driers. Igloo's roads were paved with curbs and gutters and well-lit with concrete sidewalks. The town had been laid out in a prefect north-south, east-west grid, everything was in its place, and nothing was out of place. Trees and bushes had been planted everywhere, with yards covered in green grassy lawns bordered by clean, landscaped roadsides. Even the floor in the school gymnasium was a thing of exquisite beauty made of the finest cherrywood, an extravagance that would become the envy of every visiting team to compete with the Provo Rattlers on its shiny flawless surface.

The government had spared no expense for the citizens of Igloo, a fact made obvious in every detail and every plumbed corner. Those who had found their way to Igloo couldn't believe their dumb luck in having stumbled upon paradise in the middle of a desolate wasteland at the ragged edge of the world.

Velda and Babe looked forward to moving away from the shabby blight of Provo to the pristine grandeur of Igloo. The girls had talked with George and Billy a number of times over the past several months and gotten to know them well. Velda often dropped by the Newsy Nook to drink a soda with Billy and had learned he had lived in many places during his childhood. In some ways his stories were exciting and full of adventure, and yet, somehow sad. Velda felt sorry that Billy had grown up without ever really knowing his mother, though his stories about living with his Aunt Beula were always happy ones. She knew the woman had been like a mother to Billy and had become a very special person in his life. Having fallen in love with Billy, Velda hoped she too had become a very special person to him.

The sky and sea merged into a perfect azure blue. The smooth surface of the water as it met the cloudless sky at the horizon looked as though it were a single polished piece of lapis lazuli, the precious stone prized by ancient cultures across the world and believed by the Egyptians to guide the souls of the dead into the afterlife. Francis prayed it would guide the souls of those who lost their lives at Pearl Harbor on their journey beyond the bounds of this world. He had witnessed the surprise attack from shore and had fired at the marauding Zeros. Two waves of attacking planes had laid waste to the naval base in mere minutes, sinking several ships and damaging many others, leaving behind over two thousand four hundred dead and eleven hundred wounded. The shock and horror of that day had forever been etched deep into his memory.

Rather than being assigned seas duty in the fleet, he had been assigned to shore duty and sent to Hawaii straight out of basic training. He had been eager to see the world and believed like his older brother, Alva, that America no longer ended at its shores. With a growing number of far-flung territories beyond its continental fortress, America had become a global power. Unable to see America's growing empire firsthand, Francis had fed his hunger to learn more about the world by spending nearly all of his free time reading every book he came across at the base library. The more he learned, the more he discovered he didn't know much about many things in the world, which drove his desire to learn even more about anything and everything he could.

From where he sat on his stool in the shade, he watched with interest a small gray-winged bird, with a black head and white breast, poke its short bright orange beak into something hidden in the grass along the edge of beach and wondered how in the world an Arctic tern had ended up in Honolulu. But then he had read, Arctic terns had the longest annual migration cycle of any animal on earth. Though they flew back and forth between the Arctic Circle and the Antarctic Circle every year, he knew these small birds flew following the shoreline and weren't known to venture into the middle of the Pacific Ocean. Stranded on a rock in the middle of the Pacific, Francis wondered if the little bird would ever be able to find its way home, something he often wondered about himself.

With the tide out, the beach seemed a mile wide, and though it looked inviting, the heat of the midday sun kept everyone comfortably under the palm trees and the large cabana-topped bar, relaxing and drinking cool beer while shooting the breeze. Francis had received orders to report for duty aboard the aircraft carrier the *USS Independence*, which would be pulling into port in the next few weeks. He had come to Coconut Joe's Hula Bar to have lunch and hang out with Alva.

At first it had been hard to believe that they would end up in the same place, considering the number of countless ports around the world. Francis knew Alva was serving on the *USS Wasp* in the Atlantic when he joined the service. That the *USS Wasp* had ended up fighting in the Battle for Guadalcanal and had been sunk came as a hell of a surprise to Francis. That his brother had survived and had been brought to Honolulu was nothing more than pure serendipity. That had been nearly a year ago.

"Well, there you are, Petty Officer Third Class Barton," Alva said with a smile, as he walked up to the daydreaming Francis.

"You found me, Master Chief Petty Officer Barton," Francis said with a grin of his own, acknowledging Alva's own recent promotion.

Both men had been promoted during the last cycle. For Francis, becoming a petty officer would make his sea duty a bit more bearable. At least, he wouldn't be assigned the most undesirable work aboard ship like a common seaman. As a petty officer, he would more likely be put in charge of such work details. Alva had served more than twenty years in the Navy and had finally achieved his ultimate goal, the rank of master chief petty officer, equal to a sergeant major in the Army, the pinnacle of the enlisted ranks.

Rather than being sent back to the fleet, Alva had been assigned shore duty in Honolulu. Though staying to enjoy a tour on shore in Hawaii was tempting, Alva had put in for retirement and hoped the Navy would let him go now that the war had turned with real prospects for an end in sight.

"How many of those've you had?" Alva said.

"Not near as many as I plan to," Francis said, holding up an empty bottle of Primo Island Lager, Hawaii's favorite local brew.

"Bartender, two ice-cold Primos," Alva said, sliding onto the stool next to Francis.

Two bottles of Primo soon landed on the counter. At twenty-five cents a bottle, prices were high on the beach, but no one was complaining. Taking in the panoramic view of all the tanned shapely ladies clad in skimpy swimwear was well worth the premium pricing to a bunch of lonely, beached squids.

"Cheers," Alva said. "Next round's on you, little brother."

Clinking their bottles together, the two men took long pulls on their ice-cold brews. News from home was shared. Bart had been drafted and the last letter anyone had received from him had been postmarked from somewhere in Europe. Herman was also in the Army and had been stationed in San Diego at the outbreak of the war. To everyone's surprise, his most recent letter was postmarked from Brisbane, Australia. According to Herman's letter, American soldiers earned double their Australian counterparts, turning them into kings in the land down under. In a country suffering from strict rationing and shortages, American soldiers and sailors were the big spenders in town. Not only did they have access to chocolate, cigarettes, nylons, and coffee, they had money to burn. Their stylish uniforms and devil-may-care attitude helped them to attract the attention of Australia's fairer sex, causing more than a little friction with the local male population.

"With fighting going on everywhere, Herman and I seem to have drawn the long straws," Francis said.

"Count yourself lucky to've stayed clear of the war, so far. It damn near took my life. I'm counting the days until I can finally go home," Alva said.

"Home? Where would that be?" Francis said, meaning it.

"The Black Hills for me. I plan to set up one of those new mobile home parks in Rapid City. I've saved my money and would like to invest. With my monthly retirement checks and income from rentals, I should be able to live comfortably enough," Alva said, sounding like a man with a plan. "I also want to give Pa a place where he can settle in. He's been sent back and forth between our sisters for far too long."

Alva had never married, and now hoped more than ever that he would be able to find a good woman, when he returned home. He also wanted to take care of his Pa, who had been living with his four sisters on a rotating basis. Living in a small travel trailer, John had been pulled from one place to the next, with his daughters taking turns tending to his needs. None of the four was willing to keep him full time. With John in his late seventies and nearly completely blind, Alva wanted to put an end to the circus, believing the man deserved to spend his final days in peace and in one place.

"I have orders for the light aircraft carrier the *USS Independence*, the first carrier of its class," Francis said, wanting to hear Alva's opinion.

"I read about the new Independence class carriers. They're basically light cruisers that have been converted into small aircraft carriers. They carry about thirty aircraft, including a couple dozen fighters and a handful of torpedo bombers. They're light and fast, a hell of a lot faster than the larger ships. They'll probably be used in the final push to drive the Japanese back to their home islands. I think you picked a short straw this time, little brother. You're bound to see action before this war's over," Alva said, knowing the war was far from over and worried his little brother would now be thrown in the middle of it.

"I figured as much. No way I was gonna get out of this war without a fight," Francis said. "Bartender, how about a couple more Primos?"

With fresh bottles of beers slid in front of the two men, they once again clinked their bottles together, both men accepting that in the end, life is for the living and living is what happens every waking hour a man still draws a breath. The past was but a memory, the future yet to be written, they had the now, and it was the only thing they could be sure of, the only thing they could hold on to.

War had a way of clarifying things, a way of bringing things into focus. There really was no time to waste in life. Life was to be lived. They wanted no more out of life than to live it, truly live it. And though life happened in the now, they both believed in the promise of tomorrow and what it might bring, and more importantly, in what they might make of it.

The Fremder family had come to use Bill Barton's cabin more and more as the Detrick's children grew older. Detrick farmed the cabin's surrounding forty acres, incorporating the original Barton claim into his own. Lena had also made a homestead claim for one hundred sixty acres nearby, which eventually had been added to Detrick's growing holdings in Pleasant Valley. Life had not been easily in Pleasant Valley, but a number of stubborn homesteaders had continued to hang on through all the tough times.

With the sudden death of Gutzon Borglum on March 6, 1941, work on Mount Rushmore came to a sudden halt, until Gutzon's son, Lincoln Borglum, was called on to finish up work on the faces. Though the original design of the monument depicted the full figures of the four presidents, from head to waist, a lack of funding eventually forced Lincoln to declare the sculpture complete on October 31, 1941. Jeff Engel and Mike Robinson had done well over the eleven years they worked on the mountain. Both had banked a good deal of money and after selling their homesteads in Pleasant Valley had moved to California to invest in farmland in Capay

Valley northwest of Sacramento on the advice of Jacob Shultz, who had moved there to join his brother to grow almonds in the mid-1930s.

Jeffery's son, Jeffery Junior, had been drafted into the Army and sent to fight somewhere in Europe. Unknown to everyone except his wife, Wilma, Jeffery feared that his son may carry his father's curse. Now that Jeffery Junior was fighting on the same battlefields from which he had once turned and ran as a coward, Jeffery worried that the German bullet with his name etched into it may now find his namesake instead. If this became his son's fate, Jeffery wondered if he could live with such guilt. In years to come, Jeffery Junior would return home a war hero, causing his father to realize no German bullet with his name on it could have ever found his son, since the coward named Robert Grant had died in a battlefield hospital in Germany in 1918 and had left no namesake.

With the departure of Jeff Engel and Mike Robinson, of the original Lucky Seven, only the Determined Two, Detrick Fremder and Roy Kelly, remained on Pilger Mountain. Detrick often pondered, who would be the last man standing. As had become his custom from time to time, Detrick walked over to the Barton cabin to look things over. Coming around the big pine tree with its rope swing that stood near the house, he stopped in front of Bill's stone maker, which always reminded him of the good times they all had when they first came to Pleasant Valley.

Bill had told him of all the symbolic meanings contained in the stone marker and its Lakota *uname* design. Detrick had respected Bill's desire to leave the maker untouched as Bill's father had done when he left his stone marker in the badlands. Bending down on one knee, Detrick brushed several loose pine needles off the delicate jade pendent that rested on the yellow stone, facing east toward the rising sun.

Looking at its intricate design, he recalled Bill telling him that the carved Chinese characters meant double happiness. If only that could have been true, he thought. And then, upon further consideration, he realized it was exactly how things had turned out in the end. He had stayed on Pilger Mountain, where his family had thrived. Bill and Kate had found their paradise in Igloo, where they now thrived and from which they planned to make a new beginning.

Standing up, he once again looked down at the yellow stone and the jade pendent, which brought an additional thought into his mind, one that had stewed there since he first learned of Roosevelt's Executive Order 9066, not long after the bombing of Pearl Harbor. Without due process of the

American justice system, Order 9066 had resulted in the forcible detention of over a hundred twenty thousand people, the majority of whom were American citizens, simply because the homeland of their ancestors was at war with America.

Japanese immigrants were no different than German immigrants or Italian immigrants or any of the other ethnic or racial groups fighting America, of which many could be listed. America had not seized the assets of any of these peoples, nor had it shipped them off to detention camps.

The *why* seemed clear enough. Unequal treatment became easier when racial differences were clear. This truth about America left a sour taste in Detrick's mouth, because he knew it held true nearly everywhere else in the world where different groups of human beings came face to face with one another. That America, home of the free, was freer for some more than others, was a fact that could be easily witnessed nearly everywhere, if only those who already had the all the freedoms simply took the time to look around.

Detrick realized that the marriages of his own daughters to husbands from a wide variety of heritages, from English and Irish to French and Swedish, would have been unheard of before he came to America. Such mixing of races was not common in Europe and had almost never happened among Germans. Detrick could see that for America, a nation of people of mixed heritage, it had become increasingly difficult to sort out everyone's ethnicity.

For a system of privilege to work, the hue of a person's skin had become the measure of privilege. The lighter the more privileged, the darker the less. This simple color bar made bigotry all too easy and avoided the need of sorting out anyone's ancestry, unless someone was Jewish, of course. Under this perverse system, the reason the Japanese had been singled out and rounded up was easy to understand, the hue of their skin simply wasn't white enough.

December 6, 1943

Igloo, Fall River County, South Dakota

Little Italy to Little Italians

THE ARMY HAD WASTED no time in shipping Bart straight from basic training at Ft. Leonard Wood, Missouri to combat in Europe. Italy was believed
by British prime minister Winston Churchill to be "the soft underbelly
of Europe." In an effort to secure the Mediterranean and hopefully force
Germany to defend its flank in southern Europe, the Allies focused their
attack on Italy. If Italy could be removed from the war, Germany would
need to shift the deployment of its forces in Europe, reducing the number
of its divisions guarding the northwest coast of France, the location of the
Allies' planned invasion.

After driving the Nazis out of North Africa, the Allied invasion of Sicily began on the morning of July 10, 1943. Code-named Operation Husky,
the joint invasion forces led by Lieutenant General George S. Patton commanding the Americans and General Bernard L. Montgomery commanding the British struck the island by air and sea, landing over one hundred
fifty thousand ground forces on Sicily's southern shores.

Hitting the beach, Bart found himself in the middle of a war. He had
claimed the reason he wanted to be drafted into the Army was that he
wanted to meet the enemy face to face. Now that they were shooting at him,
he wasn't so sure it had been one of his brightest ideas. With sand flying up
from explosions and machine gun fire raking the beach, Bart ran for his life
and for the cover of rock outcroppings that dominated the shoreline.

During the initial heart-pounding minutes of the invasion, Bart had fired at the enemy, or at least in their direction, but had spent most of his time seeking shelter in the rocks from a barrage of enemy fire. As the Allied air and sea bombardment drove the enemy further inland, Bart and his platoon followed, picking off stragglers left behind by the enemy retreat. After thirty-eight days of fighting, Sicily had been liberated. Though the island was now in Allied hands, the bulk of the enemy force had escaped to the Italian mainland.

With the fall of Sicily, the Mussolini government collapsed. Soon after, Il Duce, Benito Mussolini, found himself under arrest. In a major reversal, Marshal Pietro Badoglio assumed control of the Italian government and promptly entered into secret negotiations with the Allies, despite the presence of a huge number of German troops occupying large swaths of Italy.

In September 1943, the Allies landed in Calabria and south of Salerno, pushing German forces north up the Italian peninsula step by step. To slow the Allied advance the Germans had set up a series of defensive lines that cut across the Italian peninsula from the Tyrrhenian Sea in the west to the Adriatic Sea in the east. The first, and southernmost, defensive line was the Volturno Line. After an intense battle, Allied forces broke through the Volturno Line only to run directly into the Gustav Line that blocked the way to Rome.

Try as they might to push through and on to Rome, the Allied invasion stalled in December 1943. With warmer weather in the spring of 1944, the Winter Line, as the Gustav Line came to be known, would see some of the fiercest fighting of the war. With a second front opened in Europe, Soviet forces in the east found themselves no longer the single-minded focus of the German army, allowing them to maneuver and resupply, giving them newfound life.

Bart was relieved when the Allied advance had been halted at the Winter Line. After fighting nonstop for months, he was exhausted and looked forward to spending a peaceful Christmas even if it was in an alien land in the middle of a war. As the American and British forces advanced from the North African campaign to Operation Husky in Sicily to the invasion of the peninsula of Italy, they gathered tens of thousands of Italian prisoners of war.

Unknown to Bart, of the fifty-one thousand Italian POWs that had been sent to the United States, two hundred fifty had ended up at the Black Hills Ordnance Depot at Igloo. Originally sent to Council Bluffs, Iowa, for detention, the status of Italian POWs changed when the Italian government switched sides by declaring war on Nazi Germany on October 13, 1943. To recognize the new status of Italian POWs, Italian Service Units, or ISUs, composed of former Italian POWs and lead by U.S. Army officers, were organized to serve with the Allies against Nazi Germany and the Empire of Japan.

When government transport buses, loaded with Italians, passed through Edgemont on Monday, December 6, 1943, local citizens gawked in wonder. Many found it difficult to understand why enemy POWs had been brought inland all the way to the Black Hills Ordnance Depot. While Bart huddled in the mud, near the mouth of the Liri Valley south of the strategic town of Cassino on Highway 6, the road to Rome, former Italian POWs lounged in comfort in new barracks only recently constructed in Igloo. Irony of ironies, the young men of both nations had traded places in the war against Nazi Germany. Bart with other young American boys would liberate Italy, while young Italian boys would provide the munitions to fight the war from the safety of America soil.

The arrival of the Italians had caused quite a stir at the Black Hills Ordnance Depot. At first, it was difficult to accept that the Italians, former enemies and members of the Axis Powers, were now allies, even though the battle for Italy was still underway. With nearly all of the military-aged men in the region off fighting the war, Igloo suffered from a chronic labor shortage. Though generous wages had attracted thousands of workers to Igloo, finding good labor in the sparsely populated region had been difficult from the start. The use of ISUs to fill the labor gap was seen as an answer to the long-standing problem.

The first thing the men of Igloo noticed was the high degree of curiosity the women of Igloo had in the new arrivals. Their curly hair, chiseled features, and tan complexions seemed to attract the attention of the fairer sex, which quickly heighten friction between the locals and the Italian newcomers. The peaceful utopia of Igloo, where everyone, regardless of race and background, had somehow found an equilibrium that had allowed everyone to get long, was shattered when Igloo's menfolk were forced to accept new foreign inhabitants who neither spoke their language nor followed their customs, and worst of all, who had become serious competitors for the greatest prize of all, their women.

George and Billy both worked at the ordnance depot. George lived in Igloo and Billy in Provo with his father. Though it took some time for Uncle Sam to track Billy down, having originally registered for the draft in California, upon finally receiving his official draft notice, Billy promptly joined the Navy. With orders to report by July 1 to the U.S. Naval Training Station in San Diego, California, for basic training, Billy's life went into overdrive. He was delighted that he would be able to stop by and visit his Aunt Beula on his way to basic training. Before departing for San Diego however, Billy wanted to help his father as much as possible. He also wanted to spend as much time with Velda as he could. He had fallen in love with Velda and never wanted to lose her. Knowing he had no real hold on her, he worried that by the time he returned, she may have found someone new. Though they had pledged to trust one another, he knew all too well the reality of the old saying, "Out of sight, out of mind." His father had told him that if Velda really loved him, she would wait. He knew his father was right. He also knew his mother had up and left his father without warning. Unlike his mother, who had married his father and bore his children, he feared the worst: Velda might leave him before she ever belonged to him.

Igloo's new roller-skating rink was huge with a beautiful polished circular oak floor. Couples skated arm in arm in a circle around the rink, some gliding smoothly, others unsteady on their skates. George and Billy had arrived early to stake out a good table next to the rink. Being close to the action also allowed them to watch the slapstick comedy of first-time skaters trying to stay upright.

"Hey, fellas," Babe and Velda said in unison as they walked up arm in arm.

"You two look cuter every time I see ya," George said, standing to offer the girls seats.

"They certainly do," Billy said, standing to make way.

The couples took their seats facing each other, with Velda next to Billy and Babe next to George. Billy and George quickly ran to get cokes for everyone and two large bowls of popcorn. After putting on their skates, everyone was ready to spend a fun and relaxing afternoon together.

"So, I heard you'll be shipping out in July. That's only a month away," Babe said, having just learned the news from Velda.

"Well, I got a love letter from Uncle Sam, so I decided to join the Navy rather than be sent to the front line in France," Billy said, hoping it didn't sound like he was running from the war.

"You made the right move. I read over a hundred fifty thousand men landed on the beaches in Normandy on June 6. A lot of them never made it off those beaches. The invasion and battle for Europe is now a hot war. I sure as hell wouldn't want to be thrown into the middle of that bloodbath," George said.

George was the same age as Billy but had no worries about being drafted. When he tried to enlist in the Navy, he had received a 4-F draft classification due to his bad lungs caused by a bout of pneumonia he had suffered when he was a child. Though he wanted to serve, he knew he never would.

"Is the Navy any safer than the Army?" Velda said. "The war is everywhere."

Velda worried about her brother who was fighting in Italy, where Rome had fallen just three days after the Allies invaded Normandy. With France the new battleground, she wondered if Bart would end up fighting there as well. Her uncles Alva and Francis were in the Navy in the Pacific. They had both seen the war up close. She wasn't so sure the Navy was any safer than the Army.

"Probably not, but at least I know how to swim. I'm not so good at digging ditches," Billy said with a chuckle.

Hearing the remark, Velda punched Billy in the shoulder, causing everyone to laugh.

"Well, you say you can swim, let's see if you can skate," Velda said, grabbing Billy by the hand.

Before long the foursome was skating around the rink, the girls suddenly more unsteady on their skates than they had ever been, causing George and Billy to hold them tighter than ever. No one complained and everyone tried to forget, even for a little while, that their world would soon change forever.

Billy and Velda promised to write to one another, both meaning it with all their hearts. On the morning of July 1, 1944 Ross drove Billy to Edgemont, where he boarded the train for San Diego.

With the Allied capture of Rome and the liberation of Italy, everything changed for the former Italian POWs stationed in Igloo. Once kept penned up in a designated compound ringed by fences and guardhouses, the Italians were released to roam freely inside the base. Their POW denim jump suits were soon discarded in favor of newly issued khaki uniforms with green "Italy" patches on the shoulders. What had been a low-level friction while the young Italians were penned up, heated up considerably when they began to fraternize openly with the local ladies.

Since Billy wouldn't be back until Christmas for a short two-week break, before reporting to the fleet, Velda decided to get a real job for the rest of the summer. Living in Igloo, employment was easy to find. Signing up for a job at the commissary, where jobs were always available, she was offered an opportunity to learn a new trade skill instead. With all the Italians now free and yet restricted to Igloo Base, they could no longer be treated as common POWs whose heads had been periodically and unceremoniously shaved.

This left the government with two hundred fifty shaggy-headed Italian men on their hands with no one qualified to give them haircuts. To solve the dilemma, the government decided to train several new barbers to get the job done. Learning what it paid, Velda wasted no time in signing up for the dollar-an-hour wage and looked forward to learning to cut hair while earning good money. One thing for sure, the job beat the hell out of chasing down jackrabbits for twenty-five cents a head.

Velda soon discovered she was the envy of many women in Igloo who would have died to get a position that would put them in close proximity to the handsome Italians. Velda couldn't understand all the gushing over the Italians, but then those who gushed the most, weren't exactly turning heads. Velda could see that for most of the gals wanting to get to know the young Italians better, it was the difference that made all the difference, considering many of the Italians weren't the handsomest of men. Despite being surrounded by Italian men all day, Velda only had eyes for Billy and took to cutting Italian hair the same way she used to take to shearing sheep. She actually found the two critters had a lot in common, both being covered in thick woolly coats full of curls.

It was on her third week on the job that she accidently clipped a small nick out of the top of one man's ear, causing him to yelp, "Ouch!" sparking laughter to ripple around the barber room. The laughter was less about the man crying out in pain in English and more about the fact he didn't continue with a string of swear words a mile long, the only English words the Italians seemed to know and readily employ. Everyone knew the only reason the man had bitten his tongue and hadn't let loose with a barrage of cuss words was that his clumsy barber had been a pretty young woman, which made the incident all the funnier.

No one in Igloo spoke Italian and none of the Italians seemed to speak English and yet somehow people found a way to communicate. As the weeks passed, Velda cut a steady stream of flowing Italian locks, becoming one of the best barbers on Igloo Base. Her haircuts and shaves where in high demand, with each man jokingly trying his damnedest to seduce her, though knowing his efforts were futile.

Before Velda knew it, summer was over. She had no more than started back to school when she read Billy's letter that he had reported to the *USS Shangri-La*, a new aircraft carrier that had been built at the Norfolk Navy Yard in Virginia. According to Billy, the reason Josephine Doolittle, the wife of the famous Captain Jimmy Doolittle, had attended the christening and launch of the ship was to honor the April 18, 1942 Doolittle Raid on Tokyo that had been carried out in retaliation for the bombing of Pearl Harbor.

Though very few targets of consequence had been hit by the sixteen bombers that participated in the Doolittle Raid on Tokyo, the mission succeeded in boosting U.S. morale, and in damaging Japanese morale. Indeed, these two objectives had been the real reason behind the fool-hardy mission. Roosevelt had wanted to boost American morale that had suffered greatly in the wake of Pearl Harbor. The Tokyo raid had given Americans renewed hope and had sent the Japanese the message that they were not invincible, that their homeland could be hit. The raid had such an impact on Japan's high command that Japan's naval forces were pulled out of the Indian Ocean and back to Japan to protect its homeland, thus helping to shorten the war.

Billy's ship had been named the *Shangri-La* in commemoration of President Roosevelt's answer to reporters after the Doolittle Raid on Tokyo. When ask for the name of the aircraft carrier that launched the attack on Tokyo, not wanting to reveal that the raid had been launched from the *USS Hornet*, Roosevelt had replied, "Shangri-La," the name of a mythical land somewhere high in the Himalayas. That there would actually be a ship named *Shangri-La* one day, no one could have guessed at the time, since the custom had been to name naval ships after famous battles, states or cities, or previous U.S. Navy ships. The *Shangri-La*'s name and pedigree put the aircraft carrier in a unique class of its own.

Ross had done well since arriving in Provo. His idea to run a small grocery store catering to workers in Igloo had paid off big. Since the opening of the Igloo Base, with its new housing and amenities, most of Provo's population had migrated. Ross had been able to take advantage of the migration by buying up several abandoned businesses and town lots along Bennet Street. He bought the old movie theater cheap, the owner not wanting to waste money having it moved back to Ardmore. Before Billy was drafted, they had converted the building into six apartment units, which Ross was able to immediately rent. Ross also bought the restaurant building that sat next to the theater on Bennet Street, quickly converting it into his house with a grand wraparound porch, much like the one that had been on the brick house on Bishop Ranch, when he ran cattle along the Cheyenne River north of Edgemont. Both buildings faced west and sat directly across the street from the Newsy Nook, which continued to do a thriving business.

Having built his little empire out of nothing in the middle of nowhere, Ross was content to stay in Provo, even though the town had shrunk from a population in the thousands to no more than a couple hundred souls. At night Ross would often sit on his grand front porch as he rocked in the dark, looking west toward Igloo with its bright glowing streetlights lining paved avenues and its shiny new buildings all tidy and clean. He often thought Provo and Igloo, separated by less than a couple of miles, were in fact worlds apart. Though the Newsy Nook had limited electrical service from Igloo, the residents of Provo had no running water, no sewers, no electric lights, and virtually no modern conveniences. Provo was an Old West frontier town frozen in the time of Ross's youth; Igloo was a modern wonder, a futuristic town of the coming age, an alien colony in a strange land at the edge of the world.

It had been good to have Billy home after so many years. Even in their short time together, they had built something in Provo. Though it was only a shadow of the wealth the Bishop family once enjoyed, it was at least a beginning. Now that Billy was headed to war, Ross worried he may lose the only child he had left, the only child that had returned to him. His daughters lived in far-flung states, from Florida to California. He had no idea if he would ever see any of them again. His eldest son, Joe, was out there, fighting in the war. Ross had no idea where or whether he was still alive, having not heard from him in a very long time. He prayed for all of his children wherever they were and had convinced himself that no news was good news.

December 24, 1944

Provo, Fall River County, South Dakota

Old Man Fishhook

AFTER BASIC TRAINING, BILLY had been sent directly to the U.S. Naval Training Center on Treasure Island in San Francisco to attend Gunner's Mate "A" School. One of the primary reasons he had been selected for the special training was his extensive knowledge of ordnance and munitions of all kinds, having worked at the ordnance depot in Igloo. Billy couldn't have been happier about becoming a gunner's mate striker. The biggest reason being he would be able to avoid an endless string of scrub-and-clean and chip-and-paint details aboard ship, the customary drudgery of an unrated seaman. A seaman was at the bottom of the totem pole in the chain of command. As a gunner's mate striker, however, he had a clearly defined duty aboard ship. Indeed, the defense of the ship would be his primary duty.

Not long after Billy reported for duty on the aircraft carrier the *USS Shangri-La* in Norfolk, Virginia, the ship pulled out for the Caribbean Sea on September 15, 1944, for its first shakedown cruise. From the moment he stepped aboard, Billy continued his intensive training on how to run the Mark 12, a dual-purpose gun, with surface-to-surface and surface-to-air capabilities, used on every major U.S. warship. Though the Mark 12 was hand-loaded, it had power-ramming, which enabled rapid fire at high angles against aircraft. Using standardized parts and ammunition simplified the big gun's resupply and logistics. Armed with proximity-fused anti-aircraft shells, the Mark 12 was a potent weapon that had downed countless enemy aircraft and was highly prized throughout the fleet.

As the *USS Shangri-La* cut its way through choppy seas, Billy stood on the fantail looking north as the ship bucked its way south. Billy had taken up smoking, when he discovered that smokers got smoke breaks while nonsmokers were expected to keep on working. When the chief barked, "If ya got 'em, smoke 'em." Billy soon lit up and joined the smokers. Taking a deep draw on his cigarette, he enjoyed watching a mob of seagulls as they took turns diving into the white froth churned up by the ship's screws.

"Flying rats, feedin' on garbage," the sailor to Billy's left said as he blew out a big plume of smoke.

"Yeah, the little beggars follow every ship," another sailor said with an east coast accent. "Got anything like that in Dakota, Wild Bill?"

"Can't say iffen we do. Folks ain't got much in the badlands, and don't throw out enough to feed a hungry prairie dog, that's for damn sure," Billy said in a thick western twang, touching off a ripple of light-hearted laughter.

"Well, Uncle Sam lives by different rules," the sailor said after a good laugh. "From what I've seen, he throws a damn sight more away than he uses."

The man's words resonated with Billy. He had witnessed more waste on Igloo Base than at any time in his life. War seemed to plant in the minds of men a sense of abundance where nothing needed to be saved. But then, when you can print money, there really is no limit on how much you can spend. Waste had become a kind of virtue, a demonstration of the abundance of the war economy, and yet, ironically, war itself consumed everything in its path.

Over the coming weeks, the *Shangri-La* circled the islands of the Caribbean, running a series of drills and training exercises. Billy had fired his big Mark 12 and had learned to fire and reload in a sequence of actions that soon became second nature. After a short shore leave for the crew in Trinidad, the *Shangri-La* headed back north to return to Norfolk before Christmas. A lot of men talked about the women of Trinidad and the good times they had had. The only thing Billy could remember about the island of Trinidad was the ibis with its brilliant scarlet-colored feathers, its curved slender bill used to probe swallow water, and its strange grunting and croaking calls, unlike any birdsong Billy had ever heard. He had enjoyed watching them fly in a perfect V-formation, much like geese, before circling to land, always staying close to one another. His only other thoughts were of Velda and how much he missed her.

Receiving a letter from Billy, Velda couldn't wait for him to return home for Christmas. Velda looked forward to spending ten days with Billy during her winter break from school. As the Barton household prepared for Billy's return, Bill Barton remembered how he felt about Kate when he was twenty-one and she was sixteen. He also remembered their honeymoon on Pilger Mountain, the place they had called their Shangri-La. Bill couldn't help wondering how twisted the world had become that a ship of war now bore the name *Shangri-La*; the name that had once stood only for a place of peace and tranquility. He prayed that Billy's *Shangri-La* would somehow help create a world of peace and tranquility, though he had his doubts. The war had cost too many lives already, and yet, it continued, without an end in sight.

He dreaded fetching the mail every day for fear of what he might find, with his eldest son and both brothers in the thick of the war and knowing the three of them had already seen action. The thought that Velda's beau would soon join them in the struggle bit deep. With Alva, Francis, Bart, and Kate's brother, Herman, all fighting in the war, Bill thought but for the grace of God, they had somehow escaped harm. Francis had survived Pearl Harbor. Alva had survived the sinking of the *USS Wasp*. Bart had fought to liberate Italy only to be sent to southern France to continue the struggle. Bill wondered, having so many fighting in the war, whether their luck could possibly hold out until they could all safely return home again.

Arriving back in Norfolk on December 21, Billy was given home leave before the *Shangri-La* would pull out to join the war in the Pacific. Billy returned to Provo with orders to report back to the *USS Shangri-La* in Norfolk, Virginia, no later than January 4. Over the coming days, Billy got to know the Barton family by spending much of his time at the Barton home. Velda and Billy had become a couple and they enjoyed being together nearly every waking hour.

The Newsy Nook was popular with kids from Igloo since they could come to Provo and have all the candy and soda they wanted, without their parents finding out. Johnny liked to ride his bicycle over to Provo to play with his friends in all the old wrecked and rusting car bodies and surplus ammunition crates that seemed to be stacked up everywhere in town. Sandy liked to run free and wild all day. While dogs were allowed on Igloo Base, they had to stay on a leash. Sandy, having grown up in the countryside, didn't take to being tied up all day. Sandy was getting old and there was just no way to teach an old dog new tricks, life on a leash would never sit well with him.

Riding over to Provo, Sandy ran beside Johnny's bicycle happy to be off base and free of his leash. Johnny had been heartbroken when Sandy's running days came to an end, when school started after the summer holiday. Living on Igloo Base meant Sandy had to stay home on a leash all day for weeks on end. Johnny wasn't sure Sandy could survive that kind of confinement much longer. The last three months had taken a toll on the old dog. When he pulled up at the Newsy Nook, he went straight to the soda machine. As he drank his favorite grape soda, he shared his thoughts with the old man who ran the Newsy Nook. After listening to the boy, Ross proposed leaving Sandy in Provo to live with him, where Johnny could come to see Sandy anytime. Ross's offer was a serious one, since he needed a good guard dog and Sandy fit the bill. Truth was, Ross was lonely.

Happy to have found a possible solution, Johnny promised to bring Sandy back after he talked with his parents and sister about it. After a morning of playing with his friends in Provo, Johnny headed home. As Ross watched the boy and his dog head back to Igloo, he thought about all the years he had missed spending time with Billy. The ground covered in virgin snow and the town nearly silent made the image of a boy and his dog all the more poignant. Little Johnny at nine years old was the same age Billy had been when Ross had to send him and his other children off to Oskaloosa, Iowa. Though he had later rounded up and brought Billy and his other children to Missouri, he had been forced once again to send them all away. Billy had been sent to stay with his Aunt Beula in California. Having had Billy back for only a short time, Ross would now have to send him away again, this time to a war no one wanted to fight.

On Christmas Eve, Johnny came home just before lunch bursting with news.

"I found a home for Sandy," Johnny said confidently, as he strolled into the house after spending the morning playing with his friends in Provo.

"A home? What d'ya mean?" Bill said, wondering what Johnny was talking about.

"Well, Sandy doesn't like to be tied up all day and Old Man Fishhook said he'd take him and that I could come to visit anytime," Johnny said, excited.

"Old Man Fishhook? Who in the world is that?" Kate said, having never heard of such a character.

"You know, Fishhook, the old man who runs the little store in Provo," Johnny said, wondering why they had never heard of Old Man Fishhook, a man everybody knew.

"Oh, you mean Bishop, Ross Bishop, who owns the Newsy Nook," Bill said with a chuckle that rolled around the room as Kate, Velda, and Billy listened to the exchange.

"Bishop? Bishop? I thought that old man's name was Fishhook. I've been calling him Fishhook ever since we lived in Provo," Johnny said, confused.

Seeing the confused expression written in the pinched features on Johnny's little face sent everyone bursting into laughter.

"Ross Bishop is my Pa, Johnny" Billy said. "He never corrects anyone who mispronounces his name. Heck, he's answered to Bissel, Biscoff, Bisky, Fisher, and a lot of other names less kindly," Billy said with a grin. "But now, Fishhook, there's a name that surely takes the cake."

Once again, everyone burst into laughter, even Johnny, who had learned to laugh at mishaps and mistakes and at himself a long time ago.

"So, you think leaving Sandy with Old Man Fishhook would be something you could live with?" Bill said, wanting to make sure his son knew what it would mean to give up his dog.

"He said he needed a good guard dog. Sandy's a great guard dog and in Provo, he'd be able to run free," Johnny said, having made up his mind.

As far as Johnny was concerned, tying a dog up all day was worse than torture, especially when the dog had only known freedom. After that day, Sandy became yet another link between the Barton and Bishop families. Velda thought it was fitting Sandy go to live with Ross in Provo, since it had been Ross who brought her Stinkin' Bear, so many years ago.

Billy's visit was far too short for lovers. As the days passed quickly, the couple learned what they already knew, there was no way to stop the relentless march of Father Time. Billy had learned that George and Babe planned to marry as soon as Babe graduated. Like so many other couples, Billy and Velda vowed they would marry the day Billy returned from the war.

"You know you worried about the invasion of France. Well, as it turns out, France was liberated on August 25th while you were in basic training in San Diego. The Army might not have been a bad choice," Velda said.

"The war in Europe is a long way from being over. The tough fighting is yet to come," Billy said. "Like I said, I'm a better swimmer than a ditch digger."

"Yeah, yeah, you keep saying that. How about you show me your best breaststroke at the Evan's Plunge in Hot Springs. It's open year around," Velda said.

"You're on," Billy said. "When do we go?"

"Day after Christmas," Velda said.

"You seem to have everything planned. Do you also plan to seduce me with your skimpiest swimsuit?" Billy said with a crooked grin.

"You worry about you. I'll bring proper attire," Velda said smugly, with an elfin smirk.

"Proper attire? You've been reading Newsy Nook fashion magazines again, haven't ya?" Billy said, finding her expression out of character.

"Well, I have to admit, Ross does send over all of his unsold magazines," Velda said, having enjoyed reading all the latest Hollywood gossip and about all the latest fashion trends.

Magazines were a window on the world beyond the featureless prairie. There were many rural folk who wanted to hold the world at bay and preserve their cherished isolation. Not everyone however wished to hold back the tides of change. The advent of electricity in the remotest of rural areas and the ease of transportation with better roads combined with the explosion of information brought by telephones, radios, magazines, and newspapers had swept the old ways aside. A new world had begun to emerge.

"Be careful reading those things, they're full of bad influences," Billy said with raised eyebrows.

"So you say, Billy Bishop. Speaking of bad influences . . .," Velda said with an impish grin.

Pulling her out the front door and into his arms, Billy stopped short on the porch, where they held each other tight, neither wanting to let go. After a long, sweet goodbye, Billy drove back to Provo, wishing only to be with Velda again.

The next day, Billy and Ross joined the Barton family for Christmas dinner. Ross had never been on Igloo Base nor inside any of the new homes. He couldn't believe how modern everything was. He was impressed with the electric lights in every room. The feature that amazed him most was the flush toilet, which was a wonder to a man who had never seen a toilet inside a house that was connected to a central sewer system. The softness of the toilet tissue was also a revelation, since Ross had never used anything but crumpled up pages from mail-order catalogs for TP. He had often thought Provo and Igloo were worlds apart. His visit to the Barton home had confirmed that though the two towns were less than two miles apart, they were separated by over a hundred years. For Ross, Igloo was like stepping into some Flash Gordon story about an alien futuristic world somewhere on the other side of the Milky Way. He wondered if he would ever be able to fit in and live in such a world.

The day had been a hit. When Ross and Billy were about to leave, Johnny brought Sandy to their car and asked Ross to take care of him. Ross said Sandy was the best Christmas present he ever received and reminded Johnny that he could come to see Sandy anytime. Pulling out, Billy reminded Velda he would be back in the morning for their drive to Hot Springs.

Fortunately, the weather was fair and the thirty-five-mile drive to Hot Springs uneventful. Arriving at Evan's Plunge, the couple nearly froze to death when they dashed into the building from their warm car through a stiff bone-chilling arctic wind that had suddenly come up out of the northwest. Evan's Plunge had been built over a number of natural hot springs in 1890 when Fred Evans and other investors worked to turn Hot Springs into a European-styled spa where they had hoped people would come to resuscitate and take in the healing benefits of the natural mineral springs. The natural hot springs bubbling up out of the limestone had been used by many different peoples over thousands of years before the white man entered the Black Hills.

Known as *wiwila kata*, meaning warm waters, the Lakota and the Cheyenne both believed in the healing powers of the hot mineral-rich waters. A unique feature of the springs was that the water lacked the sulfur smell so often found with geothermal formations. The pure mineral-rich spring water boiled out of the rocks at a steady eighty-seven degrees, completely changing out the water every hour and a half in the huge swimming pool that had been built over the source of the springs.

After a long swim in the naturally heated pool, Velda and Billy felt refreshed. Velda had worn a halter bathing suit and shorts she had made herself. She was pleased with her handiwork when she found that Billy couldn't take his eyes off her. As they made their way south toward Edgemont on Highway 18, Billy suddenly remembered he had unfinished business to take care of.

"Let's swing by Craven Canyon," Billy said.

"Craven Canyon lays south of Barker Flats, I've ridden my horse in that area when we lived on Pilger Mountain," Velda said.

"Really, I'll be damned. We used to drive cattle up that way. It's amazing when you think about it. You and I grew up only a few miles apart."

"Destiny, I guess."

"Oh, really. You do remember that we met in Provo, right?"

"It was Edgemont, actually."

"Oh yeah. You're right on that count. Speaking of Edgemont, my Great-Grandpa E. J. Bishop ran a saloon in the town of Burton where Edgemont now stands, long before the town of Edgemont was established."

"Oh really. Well, my Grandpa John Barton, I'd like you to know, knew your Great-Grandpa E. J. Bishop and used to drink at the Standard Gage Saloon."

"I guess it was destiny, then."

"Of that, there's no doubt. That and a cold beer, if I know my grandpa," Velda said with a chuckle.

"A man after my own heart," Billy said with a chuckle of his own.

It was amazing how the stories of the Barton and Bishop families dovetailed in many ways since both families had arrived in the Black Hills and how they had now merged since he and Velda had found one another, Billy thought.

"Why do you want to swing by Craven Canyon?" Velda said, curious why they needed to take the detour.

"My Pa showed me carvings made thousands of years ago in the walls of that canyon. I thought you might like to take a look."

"Carvings?"

"Yeah. Drawings of different kinds of animals and such. No one knows who made them."

"There're many mysterious things in the Black Hills. We have a dinosaur vertebra my Pa turned up when he was ploughing a field in Pleasant Valley. It's huge, about the size of a coffee can. We've used it as a doorstop since I was little girl."

"There's a lot of petrified wood up that way as well. The hills are old, very old."

"It's why my Grandpa Bill back in Iowa and my Great-Grandpa Pappy Breeden believed the Black Hills, one of the most ancient formations in the world, holds spiritual powers, powers humans don't fully understand. It's why they felt so strongly about preserving the beliefs of the native peoples of the region who were closer to these forces before the coming of the white man," Velda said, having always felt the Black Hills held spiritual powers beyond human understanding.

As Billy drove up Red Canyon Road, he thought of the wonder of the hills and how they must have looked during different periods over time. The road up Craven Canyon was rough, but before long he found the rugged cliff face he was looking for. Stepping out of the car, he pointed about halfway up the steep wall of stone.

"About halfway up, can you see those figures carved in the rock?" Billy said.

"Yes. I can see 'em. Let's take a closer look," Velda said, having never seen ancient petroglyphs.

Climbing up the rock face, they were able to see the figures up close. The worn carvings of bison, deer, antelope, bear, and cougar had survived thousands of years in silent testament to those who had come before. Lightly tracing the carvings with the tips of her fingers, Velda felt as though she were able to reach across millenniums to the day the carvings were first created. As she pondered the ancient carvings, she wondered what she would leave to future generations, if anything.

"Velda, will you marry me?" Billy said, kneeling down on one knee and holding up a diamond ring in a small felt jeweler's box.

Caught by surprise, Velda looked behind her to see Billy with the goofiest grin on his face she had ever seen, kneeling while holding an open ring box high up over his bowed head.

"What in the world are you doing? Are you crazy?" Velda blurted, finding herself completely at a lack for words.

"Crazy about you. Will you marry me?" Billy said, still on one knee and once again hoisting the box high over his bowed head.

"You know I will. Yes. Yes. Yes, Billy Bishop! I will marry you!" Velda said, snatching the ring out of the box and putting it on her finger.

Her heart pounded as she looked at the little diamond perched atop a thin gold band as it sparkled in the afternoon sun. She knew instantly the most important thing she would leave for future generations would be her and Billy's children. Finding a smooth rock face lower on the backside of the formation, Billy and Velda carved their own petroglyph, their initials tied together with a plus sign and framed in a heart, both of them laughing at what future explorers might think thousands of years in the future when they discover their strange etchings and try to figure out what they could have possibly meant.

Spending more than a week swimming, roller-skating, going to movies, and taking long drives in the countryside, the couple had grown inseparable. After attending a movie at the Elks Theater in Edgemont, the young couple decided to take a stroll around town, which ended at the city park with its huge gazebo.

"Do you remember when we first met?" Velda said.

"*Casablanca*, right?" Billy said.

"Yes, it was the weekend that *Casablanca* was in all the theaters," Velda said.

"Great movie. It won Best Picture in 1943 for movies released in 1942. Altogether, *Casablanca* won three Oscars," Billy said, having read all about it.

One thing about running a store full of magazines was that the latest gossip was always at your fingertips and stories about movie stars filled the pages of more than one publication.

"Well, tell me, Rick old boy, do you remember anything about when we met?" Velda said.

"Not an easy day to forget."

"No."

"I remember every detail. The Moguls of Edgemont wore gray, you wore blue."

"Moguls?"

"Yep. That's what they call their school mascot here in Edgemont."

"What's a Mogul?"

"It's the name for a kind of train engine, I think. This being a railroad town, I guess they thought it worked for them."

"So, they wore gray?"

"Yep, that's how I remember it. And you wore a blue coat. You really did, you know," Billy said.

"I actually did, didn't I? I wore my favorite blue coat. Do you remember everything?"

"When it comes to you, yes."

"Really?"

"Who could ever forget anything about somebody like you?"

"Well then, kiss me. Kiss me as if it were the last time," Velda said, quoting Ilsa's famous *Casablanca* movie lines as she leaned into Billy's strong arms.

Billy swept her up into his arms, embracing her into a world of their own as only true lovers can create. After a long kiss, they walked back to the car holding each other tight.

Just before getting into the car, Billy tipped Velda's chin up with his cupped hand and said, "Here's looking at you, kid."

"I wondered when you would get around to saying that," Velda giggled.

"I wouldn't do Bogie justice, if I didn't," Billy said, as he pulled Velda closer.

Though their final kisses delayed their departure for Igloo, neither minded one little bit. Billy would be leaving the next day and Velda would be returning to school.

The next morning, once again, Ross drove Billy to Edgemont to catch his train, this time to Norfolk. Both men feared they may never see one another again.

"Son, this war will be over soon. You just need to keep your head down until it is," Ross said as they embraced in front of Edgemont's Union Station.

"Well, as a gunner's mate, Pa, it might be tough for me to duck. I'll just have to shoot straighter than they do," Billy said, with a knowing grin.

As his train pulled out of Edgemont, he knew he had to steel himself for the challenges ahead. Pulling a photo of Velda out of his wallet, he looked at it for a long time, wishing things were different, that there was no war, and that they could be together. When he tried to look into the future, he could see nothing, no hint of things to come. Like it had been since he was nine years old, he was like a leaf in a whirlwind, tossed and turned, this way and that, at the whims of a fate that seemed out of his control.

Tucking the photo back in his wallet, he made up his mind that from this day forward, he would take charge of his own destiny. He was done with letting events define him, he would henceforth write his own story. In his story, he would come back to Velda, and with her, they would make a new life together, one of their own making.

With no fanfare nor apology, U.S. Major General Henry C. Pratt announced Public Proclamation No. 21, which informed a war-weary nation that Japanese Americans could be released from detention and return to their homes, effective January 2, 1945. Why this decision had been made prior to the fall of Nazi Germany or the defeat of the Empire of Japan, no one knew, and no one cared to offer an explanation. After rounding up over a hundred twenty thousand Americans, depriving them of their possessions, their homes, and their jobs and shipping them off to isolated detention camps in the middle of nowhere, the U.S. government deemed it sufficient upon their release to provide each detainee no more than twenty-five dollars and a train ticket.

Japanese Americans were known as Nisei, the Japanese word meaning second generation. At the beginning of the war, Nisei in the uniformed services were discharged and Nisei civilians of draft age had been classified as 4-C, "enemy aliens." Nisei from the Hawaii National Guard were eventually allowed to form the 100th Infantry Battalion. This Battalion of roughly twenty-seven hundred Nisei was later merged with the 442nd Regimental Combat Team, made up of fifteen hundred Japanese Americans who had enlisted straight out of Japanese detention camps on the mainland. Shipped to north Africa, the 100th Battalion 442nd Regimental Combat Team fought at the front lines of the Allied invasion and liberation of Italy and later in the invasion of southern France.

Dubbed the most decorated combat unit, the Nisei soldiers of the 100th Battalion 442nd Regimental Combat Team received more commendations for bravery than any other unit in history. Among the long list of honors were twenty-one Medal of Honor recipients and more than four thousand Purple Heart awardees. The irony of all this patriotic heroism was that for most of these men, their families were held in captivity behind barbed wire fences with watch towers during the war, while they fought, bled, and in many cases died for the country of their capturers. A further irony of ironies was that of the ten Americans who had been convicted of spying for Japan during the war, none had been of Japanese ancestry.

Seemingly untroubled by an unjust policy that had imprisoned an entire race of people and caused horrendous suffering, J. Edgar had turned his attentions to ponder a more serious matter, the need to find fresh hunting grounds. After the Great War, attorney general A. Mitchell Palmer had established the Radical Division of the Bureau of Investigation, giving J. Edgar Hoover his big break to oversee efforts to counter the threat of communism, when communist Bolsheviks toppled the czar of Russia. In doing so, Palmer had succeeded in igniting the nation's first Red Scare. The fear of union organizers turning America's workers into communist had expanded the powers of the Bureau and had helped to hold labor unions in check. In the following years, the Red Scare had faded as the Bureau pursued the expansion of its domestic powers during prohibition and during the crime spree created in its aftermath.

Now with the Yellow Scare no longer high on the minds of Americans with the pending defeat of Japan and with China already in shambles, American was in need of a worthy advisory. Without a menacing Germany to defeat, Stalin, by grabbing territory formerly occupied by Nazi Germany, had provided the accelerant J. Edgar had needed to ignite a new Red Scare.

In a unipolar world, America would need a boogeyman. Stalin and his Soviet armies of brainwashed communist slaves provided a ready-made nemesis, one that would provide whales aplenty for decades to come. Indeed, J. Edgar dreamed of harpooning large red whales emblazoned with bright yellow hammers and sickles inside and outside of American shores.

"There she blows, man the harpoons boys, there are whales aplenty," J. Edgar whispered to himself as he looked out of his office window and daydreamed about the many bloody hunts to come. America was at its apex of power with over twelve million men in uniform at the beginning of 1945. When the war ended, there would be no way America could return to prewar troop levels. Europe and Asia had been laid to waste, leaving America as the sole superpower in the world.

America had secured its northern boarders in the War of 1812, its southern boarders in the Mexican American War of 1848, and its place on the world stage as a New World and Pacific Power in the Spanish American War of 1898. By playing a critical role in winning the Great War in 1918, America had emerged as a global power. By winning the war in Europe and Asia, America would supplant Britain and all other nations as the ruler of the seas and dominant military force in the world. Pax Americana, and the rightness of the American way, would define the future shape of the world and all who lived in it. Of this, J. Edgar was certain.

May 8, 1945

Provo, Fall River County, South Dakota

One Down . . .

BART HAD NO IDEA the Seventh Army would be involved in one campaign after another. After driving the Germans out of Sicily, the Seventh Army had marched up the Italian peninsula all the way to Rome, where they liberated the country. From there, they had formed the lead element in Operation Dragoon, the invasion of the southern Mediterranean coast of France. Mopping up scattered German units stranded after the hasty retreat of the bulk of the German army, Bart's unit trudged across southern France to Alsace on the German border by mid-September 1944. After stiff resistance at the border, they broke through as an element of Operation Touchstone, eventually crossing the Rhine and capturing the cities of Nuremberg and Munich. Bart's unit then pushed on, reaching Austria, and had just crossed the Brenner Pass into northern Italy, having fought in nearly a full circle from Rome through southern France and central Europe and back to Italy, when suddenly and without fanfare, they learned the news that the war had ended on May 8, 1945.

Hearing the news, Bart's platoon had been halted in its tracks, so everyone could process the magnitude of what had happened. The war was over. The men had been ordered to sit and rest. Many of the men who had squatted on their down-turned helmets struck up a smoke and sat in silence, deep in thought, as they took in the breath-taking panorama of the deep Brenner Valley below, with its green meadows and steep tree-lined cliffs.

As Bart sat stunned by the news, his emotions welled up inside him until he found himself crying like a baby. Tears streaming down his cheeks, he couldn't believe the war was really over. Since landing in Sicily, he had fought nonstop for nearly two years. Looking around, he discovered there wasn't a dry eye among his fellow warriors, none of whom caring what the others might think. Theirs were the tears of joy; they had somehow survived, when so many of their comrades had not. Without an enemy to fight, each man found himself pondering the same thought: What now?

Pulling himself together, Bart stood up not really knowing what he would do next. Reaching into his pocket he pulled out the Lakota turtle amulet his father had given him and turned it between his fingers. There had many days when he had held onto the amulet as if his life had depended on it, and in many ways it had. There was no way to prove that the amulet held any mystical power or whether it had done anything to help him survive. All he knew was that he believed it did and that faith could move mountains. He couldn't wait to return to the mountains of his birth to be reborn and begin anew.

He had heard a lot about the new benefits for veterans that included college tuition, low-cost housing loans, and unemployment insurance. Going to college was something no Barton had ever done. He hadn't really thought about it much until now. He was determined not to pass up the opportunity. If the war had taught him anything, it had taught him life was short, and could at any moment be cut a damn sight shorter. He wanted to live his life as fully as possible, and he planned to do just that.

Herman had been among the first Americans to arrive in Brisbane. By 1943, the number of American troops in Australia had reached one hundred fifty thousand. U.S. naval forces maintained a presence in Sydney and Perth, with ships anchored in both harbors. Herman had witnessed firsthand the Americanization of the British colony. The invasion of American fashion, Coca-Cola, coffee, hotdogs, and hamburgers swept the country, driven by a tidal wave of American manufactured goods and Hollywood movies. By the dawn of 1945, American goods had dislodged old British staples and accounted for two-thirds of Australian imports.

While Herman had been bottled up in Australia, America had marched across the globe and become the sole superpower in the world. He had seen with his own two eyes how the war had changed Australia, what he had yet to discover was how it had changed America forever, even in his isolated corner on Pilger Mountain hundreds of miles from the nearest metropolitan center.

The news of victory in Europe had been celebrated in Australia, a country that had enlisted 10 percent of its population into the ranks of the Australian Army, sending four hundred thousand men to fight overseas. Herman counted himself one of the luckiest men alive, having been able to spend the war in the relative safety of Australia. Learning American troops were being sent home from Europe had given him hope that he just might survive the war. He couldn't wait to return home to Pleasant Valley.

Francis had sailed out of Pearl Harbor on the *USS Independence* straight into the war. In August 1944, they had struck Japanese installations on Marcus Island and by November they had struck the heavily fortified island of Rabaul, scoring a number of successes until they were hit by a torpedo in a counterattack, causing serious damage to the ship. After repairs in San Francisco, they had returned to the war and had engaged in a series of sea battles around the islands of the Philippines. On October 24, 1944, in the Sibuyan Sea, aircraft from the *Independence* sank the battleship *Musashi*, one of only three Yamato-class battleships, the heaviest and most power-fully armed ships in the Imperial Japanese Navy.

It was after the April 1 invasion of Okinawa in 1945, where the *Independence* had conducted pre-invasion air strikes and combat air patrol, that the news of the end of the war in Europe reached Francis. Francis had seen firsthand how grudgingly the Japanese had given up territory, often fighting to the last man. He wondered how much more the enemy could take. Even with the destruction of their navy, the loss of their empire outside of their home islands, and the invasion and loss of Okinawa, the Japanese contin-ued to fight as though they still had a chance for victory.

Francis had seen plenty of men refuse to give up when there was noth-ing left to fight for, the Japanese however were the toughest and stubbornest people he had ever seen. Thinking back, he remembered the day his father had decided it was time to leave the badlands and the day his brother had decided to give up on Pilger Mountain. Defeat is always a tough pill to swal-low; he had watched his father and his brother damn near choke on theirs.

Without accepting defeat, however, there is no way for a man to move on. He wondered how long it would take for the leaders of Japan to finally accept this simple truth.

Francis had come to understand firsthand why Alva was concerned about America's future. If America sought to hold onto its dominant role in the world, the country would remain an armed camp and would forever be embroiled in far-flung engagements overseas. America had grown its military from a little over three hundred thirty thousand men in 1939 to over twelve million by 1945. Francis could see no way for the country to return to blissful isolation anytime soon, if ever. He wondered if average Americans understood what this meant for themselves, their children, and future generations. What was clear to Francis was that America had gone through a metamorphosis. America had been forced to emerged from its isolationist cocoon to confront its enemies head on. Francis now feared the beast that had crawled out of that cocoon. He worried that America may continue to wield its mighty instruments of war to dictate its preeminence in the world, long after the war ended, diplomacy be damned.

Alva had learned the war in Europe was over while sipping on a cold Primo beer at Coconut Joe's Hula Bar. Francis had been back a few times since shipping out on the *Independence*. Each time Francis came back, he brought more stories of the war, a war Alva no longer wanted any part of. He had enjoyed his shore duty in Hawaii after so many years at sea. Finally receiving his retirement papers effective July 1, 1945, he looked forward to returning home. He knew that though victory over Japan might come soon, the killing was a long way from being over.

His plan was a simple one. He would get back to Rapid City, the gateway to the Black Hills, as quickly as possible and buy enough land to build a house and set up his trailer rental business. He also planned to provide hookups for travel trailers, which would give him additional income, during the tourist season. He had saved up a sizable bankroll over his twenty years in the Navy, and by taking advantage of the government's new housing and business loan programs for veterans, he believed he could borrow what he needed and get started right away. He was confident he could make a good living off rentals and trailer hookups, while drawing his monthly military retirement checks. The fact that the U.S. Army had trained thousands of pilots, gunners, radio operators, and navigators at the Rapid City Army Air Base during the war gave Alva confidence that his plan was a good one. Like Igloo, the Rapid City economy had experienced a considerable boost from all the government money flowing into the area. Unlike Igloo, Alva believed the Army Air Base would continue to operate after the war and might even be expanded in coming years.

For his plan to work, he needed to beat the coming rush of men returning from the war. He had marveled over the years at how his big brother had always been one step ahead of the competition. He wanted to follow in his footsteps. He knew his big brother was already making his moves. Bill's last letter outlined his postwar plan to buy a restaurant and boarding house in Deadwood, where the economy would boom again once the war ended. Alva believed, like his brother, there was no time to lose.

Billy had sailed out of Norfolk on January 17, 1945. After passing through the Panama Canal, the *Shangri-La* had picked up aircraft and supplies in San Diego to transport to Pearl Harbor before setting out in April to engage in their first strike against the Japanese on Okino Daito Jima, a group of small islands several hundred miles southeast of Okinawa, where they destroyed radio and radar installations.

After providing support for the invasion of Okinawa, the *Shangri-La* launched air strikes on Kyushu, Japan's southernmost home island. Unlike their strikes on Okinawa that had met with little resistance, their strikes on Kyushu turned out to be more costly than expected. Flying from air bases on land, Japanese aircraft had swarmed around the *Shangri-La* like a riled-up hive of angry bees. Desperate to drive off the enemy attack, Japanese pilots launched *kamikaze* attacks on the *Shangri-La*. Billy, as a gunner's mate striker had been assigned to reloading duties. When his gunner's mate was killed in a barrage of enemy fire, Billy had stepped up and manned his big Mark 12. Following the training that had been drilled into him, Billy took control of the big gun and threw a torrent of lead into the air at the marauding aircraft, scoring several hits. As he watched one plane after another dive harmlessly into the ocean, some planes striking the waves less than a hundred yards from the hull of the ship, he couldn't help but wonder at the fate of the pilots and the loved ones they left behind.

Having suffered heavy casualties, the *Shangri-La* headed for San Pedro Bay, Philippines, for repairs and rest and recuperation for the crew, many of whom having been badly shaken. Still licking their wounds, the crew was relieved to learn the ship would stay in port until the end of June before reentering the war.

The crew of the *Shangri-La* had received the news of victory in Europe before arriving in the Philippines. Billy was happy to know the fighting had stopped on the other side of the world. Having experienced firsthand the fierceness of Japanese resistance, he knew that the war in Asia wouldn't count the last of its dead for some time to come.

Billy and the rest of the crew of the *Shangri-La*, happy to have survived, hit the streets of San Pedro with a strong thirst for cold beer and good times, both of which they had no trouble finding at the first bar outside the gate.

The year 1945 had started out with the promise of a fourth term for President Franklin Delano Roosevelt. Upbeat after a fourth electoral victory, the mood of the nation soon turned to concerns for Roosevelt's heath. Little more than a month after having been sworn into office, Roosevelt passed away, on April 12, 1945. Just twenty-six days later, on May 8, 1945, President Harry S. Truman, who had moved into the White House only the day before, was informed the Germans had surrendered. Incredibly, for a man who had unexpectedly ascended to the presidency overnight, Truman had also inadvertently received the birthday present of a lifetime; since, in a strange twist of fate, May 8, 1945, happened to be Truman's sixty-first birthday.

News of victory in Europe had come to Bill and Kate along with the reminder that when the war ended, the full-time labor contingent at the Black Hills Ordnance Depot would be scaled back considerably. Igloo had grown into a community with well over four thousand residents, making it one of the largest towns in West River. Surrounding towns had also grown as their economies boomed with the increase in government money flowing into the region.

The end of the war in Europe had prompted the Italian government to request the immediate return of all Italian prisoners. Interestingly, Bill had learned that the request had been turned down by the U.S. government; the main reason being that the war was not over, and that prisoner labor was still needed at least until November 1. Upon hearing this, Bill could read the handwriting on the wall as well as anyone else, he and Kate couldn't count on continued employment after the end of the year, since beyond that date, it was likely they would both be losing their jobs, as the ordnance depot scaled back operations. The simple fact was that there would be little work to do on an ordnance depot during peacetime.

Kate had already received notice that when America's troops returned from the war in Europe, women would need to step back to be replaced by returning veterans. The handwriting on the wall Kate could clearly read was that women would once again be asked to return to their traditional roles as housewives and homemakers. They would no longer be welcome as team members in an all-male workforce. She wondered if simply returning to the kitchen could ever be possible again. Having been asked to step up and do a man's work, women had answered the call and soon demonstrated they were ready, willing, and able to do so. For Kate, men and women working shoulder to shoulder had changed everything in the relations between the sexes. Kate believed there would be no way for America to put that genie back in the bottle. She wasn't sure when, but she knew women would be the equals of men someday.

With over three million American military personnel in Europe, Africa, and the Mediterranean at the end of the war, bringing troops back home to America would be no easy task. According to Bart, to get the job done, Operation Magic Carpet had been launched to bring the troops home as quickly as possible. Wasting no time, American troops in Europe were soon herded onto commercial cargo ships and merchant marine and coast guard vessels for their return home at the rate of four hundred thirty-five thousand a month. Bart planned to arrive in Norfolk in early November and to make it to Igloo for Thanksgiving. Hearing this news, Bill and Kate knew they had no time to lose before an armada of ships filled with returning veterans, first from Europe and before long from the Pacific, would swamp American shores and forever remold the country.

The news of the Allied victory in Europe gave Velda hope that the war in Asia would also soon be over. Everyone looked forward to Bart returning home. Considering he had never been to Igloo and had only known the tough life the family had lived on Pilger Mountain and in Custer, Velda figured he would be more than a little surprised by how prosperous the Barton family had become in recent years. She was sure Bart would have plenty of wild tales to tell.

All the talk about their parents losing their jobs in coming months had caused quite a stir in the Barton household. Bill and Kate had informed Velda and Johnny that they had made plans to move to Deadwood at the end of the year. The reason for the sudden move was that they had bought the Copper Kettle Café, a popular downtown restaurant, and the Water Street Rooming House, that had family living quarters and a dozen small rental units. Their plan was to grow their businesses with the coming economic postwar boom. If they moved over the holiday, Velda and Johnny could finish up their school year in Deadwood.

Velda would be seventeen in November and would graduate the twelfth grade in May 1946. She had looked forward to graduating from the Provo Secondary School on Igloo Base with Babe, her best friend. Like her eighth-grade graduation in Custer which she had been forced to miss, she was now being told she would miss her twelfth-grade graduation as well. As with so many of her parents' best-laid plans, this one didn't sit well with Velda.

Though Johnny was also upset, he was more upset about no longer being able to see his dog, Sandy, than in being forced to move to Deadwood. He was tired of living on the bleak treeless prairie and looked forward to returning to the green forest of the Black Hills, where he had grown up. He often touched his cougar talisman hanging around his neck to remind himself of where he came from and where he belonged. He was his Grandpa John's namesake. He wanted nothing more than to follow the sun to the horizon and beyond but knew deep down that he would always return to his beloved Black Hills.

Velda would often read and reread Billy's letters as she sat for hours staring at the engagement ring Billy had given her before returning to the fleet. If America defeated Japan soon, she wondered if Billy might be able to come home before Christmas. If he could, she had made up her mind that she would marry Billy Bishop the day he stepped off the train. If the stars aligned, she would make her life with Billy in Igloo, and from there, wherever they decided to go. Deadwood was her parents' dream, hers was a life with Billy.

The Newsy Nook was quiet during much of the day. Sandy had become Ross's constant companion, following him wherever he went. Sitting behind the main counter, Ross listened to the afternoon livestock reports between country western songs either pining away about a lost love or roaring on about a rowdy drunk. Stroking Sandy's head, Ross looked out his little store's front door through dancing dust motes and panned the newspaper and magazine racks set up on both sides of the entry. News of the Allied victory in Europe was splashed across the front pages and front covers of every newspaper and magazine on display. Even so, the war continued in the Pacific.

Billy's letters had been few and far between, but then Ross himself hadn't written more than a letter a year to anyone in his life. Somehow, he was confident Billy would return. What he worried about was whether Billy would be able to find work when he did. The end of the war was sure to bring operations at Igloo Base to a near standstill. Without a hot war, Igloo would become no more than a munitions storage facility. He wondered how many men they would need to maintain a skeleton crew on the ordnance depot. Being from the local area and a returning veteran, Ross hoped Billy would be able to land one of the coveted positions when he returned home.

He knew Billy planned to marry Velda as soon as he got home. Without work, there would be nothing to keep the couple in Provo. Ross had to admit, his biggest worry was that he would lose Billy again, and this time, probably for good. But then he figured, everybody has a life to live. Ross had lived his and was at peace with how things had turned out. Regret never changed the past nor served any good purpose, it only made what a man had accomplished in life seem all the less. Each man lived his life his own way. It was up to him what he made of what came his way. He wanted nothing more than for Billy to live his life free of the past.

September 2, 1945

Tokyo Bay, Tokyo, Japan

Ashes to Ashes

PRESIDENT TRUMAN'S ANNOUNCEMENT THAT Japan had surrendered unconditionally on August 14, 1945, sent the country and the world into spontaneous celebration. The war was finally over. In coming days, on September 2, the military and civilian leadership of the Empire of Japan formally signed the Instrument of Surrender in Tokyo Bay aboard the battleship the *USS Missouri* with Supreme Commander of Allied Forces Army General Douglas MacArthur presiding. To demonstrate the might of the Allied forces marshalled against Japan, over three hundred warships joined the Missouri when it sailed into Tokyo Bay. At the end of the signing ceremony, over two thousand war planes flew in low formation over the *Missouri*, darkening the sky as the roar of their engines shook the ship's deck and the streets of the city of Tokyo, where Emperor Hirohito sat alone on his Chrysanthemum Throne. The massive show of military might drove home a simple message to Japan's official delegation and every citizen of the Empire of Japan, including their secluded emperor, unconditional surrender had been Japan's only viable option of the only two it had been presented: survival or utter annihilation.

Victory over Japan was no more than ashes in the mouths of its victors, however. Beyond the honor of the atomic bombings of Hiroshima, killing over a hundred thousand people, and Nagasaki, ironically Japan's only city with a large Christian population, killing an additional one hundred thousand people, American B-29 bombers had firebombed sixty-seven other major cities, leveling more than 50 percent of their structures and resulting in the deaths of over five hundred thousand people. Of the hundreds of thousands of deaths from indiscriminate bombings, nearly all were civilian.

In winning the bittersweet victory, America had lost over one hundred ten thousand men and had suffered more than double that number of wounded, many of whom seriously. The wars in Europe and Asia had all tolled cost sixty-five million lives, divided nearly equally between the two main theaters.

With the war ended, the *Independence* and the *Shangri-La* joined the Pacific's version of the Magic Carpet Fleet. Unlike the European version that had used commercial cargo ships and merchant marine and coast guard vessels, the Pacific version was made up of three hundred sixty-nine ships of war, including assault transports, battleships, cruisers, aircraft carriers, and hospital ships. With the demobilization of the Pacific underway, President Truman ordered ship commanders to bring home as many soldiers and sailors as possible by Christmas. Bunks were soon welded into place, stacked four deep, as aircraft carrier harrier bays were converted into troop transports. Ships of every stripe gathered troops from southeast Asia, the Philippines, Formosa, China, Okinawa, and all the islands in between until each, filled to capacity, headed for ports on the American west coast at full speed.

Unbeknownst to one another, both Francis and Billy had been among the hundreds of thousands of soldiers and sailors that had been given early discharges. Billy planned to head straight to Provo and to arrive before Christmas, God willing. He had decided he would marry Velda the first chance he got. Having witnessed more than a few deaths, he had seen just how short life could be and didn't want to miss a second of what he still might have left. Francis had decided to take up his brother Alva's offer and return to Rapid City, where his brother had built a new home and had taken in his father to live together.

Herman had also been discharged early and had hopped on a troop transport in Sydney determined to make it back to Pleasant Valley by Christmas. All three men looked forward to making it home by Christmas as their ships streamed across the Pacific headed for American shores.

Alva, having retired in July, had already taken the first steps toward his postwar dream. Returning to the Black Hills, he had purchased ten acres of land in Rapid Valley on the outskirts of Rapid City, where he quickly built a new home and laid out his plans for the land's future development. He had joined Bill, Kate, Bart, Velda, and Johnny for Thanksgiving dinner and birthday cake in Igloo. It was then that the Barton family decided it would be a great idea to have everyone come together again for a final Christmas holiday in Igloo. They all agreed that 1946 would bring big changes for everyone, with each of them looking forward to pursuing their dreams and building their postwar lives in a booming postwar economy. They had all discussed the arc of their lives, and all that had passed, and had agreed they had much to be thankful for. They had never had higher hopes for a brighter future in the nation that had just conquered the world.

Entering the Strait of Juan de Fuca, the *Shangri-La* had turned south into Admiralty Inlet, passing the many islets and skerries straight down the Main Basin past Bainbridge Island, before turning southwest up Sinclair Inlet to the Puget Sound Naval Shipyard, near the city of Bremerton on Kitsap Peninsula, across from the city of Seattle. The shipyard, established in 1891, had the primary mission of repairing Pacific Fleet warships that had been damaged in battle. On December 9, 1945, its docks were teeming with men pouring off landed ships eager to get home. The scene was a familiar one in naval ports from Seattle to Portland to San Francisco to Los Angeles and San Diego. Trains were soon clogged with hundreds of thousands of men trying to head inland and home. Though the Navy had handled the demobilization across the Pacific with military efficiency, that efficiency ended at the shoreline.

Desperate to get home for Christmas, men unable to purchase tickets for seats on overbooked passenger trains and buses soon packed themselves into quickly purchased used cars, hopped on freight trains, took to the highways to hitchhike, or simply started walking east hoping to rely on the kindness of strangers. America's warriors had come home victorious. The mood of the nation was high. Though the troops were met with good cheer everywhere they went, they found themselves a long way from home with no means to get there.

After spending ten impatient days in port, Billy was finally discharged from active duty on the morning of December 19, leaving him only five days to get home for Christmas. With his discharge papers in hand, Billy stood on the docks in his crackerjack uniform with his Dixie-cup hat cocked to one side and his seabag balanced on his left shoulder, while he considered his limited options. His problem, like that of nearly every other man standing on the dock, was that he had no way to get home. In his case, he had no way to cover the twelve hundred miles he needed to travel to get to Provo. He had five days, which seemed like a lot, but he knew it might not be near enough. With few other options, Billy decided to hop a freight train on the Northern Pacific Railroad and to head straight west to a point somewhere along the line where he might be able to hop another train going south into the Black Hills. Riding the rails in the dead of winter through the Rocky Mountains and across the northern Great Plains was not a journey he looked forward to, but he knew he had little choice in the matter if he wanted to make it home by Christmas.

Seattle's Union Station stood on the corner of South Jackson Street and 4th Avenue. Arriving at the station, the first thing Billy noticed were the large scrums of uniformed men gathered along the tracks several blocks up the street from the station. It was clear, he wasn't the only sailor trying to get home nor the only one who thought hopping a freight train might be a good idea. Seeing police officers and railroad bulls patrolling the tracks, Billy wondered how any of the sailors trying to hop on trains near the station could possibly be successful. To hop on, he would need to get further away from the main terminal, somewhere further out of town.

"Hey, bubby, you need a lift?" a bearded man yelled at Billy out of the rolled-down window of a banged up pickup truck on the other side the street.

"I need to get to the edge of town," Billy yelled back.

"Hop in," the man yelled as the passenger door swung open. "Just throw your seabag in the truck bed."

Climbing into the pickup cab, Billy was surprised when he realized there were two men in the pickup. The man who had been riding shotgun had scooted over and now sat between Billy and the driver.

"I'm Tom, and this is Pete," the driver said with a funny chuckle as he pointed his right thumb at the man in the middle.

"I'm Billy, glad to meet you fellas. Thanks for the lift," Billy said, happy to have stumbled onto a bit of good luck as he quickly shook hands with both men.

"Headed home?" Tom ventured.

"Yeah, we pulled in over a week ago. It took a lot of time and paperwork, but I'm finally a free man," Billy said, relieved his active duty military service had ended. "I'm just tryin' to get home for Christmas."

"Got all your war booty and worldly goods in that seabag, I bet," Pete said, his voice high pitched with a nervous edge.

"If you know anything about the military, they ain't payin' in gold Sovereigns these days, that's for damn sure," Billy said, as he felt the hairs on the back of his neck stand on end.

Billy knew something wasn't right and only hoped he could get to the edge of town and out of the pickup without incident. Billy felt increasingly uneasy as they speeded further and further away from prying eyes.

"Edge of town's not far. We'll just follow the tracks east," Tom said.

"How about a cigarette," Pete said, looking at Billy.

"Sure. Tom, you want one too," Billy said as he tapped a couple of cigarettes out of a fresh pack of king-size Pall Mall.

"Hey, these are the longer ones," Pete said, taking his smoke. "They give you guys in the military all the good stuff. Yep, these are king size, I saw the ad. They just came out, didn't they?"

"Yeah. It is longer, all right," Tom said, firing up his cigarette and admiring its length.

Soon all three men had lit up, filling the cab with smoke. Billy and Tom cracked their side windows to clear the air.

"They must've given you boys severance pay 'fore they sent ya home, right?" Pete said as he blew out a large plumb of smoke and twisted his king-size Pall Mall between his pale thin fingers as he studied its extra length.

"No, they said they'd send it to us. God knows when or how. They gave us just enough to buy a train or bus ticket home," Billy said. "Of course, there're no tickets to buy. So, here I am, lookin' to hop on a freight train."

As the men enjoyed their cigarettes and drove east in silence, the streetlights became scarce and the night darker by the block. Temperatures had plunged and Billy was glad he had decided to put on his peacoat and stocking cap. He had filled his peacoat pockets with the few valuables he had stowed in his seabag back in Seattle, not wanting to carry anything valuable in a seabag that could get lost in transit. He didn't own anything worth much but didn't want to lose what little he had, nor did he want to lose the over three hundred dollars he had stuffed in his socks.

"I think I'd like to see what might be in that seabag," Pete said, breaking the silence. "Be alright for us to take a look, Billy?"

In one swift fluid motion, Pete straightened up in his seat, slipped his left hand into his coat pocket and, in a blur brought his hand back out, flipping his wrist and throwing a seven-inch razor-sharp knife blade into its open and locked position. Pointing the business end of the knife at Billy, he repeated his request through clinched teeth.

"I think we'd like to see inside that seabag and inside your coat pockets, Billy," Pete said with a gritty mean edge in his voice, as Tom began slowing down the pickup and pulling over onto the apron of the highway.

Knowing it was now or never, Billy flicked his burning cigarette butt straight into Pete's face, causing burning embers to explode across the man's ape-like features as the cigarette hit him square between the eyes. With red hot ash showering across Tom's side of the cab, Tom quickly swerved and slammed on the brakes. Caught off guard, Pete's hands reflexively jerked up in a defensive motion, when the cigarette struck him in the face. With Pete's knife hand raised and his midsection exposed, Billy slammed his left elbow as hard as he could deep into the man's exposed ribs. As bones cracked and give way, the elbow dug deep into Pete's abdomen, doing serious damage, causing air to shoot out of his lungs, leaving him breathless. His lungs collapsed and diaphragm paralyzed, Pete dropped his knife and grabbed at his throat as he desperately gasped for air. Tom, having brought the pickup to a dead stop, turned in his seat to see what had happened to his partner, giving Billy the opportunity, he had hoped for.

Though the pickup cab was tight and crowded with three grown men in the front seat, Billy had just enough room to throw a jackhammer of a rabbit punch with his right fist straight into the end of Tom's nose, smashing it down against his once smug and chuckling lips, sending sparks flying from his lit cigarette and blood splattering from his busted nose across the inside of the windshield. With both men busying dealing with their injuries, Billy jumped out of the cab. Just as he reached to grab his seabag out of the pickup box, Tom, having regained enough of his senses to know what Billy was trying to do, punched down on his gas pedal, causing the pickup to fishtail as it rapidly accelerated, its rear tires spitting out gravel in every direction until it climbed back up onto the paved road and sped off into the night.

Billy, standing on the side of the road, took inventory. They had gotten away with his seabag but would soon discover they had nothing more than a bag full of dirty laundry, all stenciled with his name, rank, and serial number, just like the dog tags he wore around his neck, making the contents worthless to anybody but the owner. He couldn't believe his good luck in escaping with his valuables still in his peacoat pockets and his money still tucked in his socks. The only thing he had lost of any value were two perfectly good king-size Pall Mall cigarettes. But then, he figured, he could write off the cigarettes as payment in full for the ride to the edge of town. As far as the other entertainment, he was sure Tommy and Petey would think twice before they tried to roll another war-weary squid.

Not wanting to run into the pair again or any more like them, Billy made his way to the tracks and tried to figure out how he was going to hop on the next freight train headed east. He had no idea how fast trains would be moving at the edge of town but was sure they would be picking up speed. He didn't have long to wait until the beacon-like headlamp of an oncoming freight train was headed his way. In the bright light he could make out the crouching shapes of other men hiding along the track. The fact there were others didn't surprise Billy; after seeing the mobs of men surrounding Union Station, he knew he wasn't the only serviceman desperate to get home.

No longer having to tote his heavy seabag, Billy started to run just as the glare of the headlamp on the engine passed him. Running as fast as he could, he quickly realized that the train was outpacing him by a good clip. Other men in front and behind him were yelling at one another as they sought handholds so they could jump onto the moving train. Running at a full tilt, Billy could see no way to make the final leap. The train was moving far too fast.

Ready to give up, Billy suddenly felt something grab hold of the back collar of his peacoat. Before he realized what was happening, his feet came off the ground as his legs continued to pump, leaving him running suspended in midair. Helplessly he witnessed himself fly through the air toward the side of the train and through an open door; his confusion ended when he found himself tossed next to another man on the wooden floor of an open boxcar. Before he could fully gather his thoughts, another man flew in on top of him, and then another.

Billy watched in disbelief as two massive giants, one on each side of the boxcar, plucked up one running man after another from both sides of the track. He soon discovered that there were other men in the boxcar cheering, yelling, and rooting with money in hand as the two giants, in an all-out competition, fished up one running man after another. The yelling calmed down when the two titans ran out of runners.

"Alexi, twelve. Andre, eleven," a short little man wearing a large cowboy hat barked.

The reaction to the news was divided into two camps, those who cheered and those who groaned. As money changed hands, the side doors on the boxcar were slid closed and the men inside settled in for the ride.

"Gentlemen, gentlemen, may I have your attention, please. Welcome to the Squid Express," the short, little man said in a tall, big man's voice.

His oversized features appeared ghoulish as the deep shadows cast by the dim yellowish light of a single Coleman lantern turned down low danced on his impish face.

"We thought we'd make a little sport out of helping you fellas find your seats," he continued.

Billy joined the other men in a good laugh at the little man's joke. Like Billy, the other men who had been hoisted into the boxcar were still in a state of disbelief that they had somehow made it onto the train. To a man, they had all given up any hope of jumping onto the speeding train just when their fortunes unexpectedly changed.

"Alexi and Andre here only charge ten dollars a head for seats on the Squid Express, this being their boxcar and all," the little man said, nodding to the two giants and taking off his cowboy hat and holding it out top down as though he were a preacher passing a collection tray.

When the hat came around, Billy dug out a ten-dollar bill and dropped it in, hoping the shakedown would end there. All he wanted to do is get home but had discovered the hard way with hundreds of thousands of men returning from the war at the same time, the flood of desperate men had become a boon to those who chose to take advantage of the situation. With the war over, the comradery of men coming together in common cause was also over. He had returned to a world where it was every man for himself.

After the hat was passed and fares were collected, shorty with his oversized cowboy hat back on his head outlined the rules of the road. Essentially, everyone was asked to maintain their best behavior while passengers on the Squid Express. A latrine had been set up in one corner of the car and all food was to be collected and shared to avoid any unnecessary conflicts. Smoking was fine, but only when the train was moving across open country. When the train pulled into towns along the way, everyone was to stay silent.

Billy was relieved that all the rules were sensible and fair. Everyone in the boxcar, including Alexi, Andre, and their sawed-off pitchman, just wanted to get home, safe and sound. The only difference was the two giants and their little bubby had figured out a surefire way to get home with a bit more money in their pockets than the others.

In an attempt to relax after his close call with Tom and Pete and his heart-pounding flight into the boxcar, Billy struck up a cigarette and blew out a long stream of smoke, which swirled and danced in the dim light before slipping out a narrow slit between a set of boxcar doors that had been left ajar. Beyond the speeding train, the pitch-black countryside provided little clue as to their location. With every passing hour, Billy knew he was getting closer to home and his long-awaited reunion with Velda. Though his world had been tossed around on violent seas over the past year since pulling out of Norfolk, Billy's anchor had held firm. He had never tired of thinking of his future life with Velda. Of that, he was certain, no matter what came.

December 23, 1945

Igloo, Fall River County, South Dakota

New Beginnings

BEING AMONG THE FIRST group of servicemen to return from the war in the Pacific, Francis had been able to buy a ticket on a passenger train out of San Diego. With a flood of servicemen riding on the Magic Carpet Fleet close on his heels, he had been able to stay one step ahead and made it home without a hitch. Arriving in Rapid City, Alva had picked him up at the train station. Herman too had made it back to Pleasant Valley, also having arrived in California before the mad rush. Bart had been able to return home from Europe a month earlier and had enjoyed Thanksgiving with the family. As everyone counted down the days until Christmas, only Velda's finance, Billy, had yet to return from the war.

Alva had driven down to Igloo from Rapid City with John and Francis to join Bill and Kate and their children, Bart, Velda, and Johnny, for the Christmas holiday. Since Bill's neighbors were spending the holidays with relatives out of state, Bill had been able to borrow their house to make use of the empty bedrooms. Having so many visitors, and with Bart having returned home, there had been real pressure on Velda to give up her bedroom. Gaining use of the neighbor's bedrooms put a smile on Velda's face. She had grown tired of always having to give up her bedroom, just when she finally got one of her own.

With sleeping arrangements taken care of, the family sat round a large double dining table set up in the living. John, Ross, and Bill sat at one end of the table, with Kate, Velda, and Johnny at the other. Alva and Bart sat across from Francis, who had an empty seat next to him reserved for Billy, who had yet to arrive. The family had spent a relaxing day eating, trading jokes, and playing cards. As the evening grew late, the conversation turned to thoughts about the war and everyone's future plans. Unspoken was the growing concern about the whereabouts of Billy, who had been discharged on December 19 and hadn't called for several days since.

"I know I might have said it before, but it's hard to believe that they built Igloo Base, the town and all the surrounding facilities, in less than a couple of years out here in the middle of nowhere," Alva said, still amazed at the cost and amount of effort that it must have taken to stand up a fully functioning town and ordnance depot where only pronghorns, jackrabbits, and coyotes once roamed.

"It surely is. Hell, I laid the damn place out and watched it go up, stick by stick, and it still amazes me how it all got done," Bill said with a chuckle. "When Uncle Sam wants something, it seems money is no object. Igloo is proof of that simple truth."

"I'll second that," Francis said. "During the last several years in the Navy, I saw more things thrown away than we ever used. It seemed at times there was no limit to the waste."

"We've all seen plenty of waste over the last several years, that's for sure," Bart said. "We've wasted time, men, and materials, and have thrown more things away than we could ever have made used of. We laid to waste one town, one city, and one country after another. We didn't leave much left standin.'"

For Bart, who had fought in ground battles without relief for two long years, the war had taken a toll on his soul. He had seen more death and destruction than any man should see in a thousand lifetimes.

"I've lived through two world wars and was lucky enough not to have to fight in either one of 'em. I'm damn proud that you boys had the sand to tough it through," John said, meaning every word.

John had seen his share of gunplay in his day and knew what it was to kill a man, face to face. Though he had never fought in a war, he had fought in battles with marauding Indians and desperadoes where everyone had tried their damnedest to kill one another. He had never forgotten the horror of killing other men, their blood still stained his soul. He knew his sons and his grandson would forever live with their memories.

"Well Pa, I haven't fought in one either. I was too young to fight in the first world war and too old to fight in the second. Let's hope we can avoid a third," Bill said. "We've all lived through some damn tough times, before and during the war. We're blessed we can all be here together considerin' how many other men didn't come home to their loved ones."

"Amen, to that" Kate said. "You know we had the Italian prisoners here in Igloo at the same time Bart was fighting in Italy. They were finally sent back home in November. I guess the government sent the German prisoners who worked in the sugar beet fields around Belle Fourche home about the same time. It's been a strange time with enemies becoming friends and friends becoming enemies."

"It's not so much that the world has changed, it's that America has," Alva said, flatly.

"What do mean by that?" John said, knowing Alva had witness an America beyond its shores, an America most Americans had yet to fully understand.

John knew it might take time, but the nation would realize soon enough that America now had an outsized role to play in the world. He wondered if Americans were really ready to take on that role and stay the course for the long run.

"Frontier America had focused on domestic growth. When I was younger, I had wholeheartedly believed that our conquest of territories overseas was the true measure of America's expanding greatness. Hell, I joined the Navy believing America should rule the world one day. Well, the war has shown me our greatness is in our ideas and in the power of our example, not in the example of our power. America needs to serve as an example of the possibility of a better world, not as an occupier of lands belonging to other peoples."

"Is our example really all that great?" Bart said, still bitter from what he had witnessed firsthand on the battlefields of Europe. "We just fought a war of freedom and yet we fail to treat our own American citizens equally right here at home. I saw segregated units of black Americans with white officers, and in Italy, I saw units of Japanese Americans thrown at our front lines without regard to casualties while their families sat locked up in detention centers right here in America."

"Well at least we're trying to become a more perfect union," Kate said, well aware America had plenty of faults, particularly in the treatment of different races. "I remember when just being a German immigrant was something less than American."

"Look what they did to the Japanese Americans. They stripped them of everything, including their freedom," Bart said, angry people couldn't just treat each other with mutual respect.

"Yes. But think about what we've tried to do as a nation, at least when we listened to our better angels," Bill said. "We freed the slaves, we ended child labor, and we gave women the vote, something your grandma never stopped talking about."

"Yeah, well, I agree the nation has made progress, but each step has had its cost," Bart said, conceding that things had slowly gotten better, though all too often at the price of more than a few lives.

"Igloo's a good example of how different peoples can work and live together," Bill said, wanting to drive home his point that people can change, that the world can get better, and that people should never give up on trying to make it so. "We have Lakota, blacks, and Mexicans all working here on Igloo Base and no one cares, one way or the other. It seems, when everyone has a job and a good place to live, they become increasingly color blind. Giving everyone a fair shake seems like a simple enough formula for the formation of a more perfect union."

"You might have something there. When money was tight and times tough, folks seemed to blame everything on folks that didn't look like them, didn't act like them, didn't pray to their God," Kate said. "I still think they should have put that fifth face on Mount Rushmore."

"Fifth face? Whose face would that have been?" Francis said, surprised. "President Franklin Delano Roosevelt? We already have Teddy up there, ain't that enough Roosevelts?"

"No silly, not FDR. They were goin' put Susan B. Anthony up there, but ran out of money," Kate said.

Kate believed that had a woman been included, it might have prompted the nation to rethink the role of women in American society.

"You're kidding," Francis said, having never heard of the idea.

"Nope. It was all the talk back in 1937, but Congress, unwilling to appropriate the additional funds needed, decided to finish the four faces originally proposed," Kate said, disappointed. "But there's another example of how America is trying to form a more perfect union."

"I know we have been trying, and I wouldn't live anywhere else in the world, but I think we need to mind our own damn business," Bart said, convinced America was now headed down the wrong path. "I don't agree with America becoming the world's policeman."

"I couldn't have said it better myself," Alva said. "I'm retired military, and I no longer agree with the desire by those yahoos in Washington who seem to want to rule the world. We've got enough problems here at home. We should use the new United Nations and work closely with our allies to bring this world to a better place. There's no need for America to go it alone and to have a military outpost in every country."

"I'm afraid folks have gotten spoiled by the new war economy," Bill said. "Things were bad before the war. There weren't any jobs and there wasn't any money. People scraped to get by. They had to make do. Hell, we lived in a surplus Forest Service squad tent for two years. Now, things are booming, just like they did back in the '20s after the Great War. Everything today is new and shiny and modern. No one wants to return to the grime and misery of the past."

"I for one have seen enough tough times," Francis said. "I would've never dreamt it, but with Uncle Sam offering to pay the bills, I can't wait to go to college."

"You and me both, I plan to get a degree in finance. There's plenty of money to be made in finance with all the markets sure to go through the roof in coming years. Herman told me he was also planning to attend college to get an engineering degree. Like us, he'll be the first in his family to have a college degree," Bart said, realizing the military had shown them all how a higher education was the key to a better life.

The military had become America's great homogenizer, taking in men from every background and region and grinding them down into a one-size-fits-all world, where advancement was based solely on merit. The military was a ridged uniform world where everyone, no matter their background or birthright, had an equal opportunity to better themselves. For most men, this kind of meritocracy was a new experience, having been raised in communities where those who had and those who didn't have had remained the same for generations. Breaking free of poverty in such closed communities, particularly in isolated rural communities, had been next to impossible and something very few ever did, or even dreamt of doing. The government's offer of a free college education for returning veterans was tough to turn down and soon became the path to a better life for millions.

"We've all seen it boom and we've all seen it bust," John said almost to himself. "Life is more than money. The best things in life happen even when you don't have any. Folks need to remember that."

"That they do, Pa," Bill said, remembering all the good and bad times they had lived through over the past twenty years and knowing all too well what being penniless felt like. Bill for one swore he never wanted to experience that hollow helpless feeling again for the rest of his life.

"It's pretty clear from everything I've seen, the main thing that's been stoking the America economy in recent years has been the war. Plenty of people have profited by supplying the American war effort. Is war the price of our continued prosperity?" Francis wondered out loud, his mind filled with images of a world unable to free itself from a state of perpetual war.

"Unfortunately, I don't think there's any jumping off this train anytime soon. It's already left the station," Bill said, knowing his little brother's question begged for a better answer, an answer Bill didn't have and didn't want to think too deeply about.

Bill only hoped things would continue to boom. In truth, though he had mixed feelings, he wasn't particular how. He had lived a life that had been twisted and bent by whimsical forces beyond his control. Now that he had clawed his way back onto his feet after years of sacrifice, he was determined to ride the cougar this time, rather than play the role of the mule deer and once again be devoured by it.

"Question is, little brother, will America choose to find a way to build its economy without the need of war," Alva answered, believing America's challenge would be in taming its war machine and in finding a path back to peace for its people and hopefully for the peoples of the world.

Alva's words hung in the air for a long moment until Kate said, "Speaking of trains, Velda, have you heard from Billy? I hope he hasn't lost our phone number."

Kate and Bill had a telephone installed in their new home soon after moving to Igloo. Though all the phone lines where party-lines, no one cared that they had to share their phone line with others. The added convenience of actually having a telephone in the house was like living in the world of the future. Having the ability to call anyone anywhere in the country at any time was nearly unbelievable to people who had lived where news had come on horseback not so many years before.

"The last time he called was from Bremerton the evening before he was discharged on December 19th. That was nearly four days ago," Velda said, her face etched with concern. "I'm getting worried. I hope nothing's happened to him."

"If he left on December 19th, he's only been on the road three days," Francis said. "It took me almost three days to get here from San Diego. Coming from Seattle by train might take a little longer, that's all."

"He couldn't get a train ticket, so I'm not sure how he's comin' home," Velda said, her voice unsteady.

"Maybe he hopped a freight train. That would explain why he hasn't called. He'll make it," Francis said, hoping his words would help to calm his niece's concerns.

Francis knew very well that if Billy left Seattle on December 19, he had actually been on the road for four full days. Even if Billy had experienced a few delays, he feared four days was too many without any word.

"If Billy said he'd be here by Christmas, by God he'll be here," Ross said, his words firm though his voice remained calm and reassuring.

Velda had driven over to Provo to bring Ross back to Igloo for the afternoon. Ross had listened to all the talk around the table about the war and America's place in the world and couldn't agree more that the country needed to stick to its own knitting and not try to remake the world in America's image; leastwise, not until a few more improvements could be made right here at home. Most people around the world just wanted to live their lives in peace. They wanted jobs, a good safe place to live for their families, good healthcare, and a future for their children. All the other trappings of modern society with its shiny new gizmos were optional. As for Billy, Ross was certain he would make it home by Christmas; he didn't know why he felt so strongly about it, but somehow deep down in his bones, he just knew.

Johnny too had listened to all the adult talk and hadn't agreed with a lot of it. He wanted America to be number one. He wanted to serve in the military like his big brother and his uncles. He wasn't convinced that Pax Americana was a bad thing, if it meant all the nations of the world now bowed to America. He knew what being poor was. Though he hadn't been bullied at school the way his brother and sister had been, he had felt the shame of having nothing and being thought of as being less than other people. He liked the fact his family now had money, that they had grown wealthy working for the government, and that they had a fine house to live in. He was proud his parents now owned businesses in Deadwood and that the family would be prosperous and respectable. He liked what a booming economy could provide. He was happy America had won the war and had come out on top. If America had to go to war to stay wealthy, he swore to himself he would be among the first to sign up to fight. He never wanted to be poor again no matter what it might take. Still young and naive as to the ways of the world and as to the true cost of war, what Johnny failed to fully understand was that he might be called on to give up his life for the enrichment of others, who may care little about his sacrifice.

The air was cold as it flowed in through the open door of the boxcar. Billy had dozed off and when he awoke the door was open and the boxcar nearly empty. Several other men were either curled up sound asleep or milling around gathering up their things as they readied themselves to hop off the train. Billy walked over to the open door and looked out across a snow-swept countryside. The frigid wind stung his face. From the looks of things, the train had been brought to a halt due to drifting snow. The lights of a good-sized town lit up the underbelly of low-hanging clouds not far off to the southeast. The men who had already hopped off the train had walked in single file through hip-deep snow toward those lights; lights Billy knew seemed closer than they really were. Feeling the arctic cold burrow into his peacoat, Billy hopped off the train, turned up his collar, and followed the well-worn trench through the snow.

Reaching town, Billy could see that most of the men had made a bee-line straight to a large well-lit café on main street. Catching sight of a wiry old man wearing a well-worn cowboy hat climbing up into the cab of a semi-tractor-trailer parked in an alley on the other side of the street, Billy decided to try his luck. Running over to the semi's cab, Billy waved his arms to get the driver's attention.

"Where you headed?" Billy yelled, desperate to get home.

"Headed to Pierre and then on to Rapid City," the driver yelled back.

Billy couldn't believe his ears. He must have slept through all the way to Bismarck, North Dakota. He had thought about hopping off the train several times to try his luck finding a train headed south. The problem with the plan was that drifting snow had blocked the tracks, on and off, for nearly three days, stopping anything moving south. For days, nothing moved in any direction other than due east, if it moved at all. With no other option, he had stayed on the train, hoping the weather would eventually let up.

"Do you have room for a rider?" Billy said, hopeful.

"You comin' back from overseas?" the driver said, noticing the hitch-hiker was wearing a Navy peacoat with a sailor's stocking cap on his head.

"Yep. Just got back from the Pacific. I'm headed home for Christmas," Billy said.

"Well then, hop in, sailor," the driver said as a broad, friendly smile creased his rubbery features, exposing his crooked tobacco-stained teeth. "We're all damn glad you boys beat the tar out of them bastards."

"We did that alright. I don't mind tellin' ya, you're a godsend. My name's Billy. If I can get to Rapid City, I should be able to make it home by Christmas," Billy said, excited to have struck gold.

"Glad to meet ya, young fella, my name's Sam," the driver said. "Always ready to lend a hand to a war hero. Where's home?"

"Provo, south of Edgemont," Billy said.

"Provo? Ain't that the little town next to Igloo?" Sam said, seemingly surprised.

"Yep. My Pa runs the Newsy Nook grocery store down there," Billy said.

"Well, I'll be damn. Your Pa must be Ross Bishop," Sam said matter-of-factly. "I've known Ross nigh on fifty years. We rode up the western Chisholm Trail from Texas together back in 1900. He and I were just sixteen at the time. By God, this is a small world."

"It sure as hell is. He told me about that drive. The last of the big cattle drives. So, I guess you know what happened to our ranch along the Cheyenne?"

"Yeah, Ross told me. Too many folks lost everything in the thirties. I lost my place in Montana, and like your Pa, I lost my wife and kids too. After kickin' around for a few years, I ended up driving trucks for a livin'."

"How'd you know where my Pa ended up?"

"I've delivered several loads down to Igloo. That place is a wonder to behold. Just happened to stop in at the Newsy Nook on my way back to Edgemont. We had a hell of a time catching up after so many years. Your Pa has a heart of gold. Always quick to lend a helping hand and never askin' nothin' for it. I'm damn glad I can return an old favor; one I have owed your Pa for far too long. It's a pleasure to lend a helping hand to the son of Ross Bishop."

For the first time since returning to the United States, Billy felt truly happy to be home and proud of who he was. As they drove south, Sam told Billy of all the wild times he and his Pa had together and about all of his travels as a driver. Billy shared his experiences during the war and his dreams for the future. Both men enjoyed the drive through the snowy night, both feeling the time had passed far too quickly.

On the morning of December 23, as the sunrise reddened the sky in the east, Sam dropped off his load in Pierre and headed west toward the Black Hills. A little past noon, Sam pulled up in front of the Rapid City train station to drop Billy off. Sharing a hearty handshake and waving a heartfelt farewell, Billy watched as Sam drove off in search of his next destination. Wasting no time, Billy headed for the nearest ticket window with high hopes.

After a light diner, Velda volunteered to take Ross back to Provo. Though there was snow on the ground, the road was clear and the drive a short one. At the Wallace Street railroad crossing, Velda noticed mule deer tracks in the snow headed north right through the heart of Provo. As the weather got colder and food sources on the prairie became more scare, the deer naturally gravitated toward the shelter of the hills to spend the winter. This natural migration kept the cougars busy, as the cycle of life continued to turn, fulfilling its own reasons.

She hoped she would also one day return to the shelter of the hills. She wanted nothing more than to return to the Black Hills where she had grown up, the place where she hoped to fulfill her own destiny. Without thinking, she reached up to touch her cougar talisman feeling its energy. Her thoughts soon turned to Billy and what might have happened to him. It had been far too long since his last call.

"Tomorrow's Christmas Eve," Ross said, breaking the silence when he witnessed a look of concern cast its dark shadow across Velda's face. "Don't you worry, Billy'll be comin' along, you'll see."

Looking over at Ross, Velda thought she saw a knowing glint in the old man's eye that somehow reassured her that all would be well. Pulling a U-turn in front of the Newsy Nook, Velda stopped in front of Ross's house.

"Now that's service with a smile," Ross said with a grin and a grunt as he stepped out of the car directly in front of the gate to his house. Before shutting the car door, he leaned his head back into the car and added, "Don't you worry none, Billy'll make it."

As Ross made his way up the steps to his house, Sandy came running and barking, happy to see his master return home. Sandy was going on eighteen but still had plenty of spunk. Velda hadn't seen Sandy in a while and decided to say hello. Getting out of the car, she called to him, and the old dog came running. Jumping up to lick her on the face, Sandy acted as frisky as a pup, prompting Velda to recall all the hours and days they had spent together.

Turning to send Sandy back to the house, Velda heard the distant horn of a train coming from Edgemont. Trains passed through Provo on a regular schedule as they traveled between the rail hubs of Edgemont, South Dakota, and Alliance, Nebraska. Knowing the train would soon reach the Wallace Street railroad crossing, Velda decided to spend a little more time with Sandy and wait for the train to pass before driving back to Igloo.

As the train came into Provo it blew its horn at the Wallace Street crossing, but instead of continuing on, it screeched to a halt at the depot to make a brief stop. Blowing its horn once again, the train lurched forward and continued its journey southeast toward the Nebraska border. The unexpected stop and start of the train left behind huge plumes of smoke and steam swirling in the dim light of the station's lone streetlamp, shrouding the depot platform from view. As Velda looked south toward the depot, the whole scene took on an eerie feel as the bellowing plumes slowly faded layer by layer like something out of an old spy movie.

Just as she was about to turn to get in the car, a lone silhouetted figure emerged from the foggy mist. Backlit by the streetlamp, Velda could only make out the outline of what appeared to be a man wearing a stocking cap with his coat collar turned up. Picking up the man's scent, Sandy began to bark and then took off in a sprint. Velda's heart raced, when she realized the lone figure could be only one person, her precious Billy, returned from the war.

Without thinking, Velda too soon found herself running toward the depot as the man on the platform hopped down and started to run toward her. Meeting in the middle of the Bennet Street, Billy and Velda fell into each other's arms. Sandy barked with joy as he hopped up and down wagging his tail, while the couple remained frozen in a long embrace.

"How?" Velda said, as tears of joy ran down her face.

"I'm not sure really. All I know is I'm damn glad to be home," Billy said, stunned that Velda was somehow magically in his arms, having no more than stepped off the train.

"You remember our song?" Velda said, thinking of the first time they met.

"You must remember this, a kiss is just a kiss," Billy sang and gave Velda a kiss she would often touch her lips to recall for the rest of her life.

"And the name of the song?" Velda said, as she wiggled in his arms, pretending to pull away.

"Ah, the world will always welcome lovers," Billy said, pulling Velda closer and giving her another long kiss.

"No, Bogie, the name of the song," Velda said, playfully.

"What's in a name? We've already let too much time go by," Billy said. "We're getting married tomorrow."

"No matter what the future brings?" Velda said with a giggle.

"Is that a yes?" Billy said, hopeful.

"It's not a no."

"Then, it's a yes, right?"

"Woman needs man . . ."

". . . and man must have his mate."

"You are a clever little devil, Billy Bishop."

"And you're as cute as a button, Velda Barton."

"Just cute, huh?"

"Cuter than a bug's ear."

"I never understood how that could be cute."

"Well, it damn sure is," Billy said with a chuckle.

"Alright then. Yes, Billy Bishop, I will marry you tomorrow!" Velda said, throwing her arms around his neck and giving him a tender kiss.

"Alright then. Now, I like the direction things are headed," Billy said, pulling her closer.

"I imagine you do, little Billy. You squids are all alike. Always trying to put your suction cups on anything in a skirt. For now, I'm headed home. And you still need to let your Pa know you made it back safe and sound," Velda said, standing back and straightening her coat.

"You always goin' be wearin' the pants in the family?" Billy said, giving her a sideways look.

"Yep. And don't you ever forget it," Velda said with a serious look on her face.

"Well then. I'll just have to be a good boy," Billy said, eyebrows raised.

"Well, not all the time, I hope," Velda said, her own eyebrows raised high.

"I imagine we'll find a way . . . *As Time Goes By*" Billy said with a knowing grin.

"You really are a clever little boy. You knew the name of our song all along," Velda said as she blew him a big fat kiss, got in the car, and headed back to Igloo.

Driving back from Provo surrounded by darkness, Velda could see Igloo's shiny new streetlamps blazing in the distance. As though caught between two worlds, she knew after tomorrow her life would never be the same. During her hard frontier life, she had learned how to take life as it came. She knew it wasn't what life dished out so much as it was what you made of it that made all the difference.

With Grandpa John's words still fresh in her mind, she was determined that in this chapter of her adventure, she would be the one behind the wheel, steering a new course into a future yet to be written. There was one thing for damn sure, she thought, she wouldn't be having birthday cake with turkey ever again for as long as she lived.

She never felt freer. Her adventure had only just begun.

Epilogue

VELDA AND BILLY WERE married on Christmas Eve, December 24, 1945, by the justice of the peace at the Fall River County Court House in Hot Springs. After losing her job to a returning veteran, Kate decided it was time for the Barton family to leave Igloo. Bill, eager to cash in on the booming economy and beat the rush of returning servicemen, agreed to pull up stakes and move to Deadwood to run the Copper Kettle Café and the Water Street Rooming House in January 1946. With Homestake Gold Mine operations suspended during war, Bill knew there would be plenty of miners with money to spend looking for a good time in Deadwood, as soon as the mine got back into full swing. Going on eleven years old and soon to be a man, Johnny was already as big as his Pa and couldn't have been happier about the move back to the Black Hills. Johnny had had his fill of the open, treeless prairie and couldn't wait to return to the forest of his childhood.

Not long after the Barton family departure, employment at Igloo fell off sharply, from over four thousand to roughly fifteen hundred full-time workers by the end of 1946. Billy and Velda lived on Igloo Base for a time, with Billy working as a heavy equipment operator on the ordnance depot and Velda working at the commissary. As jobs on Igloo Base dried up, Billy and Velda moved to Provo, where they built a sod brick house for Ross to live in and moved their growing family into the Bishop House facing the Newsy Nook. While Velda and Ross ran the Newsy Nook and managed the family's apartment house rentals, Billy went to work as an equipment operator in the nearby uranium mines north of Edgemont. In coming years, the population of Igloo continued to decline as the ordnance depot slowly wound down.

Billy and Velda had three sons, each three years apart, all of whom attended the Provo School in Igloo before the family's move to Rapid City in 1959. Igloo closed in 1965, with most of its modular housing units moved to either the Pine Ridge Indian Reservation or to the nearby Wyoming coal fields. Though the town of Igloo is now nothing more than a well-laid-out grid of empty foundations, its over eight hundred concrete igloos still dot the surrounding countryside, some of which having been converted into doomsday shelters.

Returning to the Black Hills after nearly twenty years on the prairie, Velda's life had gone full circle and, at the age of thirty-one, her adventure was far from over. At this writing, Velda's adventure continues at the ripe old age of ninety-three.